Lord of my Heart

"I've never seen you naked," Aimery said. "Will you stand in the sunlight in just the glory of your hair and let me worship you?"

Madeleine blushed. "If you want," she said shyly.

He grinned. "If you'd understood me that day in the woods, you'd know what I want."

"What did you say then?"

"I told you how beautiful your curves felt," he said running his hands over her. "How sweetly heavy your breasts."

"What else did you say?"

He laughed and slid his hand down her thighs. "I promised to be slow in loving you, to stroke you to your pleasure, then when you couldn't bear it anymore, I'd take you hard and strong."

Madeleine pressed back against him. "I can't bear it anymore . . ."

He laughed against her neck, kissed her nape. "Insatiable wanton. Have pity on the poor male."

Lord of my Heart

Jo Beverley

AVON BOOKS ◆ NEW YORK

This book is dedicated to the memory of my parents,
John and Mildred Dunn.
My mother ignored any notion of sexist limitations,
and encouraged her daughters to aim as high as they pleased.
My father introduced me to the romance of English history,
and was a great admirer of Hereward the Wake.
Thus this book, more than any other, springs from them.

Thus speaks the homeless-one,
haunted by memories of terrible slaughter
and the death of his friends:
"Dawn often finds me grieving in solitude,
for no one still lives
with whom I dare share
the truth of my heart."

From *The Wanderer,* an Anglo-Saxon poem.

Castle Gaillard, Normandy, August 1064

The Lady Lucia looked up as her husband strode into the hall. There was a heavy frown on Count Guy de Gaillard's face, and he bore a scroll clenched in his fist.

"Plague? Murrain?" Lucia hazarded as she rose to accept a kiss on the cheek. "Mischief by one of the boys?"

His frown eased as he hugged her. Lucia wished she could soothe every care from his life so easily. Small chance of that in Normandy, nor would he relish it. Norman men seemed to thrive on mayhem. Being English born and bred, she would be perfectly content with tranquil, unchanging days.

She had to admit that fifty years of mayhem had done Guy little harm. His back was straight, his hair still thick, and his green eyes keen and shrewd. The only changes she saw after twenty years of marriage were the silvering of that springy hair and the darkening of his eyes, which had deepened in color as a spring leaf darkens at summer's end.

"Neither plague nor murrain," he said as he threw himself onto his great oaken chair by the fire. "Nor even, unlikely as it may seem, mischief by one of the boys. Here." He tossed the rolled parchment to her, then reached for the wine kept warm by the fire. His favorite hound, Roland, came over to rest its muzzle on his knee. Count

1

Guy relaxed and pulled gently at the dog's long, silky ears.

He watched his wife as she sat down again on the facing chair, carefully moving her exquisite needlework to one side and unconsciously arranging her woolen skirts into elegant folds. It was still a matter of wonder to Guy, the grace and beauty his English bride had brought to his harsh Norman home, though it was now a well-accustomed pleasure.

Under her skillful management there was always tasty, wholesome food on the table, even at the end of winter; the stone walls were softened by tapestries; and he and his sons wore softly woven garments edged with bands worthy of a king.

Life was good at Castle Gaillard, and he desired only to keep it so.

Lucia unrolled the parchment, and her brow furrowed slightly as she tackled the Latin. It was the only line on her comely face, and the hair which peeped out from her snowy wimple was still golden. Guy wondered with lazy admiration whether she knew the secret to eternal youth, for she was nearer forty than thirty. It must be her tranquil nature. Lucia was comfortably padded into delightful curves, and one needed a tranquil nature to stay plump in Castle Gaillard.

Being English, she was better educated than he—though he was well-lettered for a Norman—and the text gave her little trouble. "Poor Earl Harold," she remarked dryly. "First swept toward Normandy by storm, then captured by Guy de Ponthieu, now 'rescued' by Duke William and forced to swear to help him to the English throne. The earl must think God's hand against him."

"As you see from the letter," said Count Guy, "many would agree."

Lucia picked up her needlework. "I can think of no reason why God would turn against the earl, who does his duty to Christ and king as well as the next man." She sighed. "That oath is a seed for trouble, though. The question is, what will Harold do when he's safe home again? It's said King Edward's health is failing."

"What can he do?" asked Guy. "An oath is an oath no matter how obtained. No man can prosper who breaks his word. William has long claimed to have Edward's favor as heir to England, and now he has the oath-bond of the greatest earl."

"But Earl Harold won't have the giving of it, Guy. That right is held by the great men assembled in the Witan."

"Are they likely to choose William?"

She shook her head. "Not even with Earl Harold's support. They'll want an Englishman. One of mature years and proven abilities."

"Such as Earl Harold of Wessex," said Guy. "Which William will never accept now he has the man's oath to support his cause." He looked into space and cursed softly.

"A Norman worried about a nice juicy war?" Lucia commented to the air around her. "It must be old age."

To her surprise the teasing didn't lighten his concern. She extended her mind to find the problem. A blast on the castle horn turned her mind in the right direction. It doubtless announced the return of the two youngest de Gaillard sons, who had ridden out with a troop of knights to seek a band of marauding outlaws. "Aimery," she said.

Guy nodded. "No more jaunts to England for him."

Guy had three sons and two daughters by his first wife, but God had only granted him and Lucia one child. Lucia had wanted her son to learn some of the cultured English ways as well as the bellicose Norman, so since infancy Aimery de Gaillard had spent a part of each summer in Mercia.

"My family would never let harm come to Aimery," Lucia protested. "If Edwin is young yet, there is always Hereward."

Count Guy snorted. "It's my opinion your brother is half mad! Hereward the Wake. Hereward the Beserker. He clings to ways generations past. Lord knows what possessed him to put those skin-marks on Aimery."

"They are a great sign of honor in the English tradition," Lucia protested.

"And a matter of ridicule in a Norman! And what of the ring he gave him?"

"To be ring-friend to a great man is an honor . . ." She trailed off and looked at her husband, very pale.

"It is also a binding commitment, is it not?"

Lucia nodded.

"So what will Aimery do if this contest for the throne of England comes to arms with all the men of Mercia, including Hereward and Edwin, on one side, and Duke William and the de Gaillards on the other?"

Lucia had no answer. A shiver trickled through her at the possibilities.

"Your son goes no more to England till this matter is settled," said Guy firmly.

Noises suddenly broke out in the castle bailey—hooves and shouts and barking dogs. Guy went to the narrow window which overlooked the busy space. It was thronged with dogs and horses, grooms and soldiers. Cutting a clear swathe through them all were his two youngest sons. Instinctively he checked for limps and wounds. Aimery had a bloody cloth tied around his arm, but from the way he straight-armed a soldier out of his way, the wound clearly gave him little trouble.

Lucia came to her husband's shoulder, tut-tutted, and bustled off calling for hot water and her simples.

The two young men were tall and strong but otherwise utterly different. At twenty and eighteen, they were both approaching their mature build. Long, rigorous hours of weapons practice from infancy had given them strong arms and shoulders, well-muscled legs, and fluid agility in movement.

Roger, the last child of Guy's first wife, was massive like all his older boys. He looked as if a falling tree trunk would bounce off him. Aimery, Lucia's son, was of a lighter build. The tree trunk would kill him if it hit, but it was clear he would be nimble enough to avoid it.

They were both clean-shaven, but while Roger wore his dark hair trimmed close to his head in true Norman fashion, Aimery's blond hair flowed to his shoulders. One had to give the boy credit for taking pride in the English style in the face of his brothers' teasing, but perhaps he had little option now that his body was marked with tattoos. Even at a distance, Guy could see the blue rood he wore on his left upper arm and the fantastic, curlicued leaping beast which decorated his right forearm and hand.

Under Lucia's influence, all the de Gaillard men wore clothes of the finest weaving, cut and embroidered as only an English woman could. Like all Normans they wore as many English-made ornaments of gold and precious gems as they could afford, for English goldsmiths were the best in Europe.

Aimery had a taste for bright-colored clothing, and his English relatives had gifted him with particularly fine ornaments—at the moment he wore two bracelets of gold and garnet which would buy a decent property—but he should not have looked so strange. His looks came, however, all from Lucia and her family; as he reached maturity he was disconcertingly like her brother Hereward twenty years since. His style of dress made him seem a foreigner in his homeland.

Sometimes Guy felt the only thing he'd passed on to his youngest son was his green eyes.

Guy went to pour wine into two more silver goblets. His life would have been simpler if he had never seen Lucia. Simpler, but in no way desirable. Lucia was the light and warmth of his life, and her troublesome son was in many ways his favorite. He hoped the cub was not aware of it.

The young men burst noisily into the hall, bringing the smell of fresh air, horses, and blood.

". . . no need to kill them all!" Aimery was shouting.

"What point in bringing them back here to hang?" asked Roger with a sneer.

"Justice."

"Justice! Saxon pap. They were murdering outlaws, and that's all we needed to know."

Guy broke in. "Has the problem been taken care of?"

Two voices clashed, but Roger's carried through. "A few escaped, but we killed eight."

"Good," said the count.

Aimery opened his mouth, but at the look in his father's eye he gave up the argument and came to take the wine being offered.

"How were you wounded?" asked Guy.

"An arrow. It's only a scratch."

"Nevertheless, your mother is preparing to tend it."

Aimery grimaced and turned as Lucia bustled in. "It's nothing, Mother."

"That's what the last man in the graveyard said," she replied tartly. "If you're brave enough to get it, you're brave enough to bear the healing. Sit down."

He sat on the stool indicated, and Lucia began to gently unwind the bandage. Guy took pity on him and gave him something to take his mind off things. The letter.

Aimery put down his wine and took up the parchment, reading with absorption. "This—" He broke off and hissed as his mother ripped the last of the bandage off roughly to open the wound and set the blood flowing. "It's clean," he protested. "I cleaned it."

"I'll be the judge of that," she said, washing and poking.

Aimery forced his mind back to the document. "The oath must have been forced—Mother!" He took a deep breath and continued. "Earl Harold would never voluntarily swear to support the duke's claim to the throne."

Guy took away the parchment and replaced it kindly with the wine. "Then he should have died before swearing," he said absolutely. "An oath is an oath. What do you know of him?"

Aimery took a deep drink. "Earl Harold? I've never met him . . ." He stopped speaking as his mother dug deep after something. After a moment he carried on. "He's well-regarded and known to be a fine soldier. He's been running England on the king's behalf for years. He'd make a good monarch.'' He looked at his father defiantly.

''He'd be an oath-breaker,'' Guy countered.

Aimery drained the goblet and sat looking into the polished bowl. ''If the Witan chooses Harold as king,'' he said at last, ''and Harold accepts, what will Duke William do?''

''Go in force to make good his claim.''

Aimery paled, possibly because of whatever powder Lucia was pressing over the wound on his shoulder, but Guy doubted it. He'd never thought Aimery slow to understand implications.

Staring into an unfathomable distance, Aimery de Gaillard slammed down his empty goblet with a sound like a blade striking a shield.

Abbaye des Dames, Caen, Normandy, February 1066

T he visitor's chamber of the Abbaye des Dames in
Caen was a small but finely proportioned room. It
was cozy on this bitter day, for its two narrow windows
were filled with precious glass and a fire burned in the
great stone hearth. The sunshine that beamed through the
small panes of glass was deceptively golden and gaily
picked out the jewel-colors of wall paintings and embroidered cushions. The three people in the room seemed stark
by comparison.

Two were men of war—tall, sinewy, and dressed in armor and clothing that had been used long and hard. One
was old with well-grizzled hair and heavy-knuckled,
gnarled hands; the other was younger and brown-haired
but, age apart, he was the image of the older and clearly
his son.

The third person was a girl in the plain white of a novice. Her linen gown lay straight over a still boyish figure.
A thick chestnut plait hung down her back, covered by a
fine lawn veil. Her scrubbed features still had a childish
softness to them, but her lips hinted at determination, and
her large brown eyes were keen and intelligent.

The older man, Gilbert de la Haute Vironge, fidgeted
uneasily amid this elegance. He would move, and then
stop as if afraid to damage some precious item. Marc, his

son, leaned his mailed shoulders against a white wall without thought for the scrapes he would leave. Gilbert's daughter, Madeleine, sat straight and composed, the perfect image of a little nun, appearing to fit her setting like a pearl in gold.

But Madeleine's composure was a mask for desperation. Two weeks ago, on her fifteenth birthday, when the abbess had raised the question of her final vows, Madeleine had realized she did not want to be a nun. There appeared to be no choice in the matter, for she had been a deathbed offering from her mother, intended to pray for the souls of all the Haute Vironge family. This unexpected visit from her father, however, could be her chance to persuade him to revoke the pledge. If she could only find the courage to ask.

"So things are hot everywhere," said Lord Gilbert gruffly, armor and mail jangling as he moved restively about. "God alone knows when we'll next have a chance to visit you, daughter. Now that Edward of England's dead and the English have crowned this Earl Harold, there'll be work for our swords unless they come to their senses."

"Hope they don't," said Marc, picking his teeth. "There'll be spoils if it comes to war. The duke owes us something."

Gilbert scowled at him. "We do our duty to our liege for our soul's sake, not for gain."

"Some earthly rewards wouldn't come amiss. We've been loyal to the duke for decades, and what good has it done us?"

"But why haven't the English accepted Duke William?" Madeleine interrupted, wondering if they bickered their way over the battlefields of Europe. "He has the promise of the crown, hasn't he?"

Marc snorted. "If I were English I wouldn't accept a foreign usurper. And all the better for us."

Gilbert angrily rejected the word "usurper," and they were at it again. Madeleine sighed. She didn't like her brother's taste for war, but she knew there was little option for a family brought to the brink of poverty by the troubled times. And greater prosperity could work to her advantage.

Haute Vironge lay in the Vexin, the territory endlessly contested between France and Normandy, and it had suffered over the last decade. Gilbert had been a faithful vassal to Duke William during his struggle for his land, and in return the family received benefits from the duke as often as he was able to provide them.

Madeleine's acceptance at the Abbaye, which had been founded by the duke and duchess themselves, had been one such benefit. It was doubtless true that if spoils of war were to become available in England, the duke would pass some of them to the men of Haute Vironge.

The convent bell rang for nones, and Madeleine rose to her feet. The two men broke off their squabble.

"Aye," said Lord Gilbert, not quite hiding his relief. "It's time for us to go." He laid a hand on his daughter's head. "Pray for us, daughter. You'll be a full Bride of Christ soon, I daresay."

As the two men picked up their fur-lined cloaks, Madeleine grasped her courage. "Father!"

He turned. "Aye?"

She could feel her heart racing, and her mouth was suddenly dry. "Father . . . Is there any way I can *not* take my vows?"

He frowned at her. "What are you saying?"

Madeleine cast a frantic look at her brother, but he was only curious. "I . . . I am not sure I am meant to be a Bride of Christ."

Lord Gilbert's brows lowered yet more. "What? If you'd been left at home and I brought a man for you, you'd marry him at my word. This is no different. Your mother sent you to take the veil and pray for us all, and here you are."

Madeleine fought back weak tears. "But . . . but shouldn't I *feel* something, Father?"

He made a growling noise. "You're feeling soft clothes

against your body and good food in your belly. Be thankful.'' But then his expression eased. ''You're pledged here, Maddy. It'd take more money than we have to buy you out, and then what? There'd be poor pickings when it came to husbands. We're not rich and powerful. Perhaps,'' he added without conviction, ''if there's fighting in England and spoils . . .''

Madeleine cast an appeal at her brother, who had once been such a hero to her. He shrugged. ''I wouldn't like to be a monk, but it's different for a woman. The sort of husband we could attract these days you'd be better off without.''

''But I wouldn't mind just staying home and looking after you both,'' Madeleine protested.

''Staying home?'' said Gilbert. ''Maddy, in the five years since you came here, Haute Vironge has become a ruin. It's in the middle of a battlefield.''

The ache in Madeleine's chest threatened to consume her. ''I have no home?'' she whispered.

''You have a home here,'' he countered. ''A finer one than you could ever have expected except for the duke's bounty. The abbess is very pleased with you. You're a regular scholar, it would appear, all set to be a healer. Who knows? One day you could even become abbess yourself.''

He was trying so hard to paint a good picture, and every word he said was true. Madeleine managed to give her father a smile. In his way he loved her and would not want to think her unhappy.

He rewarded her effort with a smile of his own and patted her head. ''That's my girl. This is the best place for you, Maddy, believe me. The world's a harsh place. God bless you, daughter.''

Madeleine curtsied. ''Godspeed,'' she said softly, hopelessly.

But at the door Marc turned back. ''It's a hard life out there, sister. Are you sure you want it?''

Sure was a strong word, and Madeleine hesitated, but then she nodded.

"Hold off your vows, then, for a while. This English business will soon be in hand, I'm sure of it. If we end up with English riches, I'll come and buy you out."

With this careless promise he left. The tears Madeleine had dammed began to fall. Marc's talk of riches was just a dream; her longing for freedom was a dream, too, and a foolish one, as her father had pointed out.

Madeleine wiped the tears from her cheeks. But a dream could not be wiped away so easily. She stared at the picture on the wall, silk worked on silk showing Christ in the desert being tempted with worldly delights. As she was tempted.

She ached to experience all the wonders of life, not just to read of them. She longed to travel to the frozen lands of the white bear, and to the burning sands of the Holy Land. She wanted to dance and gallop a horse. She wanted to see if dragons really flew in the skies above Scotland, and what it felt like when a man touched his lips to a woman's . . .

As she left the room and made her way to the chapel for the singing of nones, Madeleine clung to the slender hope offered by her brother's careless words. She would put off her vows and hope that perhaps he would ride up to the Abbaye one day, rich and come to set her free.

Westminster, England, January 1067

"**I**'m staying in England."

Aimery de Gaillard faced his father unflinchingly, but there was tension in every line of his body.

"You will do as I say," replied Count Guy flatly, but his jaw ached with the effort of keeping his voice steady. They had been sidling around this confrontation for two months, ever since the battle at Hastings, the one everyone now called Senlac—the Lake of Blood.

Harold Godwinson and most of his family were dead. The victorious Normans had marched to London against little opposition, and there William had received the acceptance he was demanding at sword point; the Witan had named him king, and on Christmas Day the Archbishop of York had crowned him in Edward's magnificent abbey.

Now it was time for many of the Normans to go home.

William had granted lands and power to those who had fought for him—Guy had received a fine manor called Rolleston and territory near the Welsh border—and a few great lords would stay to be the cornerstones of the new kingdom. Most, however, only wanted to be back in their own lands before some opportunistic raider moved in on property or wife. It was mainly the hungry younger sons and mercenaries who would stay permanently to snarl over the

13

spoils—and pay for them with military service, putting
William's mark on every corner of the land.

It was no place for Aimery, already racked by honoring his
allegiance to William. In a few short months he had toughened
and hardened in a way no father ever wants to see. He'd had
a wound, of course, and been close to death . . .

"No."

The word dropped like lead into the fraught silence of
the small room. It was the first time Aimery had ever used
it to his father in such a way.

Guy's fist clenched reflexively. It would be so easy, so
comforting, to use it, but there was more at stake here
than his absolute authority over his son.

He turned away, ignoring the negative as if it had never
been spoken. "Tomorrow we leave for the coast," he said
briskly. "There is work to do in Normandy since William
will be much absent. I will need you at Castle Gaillard
while I am assisting the duchess with affairs of state."

He glanced back. Aimery was pale and tense. There
was nothing to read in that. He'd been pale and tense since
the battle, with three notable exceptions. Just after Senlac—weak, in pain, and distraught—he'd wept in his father's arms; as he recovered he'd twice been violently and
bitterly drunk. The healing of his wound had not brought
a recovery of health and spirits, and Guy wanted only to
get him away from England, home to Normandy and Lucia.

"You have Roger to help with Gaillard," Aimery said.

"I am leaving Roger to look after Rolleston."

That set a spark ablaze. "*Roger!* Does he know a sheep
from a wolf?"

"Does he need to? He'll keep order."

"At sword point. He'll ruin the place!"

"All England is at sword point," Guy countered. "I
need you at home."

Aimery broke a little and turned away. His hand went
to his left shoulder, where he still wore bindings to help
the healing of a deep axblow. He'd been lucky not to lose

his arm or his life. He looked out through the narrow window over the thatched roofs of the houses of London.

At last he spoke. "This is my home."

"By God it is not!" Guy roared as fear and rage broke free. He swung Aimery against the wall. "You are Norman! Or do you question your paternity?"

Aimery's eyes blazed. "I also have a mother!" He moved to twist from his father's grip. Guy unhesitatingly pressed him to the left until Aimery caught his breath and desisted.

"You are Norman," Guy said quietly, inches from his son's face. "Say it."

"I am Norman," Aimery spat back. "Though whether I'm proud of it is another matter." He took a deep breath. "The king is making England his home, Father, and he is fully Norman. Though, of course, he *claims* English blood."

Raging terror surged in Guy. "That's treason, you—" He banged Aimery against the wall.

Aimery bit back a cry.

Guy forced himself away from his son before he did serious damage. He kept his eyes on the opposite wall as he struggled for control. William's claim to England hinged on his blood-link to kings Ethelred and Cnut through his grandmother. Even though she had merely been widow of both kings and thus brought no royal blood to her grandson, it was not a matter open to debate, even by Aimery, who was William's much-loved godson.

What would Lucia say if she heard Guy had risked a healing wound to assert his will? A lot, and none of it pleasant. But Lucia was too gentle to raise Norman men. See, now that he'd stopped handling the boy like an anxious nurse, there was a spark of life in him. He swung back.

"I'll have no son of mine play the traitor!"

"Fine trust in me you show!" Aimery shouted back. "By the Rood, I killed for the king, didn't I, like a good Norman vassal? The English came to withstand an invader, and I rode them down. I drove my spear into them. I sliced off arms and heads . . .'' His teeth clenched, and he breathed deeply and raggedly, as if he had come straight off that battlefield.

"And you liked it, did you?" Guy asked maliciously. *"What?"*

Guy closed the distance between them. "Got a taste for hunting peasants, have you? Why else do you want to stick around, hey? There'll be lots of chances for that as William shows the English whose hand is on the bridle. Women and children, too, I shouldn't doubt—"

He blocked the swung fist, but only just. Aimery was of a height now and strong. God, he was strong. Gripping his son's wrist, Guy had to fight to control where so recently he had won or allowed to win.

The nature of the struggle changed. Neither of them brought the other hand into play, for that would involve Aimery's weakened shoulder. Neither tried to maneuver for better torque. Guy's sword-calloused hand gripped just below his son's hand, and just above a heavy bracelet. His muscular arm could not prevail against an arm as strong.

They were deadlocked.

They were equal.

Eye to eye, they acknowledged the fact.

Aimery took a deep breath and relaxed. There was even humor in his expression, a touch of color in his cheeks. "You can let me go, Father," he said levelly. "I apologize."

Guy released him cautiously, easing the ache out of his fingers. Aimery moved away, rubbing absently at the bruised flesh of his wrist. "The truth is," he said softly, "and it's very unworthy of a Norman, I'd be happy never to see a drawn sword again. But I can't run from it. If I'm here, perhaps I can help."

"Help? Help who? Hereward?" This was Guy's greatest fear, that Aimery would join his boyhood mentor. Hereward of Mercia had been out of England at the time of the battle but was rumored to be back now, swearing to throw the Normans into the sea.

Aimery turned in surprise. "No."

"You don't plan to help him in his resistance to William?"

There was a bitter laugh. "After all I've gone through, you think I'll turn traitor *now?*"

"Whom then?" Guy asked, genuinely puzzled. "Whom do you plan to help? William? I've told you what kind of help he'll want from you."

Aimery moved away from the window to roam the room aimlessly. "The people," he said at last. "I think I can help the English people to adjust to the new ways. There's something good and fine in this country. It would be a sin to see it trampled under armed feet, especially when they cannot prevail and throw us out. I understand both sides. No one else seems to. The English think the Normans are barbarians. The Normans think the English customs are fanciful nonsense."

"And whose mind are you going to change?" Guy asked in exasperation.

A smile twitched Aimery's lips as he looked ruefully at his father. "Everyone's, I suppose."

Guy wanted to throttle him. "The only thing they'll have in common is the desire to take you apart bit by tiny bit." But that smile had defeated him. It was the first real smile he'd seen on the boy's face in two months.

"You can have Rolleston," he said abruptly.

Aimery colored with astonishment. "But Roger . . ."

"I haven't said anything to him. There's land over near Wales. He can have that. Unless the Welsh undergo a miraculous change of nature, there'll be all the fighting he could want on the border."

Aimery was dazed and a little suspicious. "Thank you."

"Rolleston was Hereward's," Guy said gruffly, "so at least you know the place. You should be able to keep it profitable. I'll have your word, though, that you'll have nothing to do with that madman."

Once, it would have been a command, but now Aimery took time to consider the point. Guy knew he now faced a man. He felt a pang at the loss of his last child and a flame of pride at what he had become. By the Blood but Aimery had courage, the deep kind that was more than the ability to kill and be killed.

"I give you my word that I will do nothing against the king," Aimery said at last. "But if I can influence Hereward to make peace with William, I will."

Exasperation returned. Were they going to start all over again? "He's a man with power over men, Aimery," Guy warned. "Get within his orbit, and you could find yourself doing more than you intend."

"You don't have much faith in me, do you?"

"I've met the man," said Guy flatly. "He's mad, but it's a special kind of madness that burns like a beacon in the dark. If he's set his hand to opposing William, he'll hold to it to the death. God knows how many others he'll take to hell with him. I want your word you'll not seek him out unless it's to make peace with William. It's either your oath on that or you go home in chains."

His son walked the room again.

"I will do it, Aimery."

"I know," said Aimery casually. "Mother has often remarked how much I take after you."

A bark of infuriated amusement escaped Guy. The urge to knock the cub silly was overwhelming, even if he might have to call in a half dozen guards to get the job done.

Aimery faced him, and that humor was back to warm Guy's heart. "You have my word, Father."

Guy was taking no chances. He took out a small ivory reliquary from the pouch at his belt and opened it to expose the fragment of the true cross it contained. "On this."

With only a quizzical look, Aimery placed his hand on the box. "By the Holy Rood," he said without hesitation, "I swear I will not contact Hereward or seek a meeting with him unless it be to bring him to William for pardon."

Guy nodded and put the reliquary away. His hand moved

to the heavy gold band on the third finger of Aimery's right hand. "You had best give me the ring."

Aimery pulled his hand away. "No." He immediately softened his tone. "I'm sorry, Father, but I cannot give it up like that. I'm not Hereward's man as a ring-friend should be, but I hope to be able to do well for both him and the king. If the day comes when I cannot, I'll return the ring to Hereward."

"But not in person."

"But not in person," Aimery agreed.

Guy took a grip on his son's shoulders, but gently. "I still think it would be wiser to knock you down and drag you home."

Aimery shrugged slightly. *"Wyrd ben ful araed."*

"And what does that mean?" Guy asked tightly. The last thing he needed was a reminder of his son's split heritage.

"Fate cannot be changed," Aimery supplied. "And my *wyrd,* I think, is in England, Father."

Guy let go of him before he gave in to the temptation to drive his fist into Aimery's bandaged shoulder. "By the Hounds of Hell, I wish I'd never given in to your mother's silly idea of sending you to this cursed land!"

"Well," said Aimery lightly, "sometimes so do I. But it's too late now to change anything."

Before his father could respond to that, he was gone.

Abbaye des Dames, Caen, Normandy, March 1068

Madeleine hurried along to the abbess' chamber, raising the skirts of her habit to run the last little way. She had been in the herb garden instead of the scriptorium and so had not been easily found. There would be penance to do for that.

She would be in trouble for running, too, of course, but hopefully there was no one around to see the misdeed.

She took a moment to catch her breath and straighten her veil, then knocked on the oak door. At the command, she entered, and halted in surprise. Waiting for her was not the abbess, but Matilda, Duchess of Normandy. She was, Madeleine remembered, now uncrowned Queen of England as well.

"Come in, Sister Madeleine," said Matilda.

Madeleine's first alarmed thought was that the abbess had despaired of teaching her decorum and had brought in the governor of the duchy to discipline her. Or even worse, to force her to take her vows. Madeleine was delaying the matter. There *had* been fighting in England; her father and brother had been richly rewarded; there was still hope . . .

But surely such personal matters could be of no interest to the duchess.

Madeleine was gestured to sit on a small stool close to the duchess' chair. As she did so she surreptitiously studied the lady. The duchess was the patroness of the Abbaye and therefore not unknown to her, but Madeleine had never been so close to her before. She was tiny and delicately made. It was hard to believe she was married to the frightening duke and had borne him six children, but she had a determined nose and chin, and very shrewd dark eyes.

"I have sad news for you, child," said the duchess bluntly. "You received word that your father was wounded at the battle when the duke went into England. Though serious, the wound was not expected to be his death, but Our Savior had other plans. The wound never healed as it should, and from that or other cause, he was taken by a seizure some months past and has gone to his heavenly reward."

The news had been clear from the first, but the lengthy telling gave Madeleine time to adjust to it. She felt great sadness that she would not see her father again, but she could not help wondering if this loss would help or thwart her dreams.

"I will pray for his soul, Your Grace," she said, keeping her eyes properly lowered to her hands in her lap.

"There is more," said the duchess. Madeleine looked up. "Your brother, Marc, was drowned two weeks ago crossing from England."

Madeleine felt numb. Marc, dead? A tingling spread through her body . . . A goblet of wine was pressed into her hand and she gulped from it, feeling the world come back, and grief, and the end of hope.

Had Marc drowned even as he came to buy her freedom?

What a thing to think when her sorrow should all be for a young life cut short in a time of triumph.

A tear trickled down her cheek, and she brushed it away. "I will pray for his soul, too, Your Grace," she said, not knowing how else to respond. She took another drink of the rich red wine, then put the goblet down on a table.

It occurred to her for the first time that it was extraordinary the Duchess of Normandy should be here to give a simple novice this sad news. She looked a question.

"At your father's request, child, you are now under the wardship of my lord husband. He has directed me to talk to you of your future."

"My future?"

"Are you aware, child," said the duchess, "that after the king was crowned in England he gave a barony to your father in recompense for his long and faithful service?"

Madeleine nodded. That barony had been the linchpin of her dreams. "Baddersley," she said.

"It is apparently a fine and prosperous parcel of properties, centered close to one of the old Roman roads that run through England. It was part of the lands of a man named Hereward—a son, I believe, of the old Earl of Mercia. My lord husband is being merciful to those who raised their hand against him once they pledge allegiance, but this Hereward is an unrepentant rebel and so has lost his estates. The question is, who is to hold Baddersley now?"

"And Marc is dead," said Madeleine numbly.

"The property is to be yours, Madeleine."

"Mine?" she queried blankly. "It is to come to the Abbaye?"

The duchess' eyes watched her carefully as she said, "No. It is the King of England's wish that you return to the world and marry a man who can hold this land for you."

Marriage, thought Madeleine dizzily. This was her dream. This was her freedom.

And yet it clearly was not.

If Marc had brought a dispensation for her, he would have treated her with careless kindness and allowed her to choose a husband. But this plan meant she and her land were to be gifted to some man with no thought for her tastes. Powerful men were often old. Most of the Norman nobles she knew were coarse, gap-toothed, foul-mouthed, and dirty.

She looked up. "Do I have to do this, Your Grace?"

The duchess studied her. "It is the will of your duke, the King of England. If, however, you feel you have a true calling to the religious life . . ."

Assailed by a decision for which she was completely unprepared, Madeleine rose and paced the small, plain room, fiddling with the wooden cross which hung round her neck, trying to assess the two paths laid before her.

One, the Abbaye, was known and stretched smooth as far as the eye could see—tranquil, ordered, cultured . . . tedious.

The other curved quickly out of sight and into mystery. What lay beyond the moment? Kindness or cruelty? Comfort or hardship? Adventure or tedium?

Madeleine stopped for a moment before the ivory crucifix on the wall and murmured a prayer for guidance. She remembered how often she had prayed to be released from the religious life. Well, there was a saying, "Watch well for what you pray, for you may receive it."

So be it. Her honesty told her the Abbaye offered her comfort and security but nothing more profound. The prayers and rituals which transported others into spiritual ecstasy were merely routines to her, some pleasant and others not.

"No," she said. "I don't think I have a true vocation."

The duchess nodded. "That is also the feeling of the abbess, though she will be sorry to lose you. I understand you have a gift for learning, particularly in the healing arts." The duchess rose. "There are many ways to serve, my dear. These are troubled times, and the king has need of you."

Madeleine was not deceived. The king needed her to toss to some man as a reward, as men toss the still-warm entrails of their kill to a hunting dog.

"Whom am I to wed, Your Grace?"

"That is not settled," replied the duchess. "There is no urgency. An uncle is caring for the land at the moment."

Uncle Paul, thought Madeleine, unsurprised.

Neither her mother nor her father's family had proved to be fertile or fortunate. Her only remaining relative was her mother's sister, Celia, who had married an impoverished lord, Paul de Pouissey. That marriage was childless, but Odo, Paul's son by a previous marriage, had always been considered Mark and Madeleine's cousin.

Paul de Pouissey was a consistent failure and quick to latch onto any good fortune of his wife's family.

"You have been educated here beyond most young women," the duchess continued, "but will need to learn court manners. You must join my ladies. I expect to be summoned to England in the spring to join my lord. Time enough then to settle your future."

If no particular man had been chosen, Madeleine thought, then perhaps there was a chance to take control of fate. "I would ask a boon, Your Grace."

A faint touch of frost entered the duchess' eyes. "And what might that be?"

Madeleine's nerve almost failed her, but she spoke her request quickly. "My lady, I would beg to have some say in whom I am to marry."

A glance showed her the duchess was very cool indeed. "Are you suggesting the king and I would not have care to your welfare, girl?"

Madeleine hastily knelt. "No, Your Grace. Forgive me."

She watched the duchess' slippered foot tap three times. Then Matilda said, "Well, yours has been an unusual upbringing, and some allowance must be made. At least you have spirit . . ." That foot continued to tap. Madeleine stared at it, wondering if she was merely to be forgiven, or would gain something, even the slightest right of consultation.

"I will ask my lord husband that your wishes be taken into consideration," the duchess said eventually, startling Madeleine. "And I will do my best to see that your marriage is delayed a little, to give you time to adjust."

At this extra generosity Madeleine looked up in amazement. The duchess was smiling dryly. "Oh get up, girl. Your groveling has gained what you want."

Madeleine rose warily.

"You are suspicious?" asked Matilda. "That is wise. Do you know of my courtship?"

"No, Your Grace."

The duchess' smile broadened as she looked into the past. "William asked my father for my hand, and I refused. He was, after all, a bastard and none too secure in his hold on his land. I was somewhat rude in my rejection. One day William and one attendant rode into Blois and came upon me in the street with my maid and guard. He seized me and laid his riding whip to me."

Madeleine gasped, but the duchess' smile was still fond. "Later he sent to ask again, and I accepted."

"After he had whipped you?"

"Because he had whipped me. Oh, don't think I desire that kind of thing. Since that day he has never raised a hand to me, and the heavens would crack with our raging if he did. But a man who dared come into my father's stronghold and assault me so was a man whose destiny I would share."

The duchess rearranged the folds of her flowing ruby skirt. "Why am I telling you this? Because I approve of a woman willing to take a grasp on her fate and try to steer it. I will support you as far as I am able. I also point out that the responsibility for choosing a husband is not a light one. Take heed what qualities you seek."

Madeleine nodded.

"My cloak," the duchess commanded. Madeleine picked up the soft, white cloth embroidered in gold and red, and draped it around Matilda's shoulders. She pulled the ends through the heavy brooch of gold and garnet, and arranged it on the lady's shoulder.

Matilda nodded her approval. "As for now, I am on my way to Saint Lo on the business of the duchy. I will visit here again in two weeks and take you into my company of ladies."

With this Madeleine was dismissed. She stood in a quiet corner of the cloister and considered her strangely altered future with excitement and trepidation. She would be joining the court and going to England. She would be entering the hitherto forbidden world of men and the marriage bed.

The convent had not left her totally ignorant, for there was much whispered speculation about sins, especially those of immodesty and fornication. And she had, after all, lived in the world until she was ten. She believed she knew well enough what men did to women, though she hardly thought, as Sister Adela had insisted, that some women became as crazed with lust as men. And as for Sister Bridget's assertion that men sucked magic fluid from a woman's breasts in order to stiffen their member for the act . . .

All such issues were irrelevant anyway. Madeleine had been given a chance to live in the world. That meant more to her than a sweet lover in her bed.

She understood the duchess' lesson perfectly. She would need a strong man to hold her barony safe in a troubled land—one skillful in war and careful in administration. The color of his eyes, the shape of his limbs, were irrelevant.

She would take care to choose well. Then Duke William would have no pretext for rescinding the privilege she had won and imposing on her a choice of his own.

Chapter 1

Baddersley, Mercia, May 1068

Madeleine walked along the woodland path, searching the undergrowth for valuable plants. Baddersley had suffered, first under the rule of her sick father and careless brother, and now under the harsh hand of her uncle, Paul de Pouissey.

She would never understand men. What point was there in conquest if everyone starved, or died of disease? Medicinal supplies were scarce at Baddersley, and the herb garden was rank with weeds. She had brought a small box of medicinal and culinary herbs and spices—a farewell gift from the abbess—but more, much more, would be needed.

Most, but not all, of the plants here were the same as those she was familiar with back home—she stopped and picked a handful of cinquefoil, so good for toothache. When she had more skill with the strange English tongue perhaps she would be able to learn from the local people.

It was not very likely, she admitted with a sigh. It wasn't just language that cut her off from the English, but the sullen resentment they felt for their Norman conquerors. Quite reasonably, she supposed, especially when the representative of Norman rule hereabouts was Paul de Pouissey. Madeleine had never liked her uncle, and now she was coming to hate him.

Things were not turning out at all as she had planned.

After two months of training at Matilda's court in Rouen, Madeleine had joined the duchess' train en route to England, the proud owner of chests full of fine clothes, jewels to wear with them, and a tiring woman to care for them. She had new skills in music and dance, and new friends, including the duchess' thirteen-year-old daughter, Agatha, and her sixteen-year-old niece, Judith. The three young women had a common interest, for they were all to find husbands in England.

Now Agatha and Judith were at Westminster, enjoying the festivities surrounding Matilda's coronation as Queen of England—and meeting all the eligible men. Madeleine, however, was here in Mercia "learning about her land." That was how Matilda had described it, adding that such a great heiress would not want to be at court where she would be fought over like a rabbit thrown to the hounds.

Wouldn't she?

Madeleine suspected the real problem was her right of choice. The king and queen must have come to regret promising her some say in the choice of her husband.

Madeleine stretched and raised her loose brown hair from her neck. It was a warm day, even in the shade. All she wore was her shift and a simple blue linen short-sleeved kirtle. This was girdled with a plain leather belt holding two pouches for leaves and roots, but her main object at the moment was not collecting but taking inventory of nature's storehouse.

She left the path to study a low-growing bush, and her skirt caught on a twig. Impatiently she hitched it higher into her girdle, upsetting the careful folds achieved by her tiring woman, Dorothy, and achieving a length more suited to a peasant than a lady.

Dorothy would have a fit to see her so, Madeleine thought with a grin, but Dorothy was some way back resting against an oak and sewing, and so in no position to object.

The bush proved to be dwayle, as she had hoped. Madeleine stored it in her memory. Though the berries were dangerous, the leaves could soothe those who were agitated or in pain.

Back on the path she noted witchhazel, elder, and some mosses growing on an oak. She saw brambles which would bear fruit later. If the management of Baddersley continued as she had witnessed during her week here, wild foods might be all that stood between them and starvation in the winter.

She now knew why all her Uncle Paul's enterprises came to naught. He blustered and roared and plied his whip, but he could not organize people to purposeful work, nor could he look ahead and guard against disasters.

Aunt Celia was almost as bad. She had more notion of management than her husband, but her ranting abuse of any shortcoming, and her constant belief that everyone was trying to deceive her, did not lead to good service.

Angrily, Madeleine snapped a dead branch from an elm. This was her land, and it was being abused. The first thing she would do when she had chosen a suitable husband was to throw out Paul and Celia. And they knew it.

At least they were happy to have her out of sight, and so made no objection to her exploring the nearby land as long as she took Dorothy and a guard along. Dorothy complained at "being dragged all over the place," and so Madeleine left her to sit in the shade. Paul's men were as idle as they could be, and happy to guard the maid rather than the mistress. Madeleine was left to explore in peace.

She never wandered far, however. The people here were cowed but still unfriendly, and she no more wanted to meet any of them alone in the woods than she wanted to encounter an angry boar. She looked back and checked that Dorothy and the soldier were still in sight.

Then she glimpsed water through the trees. She went forward eagerly for there were many beneficial plants which grew in marshy ground at a river's edge.

A large splash halted her. Just a fish? Or some large animal? She moved forward more cautiously, and peeped out from behind a stand of willow.

A man was swimming.

The smooth line of his back was clear—long, golden, and slick with water. When he turned to swim toward the bank, she could see his face but could make little of it. Young, though. But she'd guessed that from his body . . .

Still in deep water, he stopped swimming, stood, and began to wade toward the bank. Madeleine gave a little sigh as his body was revealed bit by bit.

His shoulders were broad and sinuously strong, sloping down into hard breasts; between the flaring ribs ridges of muscles formed a perfect central cleft which was emphasized by the faint line of water-darkened hair disappearing into the river.

Naked and a part of nature, he was like a perfectly formed wild animal.

He stopped with the water girdling his hips and raised his arms to slick back his long hair. His shoulders stretched, and his upper body seemed to form a heart shape for her delight. She suppressed a breathy, "Oh!" He shook his head like a dog, sending spray to make diamonds in the sun.

He began to wade out of the water again, revealing more of his body, inch, by inch, by inch . . .

Madeleine watched, her chest rising and falling with each deep breath—

He turned suddenly, as if alerted by a sound.

Madeleine looked away, horrified by her rampant curiosity and the disappointment she felt. She knew how a man was made. She'd laid out corpses.

This man was nothing like a corpse. He was nothing like any man she had ever seen. She peeped back.

He stood like a statue, watching the far bank of the river. Madeleine followed his gaze and saw three russet hinds prick their way delicately down to the water. They were alert for danger, but he stood so still they were unalarmed and dipped their heads to drink.

Madeleine looked back to the man.

If anything, his back was more breathtaking than his

front. The smooth line from broad shoulders to hard buttocks was surely God's perfect work. The long valley of his spine could have been drawn by God's loving finger . . . She imagined running a finger from nape to cleft . . .

Madeleine shut her eyes and said a silent prayer. ". . . deliver us from temptation . . ." But it was no good. She opened her eyes a slit.

He had not moved. He stood as still as a statue and just as God had made him. There was no sign of race or rank, though she knew he was English from the long hair. Though it was darkened by water, it was blond, probably the golden Scandinavian blond much more common here than in Normandy.

But he wasn't a peasant. He was too tall, too evenly and beautifully developed to be of such low class. It needed good food from birth and long years of training in a range of skills to develop a body like that—fluid, capable of wielding sword or ax throughout a long battle, able to control a war-horse, climb walls, draw a bow . . .

Water from his hair formed a rivulet in the cleft of his spine. It ran all the way down to his buttocks. Madeleine found herself imagining catching those drops of water on her tongue, running her tongue up that sensuous valley to the nape of his neck . . .

She clapped her hand over her mouth and shut her eyes. What a thing to think!

She heard something and opened her eyes. He was gone, leaving only ripples, and so were the deer. Had such a little noise alarmed them?

The spell was broken. Madeleine hurriedly retreated and leaned against a tree—weak, breathless, and ashamed of herself. How extraordinary and dreamlike that had all been, and how wicked her thoughts. She would have to confess them.

She wouldn't dare!

Who could he have been? There were no noble Englishmen left in this area. She could almost believe him of the

faery world—a river prince, a forest king. Hadn't she seen
dark marks on his body which were surely magical?

She didn't dare investigate the river plants today. She
might be enchanted and dragged down into the water to
live as captive to a faery prince.

It wasn't fear she felt.

To be such a man's captive . . .

She tiptoed away from the river back toward Dorothy
and Conrad. And safety. Safety from faeries and her own
wanton weakness—

She was seized. A hand clapped over her mouth. She
was entangled in a cloak. In a second, Madeleine found
herself pinioned by a strong arm with her back against her
captor, silenced by a large, calloused hand.

Her fantasy had become terrifying reality, and this was
no faery prince. She struggled and tried to scream. He was
Saxon. He'd slit her throat!

He said something she could not understand, but the
gentle tone calmed her, and she stopped her futile struggle, though her heart still raced and tremors shook her.

He continued to speak in the soft, burred English Madeleine heard all day but hardly understood as yet, despite
her lessons with the local priest. Looking as she did, he
doubtless thought her one of the castle maids. She must
keep up the pretense. He was surely an English outlaw,
and if he realized she was Norman he *would* slit her throat.

It was hard to believe he was the enemy, however, for
his soothing voice smoothed away her fears. The voice,
the cloak, the heat of his body behind her, his arm around
her, all made her somnolent, as if he were casting a spell.

Perhaps he was.

Was he still naked? She imagined him naked behind
her, his wonderful body separated from hers by only two
layers of cloth. Trembles started which had nothing to do
with fear.

Held as she was, she could see nothing of him, just the
path ahead—ground kept barren by the regular wearing of
feet, the arch of trees in leaf, yellow and white flowers

blooming among the undergrowth. She heard the singing of birds, the humming of insects, and the murmur of his entrancing voice.

He said something else, and cautiously slid his hand from her lips. She guessed he had told her not to cry out. She licked her lips and tasted him upon them. His hand slid down her neck, then up again to gently press her head back against his chest. Still she could see nothing of him, but beneath her hair she felt cloth. It disappointed her that he was dressed. At that thought heat rose in her cheeks . . .

He laughed softly and murmured again as his hand stroked down her stretched neck like a trail of fire. Then it traveled further, to rest hot over her right breast.

Madeleine gave a breathy moan. Even through her kirtle and the cloak she could feel the heat from that hand as if it lay against her bare skin. Her nipple swelled into a point of unbearable sensitivity, and his hand moved in slow butterfly circles as if he knew. She imagined that deep murmuring voice was speaking of love and sinful delights . . .

She ached with a need to respond, to reach up and hold his hand against her, to turn and kiss him, but she was caught in the cloak. She wanted to speak but dared not, for then he would know she was Norman.

His right hand moved again, leaving her breast bereft. Now, following the path of her desire, it slid down to the juncture of her thighs, cupped and pressed her there. She made a wordless protest and moved back, but there was nowhere to go, and her wicked body did not really want to escape . . .

She stifled a betraying plea even as her body moved against his hand.

He laughed and blew softly over her heated cheek.

Then he picked up his spells again as his hand slid up her body, over her left breast to her neck. His fingers trailed to her nape, and he lifted her damp, heavy hair. The murmur of his voice stopped. The brush of his lips at her hairline trickled a shiver of delight down her spine as the river water had run down his.

His tongue against her skin was moist, hot, then cool as the breeze found the trail he left. He was doing as she had imagined and running his tongue down the top of her spine, but the moisture he would find there was not cold river water but hot perspiration.

Hot. So hot.

A shudder passed through her, as if she were taken by a fever. The rumble of his laughter vibrated into her. She laughed, too, enchanted into madness. She was going to speak, to turn, to seek the kiss she hungered for.

Then, ''Farewell,'' he said. She understood that.

He flipped the back of the cloak over her head. By the time she had disentangled herself he was gone.

Madeleine collapsed on the ground. He was surely of the faery world to be able to entrance her so. For all she knew that had been faery language, not common English at all.

But the cloak in her hands told her he was human and his magic was human, and all the more dangerous for it. The garment was fine green wool, woven in two shades and trimmed with red and a darker green. Not a poor man's garment. Unlikely in an outlaw unless stolen; certainly not faery.

She would like to keep it, but she would be questioned. She folded it neatly with cherishing hands and left it there, then returned dazedly to her attendants.

She had not called out. The Bible said that if a woman did not scream she could not claim assault.

How strange. How strangely wonderful.

How sad that such a man was not for her.

As far as she was concerned, he might as well be a prince of faery. Such men didn't exist in the real world, the world from which she would have to choose her husband.

But still, she could not resist a prayer that when finally she found herself in the marriage bed, her husband would touch her as the faery prince had touched her, and take

her to the end of the magical path he had opened before
her.

Aimery de Gaillard chuckled as he escaped. When he'd
ambushed the secret watcher, he'd not expected to find
such a delicious armful. He wished he'd been able to pursue the matter further—a great deal further. She had a
lovely, luscious body, and a responsive one.

At first he'd assumed she was a local wench, but he'd
soon guessed she was Norman, probably one of Dame
Celia's women. Few English had that dusky tone to their
skin. Blood from southern France or Spain lay in her
somewhere.

Clever of her to stay silent and conceal it.

And she didn't understand English. If she did she would
have reacted when he described all the wonderful things
he wanted to do with her body. He laughed again. If she
ever learned the language and remembered some of the
things he'd said, she'd be after him with a gelding knife.

He'd not even been able to steal a kiss for fear of her
seeing him up close. Aimery de Gaillard had no business
on Baddersley land, and he wanted no connection made
between him and a certain Edwald, an outlaw who helped
the people against the Norman oppressors.

An older, bearded man emerged from among the trees.
"Taking your time, aren't you? Why're you grinning like
a fool?"

"Just the pleasure of the swim, Gyrth," said Aimery.
"It's a joy to be clean again."

Gyrth was Hereward's man, but he'd been appointed to
attend Aimery during his youthful visits to England. It was
Gyrth who'd taught Aimery English skills and English
ways—the reverence for custom, the importance of discussion, the stoical acceptance of *wyrd*.

When Gyrth had turned up at Rolleston, Aimery had
known Hereward was back in England and planning resistance. Aimery's duty to William said he should hand Gyrth
over to the king, but instead he had accepted him without

question. Gyrth was doubtless part missionary and part spy, but he was also Aimery's link to the English way of thinking. He needed that as he tried to explain the new Norman laws and customs to the ordinary folk to help them to survive invasion.

It had been Gyrth's idea, for example, that they go around this part of England disguised as ragged outlaws. It was a dangerous plan but had proved useful. Though Aimery de Gaillard looked English and spoke the tongue, the English knew him for what he was—a Norman, an enemy. As Edwald the outlaw he was accepted and heard the truth. Many places were doing well under Norman lords, but some were suffering, as here at Baddersley.

"What you going to do about this place then?" Gyrth asked.

"I'm not sure what more I can do." Aimery buckled on his belt and knelt to cross-lace his braies. "I've explained the villagers' rights to the headman. If abuses continue, he should make petition to the king."

"And de Pouissey'll let him go off to Winchester and complain?" said Gyrth with a sneer.

"William's always on the move. He'll come this way."

"And treat that devil as he deserves?"

"And correct injustices," said Aimery firmly as he stood. "William seeks to rule his people in justice. Constant unrest is not making that easy."

Gyrth grinned. "It's not supposed to make it easy. It's supposed to send the Bastard back where he belongs."

"Dreams, Gyrth. William's fixed in England like a mighty oak, and he'll bring hell on it before he gives up an acre. But he's dealing fairly with all who accept him. If Hereward swears allegiance, he'll receive some of his land back."

"Receive back," Gyrth echoed in disgust. "A man's land is his land. Not the king's to give and take."

"Not under Norman law, and a rebel's land has always been subject to forfeit. William is respecting the rights of loyal men."

"What of a man's right to be free? I hear tell a lord over Banbury way's making slaves of any freemen he finds and setting them to work. Where's your just king in all that?"

Aimery faced him. "William can't know everything."

"He can be told. By you, perhaps. If you insist on living on both sides you can make yourself useful at least."

It was a challenge. Aimery nodded. "Indeed I can. We have time to visit Banbury before returning to Rolleston. We'll go there tomorrow and see exactly what's going on." He looked down ruefully at his clean body and clothing. "I wouldn't have washed if I'd known, though."

As he bundled up the rough clothing he wore as an outlaw, Aimery noted the satisfied look on Gyrth's face. "We go to observe and report, not to take action. I'll not be pushed into committing treason, Gyrth."

"So who's pushing?" asked Gyrth innocently.

Aimery shook his head and turned to lead the way to their camp.

"You've left your cloak somewhere," Gyrth said.

Aimery grinned. "So I have. Hold on."

As he returned, Aimery pressed his cloak to his face and smelled the same soft perfume he'd inhaled from her skin. Rosemary and verbena, perhaps.

Gyrth looked at him and leered. "So that's what took you so long. You must be a fast worker, lad, but was it worth the risk? I thought you didn't want anyone here catching sight of Aimery de Gaillard, Norman lord."

"She never saw me."

Gyrth slapped his knee and hooted with mirth. "By Woden, I should watch you in action sometime! Come on, though, before her husband turns up with an ax."

Wrapped in the cloak against the night chill, Aimery lay tangled in thoughts of the dusky maiden even as he sought sleep. He tried to turn his mind to plans of action, but they wove back to the curve of her hip, the silk of her hair, the heated perfume of her skin.

By the Chalice, it hadn't been that long since he'd had a woman!

He turned restlessly and pulled the cloak tighter. Wisps of verbena and rosemary wrapped around him. He surrendered and allowed his mind the path it desired.

She was comely. Unfortunately their position had given him little more opportunity to see her features than she'd had to see his, but the sweet curve of her cheek was fixed in his mind, and he had studied the back of her neck at leisure. Smooth, sun-gilded skin over subtle flesh, warm and spicy on his tongue . . .

He stirred restlessly. These thoughts were not adding to his comfort. He rolled on his back and stared up at the stars. Perhaps he should just present himself at Baddersley as Aimery de Gaillard and take the pleasure the wench was so eager to give. Aimery de Gaillard had every right to stop in at Baddersley and request hospitality . . .

This was madness. Baddersley hadn't been Hereward's principal estate, but Aimery had visited it often enough to be known. His disguise was effective, but if the Baddersley people saw Edwald the outlaw and Aimery de Gaillard within days, some of them would make the connection and talk of it.

It must have been too long since he'd had a woman if he was letting a comely wench tempt him into such danger.

Aimery awoke the next morning believing himself cured. He and Gyrth breakfasted on fish, bread, and water and set out for Banbury.

The clothes they wore were those of poor peasants—a coarse homespun tunic belted with braided leather and, for a cloak, a heavy woolen cloth with a hole cut for the head. They were bare-legged with leather sandals on their feet.

They carried large packs so as to appear to be petty merchants. If their path crossed that of a Norman patrol, it was as well to have reason to be on the road, and reason to be carrying a better quality of clothing than what they wore.

Aimery had to assume his disguise—dirty his skin and grease his hair again—and so the sun was well up by the time they left the camp. He soon pulled off his cloak and bound it on top of his pack, muttering a profanity.

"You're like a hungry boar this morning," said Gyrth.

"I could be clean and on my way home to Rolleston," Aimery complained, "instead of on a hot, dusty two-day walk to Banbury."

Gyrth grinned. "Or back beneath a certain wench's skirts. Kept me awake last night you did with all that tossing and turning."

Aimery laughed off the idea, but it was true. His ill-temper was because of the unfinished business between him and a certain dusky maiden. If he'd had his pleasure with her, he'd doubtless not give her another thought. Well, they'd soon be off Baddersley land, and the memory would fade with distance.

They traveled alert for every hazard, for these were poor times to be abroad in England. Because of this, as they walked along a ridge path, Aimery quickly spotted a flash of white down near the stream. He halted, grinning. There she was again, and well away from yesterday's meeting place. He found her prudence appealing. He'd have thought less of her if he'd found her haunting the same spot.

"What's up?" Gyrth asked, hand on knife.

"A hind down by the stream." Aimery slid off his pack.

"We've no time for hunting . . ." Then Gyrth found what Aimery had seen. "Especially not that kind."

"I have a mind to meet with her face to face."

Gyrth took a grip on Aimery's sleeve. "Give her a good look at you, boy, and she'll remember you another time."

"I doubt it. We see what we expect to see. Anyway, we're not likely to meet another time." Aimery pulled free, but he took care that the dirty bandage he wore cov-

ered the tattoo on his right wrist. That was always the
thing most likely to betray him.

Aimery slipped down the scrubby hillside toward the
stream. He'd been well-trained in woodcraft, and he was
within feet of the girl without her being aware of him.

She was nimble and graceful as she hopped across stones
in the shallow stream, studying the water. She had both
kirtle and shift tucked into her belt, and he relished the
sight of her long, shapely legs. Her hair was bound today
in a thick plait which swung heavily across her back. He
imagined unraveling it and losing himself in the chestnut
cloud.

He deliberately stepped on a twig.

She jerked around, wide-eyed, a scream hesitating on
her lips.

"Good day, Lady," Aimery said.

Gyrth was right. He was mad. Was he just going to
throw her down and rape her? They couldn't even communicate unless he revealed his knowledge of French. She
was as lovely from the front as he'd imagined, though,
with a smooth oval face, clear dark brows over beautiful
eyes, and soft, sweetly curved lips.

"Good day," she said with a horrendous accent.

"You speak English," he said approvingly.

It was the same voice, thought Madeleine, with a thrill.
And yet she was disappointed. She'd imagined her faery
prince to be a little more glamorous than this. She'd spent
many sleepless hours picturing him as a noble, daring warrior. Her mind had drifted ever closer to the entrancing
notion that he might be a potential suitor. After all, it was
rumored that Judith and Agatha were to be used to buy the
allegiance of noble Englishmen.

But now here he was before her, a peasant in rags.

They were staring at each other like simpletons.

"I speak very little English," she said haltingly.

He stepped closer. "Lucky then that I speak a little
more French." His French was the coarse peasant tongue,
but he seemed fluent.

Madeleine realized with a chill that she had revealed her nationality and she wasn't even sure he *was* her faery prince. His greasy hair was quite dark and his skin was grimy, not gold. His smile began to look wolfish to her.

She backed away . . .

"Don't be afraid," he said. "What's your name?"

Madeleine was poised for flight, but something held her back. She knew, however, it could be dangerous to tell him she was Madeleine de la Haute Vironge. "Dorothy," she said.

"Don't run away, Dorothy. I won't hurt you."

Madeleine relaxed under the influence of that same soft, soothing voice. It was him. And there was something else reassuring. Something in his smile . . .

She realized it was his teeth. They were white and even, unlikely in a ragged peasant.

She smiled. He was in disguise. He *was* her faery prince, doubtless an English noble, traveling incognito. Once she'd framed this thought, it was amazingly easy to see through the dirt and rags to the handsome face, the powerful body, and the golden hair. He had startling green eyes, she discovered, which crinkled entrancingly when he smiled.

"I'm Edwald," he said. She knew it was a lie but understood.

"How is it you know French?" She made each word clear and separate. She knew how hard it was to understand a foreign tongue when spoken quickly.

"I've traveled to France."

That argued high birth. Perhaps he was one of the sons of Harold who were trying to avenge their father. But in that case she would expect his French to be more elegant.

He spoke again. "Do you make a habit of wandering the woods alone, Dorothy?"

Madeleine glanced back down the stream. The real Dorothy was just visible, the guard just out of sight. "I have friends nearby." It was a warning as well as information.

He followed her gaze, then took her hand to draw her

away from the stream and behind a thicket. Heart pounding, Madeleine knew she should run. If he tried to stop her she should scream. She did neither.

He rested his hands on her shoulders and smiled down at her. His eyes really were very attractive. "I wanted to see you properly," he said.

The darkened skin and greasy hair muddied her vision. "I wish I could see you properly, too."

Danger flashed in his eyes, but then he laughed and shook his head. "How have you survived in this harsh world, Dorothy? Don't worry. I won't harm you even if you do hold my life in your hands."

He gathered her hands together and dropped kisses into her palms, tickling them with warm breath that stirred something hotter inside her, something she recognized as forbidden. Her conscience made her pull away, but when he tightened his hold to stop her, she did not persist.

His hands slid along her bare forearms, and inside the loose sleeves of her kirtle to her shoulders, rough skin and callouses against her smoothness. "Your skin is like the finest silk," he murmured. "You must know, though, my sweet Dorothy, that I cannot see you after today."

No one had ever touched her so intimately, and she was softening like wax on a hearth. "Why not?" she breathed.

"How can I risk it? You would know me for an outlaw and tell your king."

"No," said Madeleine with certainty, "I wouldn't."

His thumbs rubbed against her collarbones. "You should. It would be your duty."

But they blinded traitors and rebels, or gelded them, or lopped off hands and feet, Madeleine thought, shivering. "No, I promise. I will never betray you."

He freed his hands of her sleeves and drew her close against his hard body. Her conscience cried the alarm. This was wrong. She should run. Now.

But surely she could stay just a little longer. It was honey-sweet to be in his arms.

Greatly daring, she raised her hands to his broad shoulders, remembering them wet and beautiful in the sun. Her right hand found bare flesh at the nape of his neck and she cherished it, her fingers seeking the top of the valley of his spine.

"Ah, my beautiful wanton . . ." His lips touched hers as softly as a kiss of peace, but this kiss brought turmoil, and her conscience gained control.

She snatched her hands away and used them to push instead. "I mustn't!"

Laughter sparked in his eyes. "Mustn't you?" He loosened his arms. "Then fly, little bird. I won't stop you."

Contrarily, his words allowed her to muffle the alarm bells in her mind. He wouldn't hold her against her will, and she wanted to be kissed. No more than that, just a kiss.

Gathering her courage, she touched her lips to his. He laughed and dropped kisses on her nose, and cheeks, and chin. Madeleine did not want to reveal her ignorance so she copied him. She showered his face with little kisses.

He murmured approvingly and guided her lips to his, this time with a hand firmly cupping the back of her head. His tongue came out to lick her lips.

Madeleine was startled, but she resolutely did the same. Her tongue met his, mobile and warm. His mouth opened, her mouth opened, his tongue entered to play.

Madeleine gave a little moan and stopped thinking. Her body hummed, and she leaned against his wonderful chest, strong as an oak, warm as a fire-stone. His hand on her breast turned her legs to jelly. She collapsed completely against his mighty arm. He moved back and sat on a rock, pulling her onto his lap.

"Yes, darling, yes," he murmured in English.

Madeleine regained a scrap of sense and realized she'd had her kiss. It really was time to stop . . .

His mouth found her right breast. Madeleine stopped thinking again. His hands and mouth tormented her, and her body developed a mind of its own. Her hips turned to move against him. She closed her eyes.

Heat. Ache. There was a piercing ache between her legs, covered suddenly by his hand. She moaned and moved against him, then stilled as she realized what was happening.

"No!" she cried and pulled away.

His hand clapped over her mouth. An arm like iron imprisoned her. She squirmed and kicked. "For Christ's sake, stay still!" he hissed.

She obeyed because she was helpless against his strength. She was panting and shivering as if with an ague. He wasn't in a much better state.

His hand eased off her mouth. "Let me go," she whispered. "Please let me go."

She felt a shudder pass through him. "By the Virgin's milk, what's the matter?"

A fine sheen of sweat covered his skin, and his eyes were more black than green. He shifted slightly, and she felt his hard member against her thigh and jumped with fright. She pushed on his chest. "Let me up! Let me up! This is wickedness!"

He stared at her and muttered something hot and angry in English. Then in French he asked tightly, "Are you by any chance a virgin?"

Feeling as if she were accused of the blackest sin, Madeleine nodded.

Slowly he released her and stood. His breathing was deep and unsteady. "How," he said, "did a bold armful like you remain a virgin at your age? What are you? Eighteen?"

"Seventeen." Madeleine pulled her skirts down and tugged at her bodice. He'd had her half naked. She ventured a glance at him. Lord, he was angry. He looked as if he were going to beat her, and for being a virgin still. "I'm sorry," she said, then giggled nervously at the absurdity of it.

If he was angry, so was her body, screaming that it had been deprived of something it had been promised. She hurt. She wrapped her arms around herself.

He sighed and shook his head. "It was a hard day when I met you, Dorothy. Go on back to your friends and take a lesson from this."

She didn't like to part from him in anger. "I only wanted a kiss," she said wistfully.

He gave a laugh that sounded almost genuine. "Well you certainly had that. Go on. Go, or I might think better of my noble impulse."

Madeleine took a step away, and then came back in spite of his forbidding look. "It was a very nice kiss," she said softly, and reached up to brush her lips against his. Then, having some sense left, she fled.

Aimery watched her in bemusement, then rubbed his hands over his sweat-damp face. That little encounter had been intended to exorcise her effect on him and leave him at peace. Now he wondered if he'd ever have peace again. His body hurt, and his mind was tied in knots.

If she really was a virgin, she was wasting a natural talent. He'd lost his head as soon as he touched her. What a pleasure it would be to show such a fiery piece all the wonders of her delightful body, but he wasn't risking another encounter like this one. He'd be a wreck before Midsummer Day. The only solution was to put as much distance as possible between them. He began to climb the slope. A two-day walk to Banbury was just what he needed.

Madeleine stopped her flight by the stream to catch her breath. She looked back but could not see him. She had the strangest desire to retrace her steps . . . She shook her head. She knew what a lucky escape she'd had. If she wasn't a virgin when she married, she'd never be honored by her husband. She could be rejected, beaten, imprisoned . . .

She shuddered. It was madness, but just now being with him almost seemed worth whatever came afterward.

She checked her appearance, sure her wickedness would be written there. Her gown was straight and decent but, oh Lord, there were two wet circles over her breasts where his mouth had been.

The dizzy heat swept over her at the memory, and she pressed her hands against the aching nipples.

"Lady Madeleine!"

Madeleine saw her guard trotting toward her. She looked down at her telltale gown. With a little laugh, she tipped herself forward into the shallow stream.

"Lady Madeleine!" The man splashed over to her. "Are you all right? I thought I heard something."

Madeleine pushed herself up, soaking wet. "I'm fine. I just tripped."

"But earlier? I heard a cry."

"Oh, that. I thought I saw a snake." Madeleine allowed him to help her over to the other side of the stream. "You are slow to respond, though. That was ages ago."

"No, it weren't," the man protested. " 'Tweren't more than a few minutes. Dorothy and I just wondered as to whether we'd heard anything, and then I came to find you. You shouldn't go out of sight, my lady . . ."

Madeleine felt as if she had been gone from the real world for hours, days even, not just minutes. She was not at all sure she was back yet, or ever would be. As the guard shepherded her back toward Dorothy, Madeleine cast one wistful look back at the thicket by the stream.

Chapter 2

A long day of walking brought Aimery a night of deep sleep. When he awoke the next day, the encounter with Dorothy seemed to be a dream. It was just as well he didn't need to return to Baddersley, though. The wench was dangerous.

Ten miles from Banbury, Aimery and Gyrth heard rumors of the enslavement. The culprit was Robert d'Oilly, which hardly surprised Aimery. D'Oilly was a coarse French mercenary—a vicious and effective fighter without any other virtue. It was a tragedy William had had to use such as he to win England, and now thought fit to reward him with land.

Aimery and Gyrth soon fell in with a group of men walking to Banbury market. It was easy enough to get them talking.

"Took my sister's nephew. Just like that. He'd done nothing wrong."

"Hear tell the priest over Marthwait tried to stop 'em and they broke his head. Still ain't recovered his wits. Bloody Normans. Bastards, every one of 'em."

"Who's overlord?" asked Aimery in the same rough tongue the villagers were using.

One spat. "Should be Earl of Wessex, but they up and killed him at Hastings, didn't they? Now there's none but the bloody king, and a fat lot of use it'd be complaining to him."

"Worth a try, though," said Aimery. They looked at him as if he were half-witted.

"Tell you what," said one man sarcastically. "Why don't you stick around the next time the Bastard king happens to be riding by, then you can tell him. And get kicked in the face."

Aimery put an edge of authority in his voice. "I know what I'm talking about. I'm an outlaw, but I know William of Normandy has no love for slavery. If you can get word to him, he'll put a stop to it."

"He'd turn against a Norman for Englishmen?" one man scoffed.

"He'll enforce the law."

"What about our women?" cried one young man. "Those guards take what they want and none dares stop them. My sister . . ." He turned away, his face working.

"Rape is against the law, too," Aimery said firmly.

The thunder of hooves shut off the talk. The villagers bolted for the woods even as a troop of horsemen swung around the bend and bore down on them. In moments they were surrounded, and none had escaped.

It was d'Oilly's men on the hunt for more forced workers. Aimery cursed his luck. There were five horsemen, but they had a slovenly look which suggested he and Gyrth could take them with even minimal help from the villagers. But violence only ever brought retaliation on the ordinary people. Instead he worked at avoiding attention.

It wasn't easy. He was half a head taller than the tallest villager and much better built. He slouched and nudged Gyrth. Gyrth got the message, and Aimery hoped the others would play along.

One of the soldiers unhooked an ox-whip from his saddle. "Well," he said in French, "we've found a likely lot here." He changed to clumsy English. "Lord d'Oilly has need of laborers. You, you, you, and you." He pointed to the youngest and strongest, including Aimery but not Gyrth.

Gyrth instantly spoke up in English. "Sir, my cousin

here is . . ." He tapped eloquently on his head. "He can be no use to you."

"He's strong. You come, too."

Within seconds the chosen ones were cut out of the group. One man resisted. "You can't do this! You have no right. I am a free man—" The whip cracked over his head and he fell silent.

The five prisoners were herded a mile or so to the river where a bridge was being built to ease access to Robert d'Oilly's new castle. A dozen men were working there, some of them already exhausted. Aimery suspected more slaves were among the workers to be seen assembling the wooden keep on the raw motte, or hill, in the distance.

Two of the villagers were added to the men loosening rocks from the bottom of an escarpment; Aimery and another were ordered to join the weary line carrying the rocks down to the bridge. Because of his greater age, Gyrth was put to work there laying the rocks in place.

As the day passed they were offered no rest or refreshment, though the guards let them scoop water from the river to drink. The five guards slouched in the shade, cracking a whip if they thought any of their slaves were idling. They shared a wineskin and, at one point, some meat pies.

They frequently shouted comments in French which alarmed the peasants, but they were invariably just scatological insults, pointless because they must assume none of their victims understood.

Aimery understood, however, and anger grew in him. These men were the scum of the earth, mercenaries brought to England by the lure of easy pickings. The urge, the need, to obliterate them was a hunger in him far greater than the pangs of his empty stomach. He kept telling himself that violence here would destroy his chance to do greater good later, and would bring harsh retribution on the local people, but it grew harder and harder to pay attention to logic.

He hauled a leather sling of stones onto his bruised

shoulders and shambled down to the river. As he passed one pot-bellied guard, the man shouted, "Hey, big boy! Bet you've got an enormous one. Bet you stick it in your mother!" Aimery pretended to be deaf. He tried to ease his fury with anticipation of the king's reaction when he heard of this injustice, but he could taste the pleasure he'd get from slitting the man's throat.

As Aimery slouched back up the hill for another load, the man in front of him stumbled. Aimery helped him up. The closest guard sneered but made no objection. The worker's breathing was labored, his eyes glassy.

"He needs rest, lord," Aimery mumbled.

"No rest," said the guard, and aimed the wineskin at his mouth.

Aimery helped the peasant fill his sling with rocks, putting in as few as he dared. It was a mercy they were hauling the heavy weight downhill, but he doubted this man would last much longer. What would happen when he failed? If the guards had any sense, they'd take some care of their beasts of burden, but scum have no brains. They probably thought there was a never-ending supply of slaves.

They set off back down the hill, and the man began to weave. Aimery did his best to help, going in front and guiding him, but suddenly the peasant stumbled and fell to his hands and knees, his head hanging like the exhausted beast of burden he'd become.

The pot-bellied guard stirred himself to his feet and cracked his whip. "Up, you misbegotten swine. Up!" The man twitched but slumped down again.

Even as Aimery dropped his sling of rocks and ran to help, the whip cracked again and bit. The peasant twitched and gave a guttural cry, but even the pain couldn't move him. The whip whistled and cut again before Aimery reached him.

"Out of the way, dolt!" snarled the guard in French, moving closer, "or there'll be more of the same for you." He switched to English. "Move!"

Aimery turned to face the brute, whose heavy paunch and slack face revealed he was poorly trained and exercised. "Mercy, lord," he said in French.

"An honest word from a worm like you?" The guard jerked his thumb eloquently. "Scat!"

Aimery rose slowly as if befuddled. The guard paid him no more attention and swung his whip back with relish.

Aimery leaped. With an arm round the man's throat and a knee in his back, he broke his neck. As the man fell, Aimery whipped the sword from his scabbard, grimacing at the clumsy feel of it and the old blood and rust marring the blade. He kicked the body out of the way—scum, as he'd thought—and turned to face the first of the four other guards. He deliberately shambled and held the sword as if he had no idea what to do with it.

A glance showed him Gyrth leaping onto a guard and the peasants standing around terrified. "Don't let them escape!" he shouted.

"They ain't going to help you, pig's swill," sneered the nearest guard, thinner but still with the belly of self-indulgence. He showed a scant collection of yellow and black teeth. "And I ain't going to kill you quickly. Not quickly at all . . ."

Aimery raised his sword awkwardly, and the man laughed. "We'll have you dance with one foot, turd. And then we'll play blindman's buff with a real blind man . . ."

As the guard continued his pointless taunting, for he must assume his victim understood little French, Aimery assessed the situation. None of these men could be allowed to live if the villagers were to survive and his identity was to be protected. But the villagers were numb with terror.

Gyrth had killed his guard and taken his sword. The other two Normans were on him, and the sword wasn't Gyrth's best weapon. He'd need help.

Aimery swung his sword wildly as an untrained peasant would. The guard howled with laughter. He sidestepped the swing and moved in contemptuously to slice off Aimery's right arm. Aimery adjusted his grip and slammed his sword up against the other. While the guard was still stunned and his arm tingling numb, Aimery said, "God save you," in crisp French and decapitated him.

The head on the ground looked profoundly surprised.

Aimery ran over to join the other fight. The guards were wary now, and Gyrth had been hard pressed to defend himself. Aimery could no longer appear unskilled, and within moments both men gave up and turned to flee.

Aimery caught one and ran him through. The other guard turned and slashed at Gyrth, slicing into his leg and sending him to the ground.

"Stop him!" Aimery yelled at the gaping peasants.

A few moved to try, but as soon as the soldier turned with his sword they cowered back. Aimery raced after the man, but this one was lean and fleet. A glance back showed the peasants making for the woods like terrified animals and Gyrth on the ground trying to staunch the bleeding.

With a curse Aimery threw his sword after the man like a spear. But a sword is not a throwing weapon, and it only caught the man on his mailed shoulder, spurring him on to greater speed. Aimery turned back to kneel by Gyrth.

"I'm all right," Gyrth gasped. "Go after him."

"Don't be foolish." Aimery slit strips off a guard's clothing and bound the wound, grimacing at the filthy state of them. "My mother holds wounds bound with clean cloth heal better than those bound with dirty," he remarked. "We'll have to hope she's wrong."

"Wounds heal or not as fate disposes." Gyrth heaved himself up. "If I'd had an ax, that one wouldn't have lived." He looked up at Aimery. "He could write your death warrant."

"And yours."

"I'm a rebel anyway. Now so are you."

Aimery shook his head. "They were breaking the law. If my part in this slaughter becomes known, I'll claim I was freeing myself from slavery."

"If your part comes out, it'll all come out. That guard

could recognize you if he bumps into Aimery de Gaillard. Then what?''

Aimery shrugged and put an arm around Gyrth to take his weight.

"I'll be admiring your head on a pike one of these days," said Gyrth angrily. "Go back to being an ordinary Norman, lad. Either that or join Hereward and throw the Bastard out."

"I've never been an ordinary Norman," Aimery replied, "but I'll never be a traitor to William either."

"Goddammit, lad!" Gyrth cried in exasperation. "Hereward and the Bastard'll be fighting as to who gets first cut at you!"

Aimery smiled. "You should meet my father. You have a lot in common. Come on. Let's get out of here."

Madeleine tried to put the encounter with Edwald the outlaw out of her mind. In view of the suffering among her people here at Baddersley, it was her duty to marry quickly and throw out Paul and Celia. In that decision her outlaw, her faery prince, was only a distraction.

An overwhelming distraction, though, which had her standing idle in the middle of a busy day, and tossing restlessly in her bed at night. Nothing could discipline her dreams. Night after night she relived his touch on her bare skin, his hot mouth on hers, and woke feeling achingly empty.

It was a great relief when her cousin Odo rode up to Baddersley. Perhaps he could take her mind off such foolishness.

Odo de Pouissey was Paul's son and Celia's stepson, and so no blood relative of Madeleine's, but he had spent a great deal of time at her home when she was a child, and she thought of him as a brother. He was tall and strong, dark-haired like his father, and of ruddy complexion. He was jovial unless crossed, and good company. His greatest fault was a fondness for ale and wine, but no one was indulging in excess in Baddersley these days.

Odo was happy to spend his time with Madeleine, telling her stories of the conquest of England. She thought he was the hero rather too often for credibility, but they were good stories all the same. He also described the queen's coronation, making much of his privileged place at court. Madeleine was distinctly envious and gathered up any scraps of information she could about eligible young men.

"And who is highest in the king's favor?" she asked one day as she set stitches to repair a shift. They were sitting outside the manor house in the sun.

"His old cronies. Mortain, Fitz Osbern, Montgomery."

"But what of the younger men? There are many carving out great futures for themselves, are there not?"

He cast her a suspicious look, and she realized he thought she was sneering at him, who didn't seem to be carving out much. She kept her face bland.

"De Varenne is well regarded," he said sulkily, "and de Faix. Beaumont . . . and the de Gaillards, of course. The king fair dotes on them."

"It is often luck," she soothed, "that brings a man to the king's eye."

"Aye, that's the truth. But what justice is there when he panders to the damn Saxons?"

"There are English at court?" Madeleine asked, surprised. Even if the king was wooing them with marriages, she hadn't expected them to be so kindly received.

"The place fair crawls with them, smiling and bowing to get their lands back. There's not one of them I'd trust."

"But it's good they are accepting the king. Now we'll have peace."

"How's a man to get lands if there's peace? If William returns their lands, what's left for his loyal Normans? You'd best watch out, Mad," he said spitefully. "One of these days that scum Hereward'll bow the knee, and the king'll give him back Baddersley."

Madeleine's hands stilled. Baddersley was *hers*.

Odo laughed. "That gets to you, I see. Mark my words. It could happen. He's given Edwin of Mercia most of his land back. Edwin's your overlord here now, do you know? How do you fancy making your allegiance to a damned Saxon? *And* William's giving him his daughter.''

''Agatha?''

''So they say, and there are rumors the Lady Judith will be given to a Saxon cur, too. If you're not careful, Mad, you'll suffer the same fate.''

Madeleine kept her eyes on her work. There was one Englishman she could bear. They could finish what they'd begun. A familiar aching warmth stirred inside her. ''What are the English lords like?'' she asked.

''Too pretty, or too rough,'' he said dismissively. ''They wear their hair long, and many of them keep face hair, though they're tending to shave it off to please the king.'' He guffawed. ''Look like shorn lambs. They dress as fancy as a lady and flaunt their gold when it should have gone as reward to their conquerors.''

Madeleine sighed. She'd get no useful information from Odo on this subject. ''You'll get a rich reward in time,'' she assured him.

Odo reached over and seized her hand. ''What of you, Madeleine? You're a prize.''

Madeleine hissed with annoyance. He'd made her prick her finger and put a bloodstain on her work. ''I don't care to be thought of as a prize of war,'' she retorted.

He smiled. ''*I* don't think of you like that. I've always been fond of you, Mad. You could do a lot worse than me for a husband.''

Madeleine sighed. It had been clear that this was behind his visit, but she'd hoped to avoid a confrontation.

She looked at him. He was young, healthy, and strong. He was familiar. She could do a lot worse, but she could do a lot better, too. Anyone who didn't bring Paul and Celia along with him like the plague would be infinitely better. She took refuge in deceit. ''The king will choose my husband, Odo.''

''Will he? He has a lot on his mind with new rebellions

popping up every week. You could languish into an old maid here, waiting.''

''I expect to be summoned back to the queen very soon,'' said Madeleine, truthfully enough. Matilda wanted her to be a childbirth attendant. But the babe was not due until August or September. Would she be left here until then?

''Even if he does remember you,'' said Odo craftily, ''the king could use you to pay any number of debts, Mad. You could be wed to a toothless ancient, or a fuzz-cheeked boy. To a man whose taste runs to commoner women, or to one who'd enjoy hurting you. I wouldn't want to see you end up like that, Mad. I'd be a loving husband.''

''I'm sorry, Odo,'' she said, trying to soften the refusal. ''I must wait on the king's pleasure.''

She caught a flash of anger in his eyes, and her decision was reinforced. He reminded her unpleasantly of his father, who often took his fist to Celia. No, she didn't want to marry Odo.

The next day was Odo's last, and his father called for a hunt for his son's entertainment, and in the hope of supplementing the poor food available at Baddersley. Odo had recovered his good humor, and Madeleine was happy to slip back into sibling fondness. On the other hand she would be as glad to see him leave as she had been to see him arrive.

It was a fine, sunny day, and as they rode out Madeleine saw that even neglect and unrest couldn't steal the beauty of the English countryside. Once the people settled to new rule, this land would be rich, great, and good. And she would be a part of it, she and her descendants. ''Ah, England.'' She said it softly to herself, as if to a lover.

Riders, huntsmen, and hounds gathered in an open meadow deep with a rainbow of flowers. Madeleine smiled and breathed the sweet air. England had a different flavor from Normandy. England was gentle, rich in the arts, and full of music and poetry. Even though she was still strug-

gling with the language, she enjoyed the sagas and stories
of love and loneliness, hope and pain.

Normandy was harsher and rougher. Or perhaps, she
thought, looking at her uncle, her cousin, and their men,
it was just a harsher, rougher people. Now that the Norman lust for war had come to England, would it destroy
Baddersley as it had destroyed Haute Vironge? Not if she
could help it. Baddersley was hers.

She pulled a leaf from a low-hanging branch and rubbed
it between her fingers. The sap stained her skin, and the
aroma rose like perfume to her nose. Her tree, her land,
her deer, her people . . .

All that was needed was a lord capable of holding the
barony safe and making it prosper.

Not Odo.

But an English lord would be in tune with this land, she
thought. Though Edwald had said he would not return,
every time she was out in the countryside Madeleine
looked for him, hoping he would appear again on silent,
skillful feet . . .

The hounds caught the scent of a deer and ran. The horn
blew and the riders began the chase. Madeleine and Odo
rode side by side, laughing for the pleasure of the hunt.

"It's heading over that hill!" shouted Odo. "This way.
We can cut it off!"

He swung his horse, and Madeleine followed as the rest
of the riders took the hounds' line. They galloped into a
wood, heading toward the other side of the hill.

And came up against a deep, fast-flowing stream.

They both pulled up. The trees grew down close to the
banks, and the chances of working their way along the
edge of the water were poor.

"Do you think we can ford the stream?" Madeleine
asked, listening to the distant sounds of the hunt.

"No, of course not." Odo was looking at her strangely.
Madeleine shivered with unease. It was surely just the dim
coolness here among the trees. "Come on then." She

turned her mount. "Let's go back around the hill and catch up."

His voice stopped her. "Hold on a moment. Mastery's limping." He swung off and raised a hoof for inspection. "Mad, can you come down and hold him?" called Odo, struggling with his sidling horse. "I think he's picked up a thorn, but I can't get a grip on it."

Madeleine swung out of her saddle with a sigh and went to help. She took Mastery's reins, and the horse immediately calmed. After a moment she realized this was because Odo had stopped touching the beast. He came around the horse.

"Odo, what are you—"

He grabbed her.

Her cry was smothered by his wet lips and stale breath. She kicked and twisted to frighteningly little effect. Fear and suffocation made her head swim, and her clawing hands found only the tangling cloth of his cloak.

His lips released her, and she sucked in breath to scream, but he pushed her down on the hard ground, landing on top of her so that only a squeak emerged as pain shot out from her spine and hip and shoulders.

Incredibly, he was grinning. "Come on, Mad, you panted after me as a girl." One hand yanked her skirt up at the side. "Bet you had hot dreams of me in your cold little convent cell. Well, I'll make your dreams come true."

She bucked. "Odo, *no!*"

His grin just widened. Bile rose in Madeleine's throat. Frantic, she twisted and kicked, but his massive body was like a log on top of her. His shoulder pressed on her face, making it difficult to breathe, never mind to scream.

Panic choked her. If he dishonored her, the law called for castration, but the law hereabouts was Odo's father. The alternative would be a hasty wedding. Once it was done, would the king interfere? "Blessed Mary, aid me . . ."

His smile switched to an ugly scowl. "Don't call on the saints," he snarled, struggling to manage both her clothes and his without giving her a chance to move or scream. "It's time you learned your . . . duty . . . Stay still, curse you! Learned what a woman's . . . for." His writhing freed one of her hands. *"Hell!"*

Madeleine wrenched out her small knife and stabbed him in the arm.

"You little bitch!" He picked her up and slammed her back to the ground. The knife flew from her hand.

He was back on top and her skirt was now up high. His weight was full on her chest as she gasped for every breath.

"By the Grail, you need a lesson, Mad!" he exclaimed, redfaced. "When we're wed . . ."

Only half conscious, Madeleine felt a new wave of terror at the word. It brought a new burst of strength. She writhed, she shrieked. He pummeled and cursed.

He stopped.

His dead weight crushed her. Then it rolled away. Sobbing and gasping air into her burning lungs, Madeleine saw a peasant leering at her exposed body. He was stocky and grizzle-haired, with a beard and moustache which marked him as English. Muttering prayers to the Virgin and saints, Madeleine scrambled painfully to her feet, grabbed her pathetic little weapon, and hobbled back against a spreading oak.

"Allez-vous en!" she gasped. Then, awkwardly, she tried English. "Go away."

"Don't be afraid."

Madeleine started at the new voice and looked down to see another man by Odo's body. It wasn't surprising she'd missed him for he blended with the leafy earth, dressed as he was in mud-colored clothes. Even his head was wrapped with a dirty cloth that hung forward over his face.

He stood and rocked Odo with a sandaled foot. "He is not dead," he said in rough French. "Do you want him to be?"

With a gasp, Madeleine recognized him. Then doubted. Then saw green eyes and was sure. She gave a little cry and hurled herself into his arms.

He held her as she shuddered, choking back sobs. He was so strong and warm and safe. His hand gently comforted the back of her head. Then he pushed her away a little. "Shall I kill him for you?" He pulled out a long, vicious-looking knife.

The other man said something sharply. She could tell he wanted to get out of the glade, which wasn't surprising. They were English, and they'd attacked a Norman.

"No," she said quickly. She just wanted them safe. "Go. Please."

He shrugged and sheathed the knife. "You should leave this place, too."

She shook her head. "I'll be all right. It was just that he took me by surprise. Please go. My uncle's hunting here. He'll kill you. Or worse."

He showed no urgency. His hand reached out to cradle her neck and humor glinted in his eyes. "I warned you about going about the country unescorted."

"*He* was my escort," Madeleine said with a disgusted look at Odo.

"Truly a wolf sent to guard sheep." He drew her gently to him.

Madeleine relished the comfort but regarded him in exasperation. Why didn't he flee? "You said you would not be here again. It's dangerous."

He traced her lips with a gentle finger and frowned. "You're swollen. I should kill him." Then, "I had business here. You did promise not to betray me."

"I won't."

"I know. Shall I take the taste of him away?"

Madeleine sighed. "Yes, please."

He tilted her chin and lowered his head.

His friend said something. Then Madeleine heard it. Horses!

"Déguerpissez!" she hissed urgently and pushed him. "Go. For Mary's sake, go!"

Still he hesitated. "Are you sure you'll be safe?"

She pushed harder, with all her strength. "Yes! Go!"

Like wraiths they melted into the forest, and Madeleine was alone with her unconscious cousin. Her rubbery legs gave way, and she collapsed on the ground. She could feel bruises forming all over her body.

Odo. Odo had tried to rape her, but if she accused him it was as likely to lead to a hasty wedding as anything. She started to shiver again. But overlaying pain and shock was joy. Her outlaw was back, and he had rescued her, and he was as wonderful as her dreams told her.

"Madeleine! Odo!"

Her uncle's voice shattered her thoughts. She called out to get his attention, then crawled to her cousin. She didn't want him dead for then the whole Norman might would be turned to finding his murderer.

No danger of that. Odo had a large lump on the side of his head but was beginning to stir and groan.

The eruption into the glade of Paul de Pouissey, four of his men, and three cavorting hounds caught her just as she was wondering what she was going to say about her predicament.

"Odo!" Paul was off his horse in a moment and at his son's side. "Who did this?" he demanded of Madeleine, fiery anger coloring his heavy jowls.

"Not me," she said hastily. Paul de Pouissey's anger easily took a physical form. "We were set upon," she explained quickly, acting on instinct alone. "Outlaws." No, that was too close to the mark. "A band of marauders. Many of them . . . Danes, perhaps . . ."

Her uncle snarled at her babbling and whirled on his men. "Find them! Find the curs who did this to my son. And," he added quietly, "take them alive for my vengeance."

In a moment the yelling men and their dogs were off

into the wood, hunting new prey. Madeleine watched in horror. She had not intended that. But, she told herself, her outlaw was at home in the forest and would easily evade such clumsy pursuit.

Chapter 3

Aimery and Gyrth raced through the forest, their dun-colored clothes blending with the greens and browns. Then, as surely as a man walks through the streets of his town, they took to the spreading oaks and moved from tree to tree. When they had evaded the hunt, they halted on a slope by a stream as their pursuers circled aimlessly in the distance.

Aimery watched in silence as he got his breath back.

Gyrth rolled on the ground laughing. "Norman pigs," he gasped. "Stupid, shit-eating Norman pigs!" He sobered and sat shaking his head. "Why'd you have to take a risk like that, lad?"

"I couldn't watch a rape." Aimery bent down and scooped up water to splash over his face and head, then shook the excess off. She was as beautiful as he remembered, as his dreams told him. He should have killed Odo de Pouissey. The mere thought of the man touching her . . .

"A Norman sow being raped by a Norman hog?" said Gyrth. "The only thing wrong with that is the chance of little piglets."

Aimery fought the urge to bury his knife in Gyrth. "She's a woman and deserves protection."

"She's the little trollop you trysted with down by the stream, you mean." At the look in Aimery's eyes, Gyrth backed off. "So you did your noble Norman duty. You nearly got yourself killed."

"I was in no danger."

"Say that if de Pouissey catches you. That was his son you knocked out."

"I know. I know Odo de Pouissey."

Gyrth raised his brows. "Nice friends you have."

"He's no friend of mine," said Aimery. "He's a braggart lout and now my enemy."

"So," said Gyrth. "Who was the pretty maid? No servant, I'll go odds, dressed so fine and with gold bindings on her braids."

"No." Aimery hadn't really considered her appearance before. He gave a crack of laughter. "She must be the Baddersley heiress, and I almost rolled her by the stream that day. No wonder she screamed no."

"Well now," said Gyrth thoughtfully. "You could do a lot worse, lad."

"A lot worse than what?"

"Roll her by the stream—*after* you've married her. Baddersley would be in good hands then until Hereward claims it back."

Aimery was surprised by the wanting that pulsed through him. He could have her, and finish what they'd begun. And damned well teach her how to defend herself. Would she really have tried to hold them off with that little knife? He suspected she would. She was brave, if foolish, his dusky maiden . . .

"I don't see her setting up a squawk," said Gyrth, "after the way she was looking at you today."

Then Aimery came to his senses. "You should have had this tempting idea before you embroiled me in Baddersley's affairs. I've been here too often now as Edwald. If I move in as lord, someone will soon recognize me, and there's a traitor in the village."

"We'll soon find him and put an end to that," said Gyrth flatly. "Most of the people would die before they'd betray you. You're their hero."

"It would be madness," said Aimery, tempted all the same. But then he shook his head. "She'd recognize me.

It would hardly be fair to put her in a position where she would have to deceive the king or betray me. Nor to tie her to a man walking the perilous path I have chosen. My fall would ruin her, too.''

And his fall came closer every day.

He had a special fondness for Baddersley, and the people here were suffering. That was why, against his better judgment, he'd returned. Aimery had responded to the pleas of the most desperate and had agreed to help them flee. They were gathered in the woods nearby. Aimery would set them on their way to the north country, which was less firmly under the Norman heel, but he well knew some of the more warlike would head east to the Fens and Hereward. He'd seen Gyrth speaking with some of the young men, recruiting.

And that—providing soldiers for the king's enemies—was undoubtedly treason. It even went against his own aim of dissuading rebellion. But the alternative was worse: to leave the people under the tyranny of Paul de Pouissey.

Killing Normans. Helping fleeing peasants. Recruiting for Hereward. One day he would have to pay the price, but he had accepted that when he had set his foot on this path in those days after Senlac. His only regret was the pain and disgrace he would bring to his parents. There was no need to add the heiress to those who would suffer.

"I would have thought," said Gyrth slyly, "that Baddersley held fond memories for you. Aldreda, wasn't it?''

Aimery couldn't help a grin. "Yes, Aldreda of the chestnut hair and luscious body.''

Gyrth grinned back. "A man never forgets his first woman.''

And that, thought Aimery, was true.

It had been at Baddersley that he'd become a man. He'd just turned fourteen, and Hereward had decreed he was ready. He'd received his last tattoo—the hart on his right hand, which was supposed to gift him with the powers of that animal. He'd received his ring. He'd chosen his woman and made love to her there in the hall.

It was an honor to be chosen, and neither Aldreda nor her husband, Hengar, had objected. After the celebration a chosen woman spent the night with the lord, and any child born a nine-month later was considered the lord's child. It would be given favor and raised high. Aldreda had borne such a child, a girl called Frieda, though there was no way to know whether she was his, or Hereward's, or even Hengar's.

Aimery realized he should check on Frieda's welfare in these uncertain times, but he'd have to do it without meeting Aldreda, for if anyone could recognize him, it was she.

He smiled. She'd been only sixteen to his fourteen, but she'd seemed a woman grown to him—shapely, full-hipped, and with long chestnut hair. She'd been kind to a nervous boy and delicious in his arms.

There was a resemblance between Aldreda and the heiress. Perhaps that was why he had been so instantly attracted to her. He pushed the thought away. Madeleine of Baddersley was not for him. Unfortunately.

Gyrth interrupted his thoughts. "So, does that winsome smile mean you're going to try to win Baddersley for yourself?"

"No," said Aimery shortly. "It's safe now. Let's be on our way."

They climbed down the far side of the hill, heading for the camp they'd set up for the cottars. People had been quietly slipping into it over the past day. Tonight they would move everyone out.

"Why don't you want Baddersley?" Gyrth persisted.

"Because I'd like to live to see the year out."

As they drew close to the camp, Aimery halted. There were no sounds when there should be, for there were children and even babies among those who sought freedom. There was no smell of wood-smoke when they had agreed a fire was safe this deep in the woods. With a hand signal to Gyrth, Aimery moved forward.

The camp was deserted. The fire was trampled out,

though wisps of smoke still rose. Only an overturned pot and a forlorn bundle told of people recently in the area. Aimery and Gyrth walked slowly into the camp, puzzled.

A rustling sounded nearby. Aimery spun around, knife already in hand. A boy crawled fearfully out of the undergrowth.

"What happened?" demanded Aimery, still alert for danger.

"Men came," said the lad tearfully. "On 'orses. With dogs. They rounded 'em all up. Then 'e came."

"Who?"

"The Devil." The boy shuddered. " 'E said as 'ow they'd attacked his son. They're all to be flogged to death. All of 'em!" He fell to wailing. Aimery gathered him in his arms, knowing the boy's family had been among the taken.

A few other people shuffled out of the dense undergrowth, gaunt with horror.

"But they were pursuing us," Aimery said.

A woman came forward, a babe at her scrawny breast. "They were as surprised to find us, Master, as we were to be found. That's why so many of us had the chance to flee. Curse the Norman bitch!" She spat sharply into the ashes of the fire.

It took Aimery a moment to register it. "A woman was here?"

"She came afterward with the Devil, fairly begging him to torture us all. I can't understand their heathenish tongue, but anyone at Baddersley has cause to learn the word 'fouettez'. 'Whip them, whip them,' she kept saying."

"Who was she?" It must have been Dame Celia, he told himself. It must have been.

"It were the Devil's niece, Master."

Aimery couldn't believe it. "Chestnut hair, brown eyes?" he queried, praying the woman would say no.

She nodded.

He was chilled. What kind of woman was she, to do this? She knew these people were innocent.

He began to wonder if there was a different pattern to the attack he'd witnessed. Perhaps she made a practice of teasing men. In Odo de Pouissey had she finally met a man without gallantry and almost paid the price? Aimery felt some sour sympathy for Odo. Not much, but some.

"You're sure it was Lady Madeleine?" he asked again.

"Clear as day," the woman said.

"And she was begging for the people to be whipped."

"Fair desperate about it."

Hope left him. She was deceitful, lewd, treacherous, cruel. The thought that he'd been drawn to such a creature disgusted him. "She will pay," he promised the people in front of him.

The woman's eyes brightened. "Praise to Golden Hart."

It was like a shower of icy water. *"What?"*

The woman touched the design on his right hand as if it were a sacred thing. "It's what we call you, Master."

Aimery looked down. The male deer which leaped down his right forearm onto his hand was of such an ornate design that many would fail to recognize the animal, but not enough apparently. Done in shades of red, brown, and yellow, it could be called "golden." But this new name was a disaster. How had anyone ever seen the marks? He'd been careful to hide them with dirt or a bandage, but they were clearly visible now.

He remembered plunging his hands into the cool stream. The dirt must have been washed off. He had obviously been similarly careless before.

Had the design become visible when he'd been slaving for d'Oilly? Or on other occasions? How many people here at Baddersley remembered the mark given to Aimery de Gaillard all those years ago? Very few, but one would be enough if he had a mind to betrayal.

Aldreda would certainly remember. He hoped she was still kind and honest, but his faith in women was at a low ebb.

"You must not call me that," he said to the cottars. "Otherwise the Normans will soon find me."

"Yes, Master," they all said.

His eyes met Gyrth's, and he saw his own skepticism mirrored there. They would try to keep their word, but they needed a myth these days, and he was apparently it.

It would be worse than that. Any story of English resistance would be attributed to Golden Hart; the murder of the four Norman guards would be just the first. Golden Hart would be eight feet tall and carry a flaming ax. He would rip out trees by the roots and hurl them at his enemies. Soon the country would be rocking with the myth. And it only needed one Norman to study the design on his skin for the connection to be made.

His *wyrd* was likely to be a brief life and a violent end, but he was English enough to accept that. He turned his mind to practical matters and ordered the few remaining cottars to gather their belongings. They must be out of here before Paul de Pouissey organized a manhunt to round up the stragglers.

But at the last moment he sent them ahead with Gyrth.

"What are you about, lad?" asked Gyrth. "It's hazardous in these parts just now."

"I need to find out what's happening to the ones who were taken."

Gyrth scowled. "You mean you want to see if the little bitch is as wicked as they say. Have done. She has you spellbound. Cut free while you can!"

"I thought you wanted me to marry her."

"Not anymore. You get close enough to touch, lad, you slit her throat."

Madeleine sat in the solar of the old manor house of Baddersley, plying her needle under her aunt's critical eye and trying to ignore the sounds coming from outside—the crack of the lash, the shrieks, and the constant wailing misery. It had been going on for so long. Her uncle had rounded up nearly twenty runaways and herded them back to the castle. He'd ordered them all flogged.

Madeleine's convent-trained needlework was better than her aunt's, which did not prevent Celia from criticizing. Today, however, the woman had grounds for complaint, for Madeleine's hands were shaking, and her stitches were all over the place.

Celia leaned over and gave her a vicious pinch. "Rip it out!" she snapped. "How useless you are. As useless as these wretched Saxons."

Aunt Celia was thin and bony, with a mouth that was constantly pursed, as if she had bitten into a green apple. She poked her needle sharply into the cloth before her as if she wished to be poking it into the Saxons, or into Madeleine.

Madeleine moved out of reach of the woman's hard fingers and began to undo her stitches. She was working on a new cloak for her uncle, and the worse it was done the better as far as she was concerned. She couldn't believe the depths of his cruelty.

She glanced around the room. One woman, Aldreda was her name, was working at the loom. Another, called Emma, was spinning. Both looked taut with bitterness. Emma and Aldreda's daughters sat by their mothers doing plain sewing, one dark-haired, one angelically fair. Tears ran down their faces, and their hands were as unsteady as Madeleine's.

Dame Celia poked in her needle and pulled it out as if the sounds from the bailey were of music, not suffering. Her one Norman attendant, Lise, took her demeanor from her mistress. Madeleine didn't know how any human could be unmoved by what was taking place.

She was still stunned by it all. Her body was stiff and sore from Odo's abuse, her mind was still reeling from the aftermath. Why had she said those fateful words? Why not say Odo had hit his head on a branch and fallen from his horse?

Anything.

She had told her uncle these people had nothing to do with the attack, but he hadn't believed her. He didn't really care. Someone must suffer for the attack on his son, and these people deserved punishment for fleeing their place.

Madeleine said a prayer of thanks to the Virgin that she had persuaded him to make do with a whipping. She had saved the men from the loss of a foot, the women and children from branding on the face.

At first she had stood and watched the whipping, still racking her brain for some way to stop the punishment, but she had become aware of the people watching her; the hate in their eyes had been as cutting as a bitter wind. She'd fled inside. There had been no green eyes among the prisoners, no stalwart build such as that of Edwald. Had these people been found quite by chance? Had they no connection to him at all? If so, their punishment was even more unjust.

Her aunt has soon spotted her—idling, as she put it—and set her to work. Madeleine wouldn't mind the work if it would blot out the floggings, but on such a fine day the shutters stood open and there was nothing to block the sounds. At a dreadful shriek her hands clenched on the cloth in her lap. It was as well she wasn't working on fine linen or silk; it would be a mangled rag by now.

A servant crept in fearfully with a pile of clothes to be placed in a chest, eyeing the Normans as if they were the Devil. The whip-cracks and moans continued, and Madeleine pressed her fingers to her aching head. "Will it soon be over?" she asked the girl in her careful English.

Aunt Celia gave a snort of disgust.

The maid looked up and nodded, then lowered her eyes, but not before Madeleine had seen a flash of hate there, too. Why? Just because she was Norman? Reason enough, she admitted.

She started as a new wailing built. "What's happening?" she asked the maid.

"Just the children, lady," the girl muttered.

Madeleine stood in shock. Her work fell to the floor. "He's going to whip the *children?*"

The girl cowered away.

Aunt Celia said, "What are you about, you silly girl? Pick up your work. It will be soiled."

Madeleine ignored her and ran into the hall, where her uncle sat drinking, staring at smoke marks on the wall. His two vicious hounds lay by his feet.

Aunt Celia was hard at her heels. She grabbed Madeleine's arm. "What are you doing?" she shrieked. Then in a whisper, "Don't bother him, you foolish nodkin."

Madeleine tore herself out of her aunt's hold but took the caution to heart. Hating the need, she swallowed her anger and sought diplomacy. "Surely the floggings should be over by now, Uncle."

"Pretty near, I'd think," he said without interest. "What's the matter? Bothered by their caterwauling? You wanted it this way. A few lopped feet would be a better lesson, and quicker. Branding would make sure they couldn't sneak off again."

"How could they work the land footless?" she protested. "We have few enough laborers as it is. If you've whipped them too severely, who will weed the fields?"

"They're sturdy as oxen," he countered. "A flogging won't do them any harm."

"What about the children?"

"What about them?"

"You're surely not beating them, too?"

"Teach 'em early." He looked up like a surly bear, and his hands formed beefy fists. The hounds raised their heads and showed their teeth. "Go mind your affairs, Niece, and let me mind mine."

Mine. Not yours. Mine. Madeleine bit back the words. Tears of frustration built in her eyes as high, childish shrieks reached her. The worst thing in life was to be powerless.

Like one of the sunbeams striking through the dusty air of the hall, Madeleine saw the truth. She needed the protection of the king and a husband or Baddersley would be ruined. Alone she could do nothing. She needed a husband to enforce her will. It was only necessary that he be just and able. Tall or short, fat or thin, young or old—such things were no longer important; she truly believed the king would give her a husband who was at least just and able.

If this awareness had been William's intention in sending her here, then she granted him the victory; but how was she to do anything about it? She had not even the means to send a message without her uncle's consent.

She had a sudden urge to flee. To run away from Baddersley into the forest, to find the great Roman road they said passed nearby and went all the way to London. There she would surely find news of the king and queen . . .

But that would be madness and the act of a child. To go alone through unknown territory, among a hostile people whose language she could barely speak? It would be suicide. She would have to find the means to send a message . . .

"What are you standing there for, girl?" her uncle demanded. "Don't you have work to do?"

Madeleine wished she could drive a sword through her uncle's black heart. "Do not speak to me as if I were a serving wench, Uncle," she snapped.

She saw the hot anger in his eyes and the convulsive clenching of his fist. A low growl rumbled from his hounds. Behind her, Celia gave a moan of apprehension, but Madeleine held her ground. When he said and did nothing, she considered she had achieved a victory. She was, after all, mistress here. "The children are not to be flogged," she declared. "Stop it immediately."

Slowly he rose to his feet, massive and with plenty of strength in his bulk. "I have the running of Baddersley, Niece. Those children will learn early the price of shirking. Just as you will if you take that tone with me."

Madeleine couldn't help but take a step back. The hounds had risen to stand by his side, lips curled to show sharp teeth. But she responded firmly, "This is my land, Uncle. Those are my people. Stop the whippings."

His hand shot forward and gripped the front of her tunic. She was hauled up against his stale body, her face only inches from his. His foul breath assailed her as he snarled, "Shut your mouth or you go next to the post."

He meant it. He was mad.

Celia scuttled over. "Stupid girl!" she hissed. "You can't talk to a man like that!" Paul de Pouissey glared his wife into silence, then contemptuously released Madeleine.

Madeleine tried to tell herself her silence was noble— she would not be able to help the people of Baddersley if she was dead. But she knew it was blind terror that stilled her. For the first time in her life she knew what it was to be in a cruel person's power, to be abused or not at his whim.

Get word to the king, she thought. That must be her goal. Get word to the king and be rid of Paul and Celia forever. It must be possible—with the help of a traveling merchant, or one of the villagers willing to risk a journey. But she must be careful. She ignored Celia's whispered rebukes and crossed the hall to an open window that looked out on the bailey.

Oh, Sweet Jesu, they had a howling child tied to the post. He could be no more than eight. At least they were using a light whip on him, but as it bit he shrieked and cried for his mother. The least she could do, thought Madeleine bitterly, was watch. And so she did, too angry even for tears, as a half dozen children were dragged to the post and whipped, each one smaller than the one before.

Dear Lord, would they whip the babes in arms?

It stopped at long last with a child of about three carried off howling in terror—Madeleine hoped to his mother's arms if she wasn't too ill from her own punishment.

Her fear left her, or rather it was worked by her hot rage as iron is worked in the forge. She felt as hard, cold, and resolute as a mighty sword. This injustice had to stop, and she must be the one to bring it to an end.

Aimery stood at the back of the angry, silent crowd and looked at Madeleine de la Haute Vironge framed in a manor window. How could a human be so calm in this situation?

What a wonderful day she must be having. She'd tormented Odo to desperation and escaped intact. Now she was enjoying the sight of these poor children dancing and screaming at the whip's end as if it were a mummer's play.

Oh, to have her in his power for an hour or two.

Chapter 4

Madeleine's chance to write to the king came a few days later.

Her uncle summoned her. "Got to send a message to the king," he said. "There must be serfs to be had somewhere in England, though there's few enough round here. Damned priest's off to the bishop over something or other. You can write, can't you?"

"Yes, Uncle." Madeleine wondered if this was a trap.

"There's a messenger here on his way to the king. I'll send word and seek help." Paul hawked and spat into the rushes. "Can't care for the fields properly with so few. Those miscreants we punished are malingering good-for-nothings, and the people here still dribble away like water through a sieve. Cursed Golden Hart."

"What, Uncle?"

He looked up at her. "Some peasant calling himself Golden Hart. He's inciting the people to rebellion, urging them to flee their proper place, to disobey the commands of their rightful lords, to kill the Normans. The Saxon dogs are bold these days. Sons of Harold are nibbling at the south, and that cursed Hereward's skulking in the east trying to bring in the Danes or Scots. The king's too easy on them all. It's enough to make a man vomit. We need to show them the price of rebellion, as I did that bunch of runaways."

"Yet they still flee, Uncle," Madeleine pointed out.

He glowered at her. "They wouldn't run footless and branded, would they? I should have never listened to your soft whinings. You're well on the way to ruining this estate, Niece, and so I'll tell the king. With you and Golden Hart undermining it, there'll be nothing left worth the having."

That was always Paul de Pouissey's way. Blame everyone but himself for his disasters. Madeleine was intrigued by this Golden Hart though, and her heart danced. It must be her outlaw. It must. She wondered if she could contact him and work with him to rid Baddersley of Uncle Paul.

Her uncle took a swig of ale. "Damn swill," he muttered. "Can't even get any wine. Well. Go get whatever you need to write, girl!"

Madeleine hurried to the small stone chapel which nestled near the manor house, but once in the one-room presbytery, she stopped to think. Was this a chance to communicate with King William? If it was, dared she take it?

She gathered parchment, pen, ink, and knife. Could her uncle not read a word? If she was caught, the consequences would be terrible, for she intended to not just put her marriage back in the king's hands, but make clear the ineptitude of her guardians.

But this is likely to be your only chance, she reminded herself. She went into the chapel and communed with the Christ on the cross. Strengthened and fortified, she returned to the manor house. As her uncle dictated the standard obsequious flattery and followed it with pleas, Madeleine wrote,

My uncle wishes you to find him serfs for this estate, but the truth is he has frightened many away with his cruelty, killed others unjustly, and works the remainder to death. I need your help, my king. I need a better hand to administer this estate so graciously gifted to my father. I need a capable husband, and willingly submit myself to your election in this.

Madeleine was so absorbed, she almost signed it.

"Bring it here," her uncle commanded.

Madeleine swallowed. One of Paul's hounds raised its head, and she fancied she saw cruel suspicion in its eye. She rose and carried the letter to her uncle, sure he must hear her knees knocking, must see how her hand trembled as she held the parchment out to him.

He scarcely looked before awkwardly scrawling "P de P." "Write my name in full beneath," he commanded.

It was hard not to collapse with relief.

He smirked. "Bet you thought I couldn't write. Better than a cross, eh? Read it back. Let me see how it sounds."

Madeleine froze.

"Read it, damn you! If you're fooling me and can't write sense, I'll have you whipped."

Madeleine sat with a bump and stared at the sheet. Her heart scurrying, she forced herself to recollect the half-heard words. "My great and puissant liege. Hesitant as I am to disturb you during your mighty enterprise of reform-ing and civilizing this barbaric land . . ." She carried on, inventing when she could not remember, expecting a bel-low of outrage at any moment.

When she finished, he nodded. "I fancy you changed a bit here and there," he said, "but it sounds very well. Give it here." He sealed it and summoned the messenger. Within the hour, Madeleine watched her letter to the king being carried away by the long-limbed runner, safe by the most severe laws from all interruption of his journey.

The messenger was heading to Winchester. Madeleine had no way of knowing how far that was, and she knew the king might not be there. He was always on the move, particularly with new troubles popping up all over the place. But the messenger would find him and soon, very soon, the king would come and bring her a husband.

Life was not pleasant for anyone at Baddersley in the next weeks. The previous year's inadequate stores had scarcely lasted through the winter, and many people, chiefly the young and old, had died because of it. Those who had survived were weakened and dispirited.

The depleted work force was forced to toil beyond its endurance to care for crops and beasts at the same time that it built the castle. The people were subjected to blows and beatings for every small infraction. Everywhere she looked Madeleine saw weary, gray, malnourished people, and she suspected she herself was no exception. Though her uncle spent coin to buy better food, mostly for himself, even meals in the hall were poor.

Madeleine suspected that the money was running out. She knew Paul had given some to Odo when he returned to his duty, so his son might have a new sword and more fine garments in which to play the peacock. Her money. Baddersley's money, which should be used to care for the people.

There would be an accounting when the king came.

But till then she could do so little. Since Aunt Celia took no interest in charitable work, Madeleine took over the distribution of what scraps were left from the hall table. She discovered the kitchen workers were passing out baskets of good food to their families and put a stop to it. What food there was would go to those in greatest need. She did not report the thievery to her uncle, however, for fear of what mad retaliation he would take. Had he not had one poor man hanged for letting his pigs get into the cornfields?

Every day she made herself available to those with problems, particularly medical ones, but only the Norman guards and servants asked her assistance. The English remained surly. No, more than surly.

The English hated her.

They hated Paul and Celia, too, but that was a dull resentment. Her they hated in an active, burning way.

Why?

Everywhere she went she felt their eyes pierce her like sharp blades, though when she faced them, their expressions were dull and blank. Even just crossing the bailey her spine crawled with the feeling that she was a target.

For a while she had continued to go out into the countryside to collect wild plants to supplement the food. She had also hoped for a meeting with her outlaw, with Golden Hart, so she could seek his help. But one day she had been struck by a large stone, thrown with vicious intent. She had fled back to her guard and stopped her wanderings.

She talked to Dorothy about it as she prepared for bed one night. "Is it my imagination, Dorothy, that the people here hate me?"

The woman combed out Madeleine's long chestnut hair. "Why should they, my lady?"

"I don't know. Do they say anything to you?"

"No," said the woman sourly. "Hold your head still, do."

Madeleine realized her maid must be as cut off as she was. No wonder she was surly. "Would you like to share my English lessons, Dorothy?"

She felt a particularly hard yank on her hair. "No, I would not, my lady," snapped Dorothy. "The very idea. Teach them to speak proper. That's more to the point."

Madeleine sighed. "I wonder when I will hear from the king."

"Doubtless he has better things to do than bother about your affairs," said the woman, driven for once into loquacity. "Why, if matters are everywhere as they are here, he must be driven mad by the wretches. Refusing to do their work, always complaining, trying to leave their proper place as if they had a right to wander wherever they will. Heathens, that's what they are, for all they pray in a Christian church."

It was true that people continued to slip away from the manor in ones and twos. Paul put his guards on the village, but still his daily rages against Golden Hart marked another family gone. When the headman of the village came to report that the ox-herd and his family had escaped, Paul turned a deep, engorged red, then a frightening white.

"What?" he roared. "Go after him! Bring him back!"

No wonder he was in a rage; Madeleine felt a spurt of panic herself. The ox-herd was one of the essential people on any estate, and though his full skills would not be needed until harvest time, who would look after his beasts? Without oxen they would surely starve.

"No one knows where he's gone, Lord," stammered the man.

"Find him," ordered de Pouissey. He lunged forward and fastened his beefy hands around the man's throat. "Find him!" He shook the man, who made nasty gurgling noises.

"Aunt," cried Madeleine. "Stop him!"

Dame Celia shrank back. "Why? He's just another troublemaker. Let him strangle."

Madeleine ran forward and grabbed her uncle's thick arm. "Uncle, stop!"

He released the man's throat and flung Madeleine off so that she was sent sprawling on the floor. "Keep out of my way, you wretched girl!" he snarled. His hounds leaped up and stood over her, growling, keeping her on the floor at his feet. She stared at their bared fangs and could imagine them tearing at her throat.

Her uncle looked down at the headman, who was kneeling, clutching his throat and choking. "If any of the oxen die," he said flatly, "you die. Now get out of here."

On hands and knees, the man went.

Paul de Pouissey turned on Madeleine. "Interfere with me again, Niece, and I'll yoke *you* to the plow." With that he snapped his fingers and lumbered out into the courtyard to whip more work out of the laborers. With a disdainful curl of their lips the two hounds abandoned Madeleine and followed.

Shakily, she rose to her feet. She looked to her aunt, but found no help there.

"Stupid girl," the woman snapped. "Don't you know better than to interfere in men's affairs? I don't know what they taught you at the convent, but you'd better unlearn it if you want to live. No husband will put up with such as you.''

Once or twice Madeleine saw someone slip in to speak to her uncle under cover of darkness: an informer from the village. As a Norman, she should be pleased, but she hated the man, whoever he was. In spirit she felt closer to the English than to her relatives. She was terrified that the traitor was bringing a tale of Golden Hart and that she would see her outlaw dragged before Uncle Paul.

''Do we know who Golden Hart is, Uncle?'' she asked one day at the table when Paul had just finished another ranting complaint about the man. She worked at picking the flesh off a very small fish, apparently the best that could be had in the nearby river.

''A Saxon traitor,'' snarled Paul. ''When I have him I'll make him pay. I'll lop his limbs. I'll blind him slowly. I'll cut off his balls,'' he said with relish, ''and then the villagers who worship him can care for him as he crawls around in the dust like the beast he is.''

The piece of fish in her mouth threatened to choke Madeleine. He would do just as he said. Had not Duke William had the hands and feet of the rebels at Falaise chopped off?

She forced the food down. ''But do we know who he is?'' she persisted, striving for a casual tone.

Her uncle grunted a negative. ''Some say he's a displaced Saxon lord, even Earl Edwin of Mercia, though that young good-for-nothing's kept tight at William's side. Others say he's that Hereward, or King Arthur come to save them.'' Her uncle laughed. ''He's no ghost, as they'll all know when they hear him scream. Give me that dish, girl.'' He poked among the mess of greens. ''Steward!'' he bellowed. The harried man came forward to receive the bowl and contents in his face. ''Find some decent food, or God knows I'll geld *you!*''

Madeleine fled the table.

She went to the chapel and prayed for the safety of her outlaw, begging forgiveness at the same time for the treason of it. "Keep him safe, Sweet Savior," she whispered. "Guard him. But," she added wryly, "let him not entirely denude my land of people before I have a chance to see it whole again."

No message came from the king.

Instead a spell of hot weather brought sickness, causing vomiting, fever, and death. Few of the castle people took the pestilence, but it roared through the already wretched village. Madeleine knew it was the near-starvation of the people there that made them so vulnerable. She cursed her uncle even more.

See what he had brought them to! Now there were few people fit to slave on his fortifications. Work in the fields had slowed almost to nothing. Animals were barely tended and the weeds grew up strong to choke the corn. A winter famine was almost certain.

Why didn't the king come?

The villagers had always refused Madeleine's attempts to act as healer, but now she would not be put off. Summoning two guards, she went out among the people. They still glared at her, but she was growing competent in English, and she demanded that they speak to her. She gave them herbs and explained how they should be used to ease the vomiting. Once, she saw a woman throw the medicine away and could have screamed with vexation. What was wrong with these people?

She refused to give up. Even if they did not use her treatment, at least she knew she was doing her best. As she sat alone one day in the solar tying bundles of herbs, a girl sidled in and waited. It was Aldreda's fair-haired daughter.

"Yes?" Madeleine said.

"Please, Lady. There's a child sick."

"There's dozens of children sick, girl."

"My brother, Lady."

Madeleine looked up. Was this the first crack? Was she being accepted? "What's your name?"

"Frieda, Lady."

Madeleine smiled at the child, who looked to be about eight. There was no answering smile.

"Where is your brother?" Madeleine asked.

"At our house. It's between the hall and the village, Lady. Da's a forester. Ma asks that you come, but without your guards, Lady. It must be secret or Da'll throw the medicine away."

It could be a trap, but Madeleine found it hard to believe that Aldreda would plot so openly to murder a Norman lady. The penalties for the whole community would be terrible. The father's enmity was only too likely. This could be her chance to show the people she was their friend. She gathered up her supplies and wrapped a cloak around herself.

They slipped quietly across the bailey. The earthwork was up and a wooden palisade was being built on top. With so few laborers, however, the work was going slowly, and there were gaps here and there. On the far side, the stream had not yet been diverted to fill the moat, and rough bridges spanned the ditch for the carts of logs. It was alarmingly easy to cross unnoticed. Madeleine prayed that no enemy would attack Baddersley. She didn't think it could repel a bunch of children armed with sticks.

Soon Madeleine and the girl stood before a substantial thatched hut at the edge of the woodland. Aldreda came out, a shapely woman with a strong, beautiful face. She was no more warmly disposed than usual, but Madeleine told herself she would be happier when her child was eased.

"He's within," said the woman coldly.

Somewhat hesitantly, Madeleine ducked through the low door and found herself in the typical house of a prosperous family. It was small but divided to give at least two rooms other than the one in which she stood. The walls were made of sticks well packed with clay, and there was a small window, open now to the sun, with shutters that could be closed to keep out the wind. The split-log floor was swept clean, and a fire burned in a central stone hearth.

The smoke rose efficiently enough to escape through a hole above, but enough lingered to fog the room, and on such a warm summer's day it made the room stuffy.

The only furnishings in the room were two long chests and a simple loom. Tools and dishes hung on the walls.

She looked around for the sick child and saw a man. The father? He stood looking at her, just a shadowy shape in earth-colored clothes.

"Where is the child?" she asked, disturbed by the slight tremor in her voice.

"There is no child." Her heart leaped at that familiar voice. "You have been brought here to see me."

"Are you sick?" she asked, moving toward him.

He stepped back, away from her. Light from the fire, the roof vent, and the window illuminated him. He was as dirty and ragged as before, with a hood shadowing his face.

"No." The coldness in his voice finally penetrated, stopping her. Menace weaved through the room with the smoke and caught her breathing. Logic said Edwald wouldn't harm her. Instinct overrode logic.

"Then I am wasting my time," she said and turned to escape. He grasped her arm.

"Take your hand off me!" She was as afraid for him as for herself. "Harm me and the wrath of God will fall on everyone here." *Oh, Sweet Jesu. He hates me too. Why? Why?*

"That's your way, isn't it, Lady? Punishment. Death." He dragged her close. She braced her hands to hold him away.

"What do you want?" she asked desperately.

"To see if your evil has marked you yet."

Madeleine's heart shriveled. "What's the matter?" she cried. "I'm doing my best. I try to heal, and they throw my medicines away. I try to be kind, but no one sees it . . ."

"Too little, too late," he sneered. "Why are you trembling? Are you afraid for your skin, *Dorothy?* You should be. You have much guilt to expiate.''

She stopped struggling and raised her hands to his chest beseechingly. ''Am I to be held responsible for everything done by the Normans in England?''

He looked at her, and she could swear his head began to lower to hers, but then he thrust her sharply away. ''Oh no. You don't play those tricks on me twice.'' He thumped a fist against the sturdy pole as if it were her. The very cottage shuddered.

Madeleine was fighting tears. She'd held this man in her dreams as her bulwark against cruelty and suffering. Now he was striking her as cruelly as if he used his fist.

He turned to her. ''Are you really trying to heal people?''

''Of course,'' she said quickly.

Then she was filled with disgust that she was still so eager to please him when he was being so cruel to her. Had she no pride? What was he anyway? Just a ragged outlaw. She glared at him, but knew she was scrabbling for anger to cover a broken heart.

He picked up a small earthenware bowl of water and thrust it at her. ''Make your infusion.''

She pushed it back. ''Go to hell.''

Some splashed over his hands, but it was still half full when he flipped the contents in her face. She gasped and spluttered, then he was holding a full bowl again. ''Make your infusion,'' he said with exactly the same inflection as before.

Madeleine took the bowl.

She'd suffered worse in her life many a time than water in the face and her courage had remained unbroken, but here . . . here there were no rules. He could scar her, blind her, maim her.

The water rippled with her fear as she placed the bowl beside the fire. She put one of her bundles of herbs in the pot and then used the tongs to add a hot stone. With a hiss the water heated and she stirred it. The bitter aroma began

to rise. She glanced up warily. He was leaning against one
of the sturdy posts, arms folded, watching her.

"It must steep for a while," she said, her voice thready
in the leaden atmosphere."

"I can wait."

Wait he did. The silence played on her stretched nerves
like a harsh bow on a viol.

She couldn't stand this. She had to know. "Why have
you changed?"

"When we met before, you promised a good roll," he
said crudely. "You lied."

It was like a knife thrust. "And for that you turn against
me? Turn the people against me?"

"Oh, you turned the people against you on your own."

Now her anger was real. Such was her hero—a lout who
sulked because she balked at giving him her maidenhead.

A flare from the fire highlighted him briefly. On his
right hand, where it lay upon his left elbow, she could
swear she had seen a design—a head, perhaps, with horns.
The skin-marks. The skin engravings of the English nobles. She had not been wrong, at least, about his high
birth.

"Are you the one they call Golden Hart?" she asked.

She saw him tense. "What if I am?"

She put a touch of malicious pleasure in her voice. "My
uncle plans to maim and unman you and leave you in the
village dust."

"My plans for your uncle are no different. Is this why
you've learned our language? To taunt the defeated?"

"I have learned because this is *my* land."

He pushed off the post to loom over her. "Then perhaps
you should care for it instead of working your people into
the ground."

"There are so few!" she protested. "I am seeking to
heal their sickness."

"There are so few," he echoed with grim humor.
"Even the cruelest farmer learns to care for his beasts of
burden. Eventually."

Madeleine gave up. She tended to her brew in silence. Eventually she said, "It is ready, I think."

"Don't you know?" he said, sneering.

"It is ready," she spat. She took a wooden cup and scooped up some of the brew, then added cold water from a pitcher. "Where's the patient?"

"Drink it."

"Me? Why?"

He just looked at her. She longed to hurl the medicine in his face but didn't dare, which was as bitter as the feverfew she had mixed into the brew. Stiffly, she raised the bowl and drank all of the foul-tasting fluid.

"That was a waste," she said icily. "I don't have an endless supply of herbs."

He regarded her in silence.

"I'm not going to keel over dead, Saxon."

For a moment she thought he would hit her. She'd welcome the pain. It might smother the agony in her heart.

"I'll tell them they can use your medicine." He walked past her toward the door. *I'll tell them* . . . These were *her* people. What right had he to stand there and pretend to be lord over her people?

"If I still care to give it."

He swung back to face her. "You'll care, Lady, or you'll feel my anger."

"You dare not touch me. The king would flatten Baddersley and kill everyone here!"

He sneered. "There are ways," he said. "I'll get you more herbs if you need them. Tell Aldreda."

"How can *you* get herbs from Turkey and Greece?"

"Just tell her." With that he left.

Madeleine stood for a moment fighting tears. She would not cry over a man who was so unworthy. He'd clearly told the truth. All he'd ever been interested in was her body. The nuns had warned her it was always so. A bitter lesson, but one well learned. She stiffened her spine, gathered her herbs, and walked out into the sunshine—to face half a dozen pairs of inimical eyes. The glances quickly slid away. She soon found out why.

"I have a daughter sick," said one woman hesitantly. "She can't eat or drink."

Just because he gave permission. Madeleine was tempted to give curses instead of aid, but it would be a petty retaliation. It would put a black mark on her soul and destroy any chance of gaining the trust of her people.

And she wanted the trust of her people.

By the Virgin's milk, she'd supplant that worthless rogue in their hearts.

She followed the woman into the village. She visited four homes and showed the women how to make the infusion, leaving enough of the herbs to last two days.

The situation in the village was horrendous. The children and the elderly were taking the sickness worst, and despite her help she thought one child would die. She hoped she wouldn't be blamed for it. The adults were recovering better, but she still gave them strengthening potions.

What they all needed was rest and more and better food. It was midsummer and there should be plenty, but their gardens were in poor condition because they did not even have time to weed and water them properly. Nor did they have time to go into the woods to pick berries and find wild plants.

She would take up her country explorations again and gather some of the most beneficial plants to pass on to them. She would try to find ways to ease their labor at the castle. Improvements were needed in irrigation for the main garden near the manor, which was shared between village and hall . . .

As she made her way back across the earthwork, Madeleine was full of a new sense of purpose. To the Devil with Golden Hart. She would save her people herself.

Chapter 5

Aimery made his way swiftly through the forest back to his camp. He had given up acting the outlaw some time ago. It had served its purpose and become dangerous, especially once the myth of Golden Hart came to life, but he had resumed his disguise for this one visit. A fleeing family had brought news of the sickness there, and the heiress' medicines. In some way he felt responsible for her behavior.

It would seem she was trying to do some good, but that didn't warm his heart. Baddersley was a ruin and its people were wretched. Her concern came far too late. It would have been more to the point to have fed the people and not overworked them, to have been easier with the whip, then they would not have succumbed to the pestilence.

Still, he couldn't suppress a touch of admiration for her spirit. Even alone, surrounded by the enemy, she had spat at him like a cat. He'd wanted to take what she'd offered and then snatched away. He'd even enjoy the fight . . .

He caught himself up with a curse. She was a witch to be able to tempt him so when he'd seen her cruelty with his own eyes. She did nothing to control her aunt and uncle, and only cared for the people when it seemed they might die.

At the camp he found Gyrth tenderly sharpening his scramasax as he eyed another man sitting facing him. Old enemies, thought Aimery, as his squire, Geoffrey de Sceine, rose and bowed.

"Greetings, Lord. The king sends for you to Rockingham." Geoffrey was a tall, strong young man and very Norman. He wore his dark hair trimmed close to the scalp at the back, and his hand always rested on his sword. If he had any problems with his lord's fondness for English ways, he never spoke of it, though he disdainfully ignored any English he found with him.

Aimery didn't know whether Geoffrey guessed what he did when he "went Saxon," or if he reported back to William. It was not a matter he could control.

"What's he doing there?" he asked in French. Gyrth scowled at being excluded from the conversation. "Learn French," Aimery said to him unsympathetically in English before turning back to Geoffrey. "I left the king in Westminster only a fortnight ago."

"He and the queen are on progress, Lord. It is said he has gifted Huntingdonshire to his niece Judith, and so they have taken her there. The only question," he added with a grin, "is to whom she will be given."

"So there's to be an Earl of Huntingdon, is there?" Aimery peeled off the cloth he had wrapped around his head instead of darkening his hair with soot and grease. "That must have started the dogs growling. But I wonder why I'm summoned." He wondered, in fact, if this unexpected call to court meant his road had finally come to its end.

"Doubtless for the feasting which will follow the betrothal, Lord," said Geoffrey, bright-eyed.

It was possibly true, so Aimery grinned at the younger man's blithe anticipation. "And you are looking forward to fair ladies and contests with rich prizes, yes?"

Geoffrey smiled back and colored slightly. "Yes, Lord." He was only four years younger than Aimery, but he had missed Senlac and did not have Aimery's split heritage, so at times he made Aimery feel ancient. To Geoffrey, England was just a place for adventure where a man could make his fortune.

Geoffrey passed over a bundle, and Aimery took it to the nearby river where he could wash off his disguising dirt. He allowed his smile to fade.

It was only a few weeks since he'd left the court at Westminster after the queen's coronation, and to be called back again so soon was ominous. Other than those he considered a danger, William liked his vassals to be out in the country, making his authority felt. Had Aimery now been identified as a potential danger?

There had been vague, scoffed-at rumors at court about a mystical hero called Golden Hart. Fortunately the stories were so wild no one took them seriously. Golden Hart could kill three armed men with his bare hands. He could disappear at will. He breathed fire like a dragon . . .

Still, William was beginning to show an interest in Golden Hart—almost as much as in the real threat posed by Hereward—because Golden Hart was becoming a focus for rebellion at the lowest level of society, the peasantry. That was one reason Aimery had abandoned the persona.

Except for this one trip. He regretted it now even though only Aldreda had seen him. And the heiress, of course.

He admitted that he could have checked the heiress' medicines at a distance, or just trusted her good sense not to poison anyone. The bitter truth was he had wanted to see her again, to see if she now appeared as evil as he knew her to be.

And she didn't. She was still beautiful and stirred his senses in a way no other woman could. Perhaps she *was* a witch.

As he waded into the cool water, he looked down and saw the clean patch on his right hand, and the design standing out there. When had that happened? He was careful these days not to give anyone a glimpse of the mark.

When the heiress had splashed water on him.

He cursed softly. Could she have seen anything in that smoky atmosphere? He hoped not, or it was likely to be disastrous if they ever met in clean company. She would be sure he was Edwald the outlaw, and would doubtless guess he was Golden Hart, particularly if she had an opportunity to study the design.

He imagined the relish with which she would denounce him. All the more reason to keep well away from Baddersley and Madeleine de la Haute Vironge, despite the insane urging of his heart. No, not his heart, just his body, he told himself.

He gritted his teeth and struck out for deeper, colder water. He swam fiercely to wash her from his mind as he washed the dirt from his body. When he emerged from the stream, his body was clean, but his mind was still full of a brown-eyed witch.

He dressed rapidly in a white shirt and tawny linen ankle-length braies. Over his head he slipped a short-sleeved tunic of blue linen lawn, richly embroidered around the neck, sleeve, and hem by his mother. The wide neck left the fine work on his shirt still visible. He fastened a gilded belt and pulled the cloth of the tunic up around it until the folds hung at his knee to his liking. He settled the table knife and pouch on the belt so they were easy to his hand.

Instead of the rags which had bound his tattered leggings, he criss-crossed his loose braies ankle to knee with beautifully woven bands of blue shot through with gold, and finished the binding with a complicated ornamental knot. He slipped on low black boots, relishing their fit and comfort after the crude sandals held on with thongs.

Geoffrey came forward and gave him his leather sword belt. Aimery set it around his waist so that Justesse, his sword, was ready to his hand. It carried a French name, but it was an English sword, given him by Hereward and bearing ancient runes along the blade. Next the squire passed a heavy gold bracelet which was worked in a rich ribbon design and flared to fit to the shape of his arm. He slid it onto his right wrist. These days he always did his best to hide the tattoo.

Geoffrey's face was carefully blank as his lord dressed in English style, but Aimery knew he noted it and did not approve.

There was not much difference in dress between the Normans and the English, yet it was there all the same—a taste in the English for brighter colors, finer fabrics, and more vivid ornamentation. In large part it sprang from the fact that the English were more skilled in producing fine fabrics and beautiful embroidery, but it had become a subtle distinction. Geoffrey was dressed in dark blue with black and white braid for trimming. He wore no gold at all.

"You know," said Aimery mischievously as he adjusted the fit of his splendid bracelet, "any Englishman seeing you must think me a wretch of a lord not to have gifted you with *geld.*"

Geoffrey stiffened. "I do not serve you for treasure, Lord Aimery."

"Nor treasure, nor pleasure . . . If I make you very uncomfortable," Aimery said seriously, "I will release you to some other, more orderly lord." If his time was come, he didn't want Geoffrey entangled in his downfall.

The young man colored. "I do not want . . . I am happy to serve you, Lord Aimery."

"Are you? You don't look it most of the time."

Geoffrey tried to resume a formal tone. "You are a fine fighter and a good administrator. You train me well and I am satisfied." Abruptly he added, "I worry about you!" He turned fiery red. "I beg your pardon, Lord."

Aimery was genuinely touched. "No need. I worry about myself." He gripped Geoffrey's arm and said seriously, "I am true to the king and always will be, Geoffrey, but if you perceive anything I do as wrong, go to him and tell him."

"That would be dishonorable, Lord."

Aimery shook his head. "No. Your first allegiance is always to the king. No man is expected to follow his lord into wrongdoing. Remember that."

Uneasy and confused, Geoffrey nodded. Aimery pulled another piece of jewelry from his pouch—Hereward's ring.

After a brief hesitation, he pushed it onto the third finger of his right hand. It said he was Hereward's man, body and soul until death. That wasn't true. He would wear it, however, until the day when he was compelled to renounce that allegiance.

As he walked back to the camp he pulled a bone comb through his shoulder-length hair and shook some of the river water from it. Gyrth looked him over and nodded.

"English enough for you?" Aimery asked.

Gyrth laughed. "You could do with more jewelry, lad. What sort of man wears only one bracelet? What sort of lord must he serve?" He himself wore bracelets, armbands, and a great bronze-gold clasp to his belt.

"This lord gives land, not gold."

"Englishmen's land."

"Those English who have acknowledged William have kept their land."

Gyrth surged to his feet. "They are *nithing!* They hold their land under Norman barons, Norman earls, a Norman king. You are all no better than slaves, you Normans and those who bow to you. The king gives you land, but it is still his land, not yours. Alfred did not own England, nor did Cnut, or Edward. Harold had just his family land. The Bastard claims to own everything! He bursts open towns that stand against him. He builds castles and puts in his own knights. He destroys the land of those who oppose his tyranny. He establishes his forests where he will. On other men's land!"

"It is the new way," said Aimery levelly. "How is the old way better? What does a ring-bearer own but the favor of his lord? If he loses that, he is a man alone in the world."

"If he loses that, he deserves nothing," Gyrth replied. "If he survives battle when his ring-friend dies, he is a man to spit on." He matched action to word, then suddenly gripped Aimery's right wrist and raised it. Hereward's gold ring flashed in the sun; an identical ring flashed on Gyrth's hand. Geoffrey began to slide his sword from its sheath, but at a look from Aimery he stopped, albeit warily.

"Whose ring do you wear?" Gyrth asked sternly.

"Hereward's," Aimery replied, relaxed in the other's tight grip.

"And who are you?"

The correct answer was, "Hereward's man." Aimery said, "A Norman. Do you want to take the ring back to Hereward?"

There were tears in Gyrth's eyes. "The fighting time is coming, lad. If the Bastard asks you to take arms against Hereward, you must refuse, or be *nithing.*"

Aimery smoothly twisted his wrist out of Gyrth's grip. "I have sworn my liege-oath to William. I must fight for him wherever and whenever he says or be damned." He pulled off the ring and held it out. "Do you wish to take it back to Hereward?"

Tight-lipped, Gyrth shook his head. Aimery pushed the ring back on his finger and strode out of the clearing.

An hour west of Baddersley they picked up Aimery's escort of knights where Geoffrey had left them, at an inn on the Roman road. The rumor had been put about that Aimery slipped off now and then for a loving tryst with a married lady who had a husband who traveled. The guards grinned over it but were careful never to refer to his absences.

Within sight of Rockingham, Aimery called a halt. Geoffrey sighed. From a pouch by his saddle Aimery took out more jewelry. A thicker bracelet with a design in garnet and obsidian went on his left wrist, and two straight bands with bronze inlay went around his upper arms. He clipped a large clasp at the front of his belt. He took his rich blue cloak from Geoffrey and flung it around his shoulders, fastening it on the right shoulder with a magnificent jeweled ring-clasp. Thus adorned as an English nobleman he continued through the village toward the castle. It would warm the cockles of Gyrth's heart to see him like this.

There had been a stronghold at Rockingham for generations, and the hill had a settled, comfortable look to it, unlike the raw motte at Baddersley. There had been a low stone fort, and William Peverell had built rapidly on it to form a formidable stone castle on the banks of the river Welland, but as yet the palisade was still wood, and so were most of the attendant buildings which cluttered the bailey. Down by the river, the prosperous village was taking the presence of the King of England in its stride.

Aimery and Geoffrey left the men and horses at the sheds set up to handle all the extra mounts and continued on foot across the crowded bailey to the tower.

Aimery paused long enough to buy two pork pies from a stall for Geoffrey and himself. Once they found the king they could be kept waiting for hours, and he was hungry. An alewife also had a stand here, and they quickly downed a flagon. Geoffrey started a promising flirtation with the woman's daughter, who obviously plied another trade entirely, but Aimery dragged him away.

They climbed the steps to the tower entrance and were admitted by the guards. They found themselves in a great hall filled with William's court, the male part of William's court at least. If the queen and her ladies had traveled with the king, they were not in evidence. One of the first people Aimery saw among the crowd of nobles, clerics, and merchants was his cousin Edwin, Earl of Mercia.

One year older than Aimery, Edwin was a little slighter in build and had hair of tawny ginger. He was a handsome young man but had a softly indecisive mouth. Though he had succeeded his father as territorial lord over most of eastern England, he had never managed to make his influence felt. Just after Senlac he had supported the attempt to put Edgar Atheling on the throne, but that had come to nothing, and he had been among the many lords who had then rushed to pay homage to William. Like most, he had been pardoned and confirmed in his titles. Since then he had been kept at court and seemed content to tie his fate to William of Normandy.

As was his way these days, Edwin was dressed in Norman style. He was clean shaven, his hair was cut short, and he sported only modest trimming on his clothes. Once, Aimery remembered, Edwin had been fond of rich, bright clothing and ornament and proud of his flowing hair and thick moustache.

The earl's lips curled at the sight of Aimery. "Well, cousin. Still trying to be a bit of both, I see. How is Uncle Hereward these days?"

Aimery wasn't about to be needled by Edwin. "I wouldn't know. How is life at court?"

"Not bad at all," said Edwin complacently. "The king's promised me his daughter, Agatha."

"Congratulations, Edwin. She's a sweet child, but not ready for marriage yet, surely."

Edwin looked sour at this reminder of his cousin's familiarity with William and his family. "She's thirteen."

"I suppose she is. I haven't seen her for, must be three years. Has she filled out? She was a scrawny little thing."

Edwin's eyes bulged, and he pulled Aimery into a quiet corner. "Don't say things like that! You'll never get on the right side of the king the way you go on."

Aimery shook his head. "William doesn't make or break a man for saying pretty things about his daughters. You'll have to stand up to him one of these days, Edwin."

Edwin paled at the thought but managed a sneer. "I've won his daughter, Aimery. What have you won? In fact, I wonder why William's summoned you here. He keeps me by his side because I control Mercia. But why you? Been up to something you shouldn't?" he gibed. "You, Golden Hart, and Hereward?"

Before Aimery could respond, Edwin slipped away. Aimery cursed softly. That reference to Golden Hart set warning signals clamoring. He instinctively placed a hand over his betraying design. He stopped the futile gesture.

Wyrd ben ful araed. Besides, it had never been wise to take Edwin seriously.

He'd never much liked his cousin, or his twin brother Morcar. They were weak, tricky men. As a Norman he supposed he should be glad they were so easily bought, but his English half was disgusted by their base self-interest. They were fawning around the king like puppies in the hope of treats, but he knew if they ever saw advantage in turning on William, they'd do it without hesitation. It was people like Edwin who were destroying England—too peevish to settle to Norman rule, and too cowardly to oppose it outright.

Aimery looked toward the stone stairs leading up to the private room used by the king. He wondered in what state he'd descend them, but there was no hesitation in his step as he wove his way through the crowded hall. He exchanged a greeting here and there but refused all temptation to linger.

At the foot of the stairs, however, a larger, darker man swept forward to pull him into a ferocious hug. "Ho, little brother! Still in one piece?"

Aimery grasped his oldest brother joyfully and endured a massive pounding on his back. "Leo! How long have you been here? Stop breaking my ribs, damn you. Why didn't you come to Rolleston?"

"The king sent for us."

"Us?" asked Aimery warily.

"Father's here."

Something tightened painfully inside. Aimery had prepared to face King William, but he wasn't sure he could face his father, whom he hadn't seen since that confrontation in the Tower over a year ago. Aimery considered what his father might think of the way he was behaving—even if he knew only half of it—and had a base urge to slip off his English accoutrements and get a haircut.

Leo gave his youngest brother a shrewd look. "Exactly what have you been up to?" he asked. Then the indulgent look faded to be replaced by a severe one. "Treason?"

"No," said Aimery sharply, and his brother nodded. "How are Janetta and the children?" Aimery asked quickly, before his brother thought of more questions.

"Well. We seem to breed rugged little ones. Castle Vesin was visited by sickness in the autumn and five people died. All the children sickened and not one the worse for it. If they go on at this rate, I'll have a private army of land-hungry warriors."

"Just don't send them to England."

Leo regarded him shrewdly. "This is your home now, isn't it?"

Aimery nodded. "But I'm still half Norman, brother."

"Then you'd better come to the king. He gave orders you were to come to him as soon as you arrived."

"Why?"

Leo at least felt no foreboding. "Perhaps he just loves your pretty green eyes. Come on."

Aimery tossed his cloak to Geoffrey and followed his brother up the narrow stairs to the guarded oak door.

"Is Roger here, too?" he asked, just for something to say. He was aware of his heart speeding, of the tingle of battle readiness, which was just another name for fear.

"No. He's happily killing Welshmen and covering himself in glory. Why?"

"I just thought we could have a jolly family gathering. I'm surprised Mother allowed herself to be left at home."

Leo laughed. "Under protest." He dropped his voice. "Father put his foot down. I don't think he's as sanguine as the king about the stability of things here."

Or he suspected, or knew, something unpleasant was going to happen. Would William send for an old friend so he could witness his son's maiming? He might well.

Guards let them pass into a room hung with tapestries and set with rich furniture for the king of England. It was small, though, and the six men in it nearly filled it. There were two clerks working at documents; William's two closest followers, William Fitz Osbern and Roger de Mortain; the king himself; and Count Guy de Gaillard. An ominously eminent group to greet a younger son.

"Ha. Aimery de Gaillard at last," said the king in his gruff voice. "You take your time, boy." William was stocky, with short ginger hair and keen blue eyes. As usual, as this was not a ceremonial occasion, he wore plain clothes—serviceable brown wool, simply ornamented.

Aimery went forward to kneel and kiss his hand. "No one, sire, can match your speed."

The king looked him over. "You'd travel a sight faster if you weren't weighed down with gold."

Aimery didn't attempt a reply. He was suffering a flood of relief. This greeting couldn't be a prelude to ruthless justice.

The king gestured, and Count Guy came forward. Aimery kissed his father's hand, and then was drawn up for a kiss on the cheek. He could see his father was delighted to see him well, and angry at his English appearance. He would say nothing about it here, however.

"How fares your land?" asked the king.

"Well, sire," said Aimery with a relaxed smile. He'd worry about what *was* behind the king's summons later. "God granting us fair weather, we should see a good harvest."

"You are one of the few to say so," grumbled William. "I suppose your people work for you because you're English."

"Half English, liege," contradicted Aimery firmly, causing a hiss of horror from someone and a flash from the king's eyes.

But then William grinned. "Impudent rascal. Tell me, then, why do your people work well for you?"

"I try to hold to their traditions and their laws, sire."

"By the splendor of God, so do I!" exploded the king.

Aimery knew, to an extent, that this was true and tried to appease the angry monarch. "As you say, sire, it must be because I am part English."

He knew it was a mistake as soon as the words were

out. The room became as silent as if there were but the two of them in it.

"Kneel," the king said, frighteningly quiet, and Aimery fell submissively to his knees.

The king's open-handed blow rocked him and made his head ring, but it was relief which made him dizzy. This was fatherly discipline, not regal.

"Have I not English blood?" asked the king.

"Yes, sire. Through Queen Emma." It wasn't strictly true. Emma of Normandy, William's grandmother, had been mother to King Edward and widow of two English kings before she wed the duke of Normandy, but that did not give William English royal blood. It was part of the king's claim to the English throne, however, and not open to question.

The king nodded and held Aimery's eyes. There was more to this than an unwary word and regal anger. The underlying message was clear. Step beyond the line and you will be punished, beloved godson or no; punished exactly as your crime deserves.

Wariness returned. How much did William know?

Aimery again raised the king's hand, the hand which had delivered the blow, to his lips for the kiss of allegiance.

"Oh, get up!" said the king in irritation, which poorly covered fondness. "You're a tiresome cub and if I'd any sense . . . As it is, I've brought you here with a mind to rewarding you, so watch yourself. Now go with your family. You've a room here somewhere. Have you brought your lyre?"

"No, sire."

"Fool. Find one. Tonight you play for us."

Aimery bowed himself out of the room with his father and brother, wondering whether his aching jaw was going to be belabored again by his tight-lipped parent.

Chapter 6

W hen they reached the small chamber put to the use of the de Gaillard men, his father merely sighed. "Take off those damn decorations."

Aimery did so, except for the bracelet on his right wrist and the gold ring. "Normans wear them, too, Father," he said mildly.

"On you they have a pointed effect. De Sceine says you only put them on to come to court."

"They're hardly suitable for working the fields . . ." Aimery stilled at the look in his father's eye.

"I'm quite happy to bruise the other side of your jaw if you want."

Aimery said nothing. He knew it was fear that stirred his father to anger, fear for his youngest child.

"By your reports from Rolleston," said Count Guy, "you're doing well there. But I hear you slip away sometimes. Where do you go? Hereward?"

"Does everyone think me a traitor? I gave you my word, and I've kept it. I haven't seen Hereward since before Senlac." He saw his father relax. "I'm half English, Father, and I'll not deny my English part, but I am true to the king."

"You'd better be. If you betray him, he'll deal harder with you than he would with one he always knew to be his enemy."

"I'm sorry, Father, but I am what I am."

Guy de Gaillard grabbed his youngest son into a bear-hug. "Take care of yourself, my boy."

Aimery relished the encompassing hold, feeling for a brief moment like a child again, safe in his father's arms. Then he realized he was now taller and broader than his father. Guy de Gaillard was beginning to age while Aimery at twenty-two was in the peak of manhood. He was surprised and disconcerted by a feeling of protectiveness toward his once awesome parent. He hid it by turning away to place his adornments in his chest.

"Do you know what 'reward' the king has in mind for me?" he asked lightly.

Leo answered. "Perhaps since you're doing so well at Rolleston, he'll give you an estate of your own."

"Not very likely. He's surrounded by land-hungry followers with better claim than a half English younger son. And as long as Father lets me run Rolleston, I'm content."

"Ha!" exploded Leo. "Wait until you've a battalion of hungry sons. You'll be glad of every little manor."

Aimery grinned. "I'm in no mood to marry, Leo, and English heiresses are fought over like marrow bones."

Count Guy passed his sons goblets of wine. "I doubt William would let you marry an Englishwoman, Aimery. He dislikes the English influence on you as it is."

"There, see," said Aimery to Leo. "And I consider myself lucky. Have you *seen* some of those English widows?"

Leo was always an optimist. "Well, then, perhaps he has a lovely little Norman heiress in mind for you. Hey, perhaps he's going to give you the Lady Judith!"

Aimery choked on his wine. "Only if he's gone mad. That's a plum to catch much bigger game than me. Did you hear he's offered Agatha to Edwin? Now that's the use for a royal lady. Buy the whole east of England."

Leo had to accept the argument. "He did say he was going to reward you, though, so you'd better please him.

Let's go find you a lyre, little brother." He drained the goblet and set it back on the chest. "Come on."

And so they started a lighthearted search of the castle and town, gathering in a dozen or so young men as they went. The search for a musical instrument was a strange one and took them through a number of taverns and one brothel. When they staggered back to the castle to change for the evening, Aimery groaned. "After this, you expect me to sing?"

"You got your lyre, didn't you?"

"Hours ago."

"And you got to practice, didn't you?"

Aimery remembered singing battle songs in the guard room, and bawdy songs in a tavern—and learning some new ones, too. He'd sung pretty, soft songs for the whores, who'd turned sentimental and rewarded him suitably.

"I think I'm all sung out, Leo," said Aimery as he slipped on a fresh tunic—a rich red silk with long tight sleeves and trimming of heavy gold braid. After a moment's hesitation he put on his armbands and extra bracelet.

"Father'll have your guts," said Leo without great concern. All the de Gaillard boys had grown up buffeted, beaten, and loved by their father, and it seemed a fine way to raise sons, which is why he was doing the same with his own little tribe. "Come on, or heaven knows where we'll end up sitting."

The hall was a fair size but could barely hold the court. People jostled and fought for seats at the tables around the room. At the head table sat the king and queen, Fitz Osbern, de Mortain, Peverell, Lady Judith, and Lady Agatha. There were only a handful of other ladies present.

Agatha had filled out, Aimery noticed, but not a lot. She was fine-boned and young for her age but would improve in time. She saw him, giggled, and waved. Aimery blew her a kiss.

He did not know the Lady Judith, for she was the daughter of William's sister and had been raised in Lens. She was definitely well-filled out, a curvaceous beauty with long red-gold plaits and sparkling eyes. All that and Huntingdon, too, he reflected.

He saw the Lady Judith catch his admiration. She dimpled with interest and flashed him an unmistakable look. Aimery winked at her. The man who received her would be getting a handful. A delightful handful, but a handful nevertheless.

As Leo had predicted, they had to squeeze a place where they could, but Aimery didn't mind. He found himself among friends, sharing memories and catching up on the news, both personal and martial.

"Seeing the luscious Lady Judith," said one young man, "reminds me of that heiress, the Baddersley one. I keep hoping my path might take me that way, but I'm jiggered if I even know where the place is."

"It's not that far from here," supplied Aimery. "A bit south of Huntingdon." This caused a small uproar.

"Don't say you've stolen a march on us, de Gaillard!"

"I just know my way about Mercia."

"Only too well," sneered a voice. "Full of nasty Saxon relatives, isn't it?"

Aimery looked up to meet the hot, dark eyes of Odo de Pouissey, who was squeezing into a seat opposite. Aimery had never liked the man, and now his feelings were deepened by what he had witnessed. This was the man who'd tried to rape Madeleine de la Haute Vironge, and though he hated her, the thought of de Pouissey pawing at her made him want to gut the man.

Aimery's hand tightened on his goblet. "Full of nasty Norman relatives, too. The heiress is your cousin, isn't she?"

Odo flushed with anger. "My father's stepdaughter only. And, by the Grail, what are you implying about Madeleine?"

Aimery took a grip on himself. The king would string them up for fighting at his table, especially over Saxons and Normans. To distract everyone, he said, "So, who wants a map to Baddersley to go heiress hunting?"

"The king'll have the giving of her," said one man whom the wine had pushed into sullenness. "Don't suppose it would matter if she grew devoted to me, so what's the point?"

"True enough." Mischievously, Aimery added, "And it might be hard to play sweetly on her if you find she squints and has the temper of a harpy."

It did not markedly lessen her appeal.

"I could play sweetly on a monster for a fine barony," declared Stephen de Faix to a chorus of agreement. Stephen was a handsome, popular young man with a light-hearted approach to life and a taste for hedonism which often got in the way of his ambitions. He'd very much like an heiress bride. "Tell us, Odo," he commanded. "How bad is she?"

"Madeleine has a temper," said Odo. "But any woman can be managed. Gag her in bed. Ignore her the rest of the time."

"By the Rood," said another man, "I'd wed the veriest hag for some land of my own. There's always a pretty wench around for amusement. But tell us just how dreadful she is."

Odo clearly realized the advantage of painting an unattractive picture of the Baddersley heiress and dropped hints to swell the tale of horror. By the end of the meal everyone was convinced she was ugly, crippled, and foul-mouthed, and that was why the king had her hidden away.

They all would still jump at the chance to wed her.

Aimery felt a twinge of compassion for the girl. He remembered fine eyes, dark and flashing, and a shapely, fluid body. In his company she had always been moderate in speech, even when angry.

He pushed his kinder feelings down. She was doing it again, bewitching him even at a distance. He knew her to be cruel and rapacious. If one of these men became her husband, he'd know what to expect and not be swayed by a shapely body and fine eyes. So much the better.

Aimery was dragged out of his musings by the king

commanding him to play. He went into the central space,
knowing the flaring torches would highlight his golden hair
and ornaments. He saw his father's frown in passing. Perhaps that was why he was more cautious than he had intended. Instead of English songs he sang the favorite
Norman ones.

The queen requested a humorous song about a fish and
an apple, then the Lady Judith leaned forward. "Lord
Aimery, do you know the song about Lord Tristan and
Lady Yseault?"

Aimery saw the gleam in her eye and kept his expression politely distant as he replied, "Yes, Lady. I'll play
it for you." He knew Lady Judith's type and had enough
troubles without engaging the interest of one of the king's
prizes. It was as well she seemed to have a taste for the
English style, however, since that was doubtless her destiny.

As he sang he ran over the possible candidates. Edwin
was the prime one, but he had apparently been offered
Agatha. The Atheling Edgar was the only male of the English royal bloodline, but he was a boy with no power and
never likely to have any. Edwin's twin, Morcar, could be
of importance, but he hadn't achieved anything yet. Gospatric, Earl of Northumbria, was married.

Waltheof.

Waltheof, son of Siward of Northumbria, had only a
few manors, but by heredity he was one of the great men
of England. He had a sound claim to the earldom of
Northumbria, but it was his personal strengths which set
him apart. There was something about Waltheof. Even
though he was only two years older than Aimery, he drew
men to him as if with golden thread. People remembered
the stories that told of his grandfather marrying a woman
who was half faery, half bear.

If William was shrewd, and William was undoubtedly
shrewd, he would bind Waltheof Siwardson to him.

Aimery picked out Waltheof, listening attentively, a
smile on his long, handsome face. There was an air of

elegance to him, but no one who had ever seen him fight thought him weak. His dress and decoration were almost as richly English as Aimery's except that he favored darker colors. Waltheof's strange amber eyes moved and Aimery followed the gaze to Judith, who was listening to the song with rapt attention.

So, Waltheof guessed. Perhaps it was already settled. My Lady Judith, he thought, you have an interesting *wyrd*.

Continuing to sing, he let his eyes travel around the room. His gaze halted and he fumbled a note. New arrivals were entering the hall. Robert d'Oilly and a soldier Aimery feared was the survivor of a certain escape from bondage.

He forced his eyes onward, hoping he had not missed a whole verse or repeated one. The less attention he attracted the better. The whole notion was ridiculous, however, when he was sitting alone in the central space in scarlet and gold. He could only hope the contrast between his splendor and a ragged, dirty outlaw was enough to prevent identification.

As soon as Tristan and Yseault met their sad end, d'Oilly surged forward. "My Lord King!" he boomed. "I come with a tale of violence and mayhem!"

"More entertainment?" queried William. "Be welcome, Lord Robert. Have you eaten?"

D'Oilly moved to stand close to Aimery, who occupied himself in tuning his lyre. D'Oilly was a heavily built man of middle years, strong, hard, and of limited intelligence.

"Nay, sire, and I will not eat just yet," d'Oilly said. "We have a dangerous miscreant in our midst, sire."

The king looked around. "Dozens of them, Lord Robert," he said dryly. "But come, tell us your tale."

With a wave of his hand, d'Oilly summoned his guard forward. "This man can tell it better, for he was there. He is the sole survivor of a massacre."

Aimery decided his position had advantages. The man was clearly over-awed and had eyes only for the king. He would pay little attention to someone close to his side.

"Sire," the man said nervously, "I and four fellows were set upon by a giant, and all but me were slain."

The king looked at him. "Come, man. That's intriguing but not much of a story. Can you not do better? What kind of giant? How many heads did it have?"

The man's eyes widened. "One, sire. It . . . he was just a man, sire. But a tall one."

"Ah. And he killed four soldiers. With his bare hands?" he queried humorously. "Sounds like that damned Golden Hart again."

"Yes, sire," said the man.

The king regarded him more seriously. "It was this creature calling itself Golden Hart?"

The man shook his head frantically. "N . . . no, sire. But it . . . he killed with his bare hands. Or at l . . . least," the man stuttered, clearly wishing the floor would open and swallow him, "at first he did. He was building the bridge, you see, sire. Then he killed Pierre with his bare hands and took his sword. Then he cut off Loudin's head. Then he ran Charlot through. Gregoire was killed by the other."

"Another giant?" The king affected astonishment, but Aimery could see how shrewdly he was sorting all this out.

"No, sire. Another slave. He slit Gregoire's throat."

Aimery saw the grimace that passed over d'Oilly's face at the word *slave* and smiled. The man must have been under orders not to mention the circumstances. Well, d'Oilly was known for thick-headedness, and he was showing it.

"Slave," repeated the king thoughtfully. "How came you by slaves, Lord Robert? The practice of enslaving people for crimes has been out of favor for decades."

Sweat broke out on d'Oilly's brow. "Er . . . not exactly slaves, sire. Laborers. We needed people to build the castle and the bridge."

"These were tenants doing their day-labor, were they?"

"Er . . . no, sire. We needed extra work and so we . . .

They would have been paid when the work was done, sire.''

"Would they?'' queried the king. "And this giant objected to the delay in payment, perhaps, and killed four guards.'' He leaned forward, amusement gone. "You were rightly served. You will treat my subjects fairly or feel my wrath.''

Robert d'Oilly went pale, and there was an uneasy shuffling throughout the room as others decided to change their hiring practices.

After a moment, the king eased back in his seat. "I would dearly like to know how this giant did it, though. Perhaps your guards need to improve their skills.''

"He fought like a demon!'' protested d'Oilly and poked at his man. "Tell the king!''

"Aye, sire,'' said the terrified man. "He used his sword like a warrior trained. I reckon few men in this room could have stood against him. He threw it after me as I ran and almost speared me.''

The king's brows drew together, and he sat in thought. When he spoke, however, it was merely to say, "Lord Robert, I commiserate with you on the loss of your men, but you were breaking my law. Let all take heed that my people shall not be enslaved. A lord is entitled to his due labor and no more without consent and payment. We will put this matter aside as finished. There is no question, of course, of punishment of those who were enslaved. Or of murdrum fines, or *wergild*.''

After a bitter moment, Robert d'Oilly bowed his acceptance. As he turned to find a seat, the king spoke again. "If you come across this warrior giant, however, Lord Robert, I would be most interested in meeting him. Do your people not know who he was?''

"No, sire. He was merely a packman traveling through. Some even say he was a lack-wit used as a beast of burden by his master. There's no making sense of these people.''

"Hmm. I certainly doubt he was lacking all his wits or your guards must have been a sorry lot indeed.'' Then the king smiled in the charming way he could on occasion, and which made those who knew him particularly wary. "But come now, take a place and eat your fill. And let your man come sit by me here and tell me more of this wondrous tale."

D'Oilly found himself shepherded off to a table and food; the man-at-arms approached the stool by the king's chair as if it were an instrument of torture.

"Aimery," said the king, "more music, please."

Now the man-at-arms would have a clear view of Aimery de Gaillard pinned in the center of the hall with attention focused on him. Aimery smiled and began a cheerful tune.

Nothing untoward happened. The man-at-arms scarcely glanced at the musician and was soon dismissed by the king. He seemed shakenly grateful to escape the royal presence intact. Aimery could understand that.

The king then called on another to provide entertainment and directed Aimery to sit on the stool by his knee. His smile was bland. "You haven't lost your skills, Aimery."

"I hope not, sire, since they please you."

"They please me. Tomorrow I have ordered an archery contest. How are your skills there?"

"Not rusty, sire. But it isn't my strongest point."

"Riding at the quintain?"

"There I should be a credit to my masters."

"Fighting with the sword?"

Aimery met the king's eye. Was there extra significance in that question? "I believe my swordfighting to be good, sire."

The king nodded thoughtfully, then his eyes slid over Aimery's finery. "If ever I find the treasury low, I'll throw you in the fire and melt you down. Here, since you have a taste for such things." The king pulled off a ring made of twisted golden wire. It was unusual in design, perhaps Saracen work or from the dark lands beyond. One thing it wasn't was English. William pushed it onto the third finger of Aimery's left hand. "A reward, Aimery. Wear it."

Did William know the significance of the ring? That to be ring-giver meant to be a great lord; to be a ring-bearer meant to be that lord's man to death and beyond? Almost certainly he did.

Aimery bowed. "I will treasure it, my liege."

The king fixed him with stern eyes. "Just be sure to wear it. Now," said the king, as if something had been established, "what do you think of this giant?"

Aimery felt his heartbeats and worked at appearing calm. "He sounds like a peasant who lost patience with injustice, sire."

"Unusual, wouldn't you say? And that he be skilled with a sword?"

"With respect, sire, that guard would have to make a good story of it so as not to appear a coward. They were all doubtless drunk and the peasant lucky."

William smiled. "Likely enough. Now, what are your thoughts on Golden Hart?"

Aimery put on a politely questioning expression. "Golden Hart, sire? He's supposed to be a rebel, a rebel of the people. I suspect a myth is growing up rather than that it is a real individual."

The king was watching him like a hawk. "Is that all you know?"

Aimery avoided that. "I don't think Golden Hart offers a serious threat to your realm, sire."

"I know that," said William flatly. "No one offers any serious threat to my realm." As if to prove the point, William gestured to Edwin of Mercia, and the earl hurried forward, eager to please. "Earl Edwin, tomorrow we will have a trial of arms. It would please me to see some of the English skills, the spear and the ax. Would my English subjects be willing to arrange this? My showy mongrel here will doubtless take part."

Edwin bowed eagerly. "Of course, Your Majesty."

* * *

Aimery had not done much English fighting for years, and the next day he performed only moderately at it. His spear skills had been kept up in hunting, and he hit the center twice. With the ax he felt lucky to hit the target each time. The throwing ax was not as heavy as the battle-ax, but it was heavy enough.

When Leo made a scathing comment about his perfor-mance, Aimery said, "Look, an ax is for hacking people apart, and with brute force more than skill. It makes as much sense to throw one as it would to throw your horse. And it's about as hard. If you don't believe me, try it."

So Leo did. With his massive build he did quite well but missed the target one try out of three. He came back easing his shoulder. "Whew. I think I'd rather throw my horse. Tell me, what do you do in a battle when you've thrown your ax?"

Aimery laughed. "I've always wanted to know that. I think it's a noble last gesture before going to Valhalla."

"Talking of noble gestures," said Leo, "the king gave me the job of arranging the sword matches. I've lined you up against Odo de Pouissey."

"Am I supposed to appreciate that?"

"Yes. There's clearly no love between you. Sword work's no game. It's always better for a bit of feeling."

"The man's a fool when he's drunk and a bore when he's sober. I've better things to do with my time than to squabble with him."

Leo looked at him with disgust and then shook his head. "At times you are a damned Saxon, aren't you?"

"Yes. Come on to the butts."

Even the king took part in the archery. He did moder-ately well and showed no displeasure to those who de-feated him. He presented a silver goblet to the winner.

He left the riding at the quintain to the younger men, saying it would be foolishness for the monarch to be knocked senseless in a game.

For all that he called it a game, the quintain was serious work, the basis of the Norman style of mounted warfare which was carrying them all over Europe, and which had won them the Battle of Senlac. Aimery hit true with the heavy spear each of the three times he rode at the target; those less skillful found themselves knocked to the ground. Odo de Pouissey and Stephen de Faix also rode clear but had close misses. William awarded the prize—a handsome dagger with a carved amber pommel—to Aimery.

During the break for roast meats and ale, Odo glared jealously at the blade in its gilded sheath, so Aimery knew what to expect when the sword work began.

The weapons were blunted and the contestants wore mail suits and helmets, and carried long shields on their left arms, but it was still not a matter to take lightly. Aimery had hoped that by the time he faced Odo the man would have lost his animosity, but it wasn't so.

"So," hissed Odo as they sized each other up. "You think you can fight as well as a purebred Norman, do you?"

"Don't be a fool," retorted Aimery, watching the way Odo moved his feet and sword. "It's all in the training, and my training was thoroughly Norman." He switched feet and moved back on himself. Odo was fractionally late in matching the move. Was he clumsy or had he drunk too much, as was his way? The man had a fair reputation as a warrior.

Odo swung his sword and Aimery took it on his shield. He could have thrust into Odo's exposed body then, but that sort of deathblow wasn't allowed in a training fight, and he'd have to pay *wergild* to his family. He hoped Odo realized that—and didn't think Aimery's death worth 1200 shillings.

He'd think it worth every penny if he knew it was Aimery who'd foiled his assault on the Baddersley heiress. When he remembered that dastardly attack, Aimery began to think it would be worth paying *wergild* for Odo.

They pushed apart and swung sword against sword, then against shield. The clang and the thud and the concentration became all that mattered. One of Aimery's greatest faults, or so his teachers had always said, was that he was unable to take a training fight seriously. Now to his surprise he felt the blood-burn of war, experienced the focus that led to deathdealing. It was because of that attempted rape.

Aimery's reactions speeded as he parried and swung. He landed a hard blow on Odo's mailed shoulder. Odo staggered back and glared, then rushed in to retaliate.

It was hot fighting after that. Aimery guarded himself as if in battle, and both his sword and shield arm tingled from the constant blows. His fingers ached with the grip on his sword. Sweat ran into his eyes. He dimly heard the roar of approval at such fierce fighting, but his attention was all on his foe.

They locked, shield to shield, sword to sword, and pushed back to eye each other, both taking a moment to catch their breath. Aimery wiped sweat from his brow, and something beyond Odo caught his attention.

Someone.

D'Oilly's man-at-arms was watching the fighting.

The flicker of inattention was only momentary, but Odo took advantage. He leaped forward. Aimery raised his sword to catch the other man's blade but suffered a bruising blow on his thigh from the shield. As he staggered, he narrowly missed having the pointed end of it driven into his foot. The crowd howled at that unfair move.

He charged Odo with a hard, swinging sword, needing to beat the man down, to defeat him. As in battle the pain disappeared. He swung and blocked and locked shields as if his energy was endless. Then he landed a blow, as he intended, on just the spot on the shoulder that must still throb. Odo dropped his shield slightly even as Aimery swung back short to hammer his wrist so that his sword fell.

Odo grabbed the sword. He would have continued, but the horn sounded as the king called an end. He graciously complimented both men but gave Aimery the victory for the disarm. Odo snarled and stalked off. Aimery let his

gaze wander back to where d'Oilly's man stood. The man
looked up as if sensing eyes on him, and for a moment
their eyes locked.

Was there anything to read in that flat gaze? Nothing,
Aimery decided, that was to any purpose. If the man recognized him and intended to denounce him to the king,
there was nothing Aimery could do about it. He went to
sit with his friends and watch Leo trounce Stephen de Faix.

His brother was huge, strong, and surprisingly nimble. He
was formidable with a sword. Stephen tried his best, but
it was clear from the start he just hoped to come through
the bout with body and honor intact.

Aimery had to fight twice more. He steadfastly put the
watching man-at-arms out of his mind, and despite the fact
he still ached from his previous fight, he did well. He
might have won the contest except for the fact that his last
opponent, of course, was his brother.

"You swing from the right too often," gasped Leo as
they recovered, sprawled companionably on the grass.

"It doesn't matter where I swing from against you, you
great ox."

"True enough." Leo shook hair wet with sweat. "But
you shouldn't be so predictable. Someone should have
beaten it out of you."

"I think they tried." Aimery waved to Geoffrey, who
came and cheerfully poured a bucket of water over them
both. "I've never had a true sword hit yet, though."

"Battles. No one's studying you in a battle. If you come
up one to one, a justice fight for example, a good opponent
would spot it. De Pouissey should have. I could have killed
you half a dozen times."

Aimery sat up and slicked back his wet hair. He looked
at his brother seriously. With the state his life was in these
days, a one-on-one fight to the death was not impossible.
"Who's the best sword master hereabouts?"

"Me," said Leo with a wolfish grin. "We should have
a few weeks to work on you before I have to go home.

But if you don't learn fast, little brother, you'll be black and blue.''

Leo was as good as his word, and he showed he had been telling the truth about Aimery's vulnerability. Leo's blunt sword was too often able to land a heavy blow and, despite the padded leather they wore, some days Aimery felt he could scarcely crawl out of bed. He didn't find it any easier when his father or the king came to watch and make scathing comments. At least d'Oilly had left and taken his man with him without any suspicion being directed at Aimery.

The king announced the marriage agreement between Judith, Countess of Huntingdon, and Waltheof, soon to be earl. Some Normans were disgruntled to see such a tasty morsel thrown to an English hound, but generally the betrothal was taken as an excuse for celebration. The court moved on to the town of Huntingon in high spirits.

Despite daily belaborings from his brother, Aimery enjoyed his weeks with the court. If William had suspicions about Aimery's activities he was not acting on them, and for a while Aimery didn't have to deal with conflicting allegiances and ever-present injustice. He even began to hope the worst was over. The English nobles appeared to be finally accepting William and, apart from opportunistic raids from the Scots and Welsh, peace just might be on the horizon.

There was always the question of what Hereward would do, of course. Aimery wondered if it was time for him to try to bring his uncle and the king together, but that, too, would have to wait.

There seemed little danger of anyone realizing he was the notorious Golden Hart. In fact, the myth was now to his advantage for even as he was making merry in Huntingdon, Golden Hart was apparently murdering a Norman knight in Yorkshire, then leading a mini-insurrection near Shrewsbury.

So he hunted, feasted, sang, and whored, and felt more carefree than he had since Senlac.

Until Gyrth turned up.

The man slipped into the stables one day as Aimery was tending a new bay gelding, a gift from the king.

"Nice horse," said Gyrth. "What's his name?"

"I'm tempted to name him Bastard," said Aimery sourly. "This beast and I have yet to reach an understanding. News?"

"Not from Rolleston. Baddersley."

Aimery glanced around and moved into open ground where no one could sneak up to listen. "What's wrong?"

"Well, the little bitch's life has become a misery."

"What's happening?" asked Aimery sharply. "They haven't touched her, have they? They'll have the king down on them like the wolves of winter."

"Oh no, they haven't touched her," said Gyrth angelically. "It's the aunt. Gone mad, she has." He scratched his nose. "With a little bit of help . . ."

Aimery looked at him. "What have you done?"

"Everyone knows the aunt's easily goaded. I got talking to Aldreda, and we came up with this plan, see. If the girl could be made to look guilty of this and that, she'd be punished, and no blame attached to the village. With a bit of luck the bitch would be really hurt, and de Pouissey and his wife'd feel the king's wrath. He'd hang 'em from the walls, and we'd be rid of the lot of 'em."

Aimery was surprised at the immediate outrage he felt. It was a clever plan. "So, what's happening?" he asked.

Gyrth grinned wickedly. "You'd be amazed at the things a young woman can get up to. Let's see. She put salt in the cream and sawdust in the flour. She threw the Dame's best brooch in the fire and shaved a strip off her nasty little dog. If the girl's eaten anything other than bread and water for weeks I'd be surprised, and her aunt went after her with a carding brush one time and skinned her arm. The best was when she slashed a tunic the aunt was making for dear, sweet Odo. Went after her with a log and broke her ribs."

Aimery felt sick. *She deserves this and more,* he told

himself, but he wanted to rush to her side to protect her. "You must be mad. She's the king's ward. Put a stop to it."

"She deserves every blow! And I don't know that I can stop it. The people of Baddersley have been ground into the dust so they're barely human anymore. They've a focus for their hate, and they're loving every minute of it."

Aimery turned on him and gripped his arm down to the bone. "If the girl ends up dead or crippled, the king's rage will spill over the whole area. Put a stop to it."

Gyrth scowled. "You trying to break my arm? Why so tender-hearted? I thought you'd kicked her out of your system." At the look in Aimery's eyes he grew cautious. "I'll do what I can. They likely need Golden Hart to tell them, though."

Aimery didn't slacken his grip. "And why would that be?"

Gyrth winced and looked shifty. "Well . . . he's who set them on to it, or so they think."

"Golden Hart is dead," Aimery said. "As you are dead to me if you use that name again for any purpose." Gyrth's features tightened under the threat. Aimery let him go. "Go undo your own mischief. I'm not going to Baddersley again. When you've settled things, you stay away from the place, too. The king seems in a matrimonial mood, and he'll doubtless settle the heiress' marriage soon. It could well be to an Englishman. Morcar, perhaps. Things should sort themselves out. Just, for God's sake, make sure the girl's in one piece when the king rides up."

Aimery tried not to think about Madeleine de la Haute Vironge, but the vision of her persecuted, imprisoned, and beaten would not let him rest. Had that bold spirit been crushed? Did those fine dark eyes shift and falter?

She deserved it, he told himself. She deserved to suffer as she had made others suffer. But he longed to ride to Baddersley and protect her.

Even if he were so weak-willed, it would be impossible.

The king was keeping everyone under his eye and playing politics. William was feeding the ancient feud between Gospatric of Northumbria and Waltheof, whose father and grandfather had been earl. He was listening courteously to messengers from the kings of Scotland and Denmark, and building Edwin of Mercia's self-importance. The interesting point, however, was that Waltheof was now betrothed to Judith while Edwin's match with Agatha was unsettled.

Dangerous anger was building in the Mercian camp over this, not least because Edwin and Agatha appeared to have developed a genuine fondness for each other. In fact Aimery thought it sickening the way they hovered about each other.

The atmosphere at court was beginning to grow heavy, yet William continued to be jovial and to promise all things to all people.

There had been no further mention of Aimery's reward, and he was beginning to think he could request permission to leave when the king drew him apart.

"I've watched you, Aimery, and it eases my mind."

"Sire?"

The king looked out over the crowded hall, noting who was talking to whom, who was smiling and who frowning. "These are hard times, my boy," he said, "and this situation is not of my making. I seek only the good of my English subjects."

"I know that, my liege."

William nodded and looked directly at Aimery. "You will always act for my good, will you not?"

"It is always my intent, sire."

William grinned and took a grip on Aimery's arm. "I am giving you the Baddersley heiress."

Aimery froze, unable to make the appropriate response.

The king removed his hand. "Do I gather," he said coldly, "you are not delighted?"

Aimery collected his wits. "I am overwhelmed, sire. But I have Rolleston to run."

"Rolleston, according to you, is running on greased

wheels. I hear Baddersley is in a poor way. Are you afraid of work?''

With relief Aimery saw the king was not angry, merely intrigued. "You know the place, don't you?" asked William. "It belonged to that scourge, Hereward, along with Rolleston. Is it not a desirable manor?"

"It is in a strong location, sire, and the manor holds rich land, well drained."

"Tell me then straight out why you alone of all the young men are not slobbering over the prize."

Because it's to sign my death warrant. There's a traitor in Baddersley village who'll betray me for a few pieces of silver, and if I escape him, the heiress will recognize me and report it to you . . . Aimery found an explanation which contained an element of truth. "Rumor has it the heiress is ugly in body and mind. I was raised in a happy home full of love and graciousness. Even for a fair estate I do not want to marry such a woman."

The king moved forward and gripped Aimery's shoulders strongly. Aimery saw tears in his eyes. "Well said! I, too, know the value of a gracious wife. You are wise beyond your years." But then he gave his godson a shake. "But what if rumor lies and she is fair in all respects? What then, eh?"

The humor in the king's eyes told Aimery that William knew the heiress was comely. "Then I am a fool," he said, "and have thrown your generosity in your face, sire."

The king released him and paced backward and forward, deep in thought. "Very well," he said at last. "We shall throw it in the lap of fate. Follow the *wyrd*, as our Viking ancestors would have it."

There was almost a hint of mischief in the king which made Aimery very wary.

"The queen will rest here for a while," William said, "but I have a mind to see some of the new castles. We will visit Baddersley and the heiress. Does rumor tell you the lady is to choose her husband?"

"No, sire." Aimery was assessing all the angles of this disaster, seeking an escape route.

" 'Tis truth. So, I will take care to have only married nobles with me other than you, Stephen de Faix, and Odo de Pouissey. De Faix is a man who easily finds favor with women, and de Pouissey is known to the demoiselle. I believe she was fond of him as a child. All three of you are worthy, and the lady will have her choice." He looked sharply at Aimery. "Do you regret your decision now?"

"No, sire. I will abide by God's and the demoiselle's wish." Aimery was dismissed and could find peace to consider it all. What a hell-made situation.

It would only be a matter of time before the heiress recognized him as Edwald and screeched it to the king. From there to Golden Hart and d'Oilly's giant was a small step.

Even if that didn't happen, he had no wish to marry a woman who could beg to have innocent people flogged.

But she'd surely never choose de Pouissey after that attack, which left only de Faix between him and a life of misery. He thanked Christ that de Faix was the sort of man young women found very pleasing, even as he tasted gall at the thought of her in any other man's arms.

Madness. Witchcraft.

Then he remembered Gyrth's tale, which posed another problem.

If they arrived at Baddersley to find the heiress a beaten wretch, someone would pay, and he feared in the end, as usual, it would be the ordinary English people.

Chapter 7

Madeleine lay listless in her bed, thinking drearily of her noble resolve.

She had tried. She had scavenged all the food she could and given it to the most needy. She had supplied medicines and advice. She had even worked in the manor garden herself, pulling weeds and carrying water. She had deflected her aunt and uncle's cruelty wherever possible.

She had done some good, she knew she had, and yet the people here were no more kindly disposed and the world had gone mad. Strange accidents had begun to occur, and acts of malice against her aunt; and they always happened in such a way that Madeleine looked to be at fault.

She had endured day after day of accusations and blows and kept a core of strength. That had withered away when she had learned the truth.

Aldreda had slipped up to her. "Do you ever wonder why we're doing this, Lady Madeleine?"

Madeleine had realized in that moment that all her troubles were a plot by the Baddersley people. That knowledge had been more painful than any blow. "No," she said numbly. "Why?"

"Orders," said Aldreda. "From Golden Hart. The next time your aunt strikes you, remember it comes from him."

It was doubtless true. He had promised to punish her, though for what she did not know. She shouldn't care. He

was cruel and worthless. But Aldreda's words robbed
Madeleine of the last of her strength and spirit, and she
took to her bed.

She tried to eat the food Dorothy brought to her, but
took very little. She watched the shadows mark the pas-
sage of the sun on beautiful summer days. If ever the king
did come, she would ask to return to the Abbaye. Surely,
she thought, this hell was a judgment on her for leaving
the convent when it had been her mother's dearest wish
that she go there. Punishment, too, for lusting after that
outlaw.

True, the king had sent for her, but if she had resisted
and pleaded a true vocation he could not have insisted.
And no one had forced her to behave lewdly down by the
stream. These were the only blots on her conscience which
could account for God so turning his face against her. She
understood how Harold Godwinson must have felt when
he saw the Norman army carrying the Pope's banner, saw
the winds change in their favor, and knew God was dis-
pleased.

She was idly watching a spider build a web in the corner
when her aunt burst into the room. "Why are you lying
here, girl? You are not hurt. Get up, get up, and go out
in the sun. You are as pale as a ghost!"

"Leave me alone."

Her aunt lunged and dragged her up by the hair. "Get
up! The king is coming!"

Madeleine just stared, and Dame Celia shook her. "You
must look pretty. He doubtless brings your husband, and
if you find him not so kind as dear sweet Odo, then it will
be a judgment upon you, you ungrateful girl!"

Madeleine beat off the woman and dragged herself to
her feet, dizzy and weak. "The king?"

"Is coming here! The place must be freshened." Dame
Celia waved her hands like a crippled bird. "We have no
tapestries, few beds. No fresh rushes . . ."

She reached again to grab Madeleine. "You can't shirk
the work, you lazy slut!" Madeleine pushed her away and

Celia scuttled across the tiny room and opened a chest. She pulled out a length of cloth. It was slashed into ribbons.

Dame Celia shrieked, "Wretches! Wretches! It isn't our fault these people are so devil-ridden. It's that Golden Hart! Golden Hart. The king will find him, then we'll see." She glared at Madeleine. "Don't just stand there. Do something!"

"The king is coming." Madeleine repeated the words, and hope began to uncurl within her.

Dame Celia hurried back to pinch Madeleine's cheeks, though not viciously, and push her fingers clumsily through the girl's tangled hair. "He must see how we have cared for you. We have cared for you, haven't we?"

Madeleine began to laugh. It turned hysterical, and her aunt slapped her, but again not viciously. "See!" she hissed. "You make me do these things. As God is my witness, I have done my best! If you complain to the king of my treatment, I will be forced to tell him the cause— your wicked ingratitude, your madness, your lewdness—"

"I am pure!"

"If your husband casts you off, it won't be my fault," her aunt gibbered on. "No one can blame me. No wonder the convent threw you out."

"No one will cast me off! I am a virgin."

"All that sneaking off to the woods," Celia ranted. "Up to no good, I'll be bound. Odo had a lucky escape!"

Madeleine saw the woman was beyond all reason. "Yes, Aunt," she said soothingly. "I'm sure that's true. Why don't you rest?"

"Rest? Rest?" the woman shrieked, waving her arms about. "How can I rest with the king about to arrive! Paul says he can travel like the wind. He could be here at any minute. Any minute!" She scuttled out, calling conflicting orders to anyone she met.

Madeleine was weak from hunger and inaction, but a sense of purpose rose in her. Liberation was at hand. Moreover, Baddersley was hers, and it should greet the

king with some pride. She must take matters in hand, and
it looked as if she was finally to be allowed to do so. She
had Dorothy comb her hair and then bind it up in a coif
for working. Wincing a little, for her bruised ribs still
ached, she changed into a serviceable kirtle of brown linen
and went forth to take charge of her home.

Dame Celia was in her chamber wailing and gibbering.
Madeleine mixed a soothing brew that would keep the
woman asleep for the next day. Paul de Pouissey was in
as great a panic as his wife, but was putting it to use by
bullying his men and the servants to try to finish the palisade. He wouldn't succeed, but at least he was out of the
way.

Madeleine checked the food stores and found that, now
fresh crops were available, they were adequate if not abun-
dant. The king's visit would lead to shortages later, but
she could not concern herself with such matters now.

There was plenty of ale and mead, but scarcely any
wine. She tried to get coin from her uncle to buy some,
but he refused, saying there was none to spare. He had
sent out to hire men for coin to come and work on the
wall.

Madeleine had a late calf killed. That would provide
tender meat and a stomach for making custards and curd
tarts. She had other pastries prepared. She called in Hengar, the chief forester, for a report on the game. It seemed
there should be sport for the king and more meat for the
table. The man was markedly ill-at-ease, and she remembered he was Aldreda's husband. She supposed the people
here would expect her to complain to the king. She
wouldn't, for it was her aunt and uncle she wanted rid of,
but she wouldn't say anything to reassure them. Let them
sweat over it.

She inspected the stables and found them in poor condition. She was fond of horses and didn't see why they
should suffer. She stole some workers from the defensive
construction and soon men were at work to mend matters.

It seemed to her the wooden castle was a poor example

and the palisade far behind plan, but that was her uncle's problem, not hers.

There were only three beds at Baddersley—her uncle and aunt's great bed which was in the solar, and two narrow beds in two sleeping alcoves. One was hers, and one was kept for Odo, or any other traveler of rank. She had the mattresses hung out to freshen and the bedding washed. She ordered straw to make the simple coiled mattresses which would do for most.

She discovered a number of bolts of cloth stored in a chest and still intact. One was a fine brown wool with a pattern in the weave. She had it hung on the wall of the solar, which would be the king's room. It was not thick enough to give winter warmth, but it softened the bleakness of the bare wooden walls.

When they'd done what they could for the stables, she set the carpenters to work making extra trestles and benches for the hall. Laid flat at night, they would form the bases for the straw beds. Her uncle complained the men were needed for the building, but she stared him down.

She found she could stare anyone down these days. She knew her uncle and aunt dared not harm her with the king's visit so close, but she did not understand the change in the English. There was no warmth in them, but that biting hatred had gone. They listened blank-faced to her instructions and did exactly as she said. Fear of the king must be goading them.

During four days of hard, meaningful work, Madeleine healed. She began to eat heartily and sleep well. On the third day she found herself standing in the courtyard looking with pride at her home and her land. It was a good place. With proper care it could be a fine home, and it was for her to give it that care.

She heard her uncle bellowing at someone, trying to get more work from some poor soul than was humanly possible. In the house she knew Aunt Celia was lying on a narrow bed complaining because the great bed was being kept in readiness for the king. Baddersley must be rid of these two, and that could only come with Madeleine's marriage.

She reviewed her preparations with concern. Much of it was shoddily done, but time was short. The king could come this very day.

The new trestles were shorter than the old, and the old really should be mended; many of the benches were rotten. But Uncle Paul had demanded the carpenters back so frantically that she had given in. There weren't enough rushes to make a proper covering for the floor, and there was no time to make even the simplest hangings. They had tallow dips but few good candles. At least the nights were short.

Finally, Madeleine gave some thought to her appearance. It was important to her that she first meet her husband dressed as a lady of rank and dignity. The queen had provided her with a rich wardrobe, most of which she had not worn. When she went to the locked chest in which she had stored all her finery, she remembered the high hopes and spirits in which she'd left Normandy. Some trace of that optimism returned.

The king was coming, and soon she would have a husband.

She hung handsome tunics and gowns to freshen, and checked over girdles and jewelry. She washed her hair with rosemary, and had Dorothy comb it thoroughly every night. Each day, once the hardest work was done, Madeleine dressed finely, ready for king and husband both.

It was unfortunate that she was in the kitchen in her work clothes when the watchcorn on the tower sounded his horn. It could only mean the king was in sight.

"Stars and angels!" Madeleine gasped. She'd had three pigs killed and hung days ago, and today decided they had to be cooked before they spoiled. She'd been showing the cooks how to prepare a stew using some of her precious spices so it would last a few days.

At least they would have food for the meal today.

She fled to her small room, calling for Dorothy, and together they scrambled her out of her linen into silk—a pale green silk kirtle, well embroidered around the hem and cuffs in blue and yellow, and a sky blue silk tunic, edged with red and green, with a red silk lining showing on the turned back elbow-length sleeves. She tied a red girdle and let Dorothy arrange her folds as she struggled to unpin her hair. She had been torn between greeting the king with loose hair as a maiden, or with plaits and veil as a lady of substance. Now she had no choice.

As Dorothy dragged a comb through her long hair, Madeleine stood by the window, watching for the first appearance of the king. The first horse arrived as Dorothy said, "There. That'll do."

Madeleine grabbed a twisted gold fillet and raced for the door. She breathlessly joined her uncle and aunt, hoping she didn't look quite as desperate as they. She fitted the fillet over her hair just as the king's party rode in through the unfinished gate of the unfinished palisade.

There were about thirty men, mostly soldiers but some scribes and clerics—the work of the kingdom continued wherever the king chose to travel. Five leashed hounds and their handlers followed. Most of the men had hawks on their wrists.

Madeleine bit her lip. No one in Baddersley kept hawks, and there was no mews.

With Uncle Paul's guards to include, the hall was going to be hard put to fit everyone.

Would the food last?

The king rode in front on a fine dark horse. He wore mail but no helmet. He looked quite ordinary with his thinning gingerish hair and no signs of kingship other than his banner. Had she expected him to be wearing his crown?

Was her husband here?

Madeleine scrutinized the arrivals, but the men all looked the same—large mailed shapes topped by conical helmets with long nosepieces. She dragged her eyes back to the king. As soon as his horse arrived at the hall doors, Paul de Pouissey went forward to kneel. Dame Celia and Madeleine curtsied.

William swung off his mount and flung the reins to a waiting noble, then gave Paul his hand to kiss and raised him. Without much approval, Madeleine noticed. The king's shrewd eyes traveled around, missing nothing. He was not ordinary at all, she realized. She sensed the power that had brought him from bastard son of a petty duke to King of England.

He had a word for Dame Celia, then came to Madeleine. She licked her lips nervously as she curtsied again.

"So, demoiselle," he said gruffly. "I have brought you a husband."

"Oh." Madeleine knew she should thank him, but instead she looked around for the chosen one.

The king laughed. "Later. Now I want to see this place." He offered her his hand and led her into the hall, leaving her uncle and aunt to follow.

Dame Celia immediately scuttled off, screeching, "Wine. Wine for the king!"

Madeleine swallowed. "We have no wine, sire."

"Ale is better after a dusty journey," said the king as he looked around. "This place has a somewhat Spartan appearance, demoiselle. I'm sure in Hereward's day it was richer."

Madeleine gestured for ale to be brought forward. "I fear he must have taken his possessions when he fled, sire."

The king took one of the only two chairs in the wooden hall and gestured Madeleine to the other. Scowling, Paul was forced to sit on a bench. A servant crept forward with a flagon of ale. Madeleine took it to serve the chief guest as was her duty as lady of the hall. The servant backed away, pallid with terror.

William took the cup of ale. "Thank you, demoiselle." He added dryly, "I wish all the English were so awestruck at my appearance."

"Indeed, sire," said Paul, leaning forward eagerly. "We rule the wretches here with a firm hand."

The king took a deep draft of ale. "A good brew, demoiselle." He gestured. An older man and a younger, the younger very large and dark, came forward. Was this her husband, Madeleine wondered with a fast-beating heart. He looked pleasant.

"Demoiselle, I present to you Count Guy de Gaillard and his son Lord Leo de Vesin. They will keep you company while I go apart with Lord Paul. With such a firm hand, he must have good things to report to me."

Madeleine saw her uncle swallow as he rose to lead the king to the solar. She wished him well of the interview.

Guy de Gaillard considered the young woman his son had been offered and experienced the familiar desire to knock Aimery's head against a stone wall. She was a gem. Not a legendary beauty, but wholesome and comely with clear skin and white teeth. More to the point, there was a flash of spirit and humor in those fine brown eyes. Though there was no physical similarity, Madeleine de la Haute Vironge reminded him a lot of Lucia when he had first set eyes on her.

He glanced around in search of Aimery but couldn't see him. Where in Christ's name had he gone? Odo de Pouissey had disappeared, too, but perhaps he was paying his respects to his stepmother. Stephen de Faix was hovering, looking as if he couldn't believe his good fortune.

"So, Lady Madeleine," Guy said. "How long have you been in England?"

"Only eight weeks, my lord. I came over with the duchess . . . the queen, I mean."

"Ah, yes. She sent messages and gifts for you. She regards you highly. I believe she hopes you will rejoin her ladies before her child is born."

"She is well, my lord?"

"As best I can tell. And do you like England?"

"It is very beautiful," said Madeleine, "and could be heaven, I believe, were it not for strife."

Count Guy chuckled. "For some people heaven *is* strife." At Madeleine's surprised look he added, "Most Normans think life dull without a fight, and the Vikings, of course, thought heaven was Valhalla, where men could fight every day and die, then be revived to fight again the next. You must meet my youngest son," he went on, "who can explain all this kind of thing better than I."

"He is a scholar?"

The younger man laughed. "Aimery's over-educated perhaps for a Norman, but no cleric. You'll see when you meet him." He, too, looked around. "I don't know where he's gone. I think I'll go and find him." He rose to his feet.

Dame Celia came scurrying over to take the vacated seat next to Madeleine. "It is so nice to have Odo back home again, isn't it, Madeleine?"

"This is hardly his home, Aunt," retorted Madeleine.

Dame Celia reached to pinch Madeleine, then drew her hand back. "We won't have enough food," she snapped. "You were in charge of food. I don't know what you've been doing, you lazy girl."

Leo shared a look with his father and escaped.

Aimery was making a spurious concern over his horse an excuse to stay well out of the heiress' way. Let Stephen and Odo fight over her, and then perhaps she wouldn't take a close look at him. He had little hope that she wouldn't recognize him if they spent much time together.

He remembered how she'd appeared, curtsying to the king, radiant in a tunic of rich blue embroidered with red and gold worn over a green kirtle, equally well trimmed. Her long hair had hung loose under a gold circlet, gleaming all the way down to her hips, where it swung against the curve of her bottom as she turned to go into the hall with the king.

Clearly all Gyrth's concerns about mistreatment had been nonsense, and he'd worried for no reason. Instead, she was more beautiful than he remembered. Now he just had to remind himself ten or twenty times a day that she was a heartless witch . . . a hundred times a day, perhaps.

"Well now," said Leo, coming over to slap him none too gently on the back. Aimery had shed his armor, and the buffet stung. "Don't you wish you'd snapped her up? A cozy armful."

"That depends on her nature," said Aimery bleakly, and his brother shook his head.

"Sure you don't have boils on your behind? You've grown more surly with each mile we rode coming here." Leo looked around. "Not that this run-down place looks all it's made out to be. I want to get a closer look at the keep."

Leo bellowed for his squire and shed his armor, too, pulling on a well-embroidered tunic, then he and Aimery wandered around. Leo poked and prodded everything. "This has been built too fast," he said, peering at the ten-foot thick stone base to the wooden keep. "The stones aren't fitted close enough."

At the palisade he pushed at a great log set in the ground and it moved. "Hey you!" he shouted at a laborer nearby. "When was this done?"

The man looked up, terrified, and gabbled something in English.

"What did he say?" Leo asked.

Aimery translated. "He asked, of course, what you said. Doesn't it occur to anyone to learn the language?" Then he remembered it had occurred to one person.

"Ask him what I asked him," said Leo impatiently.

They soon established that the whole section had been put together in a week. The man said he knew it wasn't done right, but it was the lord's command.

"If you become lord here," Leo said, "you'll have to rip this all down and do it again."

"And you wonder why I don't want the task. Let's look at the stables," said Aimery. "I'm wondering how our mounts are faring."

They found their horses adequately housed, though the

squires were having to do more work than usual as the manor seemed short-handed. At one end of the stables was a makeshift mews where crude perches were being hastily knocked together. Aimery was grateful he had no bird with him.

Leo set again to asking questions, using Aimery as translator, and they soon discovered the Lady Madeleine had put the stables and storehouses in order.

"Rich and efficient," Leo approved. "If I were you I'd change into my finest and start dancing attendance. Gift her with some of the bullion that offends Father so. You could buy half the women in England for that lot."

"Are you suggesting she's that kind of woman?" Aimery asked dryly, leaning against the door jamb of a grainstore.

Leo laughed. "They're all that kind of woman. They decide how much they're valued by how much you spend. Give her the bracelet with the blue and garnet inlay."

"It's warrior's *geld*. Do you think she's a fighter?"

Leo at last caught the resistance in his brother's tone and studied him, puzzled. "You still don't want her? What is it? You've a true love somewhere? Marry her. If you can't, marry the heiress and keep the other for variety."

Aimery laughed. "If you have a little variety tucked away back home, I don't know Janetta."

Leo acknowledged the truth with a humorous grimace, but any further comment was cut off by the horn, summoning everyone to the evening meal. They made haste toward the manor house.

The great hall of Baddersley manor was fine in its own way with carved rafters and paneling. Perhaps only Aimery, who had visited here in better times, missed the handsome hangings, the massed arrays of gleaming weapons, and the carved and gilded furniture.

The high table was well laid, with a brightly embroidered frontal to hang down and conceal the diners' legs, and snowy covering cloths. The two great chairs stood behind, and the king and Madeleine were already sitting in them. To Madeleine's right sat Paul de Pouissey, looking sullen and frightened. To the king's left sat Dame Celia, looking frantic. On her other side Count Guy was attempting some kind of rational conversation. He looked up to see his sons and made a quick expression of despair.

Trestle tables of irregular sizes and heights crammed around the walls of the rest of the hall so it was difficult to work through to a seat. The tables were covered by a hotchpotch of cloths, some with ragged edges, showing how hastily the room had been prepared. When Aimery and Leo found a place, they eyed the cracked bench with misgiving. As they gingerly lowered themselves, it swayed and creaked. Two other men came to join them.

"Sit carefully, friends," boomed Leo, "and there's a chance we'll survive the meal upright."

Aimery saw the heiress color and cast a swift, angry look at his brother. Her gaze passed over Aimery, then flicked back. She frowned thoughtfully, but then a great crack and a shout turned her attention elsewhere. Either other diners had been less cautious, or their bench had been even more decrepit. Across the room a line of sitting men disappeared from view.

For a moment, nothing could be seen except a waving arm and then, unfortunately, a flailing leg kicked the table and sent it flying to partially demolish the one next to it.

Aimery saw Madeleine half rise, then look anxiously at the king beside her. William was guffawing with laughter. A wild screech rent the air, causing the king to turn, mouth still wide, to look at the lady on his left. Dame Celia was shrieking something and pointing at Madeleine. Count Guy was attempting to control her. The lady's wimple slid half over her face, and she clawed at it, finally dragging it off to reveal a nest of messy gray hair.

Madeleine said something, though from where Aimery sat her words were drowned by laughter and the curses of the downed men. Dame Celia hurled her headcloth at the girl. It hit the king full in the face.

Silence fell.

The king pulled the cloth off, looking with astonishment from the boggle-eyed lady to her husband. Paul turned red, then white, and leaped to his feet. He crossed to his wife and swung a hand to deliver a mighty blow. His arm was gripped and stopped dead by a stern-faced Count Guy.

The tableau held for breathless moments. Then the king said into the silence, "I hardly think that would effect a cure, Lord Paul. Your wife clearly needs rest. Tomorrow you had best leave here and take her back to her homeland. I suggest you may wish to give her into the care of a convent for some time to recover her wits. I vow, this England is enough to drive anyone demented. Perhaps you had best take her apart now and care for her."

Stiffly, Paul recovered his hand from the count and took his wife's arm. As they left the room, the king's voice went after them. "Care for her gently, Lord Paul."

Conversation started again with a murmur and rapidly grew to bedlam. Aimery returned his attention to the fallen table and found little was being achieved. The servants were being dull-witted or deliberately obstructive, and those gentlemen nearby were finding great amusement in pinning the fallen down and trying to get the boards on top of them.

Exasperated, he said, "Watch the bench, my friends, I'm going to stand on it." Having accomplished this, he took his life in his hands and leaped over the table to the central floor and crossed to the tangled mess. Giving crisp instructions in French and English, and using force on one mischievous knight, he got the diners up and the table set on its legs again. A brief discussion with the groom of the pantry brought two chests to take the place of the splintered bench.

"And be grateful," he said tersely as the men sat down. "You probably have the most solid seats in the place."

As he turned to go back to his place, he gave the high table a deep, ironic bow.

''My thanks to you, Aimery,'' said the king. ''But I cannot allow you to risk yourself by vaulting over the table again. See, there is a vacant seat here beside the demoiselle. Come, take it.''

Chapter 8

Aimery obeyed, cursing his habit of trying always to put things right. Now he'd brought himself to everyone's attention, including the village people ordered in to supplement the hall servants, and the heiress, of course. Then again, a meeting with her could not be put off indefinitely.

As Aimery took the stool to Madeleine's right, the king said, "Demoiselle, I present to you Lord Aimery de Gaillard, son of the Count de Gaillard, whom you have met. As you see, he is a very useful young man."

Madeleine was scarcely paying attention. She was furious and mortified. She had done the best she could for this meal, but months of neglect and, she suspected, deliberate sabotage, could not be undone in a few days. She supposed she should feel grateful to this young man who had competently sorted out the mess so that at least the food could be served, but she found it difficult. Something in the ironic way he had bowed struck her as insulting—not to William, but to her and her household.

Still, she couldn't ignore his efforts. "Thank you for your assistance, sir," she said flatly, looking down at the trencher before her.

"I was hungry," he said coolly, "and that contretemps was holding up the food."

She flicked her eyes sideways and saw, what? Indifference? Dislike? What reason had he to dislike her? Young

Norman lords were supposed to want to please her, and certainly the one she had met thus far had tried hard enough. Stephen de Faix was handsome and charming.

But then, she realized with surprise, this wasn't a Norman. His shoulder-length blond hair told her that. She had noticed it earlier and wondered. He met her gaze with clear green eyes. She gasped. It wasn't possible.

"Who are you?" she whispered.

"Aimery de Gaillard, demoiselle."

"You are Saxon!"

His fine lips twisted. "Do you fear to be murdered in your bed? I am Norman. My mother is English. She is a lady of Mercia."

She shook her head at her foolishness as she realized he was speaking in perfect Norman French. He was the youngest son of Count Guy de Gaillard, distant relative and close friend of King William, the son who could tell her about Valhalla. She saw what the count meant. He looked like a Viking barbarian with his flowing yellow hair and gold bracelets, but he clearly could not be a Saxon outlaw.

She wondered if he was married. It would explain his indifference. She had discovered his brother Leo was married and had been a little disappointed. Leo de Vesin appeared to be both kind and trustworthy.

A platter of pork was placed before the king, and he selected a few pieces before waving it on to Madeleine. She took one piece of the meat. "May I help you to some, Lord Aimery?"

Aimery murmured his thanks and let her pick a few choice lumps of meat to place on his bread. For a moment he'd thought she recognized him, but it appeared not to be so. If he could only keep his right hand out of her sight he might avoid detection.

Their goblets were filled and a dish of beans came by, then fine white wastel bread. That appeared to be the sum of their provisions, and he saw Madeleine anxiously watching the dishes progress around the room. Probably some men would end up eating more beans than pork.

The liquid in his cup turned out to be mead. He leaned closer to the heiress. "I hesitate to add to your worries, Lady Madeleine, but the king dislikes mead. If you have no wine, you would do better to offer him ale."

She flushed and cast him a look that was both worried and annoyed, then beckoned a servant. Within minutes the king was offered a clean goblet and ale. He nodded his thanks.

"Do you have other suggestions?" Madeleine asked, aware that her tone was unfairly tart. She could not explain her antagonism to Aimery de Gaillard. She did not know him and had scarce looked at him since he had sat down beside her, yet she felt as if hedgehog spines were springing up along the side of her body. It must be because she'd developed an antipathy to green eyes.

"Relax," he said in an indulgent tone that rasped her nerves. "The king's no glutton or lover of ceremony for its own sake. The food you have is properly prepared and adequate. It is clear matters have not been well run here."

She gritted her teeth. "I have only just started to take a part in the running of Baddersley, Lord Aimery."

"Then perhaps you are slow to see your duty, my lady."

Anger turned her head toward him. "I have only been in the country since April!"

"A place can come to rack and ruin remarkably quickly, can't it?" he said with an insincere smile, and passed her a basket of nuts. "May I crack one for you, Lady Madeleine?"

"You may crack your head, sir!" Madeleine hissed, then stiffened when the king chuckled.

"By the Blood, Guy, they argue like man and wife already."

Already? Madeleine looked from the king to Lord Aimery in horror. *This* was to be her husband?

Never.

"Sire," she blurted, "you promised me a choice!"

She saw the flash of annoyance in the king's eyes and bit her lip, but any ill-humor was quickly hidden by a smile. "And I am a man of my word, demoiselle. There are three eligible young men present, all unattached, all fit to help you here at Baddersley. You will have your choice. But then you will wed your choice. Unfortunately I have to deprive you of your aunt and uncle. I cannot leave you here unprotected."

Madeleine felt the blood drain from her face. A chill passed through her. Within days she would be married? To whom?

As if reading her thoughts, the king said, "Your choices are Lord Aimery, Lord Stephen de Faix—the man in blue over there—and Odo de Pouissey whom, of course, you know. Become well acquainted with them, demoiselle. Test them if you will. In two days you will wed your choice."

The king turned back to Count Guy, and Madeleine became aware that someone was pressing her goblet into her hand. The one with green eyes. She took a deep draft of the mead. She'd once thought she would like to marry a blond Englishman, but that had been before he had so cruelly betrayed her.

So this was to be her choice; Odo, whom she might once have chosen except for his parents; the green-eyed one who didn't like her and who reminded her all too keenly of a vicious rogue; and the pleasant young man who had flirted with her earlier.

She looked at Stephen de Faix. He was smooth faced, with curly chestnut hair which he wore cut short but not in the extreme fashion Odo favored. Madeleine thought she could categorize her choices by hair—short, medium, or long. She bit her lip on a giggle which was part hysteria.

The choice was obvious. Stephen de Faix. Her husband.

But the decision did not settle her nerves; it made her uneasy. It was just the stresses of the day, she assured herself, and having the choice forced on her so suddenly. In time she would grow accustomed to the idea.

"Stephen's a very pleasant fellow," approved the green-eyed devil to her right. "He's remarkably courteous for a Norman, competent in war, moderate in drink."

Madeleine faced him. "Are you not all those things?"

"I'm too courteous for a Norman," he retorted. "I don't like war, and I drown my sorrows in a pot." To prove it he drained his cup and summoned a servant for a refill.

She didn't believe him, which left only one interpretation. He didn't want her. She didn't want him either, but his rejection hurt all the same. "You want me to marry Lord Stephen?"

"I don't think Odo would suit you," he said with a shrug. "But then, I don't know much about you."

Madeleine fixed a smile on her face. "*You* do not want to wed me and have Baddersley for your own?"

Without apology he shook his head. "I have enough to do running Rolleston for my father." He cracked a nut with an efficient tap of a very solid gold bracelet and offered her the meat. "It's in East Anglia. Not the most peaceful spot."

She took the nut absently. "But Baddersley would be yours alone if we were wed. Does that not appeal?" Why, wondered Madeleine, am I saying these things? It's as if I'm begging him to woo me.

"In English law the barony is yours by right, Lady Madeleine. Your husband will merely be your defender." He cracked another nut and popped the flesh into his mouth. He had very strong white teeth.

Just like another man. Madeleine stared. His face had a similar shape . . . No, it was her foolish imagination again, seeing him in every man of that type.

But he was behaving very strangely. Everything about him was strange. She'd never seen a man wear a tunic of such bright green. She'd never in her life seen a man glitter so. He wore a fortune carelessly and far outshone the king.

Perhaps he had been honest when he said he didn't like war. He was not heavily built, and he had the look of a man who spent more time in his clothes than his armor.

Her father and brother would never have wasted money on needlework that could be spent on horse or sword. She certainly would not want to marry a man who couldn't fight. On the other hand, the notion of being Lady of Baddersley in more than name was startling, but wondrous.

"Are you saying that if I were to wed you, Lord Aimery, you would regard Baddersley as mine? I think perhaps you do wish to marry me, to tempt me so."

"The idea of having the power here is attractive to you?" he said with a distinct sneer, but Madeleine didn't care.

"Power." She rolled the word around her mouth like a honey-cake, savoring it.

Aimery realized he had made a serious mistake. More than one, a whole stream of them. How could this girl scramble his wits when he knew her for what she was? When she looked at him with those heavy-lidded brown eyes, a mist seemed to float over his reason.

For weeks he'd carried a picture of a wicked harpy in his mind, but now it kept slipping away from him to be replaced by Dorothy, sweet and flustered by the river. He'd wanted her to know her position under English law, but now he saw his error. Here she was, true to form, gloating at the thought of being the absolute power at Baddersley, doubtless looking forward to wielding the whip with her own hands.

Aimery had no time to pursue the matter for the king called on him for a song. As he bowed and went to fetch his lyre, Aimery knew sourly that the king was going to do his best to push the girl into choosing him, and he would not be able to refuse the "honor" a second time. He would have to apply himself to becoming unpalatable to the heiress without letting the king or his father suspect what he was doing.

At the same time he must be sure not to give Madeleine de la Haute Vironge opportunity to recognize him or see his tattoo. She didn't seem to recognize his voice speaking noble French, but it was hard to believe she wouldn't one day look at him and see Edwald the outlaw.

And there was always the danger of one of the local people letting something slip. Aldreda had already winked at him.

All in all, he thought with a sigh, it was enough to send a man on a pilgrimage, a decades-long pilgrimage.

By the time he returned, the rickety trestles had been dismantled, and men were wandering about draining replenished cups. The windows stood open, and the evening sun lit the room. Madeleine and the king still sat in the big chairs, and it occurred to Aimery that she was the only lady here. Her position was strange, and he suspected the king had manipulated it to be so. She was being given some say in her marriage, but her choice was being skillfully limited.

William was set on the girl choosing Aimery, and he would use every trick to achieve his end. When William of Normandy determined on something, the chances of avoiding it were small indeed. On the other hand, the king had promised the girl a choice, and he would not go back on his word. That was the only hope.

Aimery must direct her firmly toward Stephen de Faix. Stephen was indolent and self-indulgent, and he lacked a necessary streak of ruthlessness. But that, Aimery reminded himself, his wife would supply in full measure.

As he tuned his instrument, Aimery ran quickly through a list of songs, wondering which would appeal least to his proposed bride. He discarded all the lyrical ones about the beauties of the seasons, and also the ones with a romantic tale. He knew they appealed to the ladies. How would she react to a stirring battle saga? She was obviously not softhearted, and so it might appeal.

Nevertheless, it must be one of those, and so he chose the most harsh and bloodthirsty of the lot, an old Norse tale he had himself translated into French at William's request. It told of Karldig who, trapped by his enemies, fought to the death with all his men around him. The Norse code dictated that no true man could outlive his leader, his ring-giver, and the followers of Karldig adhered to the code with high spirit. The story was told from the enemy's point of view, for Karldig and all his men perished. The storyteller, though supposedly one of the enemy, gloried in the nobility of it all; he lauded each man sent to Valhalla, related with relish each wound, each lopped limb, each pierced eye.

It was not one of Aimery's favorite songs. As he expected, however, it pleased his male audience. Soon they were pounding on seat and floor in time with the rhythm of the piece, shouting out the most bloodthirsty parts. Chanting on automatically—for it was more a chant than a song, with Hereward's old hall shaking to lusty voices, Aimery was suddenly overwhelmed by a memory of Senlac—the battle cries, the screams, the deafening crash of weapons, Harold falling, and his housecarls and family fighting grimly on to die beside him. The smell of blood, the spilled entrails, the severed limbs . . .

He came to himself, and to the realization that the song was finished and yells of approval were shaking the rafters. He struggled to gather his wits. There were calls for more, but he shook his head and offered the instrument to Stephen.

His rival took it with a grimace. "You devil. How am I to follow that?"

"You have to please the demoiselle, not these bloodthirsty rogues. Sing her a pretty song."

Stephen cast a dubious look at the heiress, and Aimery followed it. She looked thoughtfully intent, and her eyes were rather bright. She did not look disgusted.

Aimery slipped out into the peaceful evening before he could be summoned back to her side. A man should be glad of a strong, courageous wife, but he found the Baddersley heiress too bloodthirsty for his taste. He heard Stephen begin a melodious ballad. The man had a pleasant enough voice and a taste for Frankish music with more tune and less martial themes. What woman would turn down Stephen?

Standing in the courtyard with his back to the new motte and keep, Aimery could almost imagine he was back at Baddersley in Hereward's day. The hall would have been full of song then, too. Hereward liked the song of Karldig for he gloried in the old Norse ways. It would have been sung in English, though. Aimery looked at the countryside, at rolling fields stretching toward the forest—which was farther away now, he saw. Many trees had been felled to make the castle.

The illusion was shattered, and he knew the past was gone forever. There were fewer fields under crops than there used to be, and fewer beasts growing fat. And the people, the people were very different. There were fewer of them, too, and they were pale and thin. Many had boils and other scabrous signs of poor feeding. They slid around furtively, eyes to the ground. There was no whistling and laughter as they worked, no children playing. Even the cats slunk through the shadows in search of rats.

The work of Paul de Pouissey and his niece.

It could be made good again. The thought slipped into his mind, and he shook it off.

"Too much mead?"

Aimery turned to face his father. "No. Just wondering how a prosperous manor could be brought to such a state."

Count Guy sat on a pile of logs by the unfinished palisade. "I keep forgetting you must know this place well."

"Not well. Hereward preferred Rolleston. But I came here once or twice."

"I'd think you'd relish a chance to put it in order."

"I have enough to do."

Aimery saw an irritated muscle twitch beside his father's mouth and braced himself for a battle, but Count Guy merely said, "I'd give a lot to know what's going on in that head of yours. The king's patience isn't infinite."

"He's hardly likely to banish me for not wanting to wed Madeleine de la Haute Vironge."

Count Guy let out a long breath. "Aimery, something has scrambled your wits. I'd like to think it was love, but if it is, you're not making sense. If you love another, tell the king. As he loves his queen, he'll forgive that. Otherwise, consider carefully what you are about. William is your fond godfather. He is also duke, and now he's king, and those things are paramount. If you do not serve him, you will lose his favor, and there will come a day when you will need it."

"I serve him."

"Look at me," said Count Guy sternly, and Aimery met his father's eyes. "You serve him as you see fit. That is not good enough. If the king wants your land, you give it. If he wants your right hand, you give him that, too. Or your life, or the life of your sons. If he wants you to marry Madeleine de la Haute Vironge, you marry her. You do not ask why."

Father and son looked at each other in silence among birdsong and the distant lowing of cattle.

"He has not asked it," Aimery said at last.

"Because if he did you would have to."

Aimery turned away and let out a long breath. "She may not want me."

"Then so be it. It is not for you to try to tip the balance."

Aimery's lips twisted. "You don't think the king has already done so? Stephen and Odo—"

"That is his right."

Aimery brought his clenched fist up to his mouth, then relaxed it. "Neither of you know what you ask. There can be no happiness in this marriage."

"Then tell us what is going on." After a moment Count Guy said, "Why do you keep doing that? Does it fester?"

Aimery realized he was rubbing at the marks on the back of his right hand. "No, of course not." He could hardly explain that the marks were his death warrant. He turned back to the hall, to escape his perceptive father.

"If I'm to do my best to woo the demoiselle, I had best return."

"Just remember." Count Guy's voice stopped him. "No woman in her right mind would choose Stephen or Odo over you, and the king and I both know it."

When Lord Aimery did not return to her side, Madeleine found herself warily involved in dialogue with the king, even as she listened to another of her suitors sing, the one she was going to marry. He had a very pleasant voice, she acknowledged, and sang prettily about a lady and a lark.

Why then did her mind keep returning to that other song with its violence and death? It had been something in the singer's face. It had carried her into battle so that she could smell the blood and hear the screams.

"I fear Lord Paul and his wife were not up to the management of this estate, demoiselle," the king said.

This was Madeleine's opportunity to list all her grievances, and yet, with her uncle and aunt already out of favor, it seemed petty to do so. "It is not easy at such a time, and my aunt is not well."

"So I see. You did write to me, demoiselle," the king pointed out, "and complain of mismanagement."

So he had received her letter. "My uncle is overly harsh, sire," she admitted. "It is not a productive way to handle people . . ." Under the king's eye she found herself adding, "He hanged a man for letting his pigs into a cornfield."

"Carelessness, certainly," remarked the king with a raised brow, "but hardly a hanging matter."

Another silence grew. Madeleine found she could not look away from those pale blue eyes. In the end she was compelled to say something, anything. "He whipped children once when some of the families tried to escape . . ." Madeleine wondered why that particular event had broken out.

"Children?" repeated the king, and there was that in his eyes which chilled her. Dry-mouthed, she nodded.

One finger tapped the table in front of him as William asked quietly, "Do you mean youngsters? Twelve? Thirteen?"

Madeleine watched the finger in preference to meeting his eyes. She shook her head and swallowed nervously. She knew now why William was feared. "I think the youngest was three, sire," she whispered.

"By the Blood!" William's fist crashed down, making the boards jump. The whole hall fell silent. "Leo," the king called. "You are a father of doubtless troublesome boys. For what cause would you whip a three-year-old?"

Leo blinked. "Do you mean spank?"

The king looked a question at Madeleine and she shook her head. "A whip," she said quietly, and the memory returned, bringing anger. "Tied to a post," she added more loudly.

There was a murmur around the room and Leo de Vesin said, "For no cause under the sun, sire."

The king nodded and lapsed into silence. Slowly the hall filled with voices again, but many of the men watched the king, wondering where the reverberations of his silent rage would be felt.

Madeleine waited in terror. Would the matter somehow be laid at her door?

"And you, demoiselle?" asked the king suddenly, so that Madeleine jumped. "Has he ever whipped you?"

"Sire, I have no wish—"

"Answer me!" he snapped.

"No, sire."

"Yet I see a bruise by your eye."

"That was Aunt Celia, sire. She . . . she is not well."

"I think perhaps I should apologize, demoiselle. I sent you here without much thought. As your father had left the barony in his relative's hands, I assumed it would do well enough until I had time to look into matters. What do you want me to do with Lord Paul?"

"Do, sire?"

"I'd be within my rights to hang him for the mismanagement here."

"No, sire," Madeleine said hastily. "Not that."

The king nodded and took a drink of ale. "That's as
well. I haven't ordered any man killed since I came to
England, and if I can I'll keep it that way. I can tie him
to his whipping post and strip his back."

"No, sire." Bile rose in Madeleine's throat at the
thought of it. If she had her way, no one would ever be
whipped at Baddersley again. "I just want him to leave."

The king shrugged. "You are too softhearted, but I suppose it comes of being convent-raised. I'll send him back
to your father's place at Haute Vironge. That's a ruin now,
sad to say. I don't suppose de Pouissey can make it any
worse. If he crosses me there, I'll banish him." He looked
at Madeleine and smiled. To her his expression was pred-
atory. "Your situation here has been unfortunate, but
things should be better soon. All you have to do is choose
the right husband."

There was emphasis on the word "right." "Will I really have my choice, sire?" Madeleine asked warily.

"Have I not said so?" replied the king with a mild good
humor she distrusted. "Even after receiving your petition
for aid, I have been fair. I have brought you three able
young men to choose from, all different, all proven in war
and loyalty."

The words escaped her. "But that . . . but Lord Aimery
is part Saxon!"

The king fixed her with a look which was enough to
make a bolder spirit crumple. "So am I," he said. "Most
Englishmen acknowledge my right to the crown, and in
return I raise them as high as any man of Normandy. I
have given my dear niece to a full-blooded Englishman as
wife, and promised my eldest daughter to another. Do you
rate yourself higher?"

Madeleine was petrified, but before she could stammer
out an apology his expression lightened. "But I have mis-

understood you, of course. You have seen Lord Aimery's advantage. His Mercian heritage means he is more able than most to handle the English, who are, after all, a funny lot."

That was one way to put it. Madeleine had a queasy feeling she knew now who was the "right husband." It would never do, but she was not up to telling William that just yet. "I do find the people here hard to understand, sire," she said, hoping to turn the subject.

"Talk to Aimery. He understands their ways."

"Lord Stephen seems a pleasant man, sire," said Madeleine desperately. "Does he come of a good family?"

The king's shrewd glance seemed to see right down to her stockings, but he followed the lead. "Aye. And he sings a pretty song. And Odo tells a funny joke now and then." William's look said, "Wriggle as you like, demoiselle, you will do as I wish in the end."

Marry that Saxon, with his long hair, his load of gold, and the bright green eyes which reminded her of a bitterly shattered dream . . .

"What do you know of a man calling himself Golden Hart?" the king suddenly asked.

"Golden Hart?" The second after she had repeated the words, Madeleine was recalling them to her mind to hear the inflection, was wondering what expression had been on her face. Why did she care? If Edwald fell into the king's hands and ended up blind or maimed, why should she care?

"I understand from Lord Paul that he is the bane of the area," the king prompted, watching her shrewdly. "He places all his troubles at that man's door."

"My uncle has spoken of him," said Madeleine carefully. "He does blame him for all our troubles, but I have no way of knowing the truth. People flee, and folk say Golden Hart has helped them, but they flee because conditions are so poor. Sometimes," she said boldly, "I think Golden Hart is as much a myth as the faeries."

The king was watching her far too closely. "Perhaps

you leap to conclusions about the faeries, Lady Madeleine. You must talk to Waltheof Siwardson about it. He is the grandson of a faery-bear.''

Before she could respond to this extraordinary suggestion, the king continued, "As for Golden Hart, he's real enough as such things go. His presence had been felt in other areas. You don't agree with your uncle, then, that a sweep of the forest hereabouts would drive him from his lair? He told a tale of you and Odo being attacked by the man.''

Madeleine hesitated. Now was the moment to reveal what she knew. "We were attacked by a few ruffian outlaws, sire," she found herself saying. "If any of them were Golden Hart, he is not the magical character he is said to be.''

What was wrong with her? She wanted him in chains, didn't she?

"They never are," said the king dryly, considering her thoughtfully. "I'll have the rogue in my hands one day and prove it." He looked past her. "Ah, Aimery.''

Madeleine became aware of a shadow over her lap and looked up to find Aimery de Gaillard looming over her.

The king rose. "Pray keep the demoiselle company, Aimery. I must have a word with Lord Paul if he's to be on his way tomorrow.''

Madeleine didn't look at her new companion as he sat. She tried to think of an excuse to escape. She couldn't face another verbal battle.

"You look exhausted," he said soberly.

Madeleine realized her eyes had almost shut and forced them open, made herself sit up straight. "It has been a hectic day.''

She risked a glance at him. When she'd first seen him in the hall, he'd caught her attention by the strangeness of his flowing blond hair and gaudy dress, but now he made other men look dull. Why, she wondered, was she so certain she should not marry Aimery de Gaillard? When he wasn't poking fun or sneering, he was quite attractive. She shouldn't let his resemblance to a certain lecherous wretch sway her.

Edwald was a crude outlaw who had played with her for his own amusement, and then turned the local people against her when she would not satisfy his lust. Aimery de Gaillard was a Norman, and an honorable man.

"Why do you stare?" he asked sharply. She noticed his right hand had formed a fist. There was something about it . . . He suddenly moved it so it supported his chin, and whatever had teased at her tired mind swam away.

"Did I stare?" she asked, confused. "I beg your pardon. My mind wanders."

"I think you should go to bed," he said, almost gently. "Tomorrow will be even more hectic and," he added, "these men are fast sinking their wits in your mead and ale."

She looked around and colored as she realized many of the men were drunk. The tone of the talk and singing was distinctly bawdy. She rose quickly to her feet, and he did the same. "I will escort you to your chamber," he said.

She led the way, suddenly nervous about her safety. The curtain which separated her alcove from the corridor leading off the hall had always seemed substantial enough, but now with these strangers present she felt insecure.

When she stopped at her room, he held back the curtain for her to pass. "Don't worry, demoiselle. I don't think anyone would be so foolish as to disturb you, but I'll post a guard who can be trusted. After all, you need your sleep. You have a momentous decision to make tomorrow."

The sun had set. There was only the red glow from a nearby torch, and dim evening light through the small window of her room. His arm was raised against the frame, holding the heavy curtain. The strong muscles of his forearm, bound by gold, dusted with golden hair, were right before her eyes.

Madeleine shivered, and it was not fear. "Why do you not want to marry me?" she whispered.

"I have no desire to marry anyone, Lady Madeleine. That is all."

"You are celibate?" She hoped the dimness hid her embarrassment at asking such a question.

She saw the white of his teeth as he grinned. "No."

"There is . . . is someone you love but cannot marry?"

"No. There is no one I want to marry." He put his hand on her back and gave her a little push into the room. "Good night, Lady." He dropped the curtain between them.

The place on her back where his hand had pressed felt heated, as if she had rested it against the hot stones of the bake oven. Madeleine raised her hands to her burning face.

Why was she drawn to him? Why repelled? It was all beyond reason.

Dorothy had left water. Madeleine washed her hot face, stripped down to her linen smock, and lay on her bed.

She tried to think of the other contenders for her hand and property. Odo was out of the question, though the king could not know that. Lord Stephen, however, seemed an excellent choice. He was handsome, courteous, and witty. He sang tolerably of pleasant things . . .

But not as Aimery de Gaillard sang. His was an extraordinary gift, especially for a man whose trade was war. His voice was pure and clear. It was also expressive. When he'd sung of that dreadful battle, Madeleine had been transported to war. What would it be like if he sang of love?

Her body moved under the sheets, moved as it had under Edwald's hands. This was madness, sweet, sweet madness . . .

She awoke in the night from tangled, heated dreams of blond outlaws, her aunt, and the king, aware of something of vital importance. Something she had seen, or half seen. For a moment it had been clear, but now it had disappeared like a summer morning mist.

When she woke again to a new day's sunshine she remembered the urgency, but had no trace of the cause.

* * *

Aimery returned to the hall and found Leo. Together they downed a number of goblets of mead. Leo wanted to discuss the potential of Baddersley in the right hands. Aimery was determined not to and raised the subject of hawking. He was finding his response to the heiress distinctly troubling. He was having to fight to hold on to his animosity and was even concerned about her future.

It was impossible to let her choose Odo. Even if she was willing to overlook his attempt at rape, Odo would be a heavy-handed husband and lord, almost as bad for Baddersley as his father.

Stephen would be better. He'd be kind enough to Madeleine as long as she didn't question his amorous adventures. He'd pay little attention to Baddersley, however, and he'd drain everything he could from it to send back to Normandy, where he had a small, impoverished estate of which he was very fond.

The thought of Madeleine in Odo or Stephen's bed brought a bitter taste to Aimery's mouth.

"What's the matter?" asked Leo. "*Do* you have saddle sores?"

"Of course not." Aimery sighed. "I'm just wondering how to turn the heiress off me without Father or the king noticing."

Leo shook his head. "There's no understanding you. You won't even have the uncle and aunt to contend with anymore. Wasn't that something, when the heiress let on what had been happening? Whipping three-year-olds, for God's sake."

"What?"

"Weren't you there? She told the king that Paul de Pouissey had tied children to the post for whipping. William was livid. He offered to have the man flogged for her."

Now Aimery recaptured his bitter feelings about Madeleine de la Haute Vironge. "That should be entertaining."

"Oh, she declined the treat. He's just to be sent to do his worst with the Haute Vironge property, which is in an advanced state of decay and in the middle of a war zone."

"She declined?" Aimery said with a sneer. "You surprise me."

"Well, perhaps she's not vindictive." Leo glanced at his brother, who looked as if he wanted to flog someone himself, God knows why. He sighed. "A good sleep. That's what we both need, though where, I'm not sure." He looked around the hall where some men had pulled out the straw mattresses and bedded down in their cloaks while others continued to carouse. The king had invited Count Guy and his two clerics to share the solar. It was everyone else for himself.

"You're right," said Aimery and stood. "I'm going to sleep outdoors. Get the smell of this place out of my nose."

Leo shrugged and followed his normally even-tempered brother.

They found a quiet corner not far from the stables and wrapped themselves in their cloaks. It was a warm, starry night, and Aimery looked at the patterns of the stars.

The little bitch. True enough, she must have some scores to settle against Paul de Pouissey, but to foist off on him her own crime . . . He could just imagine her sitting there telling the king all about it. She'd probably had tears in those big brown eyes at the terrible cruelty of it all.

But he'd confirmed the evidence of his own eyes. She had begged for the whippings and watched for a while before growing bored. When she heard it was time for the children to suffer, she'd run back to the window so as not to miss the show.

When would he learn? She was a vicious woman and all the more dangerous for not appearing so. By the Rood, he hoped she did choose Odo. He was just what she deserved.

* * *

The next morning, Madeleine dressed carefully for such a momentous day. She chose a fine linen kirtle woven in browns and reds and edged in black. As it promised to be hot, she wore no tunic. Dorothy raised the folds of the full garment with a gilded girdle so a good section of creamy shift showed beneath the hem.

"There, my lady," the woman said. "Fit for a king, if I do say so myself. Now the hair."

Madeleine had Dorothy plait her thick hair. She was pleased to have worn it loose yesterday, but it was time to be decorous. "Weave in those red ribbons," she instructed.

When her woman had finished, the fat glossy plaits were cleverly interwoven with scarlet and gold ribbons which bound the ends in an ornate pattern. "Very nice," Dorothy approved, and then surprised Madeleine with some extra speech. "They say Lord Paul and Dame Celia are to leave, and you are to choose one of the men here to be your husband."

"That's correct."

"It's not right, a girl like you choosing a husband."

"I'm allowed to choose from among only three," Madeleine pointed out. "All vouched for by the king."

"You'll make a mistake. I know you will." Madeleine turned, offended, then saw Dorothy was not really questioning her judgment so much as fretting.

"Why, Dorothy," said Madeleine. "I think you care."

"Of course I care," snapped the woman, banging down the comb. "A girl like you. And such things as has been going on. A fine state of affairs. And now this." She folded and refolded Madeleine's blue tunic. "I don't much like Odo de Pouissey," she muttered.

"Nor do I," said Madeleine, rather touched by this unsuspected side to the taciturn woman.

"Good." Dorothy finally put the mangled tunic away. "Do you want a veil, my lady?"

"No, it will only get in the way, and I think I'm going to be busy." Madeleine stood and twitched out her folds again, studying the maid. "What do you think of the others?"

"Don't know." Dorothy threw the washing water out of the window. "That Saxon one—the people here like him."

"I suppose they do, but they don't know him any better than I do."

Dorothy straightened the bed. "He's been here afore. Under the old lord, Hereward."

"Ah." Was that the problem? Did he resent her ownership here? Then Madeleine looked at her woman in surprise. "How did you find this out, Dorothy? Have some of the people here learned French?"

"Not them." The woman snorted. "Or not more than to follow the simplest order. I've learned enough of their talk to get by. Had to, didn't I, or how would anything get done?"

"And they favor Aimery de Gaillard, do they?"

"They favor one of their own." Dorothy turned and scowled at Madeleine. "Well, go on. You've a choice to make, so go make it, and remember, when you've made your bed you'll have to lie on it."

Which wasn't very reassuring when it was a marriage bed that was under discussion. Madeleine walked toward the hall thoughtfully.

So Dorothy, too, thought Aimery de Gaillard the best choice. Madeleine remembered how she'd felt last night in the half-dark, with his body warm and strong beside her. She tried to imagine what it would have been like if he'd leaned forward and pressed those firm lips against hers.

Would it be like it had been with Edwald? Just because he looked a bit the same didn't mean he would have the same effect on her. Except that it would appear he did . . .

She entered the great hall in a daze. He was talking to his brother. He really was a beautiful man.

He looked up. She smiled at him.

He smiled back, but it didn't reach his eyes. They stayed

cold. No, not cold. Hot with something very unpleasant. After a long moment during which it was as if they were alone in a harsh, forbidding world, he bowed.

"Good morning, Lady Madeleine. I hope you slept well."

It sounded like a warning.

Chapter 9

The first order of the day was the departure of Paul and Celia de Pouissey. Madeleine was going to bid them farewell, but the king forbade it and sent Count Guy to see them on their way. Though she was left without any lady of rank to be her companion, Madeleine felt her spirits lift. Baddersley was hers, at least for one day.

But then she would have to marry Stephen de Faix. What other choice did she have?

Everything about Aimery de Gaillard now spoke of his dislike for her. He'd made it clear last night that he didn't want to marry her, but today his feelings were stronger and more unpleasant. She could not possibly choose him.

Still, her eyes were constantly drawn across the hall to where he stood with some men, including that large, dark brother. Some joke must have been told, for he suddenly laughed in an open, boyish way, his teeth white in his golden skin, his eyes crinkled with delight.

Tears threatened because he would never laugh like that with her . . .

She dragged her gaze away.

She saw Odo alone, scowling at the other group. He must have just returned from bidding farewell to his father and stepmother. She realized how difficult and awkward the situation must be for him and felt genuine sympathy. Despite that, and Odo's attempts to ingratiate himself and recall the happier times of their youth, she could never choose him either. After that attack, she could hardly bear his touch.

So it had to be Stephen and, she told herself firmly, there was nothing wrong with that. Where was he?

He breezed into the hall, his russet hair a little disheveled, his eyes warm, his mouth relaxed in a smile. He would make a pleasant companion in life. But there was something about his expression that itched her with disquiet. It was cat-like. Self-satisfied. Satiated.

Her eyes traveled the three again desperately; the one who hated her; the one she hated; and the one whom she would *have* to choose when every instinct screamed it would be a terrible mistake.

A servant approached with a question. Madeleine grasped the excuse and hurried off to make sure all the arrangements for the king's stay were still in order. Everything was going surprisingly well. To her relief she was discovering the hall servants were competent when they were given clear orders and not scared out of their wits. They could be trusted with the day-to-day running of the hall.

Moreover, the Baddersley people no longer regarded her with malevolence. They even at times treated her as their lady and protectress against this group of Norman invaders, which included that terror, William the Bastard. Some of them could be said to be desperate to please. Even Aldreda was courteous. She was obviously afraid Madeleine would seek revenge against her for past malice. She addressed Madeleine with quiet respect and kept her eyes properly lowered.

When Madeleine glanced back into the hall to check on matters, she saw the woman laying cloths on a table. As Aldreda left the room, she went out of her way to pass by Aimery de Gaillard. She said something. He looked up with a smile and replied. Aldreda laughed and carried on with a distinct sway to her full hips.

Madeleine bit her lip. Could they be lovers? Aldreda

was some years his elder but comely. She told herself she didn't care and returned to the kitchens to check the food.

There were piles of warm fresh bread ready to go out for breakfast, along with ripe cheese and strong ale. Three well-grown lambs were turning on spits for later eating, and a good number of chickens were being prepared. Pies and puddings were also in hand, and her custard was ready. Tonight's feast, she vowed, would do justice to Baddersley.

She gave encouragement and praise as she went, and an occasional suggestion. She commiserated with the cooks over the lack of spices, and produced a few more from her seriously depleted supply. Somehow, Madeleine vowed, she would get more. One of her greatest problems, she was discovering, was lack of coin. If Baddersley had made any money in the past year, it had disappeared.

As she crossed the bailey from the kitchens to the hall she was aware of a pleasant sense of purpose and command, but also all the burdens which came with authority. She sighed. If it came to the worst, she had the jewelry given her by the queen. She would sell it to preserve Baddersley. She wondered if Stephen de Faix had money to put into the place. She thought of Aimery de Gaillard's gold ornaments. They'd keep Baddersley going with ease . . .

She saw a flash of gold and realized it was him. He was talking with a woman just outside the hall. Aldreda!

Madeleine watched, tight-lipped, as the woman swayed against him, placing her palm on his chest. He put a familiar hand on the woman's hip, tipped her chin, and kissed her quickly on the lips before returning to the hall. Aldreda watched him go, radiating sensual satisfaction.

Well, thought Madeleine bitterly, it was clear what Aimery de Gaillard had been up to last night. No wonder he hadn't been interested in a mere heiress. Men! They were all the lowest form of life to creep the earth. She stalked into the hall in a fit state to poison the lot of them.

The king was still working with his clerks and advisers. Messengers had arrived overnight, and even as she stood in the hall, another ran in. No one would break their fast until the king was ready, and so Madeleine slipped off to the chapel for Mass. Today of all days she needed God's countenance.

There were few people at the service. The king's clerics and the hall servants were all busy. Clearly most of the nobles were not pious. Stephen slipped in and knelt on the stone floor beside her. His presence was part of his courting but still, it showed concern for her interests. Her earlier outrage was soothed. If her husband at least cared enough to try to please her, it would be something.

As they walked back to the hall afterward he talked lightly of all manner of inconsequential things and managed to drop in a great many compliments. It was a silly performance, but it left Madeleine feeling lighter in heart and spirits. As they entered the hall she smiled on him with genuine warmth. Her future did not seem quite so bleak.

The king was just coming out of the solar. He saw them, and a faint frown weighted his brow, then he smiled. "Good morning, demoiselle. I see you add piety to your many virtues, but what else should we expect from one raised in a convent?"

Madeleine curtsied and returned his greeting, then went to sit by him as the food was brought in. He drew her out to talk of the area, its land, and its people, but Madeleine sensed he had other concerns. Had one of the messengers brought bad news?

When silence threatened she said, "It is a shame work follows you everywhere, sire. Every man deserves an interlude."

He laughed. "I chose my course. No man who wants an easy life should reach for a crown. But one of my messengers should set your mind at ease about that Golden Hart, Lady Madeleine. He is not lurking in your forest. He is raising the peasants of Warwickshire."

So he wasn't Aimery de Gaillard. She hadn't realized until this moment how that suspicion had lurked in her.

Madeleine felt like laughing at her own foolishness. How had she ever believed anything so unlikely as Edwald being a Norman knight in disguise?

"Is there to be another battle, sire?" she asked.

"No, no," he reassured her. "It is a minor matter and my sheriff there will handle it. Hopefully we'll have the rogue by the heels this time, though."

"What will you do with him, sire?" she asked. Despite everything, she did not want to see Edwald punished.

"That depends. I don't waste talents, Lady Madeleine. You don't cut the throat of the fiery, rebellious horse. You tame it. If, that is, it will come to bridle. But," said William jovially, "if your forest is free of the human hart, I hope you can offer us some of the animal kind to hunt."

"Of course, sire. And boar, and many smaller animals. My men have been out in the forest for days, marking the deer trails, noting all the signs of venison." The words "my men" rolled sweetly off her tongue. She looked around the hall with heightened pride.

"Excellent!" The king announced the entertainment to the men. They all cheered.

Madeleine breathed a sigh of relief. A day's hunting would help feed the men. It would also leave her in peace to continue to put her hall to rights.

Then she found she was to accompany them.

"But, sire, I need to stay here and arrange for your greater comfort."

"Your servants seem tolerably able, demoiselle," he said implacably, "and you have little enough time to weigh your three choices. We cannot allow you to waste any of it."

She should tell the king her choice was already made, but she quailed at the thought. He wanted her to marry de Gaillard, and braver people than she had put off telling William of Normandy something he didn't want to hear. Perhaps, she thought desperately, something would come up to delay the decision—the rebellion in Warwickshire, plague, a Viking invasion . . .

Anything.

But nothing was going to delay the requirement that she go hunting.

She muttered about kings, queens, green-eyed devils, and the world in general as she went off to put on riding clothes—low boots and braies under a blue linen kirtle. She had Dorothy quickly make her hair into one long plait, which she then bound up with a scarf. She pouched her gown up over her belt, making it not much longer than the men's, and went out to mount, one woman among twenty men.

And to think she had once thought such a situation would be exciting.

Everyone hoped for boar or hart, but many also carried hawks on hand to bring down tasty birds. Most carried bows in the hope of small game such as hare or badger. Madeleine had no hawk, but she had a bow and brought it. It was not a talent taught in the convent, however, and she was only just beginning to gain any skill with it. She knew she was unlikely to use the bow, for if she did she'd probably shoot wild from simple nervousness, and the men would laugh at her.

Her teeth clenched at the thought of the green-eyed Saxon laughing at her. Then she wondered in despair why her thoughts spun around him like thread around a spindle.

He showed no sign of approaching her, thank the Virgin, but just in case, Madeleine rode with Odo on one side and Stephen on the other. Their efforts to please soothed her jangling nerves. Stephen's dry wit amused her, and even Odo made her smile with a story of a childhood adventure. But then he leaned sideways and put a hairy hand on her thigh. She moved her horse out of reach. He flashed her an ugly, sullen look, and Stephen smirked like a cat in a dairy.

Madeleine decided it was extremely unpleasant to be a dish of rich cream.

It was a lovely summer day, though, and Madeleine decided to enjoy it despite her predicament. It was warm with just enough breeze for comfort. The trees were a lush green, and the blue sky was clear except for occasional puffs of lambswool clouds. They rode among a riot of flowers—buttercup and celandine, daisy and poppy—all busily worked over by bees. A foolish hare hopped out of a hole and raced across a meadow. Someone drew a bow, and soon there was a hare hung at a saddle bow, meat destined for a pie-dish, fur to trim a hood or line boots.

This first small kill delighted everyone. Stephen started a song about hunting a leveret, and soon everyone joined in except Madeleine, who did not know the words. It was a long, merry song and very foolish in parts. Then she realized there was a double meaning. If the saucy little leveret with the naughty white behind was a girl and not a rabbit, some of the sillier lines made sense; especially where the arrow went.

She felt herself color. Odo sniggered. Madeleine frowned at Stephen, but he only winked. Madeleine didn't like the look in her intended husband's eye. It was not just coarse amusement; he was enjoying her discomfort. Men!

Aimery de Gaillard was behind her. She had no intention of turning to look, but she could imagine him, too, grinning at her naive embarrassment.

By the Blood, there must be an honest man in England who wanted to marry an heiress and do well by her. Why did she have these three to deal with? She glared at the back of the King of England, the author of all her troubles.

Stephen was called up to the king. Madeleine hoped it was for a reprimand but doubted it. All men were crude, hardhearted swine. Another horseman came up beside her. She caught her breath and turned. Then she sighed with relief. It was the other one, the brother, Leo.

"I doubt he meant to distress you, demoiselle," Leo said easily. "There's no hunting song written which doesn't serve to cover the other principle obsession of men."

"It would be more to the point," she said tartly, "for

men to keep their mind on their *proper* business, the welfare of their land and people.''

Odo chuckled. ''She's a devil's tongue on her.''

''She's also correct,'' said Leo with a dismissive look at de Pouissey. ''That's why men should marry, Lady Madeleine. It takes the edge off this obsession with saucy venison.''

Madeleine turned to him angrily, but he held up a hand and grinned. ''Pax, Lady. You can't blame us, though, for being excited about your choice. It's the most interesting point of contention since Senlac.''

''I doubt you can equate my marriage with the conquest of England, my lord. I'm not falling to the mightiest sword.''

''You could put it on that basis if you want,'' Leo said amiably, ''but I wouldn't unless you want to marry Aimery. He's the best swordsman here except me.''

''I could dispute that,'' snarled Odo.

''You tried in Rockingham. And since then he's been training with me.''

Odo was silenced. Madeleine considered the matter with interest. Was Aimery de Gaillard a skilled warrior, then, despite his professed dislike of war and his pretty clothes? She would never have supposed he could stand for a moment against such a massive man as his brother.

If so, he'd deliberately lied to her. Well, he wouldn't get away with that. ''Perhaps I should see my suitors' fighting skills,'' she mused.

''Bear in mind, Mad,'' interrupted Odo, ''that the de Gaillard family need all the land they can get to provide for their tribe of males.''

''And the de Pouisseys are rich in property?'' queried Leo dryly. ''You're certainly deficient in males.'' He turned back to Madeleine. ''I'll ride forward and tell the king you want a test of arms later today.'' He was off before she could gainsay it. Her hasty tongue had complicated everything.

''If you let them twist you to their tune, Mad,'' said

Odo angrily, "you'll be a traitor's widow before you bear the first babe."

She caught her breath and turned. "What do you mean?"

"You've only to look at de Gaillard," he said, blustering. "No true Norman would dress as he does. I've seen him talking in corners with his cousin, Edwin of Mercia. He's not a man to trust as far as a bend in the road."

"He's cousin to the Earl of Mercia?" Madeleine asked. She knew de Gaillard was part English, but had never suspected such a close link to the English nobility. And there was a blood tie to the notorious rebel, Hereward, as well. Suddenly an alter-ego as an English outlaw was not as far-fetched as it had seemed.

But Golden Hart was in Warwickshire.

So rumor said.

"Aye, he's hand in glove with the Saxons," said Odo. "And they're all just biding their time. They haven't accepted William. One day soon they'll rise again, and the Saxon de Gaillard will be with them."

Sweet Jesu, perhaps he *was* Golden Hart. She swiveled to look at him, seeking Edwald and a faery prince. But now her tortured mind could only see a long-haired Norman.

Odo's smug voice dragged her attention back. "As for Stephen," he said, "I hope you won't mind sharing his favors. He spent last night rutting in the stables."

Madeleine recalled that feline smile of satiety and knew Odo spoke the truth. This morning Stephen had just come from a woman. Lord above, what now?

"Mad," said Odo gently, "I'm the only sane choice. You know me. You like me. I didn't realize how badly Father and Dame Celia were treating you. I wish you'd told me, and I would have done something."

"I was about to," she said bitterly, "when you tried to rape me."

"No," he protested. "Not that. I was carried away by my feelings for you. You weren't really unwilling, just startled. But I frightened you, and I'm sorry." He showed a lot of his crooked teeth. "You're enough to drive any man to insanity, Mad."

That should be flattering, surely. Madeleine didn't feel flattered, but she began to wonder if she should reconsider Odo. It was something, at least, to be desired, and she probably knew the best and worst of him. She knew so little of men. Perhaps she had misinterpreted that attack. It seemed so long ago now, and if she were to marry Odo she would no longer have to take Paul and Celia along with him . . .

"The king wishes to speak to you, de Pouissey." Madeleine turned so quickly that she cricked her neck. Aimery de Gaillard was riding on her right.

She turned back to her left and saw Odo's scowl, but he could not refuse a command from the king, and so he rode forward. Warily, Madeleine turned back to the blond man, studying him. Now he looked neither Norman nor Saxon but just his own arrogant self.

He wore only a short-sleeved, knee-length tunic, a sleeveless leather jerkin, and knee-length, cross-gartered hose. But simply dressed he was not. His jerkin was ornamented with a fantastic metal design of interwoven snakes which was not only beautiful but would also turn an arrow; his belt was carved and gilded and fastened with a clasp of gold and amethyst; his hose was bright green cross-gartered with brown and white embroidery.

And of course, he wore his gaudy bracelets. She couldn't help assessing the value of even one of those hunks of jewelry.

"Do you want it?" he asked, and she looked quickly up into those cold green eyes.

"No," she denied, but then added, "Would you give it to me if I asked?"

"I'm under orders to woo you," he said flatly. "If you want my gold, you have only to ask for it before witnesses."

"I do need money," she admitted, keeping her tone equally cool. "All that bullion is a temptation."

He laughed, but there was a sharp edge to it. "You have the rare virtue of honesty. What a pity you have so few virtues to be honest about."

She felt her color flare and her anger spark. "Lord Aimery, why do you dislike me? My situation is no better than yours. I don't wish to marry any one of my suitors, but I lack the luxury of refusal. You, however, are under no compulsion, so I see no reason for your bitterness."

He reached for her reins and stopped her horse. "Lady Madeleine, none of us has more luxury of refusal than you. You can turn your back on us all and return to your nunnery. If we refuse to accept your decision, we will be flung into the outer darkness where the king's favor will never shine."

He was deadly serious. "But he favors you."

"That has little to do with it."

The riders behind split and rode around them. No one, apparently, was going to object to this tête-à-tête. Nor was Madeleine. He seemed to be in a mood for plain speaking, and perhaps at last she could make sense of everything.

"Why don't you want to marry me?" she asked, studying his face again for Edwald. It was hard to be sure. If he was Edwald, surely he'd jump at the chance of controlling a barony and using all its resources for the rebellion.

"I don't want to marry a woman I don't like."

She gasped. "Why am I so repulsive to you? In all honor, I am no more a sinner than the next person. Without vanity I have to say I am not hard to look at. Why?"

His eyes were hard. Nothing like Edwald's. "I speak English," he said, "and I know Baddersley. You are a harsh and ruthless woman. Doubtless those are excellent qualities in some circumstances, but they are not ones I seek in a wife."

"Harsh?" she queried blankly. "Ruthless?"

He slipped off his horse and stood with his hand on her

pommel. "Does that description offend you?" he asked. "I would have thought you'd glory in such terms."

She looked down at him, and then at his hand on her saddle. Madeleine's mind was fogged by the awareness of his hand so close to the join of her thighs where they were stretched across the horse, by the warm weight of his arm across her thigh. She looked around dazedly. The two of them were alone. "The hunt . . ."

"Ride on then."

Eyes fixed unseeingly on that hand, Madeleine made no move to start the horse. He hated her, and yet her body responded to him as to no other. Except Edwald.

"Speak to me in English," she said.

He was surprised, but after a moment he quoted from a poem. " 'Time and again at the day's dawning/I must mourn all my afflictions alone./There is no one still living to whom I dare open/The doors of my heart.' " The clear, musical English flowed from his tongue with a crisp beauty she had never heard before. Nothing like Edwald's rough voice.

She sighed. "What do you want?"

"Your word that you will not choose me as husband."

It should be easy to comply, for had she not decided she'd be mad to marry him? But that was before she'd found out about Stephen. "I don't know," she said. "I *can't* marry Odo. I can't tell you why, but I really don't think I can. And I don't want to marry Stephen . . ." She looked sideways at him. "Odo says he's been dallying with the castle women."

He smiled derisively. "And that turns you against him? Odo and I aren't virgins, you know."

"I suppose you've dallied with the Baddersley women, too," she said bleakly, thinking of Aldreda. He was right to laugh at her naivete.

"Of course I have." A flicker of pleasant recollection passed over his face. "It was a highly memorable encounter."

Madeleine's teeth gritted, but she knew him far better

than was reasonable, and with a flash of inspiration asked, "On this visit?"

His eyes widened. He grasped her arm and pulled her off the horse.

"What . . . ! Let go of me!"

He had her in a hard grip, one hand at the back of her neck as if he'd break it. Her heart was thundering, yet not just from terror. She remembered Odo's attack and her immediate rejection and disgust. Now she was afraid but also drawn toward something, like a moth toward a deadly flame. "What are you going to do?" she whispered.

"Kiss you."

Her lips tingled, and she licked them, unacknowledged hopes beginning to spiral up to her brain. "I thought you didn't want to marry me."

"You're not going to like it," he promised. "Either crude Odo or philandering Stephen is going to seem a treasure in comparison."

Hope shattered into acid fragments. She pulled back, but his grip tightened. It bit on an old bruise, and she cried out.

He relaxed his hold instantly and she saw his shock at having hurt her. He might threaten, but she doubted he could really brutalize her, so why was he trying to? "Why?" she asked again. "Why?"

He tightened his lips, changed his grip to a manacle on her wrist, and dragged her away from the restive horses to a mighty oak. He flung her against it and leaned forward, his hard body confining her. "I don't like you, Madeleine de la Haute Vironge. I don't want Baddersley. If you force me to marry you, I will make your life a misery."

The rough bark of the tree bit into her flesh and revived some bruises, but discomfort was drowned by the smell of leather and sweat, by the hard warmth of his body overlayed by ridges of metal and jewels. His cruel words clashed with messages her soul drank in. "I don't want to marry you either, you know!'' Even as she cried it, she knew it was an utter lie.

And he knew it, too. ''Let's make sure of it,'' he said. One hand snared both her wrists with ease. The other grabbed her jaw and forced it open as he clamped his lips bruisingly to hers. His tongue, thick and heavy, thrust deep into her mouth, a vile invasion. Madeleine gagged. She struggled but could scarcely move. Her protests produced only mewling, choking sounds.

Blackness started to gather . . .

Then, with a groan, he freed her mouth and pulled her away from the tree into his arms. His hold became not a prison but a haven. When his lips returned to softly brush hers, Madeleine didn't shrink away. When his tongue tentatively brushed against her teeth, her own tongue flicked of its own volition to greet it. It had learned its lessons well. She looked at him, bewildered. His eyes, too, were dark, confused, and troubled.

His hand played on her back as if on his lyre, soothing hurts and bringing music to her senses, promising dizzy delights. When his toying fingers found a breast, she whimpered, but it was not a protest. This magic, too, was familiar, and her body leaped to it and could not be deceived.

This was Edwald. This was Golden Hart. She smiled.

Abruptly, he drew back, as dazed as she but horrified. ''You're my death and damnation, witch.''

It cut like a blade. ''I mean you no harm,'' she protested.

His hand came up to her throat again, but gently. His thumb rubbed against her jaw. ''Then don't marry me, Madeleine.''

She wanted to cry, *Why not?* But now she knew why. The Baddersley people knew him as Golden Hart, and one of them was a traitor who might recognize him and betray him to the king. No, she reminded herself, Golden Hart was the traitor. The informer was true to King William. She couldn't want to marry a traitor. She couldn't.

He read her face. His thumb stopped its tender movement, and his face set hard. "I admit you have a wanton power over me, demoiselle, but I still despise you. Don't think you can marry me and rule me with lust."

Madeleine pushed free of him and turned away to fight her tears. "I have no intention of choosing you. I'm going to marry Stephen."

He spun her back, studied her searchingly, then nodded. "Good," he said grimly.

They just stood there.

She looked at him and saw a faery prince, a tender outlaw, a cruel traitor.

He looked at her and saw a dusky maiden, a wanton wench, a cruel bitch.

They frowned at each other as their bodies swayed irresistibly closer . . .

Someone cleared a throat.

They broke apart and looked around to see Count Guy surveying them. "You have made your choice, demoiselle?" he asked dryly.

Aimery and Madeleine looked at each other. Their eyes held for a moment before he turned on his heel and stalked over to his horse. "She's made me very happy," he said. "She's going to marry Stephen."

With that he rode away and took all Madeleine's hopes of happiness with him.

Count Guy dismounted and came over to her. "You had best mount and ride, Lady Madeleine. Your absence with Aimery has been well marked. There's no need to cause more talk."

He helped her into the saddle, and they moved off. Count Guy said, "Did he hurt you?" and she could sense the anger in him. It would be easy to get revenge by saying yes and letting this man punish his son, which he surely would.

Revenge for what?

"I can't answer that," she said accurately.

"Demoiselle," said the count sharply, "it is clear there is more to this situation than I know, but it is your life you are deciding here, yours and that of my son. I ask you to take care."

"I know it!" she exclaimed. "But what am I to do?" She turned to him in appeal. "Will the king give me more time? More choices?"

Count Guy shook his head. "He has many other matters on his mind, Lady Madeleine. This one must be settled."

They rejoined the rest of the hunt, which had halted for refreshment. Aimery was with his brother. As Madeleine swung off her horse, she was the focus of curious glances, but nothing was said. Both Odo and Stephen looked sour, but when she made no attempt to join their rival they relaxed.

Stephen soon sauntered over to her side, stroking the hawk on his wrist. With grim determination she smiled at him. As Aimery had said, what did a little philandering matter? It would mean he'd be less often in her bed.

"This is fine country," he commented, and couldn't totally hide the greed in the remark.

"Yes," she admitted, "it is beautiful."

"And fortunately not in a royal forest. The lord here may actually hunt his own deer." He might as well have said, "*I* will be able to hunt my own deer." Madeleine told herself he was her only choice and worked on her smile.

"That is very fortunate," she said. "Mismanaged as the manor has been, I fear we will need to hunt to survive this winter. Perhaps we can sell extra venison to buy corn and other necessities."

She saw him note the "we" and preen. "Surely the place must produce enough to feed the people," he said idly, as his eyes took possession of her. "They seem few enough."

"But we need more," she responded, then realized she'd taken a step backward under the pressure of that covetous look. This would never do. She planted her feet firmly in place. "They will have to be fed over the winter."

He shrugged that off. "They'll keep themselves. They always manage somehow or other, like wild beasts." He stepped closer, and she made herself stay still. He put a hand on her arm and looked into her eyes. "Don't worry, my angel, I'll—"

A heron flapped up from the nearby river. With a cry of excitement he turned and loosed his peregrine. Now all his attention was on his bird's flight. It was as well, Madeleine thought wryly, she did not seek his devotion.

She was rather touched by that charming endearment, "my angel," but knew she was relieved that the intimate moment had been cut short. She could not wipe away the thought that if . . . *when* she married him tomorrow it would be carried through to its natural conclusion. His tongue would invade her mouth, his hand touch her breast, and she could not imagine that it would bring the magic she had experienced in other arms.

Her eyes hungrily sought Aimery de Gaillard and easily stripped him naked to her faery prince . . .

She reminded herself sternly that there was more to marriage than two bodies in a bed. Stephen would be a good husband . . . Then she remembered his casual attitude toward the welfare of the people. At least, she thought desperately, he was loyal to the king.

His bird overshot, and the heron was snared by another hawk. When the bird returned to his wrist he said, "Dogsmeat," in a peevish tone and shoved its hood on roughly.

Madeleine gritted her teeth. She must stop focusing on his lesser qualities. No man was perfect. She had at least learned that lesson.

She would go to the king now, announce her decision, and have it done.

Chapter 10

She took two resolute steps, but at that moment the chief huntsman blew his horn. The hounds had found game. Everyone ran to their horses and headed for the sound. As she galloped along, Madeleine felt a sense of reprieve.

The huntsmen had found the best and most dangerous sport—wild boar. Two sows and ten well-grown sounders were penned in by the snarling dogs. A feast if they could all be killed. The men surged forward on horseback to hem the beasts in further. The long boar spears were grabbed from the servants. Madeleine hung back. She had no suitable weapon, and an angry boar was a dangerous beast. Its tusks were razor sharp, and it knew no fear of man.

The squealing sounders were easily speared from horseback, but the two adults would have to be taken on foot. There was no other way to kill a full-grown boar. Men cried out for the honor of making the kill, but the king flashed a wolfish smile at Madeleine and called on Odo and Aimery de Gaillard to make the kill.

She was supposed to view this as part of the test, but of course it was irrelevant. She was going to marry Stephen.

Both men swung off their horses and took a spear. Madeleine thought Odo looked anxious, and he had cause. Men were often killed by boar. As if to prove her point, a hound lunged in too close. Tusks slashed, blood sprayed, and the hound screamed as it was thrown aside, mortally wounded.

A huntsman quickly slit the beast's throat.

Madeleine swallowed and fixed her eyes on Aimery. He showed no nervousness, but she was terrified for him. He was a couple of inches shorter than Odo, and lighter. His easy movements suggested agility, but she found it hard to imagine him withstanding the charge of an enraged boar.

"What fun!" Madeleine looked to her side and found Stephen there, bright-eyed and flushed with excitement. He carried a dead sounder on his spear like a trophy, blood running down onto his hand. "Perfect kill," he announced.

What skill did it take, she wondered, to spear a piglet? "What a shame you don't have a chance to take one of the sows," said Madeleine, turning her attention back to the action ahead.

He laughed. "Such bloody work. Perhaps the animals will kill off my opposition, though, and here I am with you while they're down there sweating."

Madeleine glanced at him with a frown. She couldn't imagine Stephen enjoying dirty, sweaty work, and that was what Baddersley would demand. She looked away quickly before she thought of anything else about him to disappoint her.

The boar were maddened by the circle of shouting men, and by the slaughter of their offspring, but hadn't chosen a target yet. They charged a few steps one way, then another. Sometimes they ran at the horses, which were danced out of the way. The horsemen were careful, however, never to leave an escape route.

The hot little eyes turned left and right, the long, wicked tusks quivered, and froth ran off their jaws.

Aimery called and shook his spear to snare the attention of one of the beasts. It worked. The smaller one fixed its gaze on him and his flashing jerkin.

It dug up the woodland floor with its sharp hooves, then charged. But a sudden move by Odo deflected the animal to him. Hastily, Odo lowered his spear and braced it in the ground, angled to take the animal clean in the chest. Aimery turned his attention to the other animal. He shouted again, but it would not charge. He stepped closer, all his attention on the beast.

Madeleine's heart was thundering. She flicked a glance at Odo. The raging boar was hurtling toward him. He looked calm, but at the last moment he backed away slightly and flinched. The spear caught in the shoulder instead of the chest. The impaled animal squealed and thrashed. Odo hung on, but was swept sideways and crashed into Aimery.

Madeleine cried out as Aimery was knocked to the ground. The snakes on his jerkin flashed fire as he rolled through a shaft of sunlight. The other beast finally charged.

Men shouted to distract it, but the tusks were aimed at the glittering target on the ground, and the beast was deaf to all. Even as men leaped down to plunge swords into the wounded sow and still it, Aimery rolled to his knees and brought his spear between himself and the animal.

There was no time to brace it.

The spear bit true into the center of the chest. The animal's own speed carried it squealing up the weapon to the cross bar, blood gushing from wound and mouth. Under that force, however, Aimery couldn't maintain his hold. The spear burned through his grip until his hands crashed against the cross-bar, against the muscular, thrashing body.

In a final malevolent death spasm the boar tossed its head. A tusk ripped into the back of Aimery's right hand and rose, a flashing gold bracelet captured in gory, Pyrrhic victory.

Silence, then an outcry as people ran forward.

Madeleine sat stunned. If he were dead . . . He could not be dead. Surely an animal so close to death must be weak.

"Definitely glad I missed that honor," said de Faix

cheerfully. "Shall we ride down to the river, my angel, and look for more fowl?"

Madeleine stared at him. "I might be called upon to help," she said, only then realizing it was her duty to offer assistance. She urged her mare forward.

The group of men parted, and she saw Aimery de Gaillard on his feet, a cloth roughly wound around his hand and arm. It was heavily bloodstained, and he looked pale, but the wound could surely not be too serious. Relief turned her dizzy.

"Lord Aimery must return to Baddersley and have his wound attended to," said the king. "His father and brother will accompany him, but will you go with him, too, Lady Madeleine? I understand you have training in medicine."

"Of course, sire." She could swear de Gaillard looked as if he would protest. Surely, she thought sadly, he could not detest her so much he would not let her tend a wound.

"Do your best," said the king heartily. "I need every loyal right hand available." With that the hunt rode off. Madeleine reflected on the king's parting words and wondered if it was her duty to botch her treatment so as to deprive a traitor of his sword hand. When had she become so certain that Aimery de Gaillard masqueraded as a Saxon outlaw?

In his arms, when her senses spoke undeniable truth . . .

Leo fussed as he helped his brother onto his horse.

"Give up, Leo," said Aimery with a sigh. "You're as bad as Mother." He turned to Madeleine. "It's not a deep wound, Lady Madeleine. There's no need for you to sacrifice a day's sport over it."

All her bitterness returned. He'd made himself perfectly clear earlier. "It's no sacrifice," she said flatly. "I am pleased to have an excuse to return to Baddersley, but your hand can rot for all I care."

Without a word he turned his horse and headed back toward the castle. Leo moved to ride at Aimery's side, and Count Guy accompanied Madeleine.

Count Guy was studying her. His hand went to his wrist,

and she saw he had placed Aimery's bracelet there. He pulled it open and passed it to her.

He offered no explanation, but Madeleine was disinclined or unwilling to question the strange act. The bracelet was warm from Count Guy's body, and very heavy. The gold was nearly half-an-inch thick at the wrist edge, and yet it had been buckled by the boar's tusk. That had doubtless saved Aimery's arm. The bracelet had been roughly cleaned but still had traces of blood on it—his or the boar's.

"It looks old," she said. "It is very beautiful."

"It is old," said Count Guy. "And valuable. And dangerous. It is an ancient jewel of Mercia, given to Aimery by Hereward, who is a traitor to the King of England. Hereward also gave him his sword, much of his thinking, and the ring he wears on his right hand. The ring on his left comes from William, to whom he has sworn absolute loyalty on the cross. His rank and most of his training come from me. He is a man struggling under too many allegiances, demoiselle. I have tried to break his ties to some of them, but it is impossible. One day they may tear him apart."

It was as good as an admission that his son was a traitor. "Why do you tell me this?" she asked. "It does not make him an attractive husband in troubled times."

His green eyes, so like his son's, were direct. "As I said before, I understand nothing and I hope I am wise enough to realize it. You should know what you are dealing with."

"I will not choose him," she said and meant it. She would not marry a traitor.

He nodded. "That is your right. And judging from what I have witnessed, it may be wise."

When they arrived back at Baddersley, Aimery again tried to dissuade Madeleine from tending to his hand. "This bandage has stopped the bleeding," he insisted. "There's no need to disturb it."

He appeared pale and tense, which wasn't surprising in

view of the blood he had lost and the pain he must be
suffering. She wondered if he was already afflicted by
wound-fever, for he was making little sense. Despite her
angry words earlier, she could not let a man die in her
house of wound-poison.

Leo snorted. "He's always been a terrible coward."

"Stop this foolishness," said Count Guy. "Let Lady
Madeleine see to it. An animal wound can easily fester."

With a foul look at his family, Aimery snapped, "So
be it, but I'm not going to have witnesses when I cry. Go
away."

With humorous looks, the two older men obeyed.

They were alone. Madeleine flashed Aimery a wary
glance, but he was clearly not in any state for amorous
attack. She called for clean water, both cold and hot, and
led him to her room where she kept her medical supplies.

"Sit by the window in the light," she said crisply, then
realized she was still clutching his bracelet. She handed it
to him. He laid it carelessly on a shelf, then sat as she had
directed.

"Take off the bandage, please."

He did so, ripping the last sticky part off without hesitation. She leaned close to study the wound. Though he
appeared calm, she could sense tension in him, but ignored it. Many a brave man feared the healer's touch.

Madeleine concentrated on her task. It was a messy
wound, but not serious unless it festered. The tusk had
ripped a finger's length up the back of his hand and arm
through a skin design. What the design was there was no
way to tell, and it was unlikely ever to be quite the same
again.

As he'd said, the gash wasn't deep, doubtless because
the bracelet had absorbed most of the force. There was a
bruised welt where the top edge had bit into him before it
was wrenched free, but that would heal of itself. A weaker
arm would have broken in that struggle, however. She was
very aware of the muscular strength of the arm under inspection.

"Have you full movement in your arm?" she asked.

Obediently he moved elbow and wrist. Fine muscles moved sleekly under the skin. The movement caused some bleeding, but not a dangerous, gushing flow.

"It will do well, I think. I just need to clean and stitch it." She rose to instruct the servants who had brought the water.

When they left he said, "Don't stitch it."

"You'll have an ugly scar," she objected. "It would stiffen your wrist. If I stitch it, it may heal very well."

"I don't want it stitched."

Madeleine stared at him in exasperation. The great and noble warrior was scared. She walked briskly out into the hall. "Count Guy," she said, "your son refuses to let me stitch his wound, and it must be stitched."

Guy raised his brows but returned with her. As soon as Aimery saw him, he looked as if he'd like to throttle someone, doubtless her.

Count Guy studied the wound and grimaced. "It must certainly be stitched. No more nonsense, Aimery."

Aimery sighed. "Very well." His father nodded and left.

Madeleine frowned at her patient. He'd given up the argument at a word. Strange man. She poured him some mead. It wouldn't make the process more comfortable, but it might soothe his nerves.

She set St. John's wort and pimpernel to steep in mead in one pot, and soaked iris root, fenugreek, moonwort, and dwayle in honey and hot water in the other. Then she took a clean cloth, dipped it in water, and gently cleaned the edges of the wound, waiting anxiously for him to flinch or even strike out. Perhaps she should call for his very large brother to hold him when it came to the stitching.

A glance showed her he looked, if anything, preoccupied with other matters.

With a shrug she lifted the mead decoction. "This will sting," she warned. She gripped his wrist and angled his arm downward, then poured some of the fluid to stream down the wound. His fist clenched and he caught his breath, but he made no attempt to wrench away. Feeling those muscles flex, she knew she would have had no way of stopping him.

"Animal wounds are always risky"—she looked at the wound, searching for obvious dirt—"but I'm not going to cauterize it yet. I'll keep a close eye on it, and if there's any sign of infection I'll do it later."

"It would be simpler to do it now," he said, as if it were a matter of small account. Most men quailed before hot iron. Perhaps he'd never experienced it.

"It wouldn't heal as neatly, and it looks clean. It's strange how hard it is to tell," she mused to herself. "One would looks dirty but heals well. Another looks clean but kills a man."

"Thank you," he said dryly.

She looked up guiltily, knowing she should not be saying such things to a patient, but he appeared amused rather than fearful. They shared a tentative smile.

Memory of that kiss returned to leech the strength from Madeleine's limbs and confuse her. She hurriedly dragged her gaze away. She took up a needle and silk thread, willing her hands to be steady. She didn't like this job, particularly if the patient made a fuss, but it was kinder to be firm and quick than to be hesitant.

There was a skill to sewing a wound so that it healed with hardly a scar, and it was something she was good at. Even though the task made her cringe inside, she was always careful to show a calm face to the patient. She had often been complimented on her resolution in sewing a wound even as the patient jerked and cried for mercy; inside she had been flinching with every stitch and crying for mercy, too.

And now there was this extra factor to shake her nerves. The memory of his body against hers; the tangy smell of leather and that other scent which was particularly his; the feel of his strong, resilient flesh beneath her hands . . .

She reminded herself she was going to marry Stephen de Faix, who doubtless had sleek muscles, too.

Madeleine took a deep breath and pressed the swollen edges of the wound close together. Steadying herself, she pushed the needle firmly through the flesh, braced for a fight. There was the slightest movement of his arm, instantly stilled. She went in again and then tied off the stitch, not too tight, not too loose.

She moved down a little and pushed the needle in again. He couldn't stop the rock-hard tension in his arm, but apart from that it was as if she worked on meat, not living flesh. If he could control himself so well, she could do a good job.

He was not a coward then, she thought as she worked, trying to pretend this was a piece of pork she was sewing, just like the ones she had used when training at the Abbaye. How easy healing would be if one could ignore the patient's pain.

But why the fuss earlier if he could handle pain? Because he hated being touched by her? At that thought, she missed her place and had to take the needle out and put it in again. She glanced up guiltily. He gave no reaction.

Heavens, she was probably going to be the one in tears, not him.

She fixed the final stitch on the back of his hand and gave a shuddering sigh of relief. A goblet appeared before her. "You are very skillful," he said.

She took the cup and drank deeply. "You are an excellent patient," she responded. "Can I hope you will continue it and not use that arm for a day or two?"

She returned the cup, and he drank from it. They were sharing the same cup. It seemed unbearably intimate.

"That depends," he said, "on whether you insist on a fight for the maiden's favors. I don't think I'd be allowed to stand aside, and I don't wield a sword well left-handed."

"You are not to even think of lifting a sword for a week," she declared, horrified.

He raised a brow. "I think your previous experience has not been with warriors, demoiselle. If I'm called to fight, I fight."

She turned to put away some of her supplies. "I won't ask for a trial of arms."

That mad scene out in the woods had returned as if it were taking place all over again. His anger. His threats. His kiss. His pain. She closed a chest blindly and turned to him, but without words of any purpose . . .

He was studying her, puzzled. "Some of the people here were flogged some months back," he said. "What happened?"

She frowned over the question, but suddenly it led straight back to Odo's attack, and Edwald, who'd been kind to her that day for the last time. Edwald, who carried a skin design on his right hand. "Those marks on your hand," she said slowly. "Are they common among the English?"

The discontinuity of the conversation clearly didn't surprise him. "Yes," he said. "All English nobles are marked in this way."

"In the same place?"

"On the sword hand and arm."

Her earlier certainty that this man was Golden Hart had begun to waver. Now his words suggested that Edwald and Golden Hart *could* be some other golden-haired, green-eyed, handsome English nobleman.

One who turned her knees to water at a touch?

"Face marks used to be popular," he added with a wry smile, "but have gone out of fashion, for which I'm grateful." He seemed at ease.

She raised his hand. "How is it done?"

"Needles and dye," he replied. His hand rested without resistance in hers.

"It must hurt."

"No more than you sewing me up."

"But so many more needles. How old were you?"

"Fourteen. It's a sign of manhood not to flinch."

The flesh was swollen and discolored, and it was hard to see the design. Higher on his arm was the stylized rump of an animal with flying legs. It could be almost anything—horse, deer, sheep. She turned his unresisting hand into the full sunlight, ostensibly to check her work but really to study the red, brown, and yellow marks.

It was no good. She could not identify the animal, but if the hand healed well, in a few days the design would be clear once more. In a few days she'd be married to Stephen de Faix, and Aimery de Gaillard would be gone from her life forever.

He turned his hand to take hers. "What is it?"

She shook her head and pulled away to assemble her poultice and bandage, and to gather her self-control. She was in command of herself again when she turned back.

He dryly anticipated her words. "Don't tell me, it's going to sting."

Her lips twitched. "If it doesn't hurt, it's probably not doing any good."

"You remind me of my mother," he said lightly, and was relaxed enough to let out a curse when she pressed the warm pack over the wound. She quickly bound it there with gooseskin and leather thongs.

"I want to check it tomorrow," she said briskly.

"On your wedding day. What devotion."

She closed her eyes briefly. "Hardly a normal wedding day."

The silence built in the room like a nest of blades, painful every way she turned.

She met his eyes. "I'm going to marry Stephen."

He stood. "It will be for the best."

She thought he was going to kiss her, and hungered for it, but he just looked at her for a moment, and then was gone.

Madeleine swallowed tears and collapsed down on the stool where he had sat, and stared besottedly at some drops of his blood on the rush mat.

She reminded herself he was the man who had toyed

with her; the man who had caused her deep grief. He was a traitor to his king and his knightly vows. She couldn't break her heart over a man like that. She couldn't.

And yet he had always been gentle, even in his anger. Today, when he had wanted to hurt and repulse her, he had not been able to carry it through. Now that she knew the allegiances which pulled at him, she could even understand his fractured loyalties. How would she behave in a similar situation? She did not know.

He was a good man, kind and brave; a better man by far than Odo or Stephen. Still, she would not marry him. She'd be a fool to bind her fate to such as him, but more importantly, trapping him here could lead to his destruction. She had promised not to do that, and she was a woman of her word.

Sunlight flashed off his bracelet. She picked it up, cold now but still heavy, smeared with dried blood. She slipped it onto her right wrist, and with some difficulty squeezed it until the split edges joined to make a closed, flared cylinder. It hung clumsily loose, which brought to mind the shape and feel of his muscular arm.

The bracelet was valuable, and she should take it to him immediately, but she could not bear to be with him when she could not have him. She slid her arm out of the band of gold and put it away in her own jewel chest.

Tomorrow she would marry Stephen de Faix; the day after, everyone would go away and leave her in peace. Except Stephen. He'd be with her for the rest of her life.

Madeleine had no patience with whiners, and she flung herself into the preparations for her wedding. She forewarned the cooks that boarsmeat would be available for roasting for her wedding feast, and she ordered two bullocks slaughtered and spitted as well.

Tomorrow would be her wedding day, and everyone in the area would feast.

She sent the steward and three guards to Hertford with

her second best gold chain and orders to bring back casks of wine.

Tomorrow would be her wedding day, and everyone in the area would be drunk—herself included if she had any say in the matter.

She authorized the use of their stores of dried and preserved fruits with a profligate hand. She didn't know what they would do after tomorrow; she didn't care. It was as if her world was about to end.

The feast for this night was well in hand. The aroma of roasting lamb filled the hall, making everyone's mouth water. Cakes and pastries were piled high in the pantry. Madeleine turned her ferocious energy toward the tables.

Since Paul de Pouissey's departure, work had halted on the defenses, and so she had no shortage of hands to mend the trestles and benches. Few of them ended up with any degree of elegance, but soon they were level, stable, and sound.

While the men worked on that, Madeleine took two women and attacked the cloths. Rough edges were hemmed, holes were patched, stains rubbed out where possible. Again, there was no time to do a fine job, but at least the appearance of the hall this evening would be more dignified.

At all times she was aware that Aimery de Gaillard was somewhere in the manor house, but she never saw him. Perhaps he was being as careful to avoid her as she was to avoid him.

The watchcorn announced the return of the hunters. Madeleine leaped up from her stool by the window and thrust her half-finished hem into another woman's hand. She had forgotten her own appearance. Calling for Dorothy, she ran to her room, washed her face and hands, and unbound her hair. Then Dorothy was there to comb it out.

"Loose or plaited, my lady?"

It was her last night as a maiden. "Loose," she said, even as she shuddered at the implications.

She wore her finest silk kirtle and chose a scarlet velvet

tunic, banded with gold embroidery. It was too heavy for this warm weather, but she felt the announcement of her choice called for some display. She fastened a girdle of gold wire and obsidian around her waist and a fillet of gold wire around her head. "How do I look?" she asked Dorothy.

"Magnificent," the woman said reverently. "I've never seen you so . . . It's as if there's a fire in you, my lady. You've made your choice, then?"

"The choice is made," said Madeleine flatly. She went to collect his bracelet to return it, then stopped herself. The only way to get through this evening was to avoid him. Forget about him. Obliterate him . . .

Tears threatened, but she fought them back. She'd cut her throat rather than show weakness tonight.

She walked out into the hall. The hum of conversation stopped, and she received a barrage of speculative looks. Then talk picked up again, and Count Guy came over.

"If you don't intend to choose my son, demoiselle," he said dryly, "your choice of dress is unfortunate."

She looked around and found him instantly. He was wearing flame red and heavy gold. He looked up as if someone had called his name, and their eyes caught and held. After a sober moment he turned away.

Madeleine felt as if all the blood had drained from her body. She told herself it would be better when it was done. She was a practical person, after all, and once she was Stephen's wife this strange hunger for Aimery de Gaillard would seem like a child's dream. She looked for the king, intending to go to him immediately and announce her choice. He was not present.

"Is the king engaged?" she asked.

The count nodded. "More messengers. Do not think of asking William for more time, Lady Madeleine," he warned. "There are urgent matters requiring him elsewhere."

"Golden Hart?" she asked on a caught breath.

He flashed her an alert look, then shielded his eyes.

"That figment of the imagination? No. The Earl of Mercia."

His reaction gave Madeleine pause. If Aimery de Gaillard carried a picture of a hart on his arm, one person who would know about it was his father. She had to say something to disguise her thoughts. "But isn't Earl Edwin . . . ?"

"My nephew and Aimery's cousin?" he supplied. "Yes," said Count Guy with exasperation. "This morning we heard he has fled the queen's court. Now we hear his brother, Morcar, has joined him. They are raising a rebellion."

Madeleine remembered wishing for something to put off her marriage, but not this. "Will Aimery . . . will your son join them?"

The count's eyes flashed. "I would see him dead first, demoiselle. Aimery may look like an Englishman, but he is a Norman warrior, oath-bound to serve William and only William." He frowned at her. "Is that what holds you back? Do you fear he will turn traitor? He will not."

His words were firm, but she sensed the uneasiness behind them.

Madeleine sidestepped his question. "Will the king have to leave immediately, then?" she asked hopefully.

"No. He'll see you wed first. After all, Baddersley is strategically located. He'll want it in strong hands."

"I thought the question of England was settled. Will the earl really rise against the king?"

"Don't fear, Lady Madeleine," said Count Guy. "Edwin is not particularly bellicose, and I doubt he wants outright war. He's making a show of rebellion to force William's hand in the matter of his marriage."

"You sound as if you sympathize with the earl."

"He received a promise, and he and the girl have become genuinely fond, but a king has many considerations to take into account. Ah, here he is."

If the king was weighed down by a threat of imminent rebellion, it was not obvious. He was boisterous and jovial, and vocal about the day's excellent sport. As soon as food was before him he asked Madeleine, "De Gaillard's hand? What of it, demoiselle?"

"If it does not fester, sire, it will heal well."

"Excellent."

"But," Madeleine added quickly, "he should not use that arm yet in anything strenuous, sire. Such as fighting."

The king quirked a brow at her. "So I should cancel the display of your suitors' fighting skills?"

"If Odo and Lord Stephen wish to show their skills," Madeleine said impassively, "I have no objection."

"Hardly fair to leave one contender out of it. What then? Music? Riddles? Dancing?"

Madeleine braced herself. "There is no purpose in further display of skills, sire."

He sobered and fixed her with those pale, calculating eyes. "So you have made your choice. I wonder, demoiselle, if it is the wise one. Have you noticed how well you and Aimery de Gaillard suit tonight?"

Madeleine almost laughed at such lack of subtlety but remembered in time that this was the King of England. He had the power of life and death over them all. It was bad enough that she was going to thwart his plans without seeming to find the matter amusing.

"I cannot match him in bullion," she said dryly.

"He would gift you with his gold if you asked."

"I have no claim to his gold," Madeleine parried, and sought for a way to deflect the conversation. "I understand in any case that those English ornaments are for warriors, given by a leader to his men. Are they not like a wedding ring? A symbol of unity?"

William's eyes were cold. "You study the English ways, Lady Madeleine? That is good since you are to be part of my new Anglo-Norman kingdom." He looked away to pick up a chicken leg from a platter presented to him. Madeleine drew in a shuddering breath. What would the king do when she finally made her choice irrevocably clear?

He turned back, amiable once more. "In fact only the

ring is that kind of symbol, demoiselle. The *geld,* as they call it, is more a matter of rank. The strongest leaders give the most. The most favored followers receive the most. It's all a remnant of our joint ancestors, the Viking raiders.'' He took a bite of chicken, chewed, and swallowed it. "I am a modern man, however. I give my faithful followers land. And heiresses.'' His eyes cooled and threatened. "And I was foolish enough to give one heiress a choice.''

Madeleine's throat seized up, but she forced out the words. "And that choice is made, sire.''

His brows lowered, and he studied her as if he could read the sins on her soul. She waited for him to ask the name and make the announcement. But he relaxed and smiled. "Then we can put the matter aside, Lady Madeleine, and relax. Let those three hopefuls sweat for the night.''

He called for attention. "The Lady Madeleine will make her decision known in the morning. The betrothal will follow, and then the marriage. Immediately afterward we leave to go north to deal with the Earl of Mercia.''

There was a renewed burst of conversation and more speculative looks, as men tried to decide from her behavior whom she had chosen.

"They're laying bets on it, demoiselle,'' said the king. "If you feel mischievous, you could mislead the gullible.'' A new platter was presented, and he turned to grasp a piece of tender lamb. He placed it on her trencher, then took some for himself. "Enjoy the feast, demoiselle.''

The king was the one being mischievous. He guessed she would not choose de Gaillard and was giving himself time to try more tricks. What could he possibly do since he seemed determined to keep to his promise and allow her her choice? She did not know, but the possibilities stole what little appetite her general anxiety had left her.

She picked at the food and drank heavily from her mead cup until her head began to swim. Odo looked sullen, resigned to the fact that he would not be her choice. Stephen was in high spirits. When he caught her eye, he blew her a kiss, which was noted with cheers of encouragement. Madeleine almost raised her hands to ward off that invisible sign of affection.

Her eyes found Aimery de Gaillard sitting with his brother and some other men. She saw Leo de Vesin poke his brother, encouraging him to follow Stephen's example. With a grimace, Aimery looked up at her and gave a slight bow of the head, then returned his somber attention to his meal. She noticed he, too, did not seem to have much appetite.

Madeleine could not endure more. "May I retire, sire?" she asked. "I am very tired, and tomorrow will be another busy day."

He frowned at her, but then grinned, "And tomorrow night a busy night. Sleep well, Lady Madeleine."

She rose and left without looking at anyone in the hall. Tomorrow night she would have to allow Stephen de Faix to do as he willed with her body. She would have given herself into his keeping, body and soul, and would have no right to object to anything unless he beat her viciously.

But why would she even think that way about a man who seemed, if anything, too easy-going? Odo would be the sort to turn vicious, like his father.

In her room she took off her jewels and the clinging silk-velvet, feeling immediate relief from the heat. As she folded the clothes carefully away in a chest, the shimmering scarlet reminded her of Aimery de Gaillard. Had he, too, put on his most barbaric clothes as a gesture of defiance?

She sat by the window and opened one of the precious English books Father Cedric had found for her. She tried to concentrate on it and put other concerns away. As the sun set, she came across the poem Aimery de Gaillard had recited for her, *The Wanderer:*

> *Thus speaks the homeless-one,*
> *haunted by memories of terrible slaughter*
> *and the death of his friends:*

> *"Dawn often finds me grieving in solitude,*
> *for no one still lives*
> *with whom I dare share*
> *the truth of my heart."*

Had he chosen it carelessly, or had it expressed the thoughts of his heart? It seemed to echo hers. They were both, in different ways, cut off from their pasts and alone. She read on through the sad story of a man torn from his place, his loved ones, and his world.

> *He thinks of the hall, its bountiful riches,*
> *his ring-friend's great feasts in the days of his youth.*
> *A splendor now past.*
> *Where is the horse now? Where is the great man?*
> *Where is the giver of rings?*
> *Where is the joyous feast?*
> *Where is the singing?*
> *Oh, grieve for the flowing mead, grieve the great warriors,*
> *grieve the proud princes. Swallowed,*
> *all swallowed by night's fatal shadows,*
> *leaving no trace for those left alone.*

It seemed to predict the ruin of the English culture.

Madeleine grieved for that lost England, for with it into the mists of history had gone her own chance of happiness. It was Aimery de Gaillard's allegiance to the past which stood between them, and she could not follow the poet and resign herself to the workings of fate.

Tears ran down her cheeks. One day, she supposed, she would be old and shriveled, and all this would seem childish folly. But now, ah now, it hurt like the cleansing fluid she had poured into Aimery's wound.

Chapter 11

I n the dead of night Madeleine woke to Dorothy shaking her. A crescent moon shed a little light. "What?" she asked.

"There's a man here saying the king wants to speak with you, my lady."

Madeleine shook off sleep and slipped into her kirtle. What trick was he going to try now? "In his chamber?"

"Nay. In the stables."

Madeleine frowned. "In the stables? Why?"

"How would I know?" asked the woman testily. "A knight shook me awake and told me to wake you and send you to speak with the king in the stables."

The horses, Madeleine thought muzzily. Was there some dreadful disease? But the king would not be there to handle such matters. Thoughts of Odo's attack returned. Would someone, anyone, try such a trick? "Who was the knight?" she asked.

"I don't know his name, but he's one of them." Dorothy caught Madeleine's suspicions. "I'll come with you, my lady. But let's go. If it is him, you can't keep the king waiting."

They slipped out a side door to avoid the crowded hall, and Madeleine found herself in a strange place. In the gray-washed light of pre-dawn nothing in the bailey seemed familiar. She stumbled over a bale left on the ground and muttered a curse. A second later she heard Dorothy repeat her actions. As her eyes adjusted she thought she saw shapes which could be sleeping men. She supposed quite a few preferred a spot out here to a cramped corner in the hall.

She made her way toward the stables carefully, watching each step. The only sounds were quiet voices from the guards on the earthworks and the screech of some night animal become prey.

Jerked from sleep, her body was chilled and trembling even though the night was warm. She felt all the uneasiness natural to this dead time of night when spirits roamed, and in addition she feared something was about to happen which would not work to her advantage. She was immensely relieved to have Dorothy stumbling along beside her.

As she came close to the long huts which formed the stables, she heard the soft movements of horses. Then she heard voices and saw the dim glow of a lanthorn. She relaxed. Whatever the problem, it was not a secret trap.

She turned to Dorothy. "I think it's all right," she murmured, "but the king must wish to speak with me privately. You stay here."

The wide doors to the wooden building stood open, and she entered slowly, letting her eyes adjust to the different light. The lanthorn was hung in a far stall, set low so all she saw was its reflected light. The voices came from there, a quiet murmur between two people, she thought.

She walked closer and was about to announce her presence when someone gasped, "Oh, Lord Stephen!" She heard Stephen's sensuous chuckle.

Madeleine froze, knowing then what was going on and what trick the king had played. Did he really believe this would change her mind? She turned to leave. As Aimery de Gaillard had pointed out, none of her suitors were virgins.

But what a way to start a wedding day.

She heard Stephen's voice again. "Come on. That's it. Very nice . . ."

Madeleine had taken two cautious steps away—the last thing she wanted was to be caught in this place—when there was a sharp cry and the words, "Don't! I don't want—" instantly muffled.

Madeleine froze. Rape?

Stephen murmured, "You'll like it. Relax. It won't hurt. Come on, my angel. Don't fight the big strong Norman knight . . ."

My angel. She felt sick. Would he call Madeleine that in their marriage bed? She wanted to flee, but she couldn't turn her back on a rape. But could she bear to walk in and interfere when in a few hours she was going to have to marry this man? She wavered, then the sounds changed to gasps and grunts.

Mating? Or struggling?

Swallowing, she crept forward, skirts raised so they would not brush against the straw. When she reached the stall, she peeped cautiously over the boards, prepared to take the quickest look and then leave.

She looked.

She stared, unable to take in what she was seeing.

Two half-naked bodies, but there was something wrong. They were wrong way around. Stephen was . . . Madeleine's mouth fell open. Stephen's partner was a man, a youth rather. One of the stable boys.

She backed away, only to kick a wooden bucket next to her foot. She froze, not even breathing. Stephen let out a gasping cry. He rolled the flushed and heavy-lidded lad over and put his mouth—

Madeleine gathered her skirt up high, checked her footing, and fled. Outside, she grabbed a startled Dorothy and dragged her behind the pigsty, out of sight, signaling wildly to the astonished woman not to make a sound.

A few minutes passed and nothing occurred. Perhaps Stephen didn't care who saw him. Perhaps he was blind and deaf when he was . . .

Madeleine tried to pull her wits together. She had heard of such practices but never quite believed it.

"Lady Madeleine," Dorothy whispered, "what on earth is it? Was it a trick? Are you hurt?"

"A trick? Yes, a trick. Oh, Dorothy. What am I to do now?"

"Are you hurt?"

Madeleine felt as if she'd been tortured, but she said, "No. No. And we must go back to our room!" But she clung to Dorothy and trembled as they crept back across the bailey. When she reached her room again she said, "Please, Dorothy, go to the kitchen and bring me some mead. I need something."

The woman patted her shoulder anxiously and hurried off. Madeleine pressed her hands to her face briefly, then slipped through the curtain into her room.

A shadow moved.

Her scream was cut off by a hard hand.

"Be quiet," said Aimery de Gaillard, and slowly let her go.

Madeleine stared at a gray shape she could scarcely distinguish. "What are you doing here?"

"I couldn't sleep. I heard you running across the bailey. What are you up to?"

Madeleine wanted him to hold her, to rescue her again from an intolerable situation, but his tone was suspicious, not concerned. She hugged herself in despair. "Nothing. Go away. I'm safe."

"Obviously. Why were you creeping about?"

"The king sent for me. Go away!"

"The king wasn't in the stables."

"No."

He stood in silence. "It was a trick? To turn you off Stephen no doubt. What did you see? Him with a lover? I told you we're none of us saints."

Madeleine turned away from him and put her hands to her face. "Go away. Please!"

She heard footsteps. He turned her back and pulled her hands down. She couldn't help it. She swayed to rest against his broad chest. His arms came around her for a

precious moment before he pushed her away. "Stephen is
no worse than the rest of us."

Madeleine started to laugh hysterically. He hit her, sharp
and hard. She put her hand to her stinging cheek.

A hand brushed against hers, as soft as a breeze, apol-
ogetically, then was gone. "Remember your promise,"
he said. Then he, too, was gone.

Dorothy bustled in with a candle and a tankard. "What
is it?" she gasped and hurried over. She looked at Madeleine with horror. "Who hit you? The king in the stables?"

Madeleine felt numb, hopeless. "I don't want to talk
about it." She walked over to her medicine chest and took
out some poppy syrup. She poured it liberally into the
drink. She wouldn't much care if she never woke up.

But after Madeleine had taken one long swig, Dorothy
grabbed the tankard and poured the rest on the floor. She
pushed Madeleine onto her bed and covered her. "Sleep.
Things are never as bad in the morning."

Madeleine laughed at that, then cried herself to sleep.

When Dorothy woke her, Madeleine's mouth was sour
and her head was as heavy as a boulder. It took a few
moments for all her causes of misery to return to her. Then
she cursed Dorothy. She cursed the king. She wished she
were dead.

"And that's a wicked sin," said Dorothy in a fine fret.
"Come on, my lady. The king's already calling for you.
You don't have much time."

"I have all the time in the world," said Madeleine fa-
talistically. "I am not going out there. I am not going to
marry anyone."

Dorothy paled. "Because of last night?" she asked.
"Because of that blow? It's gone. It can't have been a
hard blow. There's always blows between man and
woman, but a tap like that's nothing to fret over. Come
along, do. Wash your face. I have your finest clothes laid
out."

Madeleine felt strangely calm and found all this fussing unnecessary. "I can't marry any of them," she explained. "It's absolutely impossible. I suppose I'll have to go back to the convent, but that won't be so bad."

Dorothy threw up her hands and scurried from the room. In a few moments she was back with Count Guy de Gaillard, looking magnificent in a long gown of cream linen, finely worked. With a gesture he dismissed the woman.

"What is all this, demoiselle?" he asked gently.

Madeleine looked at him. "Your son hit me."

A brow twitched, but he merely said, "Then marry Stephen, but don't think he won't raise his hand to you."

Madeleine just shook her head.

"Odo de Pouissey?" Count Guy queried.

Madeleine shook her head again.

"You are going to marry Aimery?" said the count, surprised but pleased.

"I'm not going to marry any of them," explained Madeleine. "The king will just have to provide another batch or send me back to the Abbaye. I think I prefer the latter."

Count Guy strode forward and sat down on her bed. When she tried to look away, he took her chin in a hard grip so that she was forced to face his green eyes. "Enough of this. You gained the privilege of a choice. You will make it. The king has no desire to have you take the veil and no more time to waste on your silly dithers."

She tried to pull free, and he raised his hand. "I am not averse to hitting you either, demoiselle." Madeleine saw he was speaking the plain truth.

"The king just wants me to marry your son," she spat.

"Then it might occur to you to do as your sovereign wishes. But he has given you your choice and he will not rescind it. Use it."

"I can't," she whispered, tears beginning to trickle.

He flipped her over and landed a full-power blow on her behind. Madeleine let out a cry and lay there stunned, rubbing the sting. She rolled over and looked up at his stern face.

"I am under orders to bring you out, decision made, within the hour, Lady Madeleine. And *I* follow my monarch's orders. That is a taste, but if we are to settle for beating sense into you, I'll call for a switch and save my hand."

"Aimery doesn't want to marry me," she protested.

"If he refuses, I'll beat him into reason, too. Now, do I send for a switch or do you dress and come out to your betrothal?"

He was like rock. She knew he would do just as he said and would beat her bloody if necessary on the orders of the king. And he was right in one thing. She did have a duty to the king. "You must be a horrible father," she muttered as she rose from the bed and winced.

"If you become my daughter, you may discuss the subject at length with my other children." He went to the doorway and summoned Dorothy, who bustled in anxiously.

"She is ready," he said. He turned his back to Madeleine. "If you are not in the hall shortly I will return, armed."

Dorothy's eyes widened as she looked between them.

"I will be there," Madeleine said grimly. "Just remember in the future that this was your doing."

He didn't look daunted and smiled before he left.

At the king's orders, Aimery stood with Odo and Stephen. Odo obviously had little hope and was into his second goblet of the fine wine which had suddenly appeared. Stephen was acting the part of the modest, gracious victor.

Aimery had a strong desire to wipe the smug smile from Stephen's face but told himself it was all turning out as he wished. Madeleine would choose Stephen. The marriage would take place. Everyone would leave to chastise Edwin, but he, in view of his wound, would be allowed to return to Rolleston and be miserable in peace.

He had not slept the night before and had spent the long hours fighting an almost overwhelming need to claim her.

He knew—had known perhaps from that day by the river—
that she was made for him. Every time they met the feeling grew stronger. His body reacted to her like a hound
on the scent. It was just lust, he told himself. It would
pass. It would have to if he was to keep his sanity.

Worse than lust there was liking stirring in him. He was
beginning to think her evil reputation must be a mistake.
Could a woman who had practically wept as she sewed
his wound take pleasure from the whipping of infants?

But—he reminded himself for the hundredth time—he
had witnessed her with his own eyes, there at the window,
watching. What could cause a lady to watch such a thing
through to the last agonizing moment except a twisted taste
for cruelty?

Her power over him was animal. He must fight it. He
wished to hell she would come out, pick Stephen, and get
it over with.

William was clearly as impatient as Aimery. In fact the
king was beginning to grow angry, and body parts were
likely to be lost when William of Normandy lost his temper.

With Edwin's rebellion and its repercussions William
had no time to humor Madeleine. The latest news was that
Gospatric, Earl of Northumbria, had also fled the court for
his northern lands, and there were rumors of Welsh raids.
It was just possible the English lords were finally going to
pull together, God damn them all.

When the king dispatched Count Guy to see to things,
Aimery had a fair idea of how it would go. He just hoped
Madeleine realized the futility of delay before the blood
began to flow.

What was behind the delay? She'd stated she was going
to marry Stephen, and there had been no doubt in her
voice. She couldn't be such a fool as to go back on her
word merely because Stephen had romped in the stables
with a wench. If it was that easy, Aimery wished he'd
taken Aldreda up on one of her offers and called Madeleine in to watch.

He tasted bile at the thought.

Come on. Get it over with.

Count Guy came back and reported to William. The king nodded brusquely and took a drink of wine. She was coming then. It would soon be over.

A sound alerted Aimery, and he turned to see Madeleine walk into the room. She was wearing a cream silk kirtle and a heavier cream silk tunic with a yellow wave pattern worked into the weave. The neck and sleeves were richly embroidered with gold, pearls, and amethysts. An amethyst shone in the heavy gold fillet which encircled her long, silky hair.

She looked like a goddess.

She looked pale and hopeless, like a woman going to her death. But if his father had been forced to beat her to this point, he'd left no obvious mark. She walked over to the king and curtsied low.

"Good morning, Lady Madeleine," William said coldly. "You have kept us waiting."

Aimery saw her start as she realized just how angry the king was. "I beg pardon, sire. I was taken by nerves."

"Let this be a lesson to you, demoiselle, not to seek more responsibility than you can manage." But the king's humor was easing in the face of her submissiveness. "Now to your choice. I hope you have considered well the welfare of your people here at Baddersley, and my wishes, too."

Aimery stiffened. It might sound as if William was yet again pressuring Madeleine to follow his wishes, but there was a tone there which made him uneasy. The king sounded confident. When Madeleine turned to face the three of them, he kept a stern face. Out of the corner of his eye he saw Stephen smile warmly at her.

She stepped forward like a sleepwalker, her eyes flickering from one to the other. He'd seen a man look like that once. A brigand, caught in the act and fit only for death, he'd stood at bay, wounded and exhausted, looking at three opponents and wondering which would deal the death blow. Aimery had stepped forward and done it quickly to put the man out of his agony.

This, too, went on too long, and he had to fight not to step forward and put an end to it.

"By the Sweet Savior, choose!" bellowed the king.

Madeleine shut her eyes and laid her hand on Aimery's sleeve.

There was a moment's silence, then laughter and ironic cheers. Men began to settle wagers. The king strode forward. "At last. We could have come to this point weeks ago without such strain, demoiselle, if you had not been so foolish." He slapped Aimery hard on the back. "Congratulations. Come and sign the documents."

Aimery looked at Madeleine in angry astonishment, but she stared away from him, and now was hardly the place to force an explanation. For God's sake, they'd have a lifetime to settle this! He looked at Stephen and shrugged.

The other man smiled, but there was a twist to it. "Women. There's no understanding them. At least it's put William in a sweeter frame of mind."

And that, thought Aimery, was probably the only positive thing to be said about the whole affair. He walked with Madeleine to the table where the betrothal contracts were laid out. His father was hovering over the documents, and scribes were just now inserting the appropriate details.

He was going to have to marry Madeleine de la Haute Vironge, and there wasn't a cursed thing he could do about it. Moreover, when she'd made her choice an infuriating surge of joyous lust had hit him. He was hard now. He'd fight it even if he had to take to wearing a hair-shirt.

But how did he fight the other danger—his exposure as Golden Hart? Who would reveal the truth? Perhaps Madeleine herself. Did she think to achieve rapid widowhood? That would do her little good, for she'd be forced to wed again immediately. Or did she think to hold her knowledge over his head like an ax? He'd confess to William first.

Even if Madeleine held her tongue, there was the local

traitor, who had not yet been uncovered. And if the traitor did not realize the truth, there was danger of exposure by those local people who did. It would take only one careless word. Or a malicious one. Aldreda was turning sour at his refusal to give her a sample of his mature bed-manners.

The clerk began to read out the betrothal contract, but Aimery hardly paid attention. He did note, however, that the documents were drawn up in Norman style. That would give him control over his wife and her land. So be it. If she'd foolishly made this choice because of what he'd said about English law and women's property rights, she'd soon realize her mistake.

Then he heard the next part of the document and looked at his father in surprise. Count Guy had given him Rolleston, and Aimery was now apparently giving it to Madeleine as her dower property.

"No," he said instinctively, and everyone looked at him. He couldn't bear the thought of putting Rolleston into her cruel grasp, but he looked for tact. "That makes little sense. This is Lady Madeleine's home, and she is familiar with it. Baddersley manor should be her dower."

The king shrugged. "As you wish. The other properties which come with the barony will be the family estate." His, in other words. Aimery cast a glance at Madeleine to see her reaction. It was not a switch in her favor, for Baddersley was drained and in chaos while Rolleston prospered. She appeared indifferent.

The clerk continued to read out the property rights of both parties and the provisions made in the event of the death of either party, and for their children, and in the case that there be no children, and in the case of grandchildren . . .

Madeleine hardly heard the clerk's voice as he read out the long scroll. Property rights did not matter to her. She was marrying a man who hated her.

He suddenly spoke, interrupting the reading, objecting to something. Madeleine realized he was giving her back Baddersley as her own dower property. She looked at him, bewildered, for she had not expected kindness. He did not meet her gaze.

Then it was time to sign. Madeleine's hands were sticky, but she took the pen and signed. He signed next.

Then all the witnesses, beginning with the king and including as many of the men as cared to add their name and seal. Ample witnesses to testify that all this had been done according to law and custom.

Then, smiling widely, the king took Madeleine's hand and placed it in Aimery's. She felt the reluctance of his touch. "Now to the church," said the king, "and then we can eat at last. My stomach flaps like an empty bag. You need a ring," he said to Aimery. "You have one to spare."

Madeleine sensed the tension which leaped into him, and looked at the two rings, the twisted wire one on his left hand and the solid one on his right. *Geld?* No. These rings were symbols of a union as close as marriage itself. Which was to spare? Why was this matter so important?

She sensed the danger in the air even as Count Guy stepped forward and pulled a ring off his little finger. "This was the ring with which I wed my first wife. I would be honored for it to be used."

Aimery de Gaillard took it with a breath of relief. "Thank you, Father." It sounded like the most sincere thing he'd said that day.

Father Cedric was waiting at the church door. His smile turned to a beam when he saw Madeleine's choice, and he raised his hand to bless them. *"In nomine patris, et filiis, et spiritu sancti . . ."*

All the king's train were there to witness the wedding, and many of the castle people also gathered around. Father Cedric went briskly through their declarations of intent and agreement, and pronounced himself satisfied that this was an honest union.

The king took Madeleine's hand and gave it to Aimery, gave him complete and utter power over her. Aimery slid his father's ring onto the third finger of her left hand.

"With this ring I thee wed," he said somberly. "With this gold I thee honor, and with this dowry I thee endow."

"Then you are joined together in the sight of God," announced Father Cedric joyfully, "and will receive his innumerable blessings. Aimery, be forever gentle to your wife and support her in all her endeavors. Madeleine, be forever gentle to your husband and support him in all his endeavors."

Even treason? thought Madeleine. *I most certainly will not.* She made a promise of her own. *Aimery de Gaillard will give up his work for the English or I will expose him to the king.*

Father Cedric blessed them again in the name of the trinity, the Virgin, and all the saints.

The priest turned to lead them into the chapel, but the king interrupted. "Kneel to your husband, Lady Madeleine," he said, "as custom dictates. You are inclined to be bold. Kneel and kiss Lord Aimery's hand, the hand that will chastise you if you err." He was clearly still annoyed with her.

If only you knew, sire, Madeleine thought, *that you are commanding me to do homage to a traitor.* But she obeyed and knelt to kiss the fingers of her husband's right hand, which was all that protruded from the bandage there.

Throughout the Mass, she prayed for the strength to make something of her marriage and turn her husband from treason.

Afterward, they processed back to the hall among cheers. Madeleine tried to smile, but it doubtless was not much of a show. Aimery did not even try. Oh, Sweet Jesu, she wondered helplessly, what would happen tonight when they were alone together? Had he not promised to make her life a misery if she chose him?

Then she remembered she had a weapon. She held his life in her hands.

The meal at least was splendid—a feast, not a breakfast. She had not done anything to forward it since the afternoon before, but the Baddersley servants had proved their mettle and produced tender meat, fine sweet-dishes, and plenty for all. A bullock was roasting out in the bailey for all the local people.

Aimery and Madeleine sat in pride of place, even the king taking a lower seat. They sat in silence. Count Guy leaned sideways and said to Aimery, "Talk to her. You must be able to think of something to say."

"Many things. They will wait until later."

Madeleine lost what little appetite she had.

As the meal began to wind down, the king turned to Madeleine. "Perhaps you do not understand the situation, Lady Madeleine. I and my entourage must leave shortly, but we would see this matter finished. I believe the solar has been freshened for you."

Madeleine started. "Now?"

"Now," he said. "Go along. It won't take long, and we'll believe your word before all that it is done."

Madeleine stood dazedly, and the king added, "And don't forget to tend his hand."

At this descent to the mundane, Madeleine laughed, a little laugh which sounded desperate even to her own ears.

The king sighed. "I don't know why there's such a fuss over this sort of thing. Aimery, take her, for God's sake, and get the marriage completed. I need to be on my way. I'm leaving you here to see to this place so you'll have all the time you need for dalliance. You're no use as a fighter anyway for a week or so, according to your wife."

Aimery stood and held out his hand. Rather than be dragged to her marriage bed, Madeleine allowed him to lead her to the solar.

Chapter 12

The room looked very bare. The king's possessions had already been carried out, and anything Paul and Celia had considered their own had gone with them. There were two chests, a desk, and the bed, its clean sheets folded back.

She heard the door latch fall and turned, to be grabbed by his strong left hand. *"I have no intention of choosing you. I am going to marry Stephen,"* he quoted bitterly. "Can you remember that, Madeleine de la Haute Vironge?"

"I remember many things perfectly," she snapped, struggling. "Let go of me!"

"Aren't you the sweet, dutiful wife?" he sneered, tightening his grip. Madeleine balled her fist and hammered his wounded hand. He winced but didn't release her. "That's been tried before, too." He dragged her across the room and threw her on the bed.

Madeleine scrambled off the other side. "Don't touch me!"

He stood, leaning against a bedpost. "What exactly did you expect when you picked a husband? Saintly King Edward? There aren't many men who are willing to embrace celibacy in marriage, and anyway we have an impatient and irritable king awaiting news of your loss of virginity."

"We can tell them it's done," she said desperately.

211

"Lie?" he queried. "That's your way, isn't it? It isn't mine. Get on the bed or we'll do it on the floor."

Madeleine took a deep breath. "Touch me, Aimery de Gaillard, and I'll tell the king you're Golden Hart."

She saw it hit him, but he recovered. "Madness must run in the family. Golden Hart is even now in Warwickshire."

"Clever," she acknowledged, watching him carefully. "Is it luck that others are borrowing your name or have you sent people to create just such a smoke screen?"

He appeared to be relaxed, but she could sense the tension in him. "What makes you think I'm a Saxon rebel? I'm a Norman knight."

"Golden Hart speaks French."

"So do many Englishmen. And," he added with an unpleasant smile, "how do you know how Golden Hart speaks?"

"You know perfectly well that we met! And just after the last time, my aunt went completely mad and made my life a misery. At your instigation!"

"Knowing you, I doubt she needed encouragement. The king's going to be interested to hear you've been meeting a rebel in the woods."

Madeleine gasped. "Meeting *you!*"

"Did I fuck you then?" he asked with malignant curiosity.

"I am a virgin," she retorted through gritted teeth.

His false smile was wiped away. "Then we'd better do something about it before the king comes in and holds us together like a couple of recalcitrant farm animals."

Madeleine realized with horror that she'd thrown her mightiest weapon and achieved nothing. "I mean it," she said desperately. "I'll tell the king."

"I'll be interested to see his reaction." Lightning-fast, he threw himself on the bed, rolled over, and then back. Madeleine found herself snared under him. She struggled but was utterly, terrifyingly helpless.

He had rescued her from Odo, but there was no one to

rescue her now. Even if she screamed, all those men in
the hall would laugh. She saw the fury in his eyes and
frightened misery rippled through her. "Please don't,"
she whispered. "Don't rape me."

"A man can't rape his wife, Lady Madeleine." After a
moment he sighed. "I feel very inclined to beat you, but
I have no taste for rape. Can we be *gentle* about this?"

Defeated, she swallowed and nodded.

"Good." Warily, he rolled off her. "Take off your outer
clothing."

Madeleine sat up and obeyed with trembling hands. Her
teeth were chattering, and she didn't dare look at him. She
removed her tunic, then her kirtle, leaving her fine linen
shift her only cover. "Should I take th . . . this off, too?"

"You'll probably feel better with something on in bright
daylight," he said prosaically.

At that calm tone she dared a look. He no longer seemed
angry, but neither was he as calm as he sounded. There
was a darkness in his eyes which reminded her of the way
Edwald had looked at her that day by the stream. And he
was Edwald. Immediately her body recalled the way he'd
made her feel that day, and a flicker of hope stirred in her.

"Lie down again." His voice was a little hoarse.

She obeyed, and he sat beside her. He put a hand on
her hip and stroked up until it rested on her breast. She
caught her breath. He began to rub her nipple through the
cloth. It was a mechanical act, yet similar to his actions
when he'd desired her.

She looked at him in surprise. "What are you doing?"

"It'll be easier for you if you're prepared. Relax."

Which was hard when he eased her shift down a little
and put his mouth to her other breast. She remembered
Sister Bridget. And to think they'd all laughed at her.

Was he sucking milk that was driving him wild? The
process was doing strange things to her. She was breathing
high and fast, and her body had a need to move on its
own, for no earthly reason.

While he suckled her, his left hand slid under her kirtle

to stroke her thigh. It was such a gentle touch that her fear and wariness began to melt. Then his hand moved to her private place, and she tensed. Even she was not supposed to touch there except to wash. But then she remembered a husband was allowed liberties. A husband was allowed anything. When he pushed her thighs open she swallowed, but didn't resist. She just lay there looking at the wood of the ceiling, face aflame, willing the magic to come and kill thought.

A finger slid to a special place which ached in a manner she remembered. She caught her breath. "How strange," she said with a giggle, "that what was a sin is now a duty."

He made no response. He did not echo her humor.

Madeleine closed her eyes and pulled her mind away from what he was doing. She deliberately recalled better times. That day with the faery prince—the soft voice murmuring, the gentle hand stroking, the brush of warm lips across her nape. The same golden path of warm delight opening before her.

The time with Edwald. His hungry hands and mouth. The fiery need which had been left painfully unfulfilled. Her body surged against his exploring hand.

"Good," he said flatly. "You're wet. You're very responsive. If I find after all this that you're not a virgin, I will beat you, and for any number of reasons."

His brusque tone shattered the magic. Madeleine's eyes flew open and she tensed with rejection even as he moved on top of her. He gave a sigh of exasperation and put his mouth to her breast again, rolled slightly away, and brought his hand between her thighs, rubbing gently.

She could feel his touch affect her, but the magic was gone. This was all manipulation, like pulling the tendons of a severed chicken leg. Pull this tendon and one claw shut. Pull the next and another . . .

But her breathing had fractured all the same, and her legs trembled and fell open. He rolled back on top of her, and she felt his member, hard against her. It slid into her, hard, long, finding places she had never known and yet which ached knowingly for it.

She gave a trembling moan; she rather thought it was grief.

But she was made for a man, for this man, and her body knew it. Her arms went around him, her thighs tensed to hold him. Then pain made her go rigid.

"Easy," he murmured. "At least I don't have to beat you today."

She laughed nervously. She remembered his endurance under the needle and accepted him even as the pain stretched and burned. Then it broke and he settled deep in her, letting his breath out long and slow.

He was taking his weight on his arms, but his left hand brushed away a strand of hair which had drifted across her face. It was a tender gesture which brought her close to him as she had never been close to anyone. His face was only inches away, his body overlaid her like a blanket, and a part of him was deep inside, but it wasn't that. It was an intimacy quite different that came from his darkened eyes.

"What now?" she whispered. "Do we stop now?"

"And miss the good part?" he asked with a smile. He began to move, sliding almost out then deep inside, slowly, almost tenderly, again and again and again . . .

The rhythm took over her mind and soul, pulsing in her veins and driving her back into her dream world. She recognized the path of faery delight and welcomed it. She closed her eyes and let him sweep her along, glorying in the feel of him in her arms and between her thighs. Even through his clothes she could sense the fluid muscles, the clean bones she had admired naked that day. That beauty and strength were now hers, while deep inside, her body had found its match.

She cried out as the path dropped off into a deep, dark swirling pit where he found her and joined them mouth to mouth, hip to hip.

One.

Slowly they were cast back up to reality, dazed and trembling. Madeleine opened her eyes to smile at him, but his head was lowered to her shoulder, and she could only see his golden, sweat-dark hair. He was truly her husband.

How utterly extraordinary.

He took a deep breath, rolled to his feet, and adjusted his clothing. "Get dressed," he said curtly.

Madeleine stared at his back.

He turned back. "Get dressed, unless you want to return to the hall like that."

Trembling with icy shock, Madeleine scrambled for her clothes. She found them on the floor, dragged them over her head, hurried into their protection. How could he come back from that place and be so cold, so distant?

He ran his fingers through his hair before turning to survey her. He twitched her tunic into better folds. "There's water and cloth over there. You may want to wash yourself."

He turned to look out of the window as she did so. There was, of course, blood on the cloth. She looked and saw blood on the sheet. She felt as wounded as the blood would indicate, but her wounds were not physical.

She swallowed tears and spoke. "I'm ready."

He turned back and pulled up the sheet from the bed, then with it draped over his right arm he took her hand in a ruthless grip and dragged her out into the crowded room. The trestles were down; the king was dictating something to a clerk while reading a document. Most of the men were already armed and ready to leave, but they turned as Aimery and Madeleine entered the room.

When he announced loudly, "It is done!" and waved the sheet, several men took the trouble to cheer.

As if a minor castle had been vanquished, thought Madeleine. Her face was burning, and she didn't know where to look. Count Guy came over and released her from Aimery's imprisoning grip for a gentle kiss. "Welcome, daughter."

She bobbed a curtsy, not able to forget it had been the count's ruthlessness that had brought her to this point.

Leo gave her a hearty buss. "Welcome to the family." He was so big and warm and *normal,* Madeleine almost broke into tears on his wide chest. "Aimery should bring you over soon to meet everyone. Mother wanted to come this time, and she'll have things to say about her son being wed without her here."

Count Guy grimaced. "Don't remind me. But I didn't think it safe, and now I fear I'm to be proved correct."

"Doom and gloom?" said the king as he joined the group. He, too, drew Madeleine to him for a dry kiss. "As you have married my godson, Lady Madeleine, we have a spiritual relationship. As long as you do my will you may look to me for a father's kindness."

Madeleine curtsied her gratitude even as she thought that kindness such as William's she could do without. If it hadn't been for him, she would still be safe in the Abbaye.

The king embraced Aimery warmly. "I have rewarded you richly, so serve me well."

The fondness was so sincere, Madeleine didn't know how Aimery could meet the king's eyes. She knew she couldn't, for now she was embroiled in treason herself, guilty by association and silence.

"I will look in on Baddersley later in the summer," said the king heartily, "and hope to see it in better heart and you, Lady Madeleine, already swelling with child." He glanced at the bandage. "That hasn't been changed, Lady Madeleine. You are remiss."

"We were short of time, sire," said Aimery dryly.

"How long does it take?" the king demanded. "Oh, you young people . . ." With that he turned on his heel and returned to his documents, giving a curt order for departure. Most of the men surged out to the bailey, and soon the clerks packed up all the parchment and joined them. The hall emptied of all except a few servants clearing up the debris.

Madeleine and Aimery trailed after everyone and saw the men mount. Loaded packhorses were formed into line. Dogs were brought out on leads. Then the procession was passing through the break in the palisade where a gate should be, and off down the road to Warwick.

Madeleine looked sideways at her husband. Here she was, alone with Aimery de Gaillard, Golden Hart, traitor. "You had better let me see to your hand," she said.

He gave her no trouble. Once the bandage was off, it could be seen that the wound was healing well. The design was clearly a leaping hart, but neither of them mentioned that.

Madeleine put a clean pad over the wound and bound it up with a long strip of linen. "Try not to use it any more than necessary."

"I doubt Edwin will attack Baddersley, so I should be able to avoid swordplay. I won't be able to avoid work, however. We must do the king's bidding and put Baddersley in order. Go and make an accounting of all the household goods and supplies, and I will look at it later."

With that he walked away.

It had been a curt order, master to servant, stating clearly how it was to be. Madeleine thought back to their time in bed and that mystical feeling of oneness. He must not have experienced it at all. That was disturbing, but she couldn't suppress a little glow at the thought that they would repeat the experience tonight and every night. She would have that to set against his coldness by day.

Later, however, when she sought him out with the lists prepared, she was apprehensive. Matters were a great deal worse than even she had imagined. In the few hectic days since Aunt Celia had taken to her bed, Madeleine had not had time to make a careful check of supplies. Now she found they were dangerously low, and there was no money. If there had been silver it had gone with Paul de Pouissey.

She found her husband sitting at the desk in the solar working on some figures and drawings. His own assessment of the defenses. She gave him her lists and was left standing there like a servant as he ran an eye over them. He looked up. "We are all likely to be thin."

She put the matter more plainly. "There is no possibility of surviving the winter. Even if such crops as have been sown come to harvest, it will be a poor supply."

"Someone should pay for such mismanagement."

Madeleine swallowed. "My uncle and aunt had the running of the place, as you well know. And," she added angrily, "the best people were encouraged to run away to other manors!"

"Speak softly, wife," he said, "or I will be forced to teach you manners." The silent message was understood. Don't ever mention Golden Hart.

She brought her anger under control. "What are we to do, *husband?*"

He looked over the depressing lists again. "I will buy supplies to keep us through the winter and to complete the building of the defenses. I will look to you, however, for better management from now on. I think I know," he added, "where to find some people to bring here."

Madeleine clenched her teeth. Doubtless he would "find" some of the people who had fled at his instigation. But he was being generous after a fashion and making practical arrangements for the future prosperity of her manor, so it would be unwise of her to object.

She knew he was also making it clear how their marriage would be, and that he had all the power.

When Madeleine left him, Aimery relaxed his stern features and sighed. What sins had brought him to this point? If this was William's idea of a rich reward, Lord have mercy on those he thought to punish.

Baddersley was in such a state it was hard to imagine recovery—shoddy construction, debilitated workers, empty stores. In addition, Aimery had to straighten all this out while dealing with a wife who could tangle his brain in knots with a look from those heavy-lidded brown eyes.

He remembered those eyes warm with the wonder of her body's pleasure, and the way they had driven him into the depths of passion. He cursed his weakness.

He couldn't surrender to her wantonness. She'd already tried to twist him to her will with a threat of exposure; Sweet Savior help him if she ever realized the power she had over him. He had to keep her in her place and remember that she was deceitful and cruel and never, ever to be trusted.

Day after day. Week after week. For the rest of their lives.

Yesterday, entangled in her efficient healing, he'd begun to weaken, but now he reminded himself of her true nature. She had sworn to him she wouldn't choose him, that had gone back on her vow. She'd also wanted to lie about the marriage bed.

Madeleine was as two-faced as Janus, but she had Eve's power. The first time he'd touched her he'd known it, but he'd not known then that fate would throw him into her snare.

Tight-lipped, he applied himself once more to the plans for Baddersley's defense. If he could put it into some kind of order, then he could leave—even if his only excuse was to join William against Edwin. Even fighting his cousin and Hereward was preferable to living day by day with Madeleine de la Haute Vironge.

Dinner that night was a sober affair. The hall seemed empty with just the off-duty guards, a few higher servants, and Aimery and Madeleine. True, there was his squire, Geoffrey de Sceine, but he was a quiet, intense young man who did not lighten the atmosphere.

When the tables were taken down, Madeleine thought of asking for a song or a game of chess. After a glance at her stern husband, she did neither. In the end she simply retired for the night. The sooner he came and carried her off to that special place, the sooner her world would be right again.

She wished she knew why he was so angry. So, she'd said she would marry Stephen and had been forced to change her mind. She had done the king's will by that, and what terrible fate had befallen Aimery de Gaillard? He was married to an heiress, and one he had seemed, now and then, to find pleasing. Perhaps she should tell him about Stephen, but she wasn't sure she could bring herself to speak of such things . . .

Madeleine fell asleep before her husband came, and woke at sunrise when he rolled out of bed and left the room.

He hadn't touched her.

He likely never would.

Then Madeleine truly knew despair.

> *"Dawn often finds me grieving in solitude,*
> *for no one still lives*
> *with whom I dare share*
> *the truth of my heart."*

The bard responsible for that piece knew well the human condition. To Madeleine, living with Aimery de Gaillard in this cold and barren place he had constructed— always together and yet never joined—was the tree of despair which could bear only the most bitter fruits.

She could not live with this cold courtesy. She wanted his hand to reach for her again with tenderness. She wanted to look up and see his smiling eyes upon her. She wanted to relax with him and share a joke, and see him glow with laughter as she had that once . . .

She wanted him to hold her against him and murmur soft magic as his hand explored her and brought her to pleasure. She wanted a kiss. She wanted him in her . . .

Madeleine leaped out of a bed which held nothing but torture. Plague take all men!

She went out to take up her work as mistress of Baddersley manor and lady of Aimery de Gaillard. There was solace to be found in work; Madeleine threw herself into it with a vengeance.

With supplies likely to be scarce, it was crucial that they be well kept and guarded. She organized the cleaning of the storage rooms and set boys to catch the rats. Then she studied the soundness of the structures and found them wanting. She would again have to argue with a man about the relative urgencies of defense and domestic concerns. She began to look for him, but her nerve failed her. If she sought him out, she'd have to face that coldness again, accept that he hated her. Perhaps in a day or two his mood would thaw.

If it did, it wasn't obvious. He was punctiliously courteous, but cold. Madeleine strove to be as cold in return, but as she went about her work she was burningly aware of him—on the earthwork, in the keep, training the men in their exercise area. She noticed everything he did, including, one day, a messenger he sent out. To whom?

The fact that he was Golden Hart returned like a blow. Had he enchanted her that she'd forgotten? She'd give her soul to Satan before she'd allow him to continue his treasonous activities from Baddersley. But what was she to do about it? Even now, she couldn't imagine handing him over to the king's justice.

She'd watch and wait. If she uncovered proof of his continued wickedness, she promised herself shakily, she *would* inform the king. She stopped by the chapel to beg Sweet Jesus' mother to turn Aimery's heart from treason before Madeleine was faced with such a task.

Now she had even more reason to watch his every move.

She noticed how often he stopped for a word or two with the village people, and how often the village person was Aldreda. Madeleine's reaction was an unpleasant mix of loyal fear and blind jealousy. It had been through Aldreda that he had summoned Madeleine to the hut that day. Was she a go-between for Golden Hart again? Or was their talk of a more personal nature? Which was worse?

When Madeleine checked on the work of her needlewomen, did she imagine the disdainful smirk on Aldreda's face? Madeleine had to admit that, now that food was more plentiful, Aldreda was filling out handsomely. She could only be a couple of years older than Aimery. The nuns had warned Madeleine that men's sexual appetites were insatiable. As Aimery wasn't satisfying them in the marriage bed, he could well be doing so elsewhere.

Madeleine developed a sinful hatred for Aldreda, and prayed hard against it.

Five days after the wedding the watchcorn blew a warning, and Madeleine hurried out from the hall to see two carts and a line of packhorses rolling up toward the gate. For a moment she thought it was the king again, but there was no royal standard.

Aimery was in the training square with the guards. He climbed nimbly up onto the half-built parapet around the palisade and signaled for the train to be admitted.

Madeleine realized these must be his possessions.

Aimery was in mail and glistened with sweat in the heat, but his step was light and his smile broad as he raised his hand to one of the horsemen who was just dismounting. "Welcome, Hugh! You are sorely needed."

Two hounds in the first cart strained at the ropes that tied them and were loosed. They gamboled over to fawn on their master. There were also two hawks, and Madeleine fancied their hooded heads turned, seeking his voice.

The horseman pushed back his own mail hood to reveal silvered brown hair above a square, rugged face. "So I see," he said with a twinkle of amusement. "Sweating? After a little light sword work?"

Aimery laughed and gave the man a buffet that would have felled most but merely swayed him. "There's ten lazy tubs of lard need whipping into shape, and this place to be put into some kind of order for defense. There's few available workers, and the food lacks variety and quantity. You'll soon be in a sweat, too. Down," he said crisply to the hounds, and they sat. But Madeleine could see the longing to dance around him twitching in their sleek muscles. Their bright eyes watched him adoringly.

Hugh's eyes moved past Aimery to Madeleine, and Aimery brought the man over. The hounds stayed yearningly still. "Madeleine, I make known to you Hugh de Fer. He's been my Master at Arms at Rolleston and has come here to take that position at Baddersley. With your approval of course."

A trifle belated, thought Madeleine, but she smiled at Hugh, who looked able and solid. "You are welcome, Lord Hugh." She couldn't resist adding, "Matters are improving here, and with God's help, will continue to do so. We hope not to starve."

"With God's help and my money," said Aimery dryly. Then he asked Hugh, "Have you ever come across Paul de Pouissey?"

The man grimaced. "Aye."

"Then no further explanation is needed. Come, let me show you the place." Aimery moved away, then turned back to Madeleine. "See to the unloading. There will be clothes and books, but there should also be food, wine, and spices for you to do with as you wish."

Madeleine felt gratitude to be in order, and she did feel it, but his tone was so curt that she could not find the right words. Before she did, he walked off, a casual snap of his fingers bringing the hounds to dance at his heel.

If he were to snap his fingers, she'd doubtless dance at his heel, too. She wished she could hate him, but apart from his coldness to her, everything conspired to illuminate his virtues. He was consistently fair, kind, efficient, and hard-working. His rule after Paul de Pouissey was like sunshine after a storm. No, she couldn't hate him . . .

Madeline sighed and turned to obey his order. She called for servants and supervised the unloading. Her heart lightened as she saw what he had provided. A tun of wine was rolled off to the cool stone cellar; five lime-washed hams were hung in the pantry; sacks of barley, wheat, and oats were taken to her newly cleaned granary. There was a whole basket of live eels.

Gratitude swelled inside her. Later, she would thank him as she should have immediately. Gratitude flowered into hope. Surely a man so generous could not stay cold forever.

She ordered the bound chests to be taken to the solar. There she and Dorothy surveyed them.

"Should we open them, do you think?" Madeleine asked.

"How else are we to put stuff away?" was Dorothy's practical reply.

Two small chests were locked, and Madeleine guessed they would contain the precious spices and Aimery's treasure. The others opened to reveal a range of clothing, arms, and ten books in two boxes.

Madeleine placed the two boxes on the table and could not resist exploring. Most of the books were in English, but some were Latin and French. There was a life of the great English king, Alfred, and another of Charlemagne; an account of a pilgrimage to Jerusalem—the Abbaye had owned a copy of that—and another of a merchant's travels to Russia; there was also an English herbal she itched to study. With great self-discipline, she closed the boxes. Time enough for reading when the work was done, and if Aimery would permit it.

By the time he came in, most of his possessions were carefully put away in the larger chests, layered with herbs against moths.

He had taken off his armor—Geoffrey was following with it on its hanger—and sluiced off by the well. His hair was still wet and his linen shirt and braies clung to him. He carried his sword and belt in his hand and set them down in a corner.

"Did you find the spices?" he asked.

Madeleine indicated the box. "But it's locked."

He took a key from his pouch and went to unlock the

larger chest, which she supposed to hold his treasure. He took out a key and gave it to her.

"Thank you."

He turned back and dug in his chest to produce a heavy pouch. "I never gave you a morning gift," he said, and passed it to her.

His tone was impersonal, but it was a gift.

"You gave me Baddersley," Madeleine said.

"That was already yours."

She considered him. "As you pointed out, you've given money to maintain it."

He smiled slightly. "That rankled, did it? You can pay me back when the estate is prospering."

That wasn't quite what Madeleine had intended.

She loosened the strings and opened the pouch to take out a pair of bracelets similar to his flared one but sized for a woman's arms. On each was a fanciful bird shaped of gold and inlayed with precious stones.

Geld? Such a gift, uniting them in a sense, could be of great importance, and yet she could not be sure it meant anything at all.

"They're beautiful," she said. "I've never seen such exquisite work."

"They belonged to my grandmother, Godgifu of Mercia."

"Thank you."

They stood there awkwardly. In a normal marriage a kiss might be in order, but not in this one.

Madeleine turned and put the bracelets away in her own treasure chest. Then she opened the spice box and checked the contents. Some she moved to her medicine chest, others she left where they were. A small amount she took out to give to the cook.

By that time Aimery had gone.

Chapter 13

With Hugh's arrival, matters did improve. The evening meals had been burdened by silence, for Aimery and Madeleine spoke little, and Geoffrey was taciturn by nature. Hugh de Fer, however, proved to be a genial gossip willing to carry the conversation by himself if necessary. As it was, since his stories were always of fighting, the other two men joined in. Madeleine didn't find the subject of interest, but at least she was free of the heavy silences, and in listening she began to understand her husband better.

He enjoyed discussions of theory or tactics but was cynical about heroics, and silent when it came to tallying corpses. Hugh delighted in battle; when he spoke of it his eyes brightened as if he spoke of a lover. The same talk sobered Aimery.

Madeleine thought it sad that the world offered no choice to a man of Aimery's birth other than church or war. She doubted he was suited to a religious life, yet he was wounded by slaughter. Even more than before she prayed for peace to come to England so that they could settle, she and her husband, to caring for their land and protecting their people. Hopefully he'd never have to fight again.

But as news came to them of the king's action against the rebels—of siege, ambush, and pillage—she knew this was as impossible a dream as that he come to her one night whispering words of love.

* * *

Madeleine and Aimery avoided each other as much as possible, but the day came when she could no longer put off the matter of workmen for the storage buildings.

She found Aimery at the eastern earthwork plying a shovel alongside a dozen men. His hair hung lank with sweat and he wore only loose knee-length braies and shoes. He had left off his gold, and his hand was covered only by the soiled linen bandage.

The braies were tied low across his hips and his beautiful torso was once again presented to her eyes. It glistened with sweat, not river water, but she knew it all the same. To give proof there was the blue mark on his left arm.

Would she ever, she wondered bitterly, be able to run her tongue down the valley of his spine?

Someone alerted him to her presence, and he turned, thrust his shovel into the earth, and leaped down to her.

"Yes?" he asked.

Madeleine was staring at the ridging of scars on his left shoulder. It marred the beauty of his body, but more than that, it told chillingly of a close brush with death.

"What on earth happened?" she asked.

His hand moved to rub it. "I said you lacked experience with soldiers. An ax at Senlac. Did you interrupt me just to review my scars?"

Under this rebuke, Madeleine stiffened. "You shouldn't be using that hand so roughly, and I need some men to repair the storage huts."

"My hand is fine, and all the men are needed if the defenses are to be completed. Perhaps later." He turned away.

"Later may be too late. What use," she asked tartly, "to make this place defensible if we all starve to death?"

He swung back. "Watch your tongue." But after a moment he added, "I'll send two men."

He returned to his work, and she watched for a moment, fretting about his shoulder and his hand. She forced herself to turn and walk away. His hand was healed; he only wore the bandage, she knew, for concealment—to avoid having to wear a bracelet in this heavy work.

He had lived with that shoulder for nearly two years and should know what he could and could not do with it.

Fretting about his health only reminded her of their estrangement, and could bring her nothing but grief.

And she had her workmen.

And she had her power. It was true Aimery insisted on a formal submissiveness between them, but he left her free to run the manor and supported her authority where necessary.

She made it a habit to pass through the kitchens frequently and unpredictably, alert for any dishonesty or waste. She personally supervised the collection of scraps and their distribution to the most needy. She ignored the scowls and muttered curses from the kitchen staff.

In fact she found them comforting in a way. This wasn't the same biting hatred as before; these scowls contained an element of grudging respect.

She found the same attitude in the household women— Aldreda, the weaver; Emma, the needlewoman; Hilda, who was in charge of the laundry. They were all sullen under her demand for more and better work, but they obeyed.

When she worked with them, however, doing fine work to mend or finish garments for herself and Aimery, she longed for a lighter atmosphere. In the Abbaye, some of the sewing time had been free time when talking was allowed. At Matilda's court the busy-fingered women had always been lighthearted gossips. Here, any chatter died as soon as she walked into the solar.

She was lonely. *There is no one still living to whom I dare open the doors of my heart.*

One day she had one of the cooks whipped. Wryly she remembered vowing never to use a whip at Baddersley, but the man had been stealing chickens to sell, and they were working for survival here, survival for all. There was no place for sentiment. The kitchen staff members were particularly difficult to handle, as they had become accustomed to all kinds of privileges. It had always disgusted her to see how plump they and their families were while others starved.

Even so, it was not a severe whipping, just a demonstration of her will. She made herself stand and watch as Hugh delivered the ten lashes. Afterward she gave the man's wife an ointment for his back and hoped the example would deter other wrongdoers.

Aimery joined her midway through the punishment. He did not interfere, but when it was over he asked, "What was his crime?" When she told him he nodded and walked away, but there was a frown on his face. Did he object to her meting out discipline?

That evening she asked him.

All he said was, "The household servants are yours to manage as long as you are not over-harsh."

Wearily, she wondered why she tried to understand him since the pattern of their days, and nights, was clearly set.

But day by day matters improved. The palisade was finished and sturdy, the gate was in place, and the men were now working on the keep. Aimery had advised against doing too much to it, as it would be better to build in stone later. The storage rooms were tight and dry and beginning to fill.

As she went about the castle Madeleine occasionally heard singing in the workrooms and fields. In the village there were children working, but also running around in play and getting in the way. That was good, too. She hadn't realized how unnatural it had been for the children of Baddersley to be so quiet.

But all this improvement would be as substantial as hoarfrost if she didn't make provision for winter. At this time of year even the poorly tended fields and gardens of Baddersley produced nutritious food, but when winter took hold it was her providence that would keep them all alive.

She knew she could take the weak way and expect her husband to continually support the estate, but his wealth was not unlimited, and she was determined to prove herself. He had given her this estate and was allowing her a free hand in its management. By the Virgin's milk, she would manage it.

She gave orders for most of the beans to be dried and considered what other plants could be dried for winter. She was not well-versed in this technique but knew they must lay away all that they could. A limited variety of food through the darkest months would lead to sickness, to loss of teeth and sight. On the other hand she had to consider the need to feed the people well before winter so they entered that hard time of year as strong as possible.

She wished desperately for help and advice but, even if Aimery knew about such matters, she could not burden him with more responsibilities.

She was taking a moment's rest on a bench by the chapel when a guard on the palisade called down to say travelers approached. They must be simple folk if they did not warrant the watchcorn's notice. Madeleine pushed herself up and went to offer hospitality.

Two dusty figures marched briskly up the path. As they drew closer, it became clear that the two sturdy young women were nuns. It would seem they had traveled far, yet they walked lightly. As Madeleine went to greet them she saw how bright and merry their eyes were. She also saw that they were twins.

"Welcome, Sisters. Can we offer you anything?"

They both bowed. "Bed and board," one said with a wide smile.

The other said, "We are come from Abbess Wilfreda to assist you."

Madeleine blinked. The first nun took out a parchment and passed it over. "I am Sister Gertrude."

"And I am Sister Winifred," said the other.

Madeleine could not say other than that they were welcome and, in truth, such cheerful people must be. She arranged for them to share an alcove room and for food and washing water to be provided, then she went to read her letter.

The letter from Abbess Wilfreda proved to be an introduction of the two nuns, and a cover for another, longer missive.

Dear daughter,

I cannot express how delighted I am to hear that Aimery is wed, and how infuriated that I am here in Normandy at such a time. I am sure Count Guy's delay in returning home has less to do with the king's need of his services than with his disinclination to face me.

I am enclosing a note for my son which contains urgent instructions that he bring you to Gaillard to meet me.

However, reading between the lines of the letter from my husband, and having sought out poor Lady Celia de Pouissey, I have the impression you will have heavy work on your estates this year. It would also seem that those careless men have left you without companionship or aid.

I have written, therefore, to my sister Wilfreda, Abbess of Withington, and asked that she send two sisters to assist you in your labors. If you do not need them, or find them intrusive, you are to return them to her at any time.

Know that you are welcome to our family, Madeleine, which you will find a loving one. At a word we will support you in all your endeavors. I extend the same promise from my English family. There, too, you will find the mention of my name will bring anything you require, though I know in these troubled times you may not find seeking such aid convenient.

Take care of Aimery for me. He has had two wounds since we parted, and I worry as only a mother can. I

take solace from the fact that you are trained in healing,
but if you can persuade him home to me for even a little
while, you will have done a great thing.

                  Your mother before God,
                  Lucia of Mercia and Gaillard.

Madeleine sniffed back a tear. Perhaps it was the brisk
friendliness of the first part, or the patent longing of the
end that touched her. Perhaps it was merely the acquisition
of a mother. She took the small, folded enclosure and
went in search of her husband. He was in the stables,
consulting with a groom about a horse. He came over as
soon as she appeared.

"We have visitors," Madeleine said. "Two nuns from
Withington Abbey, which is apparently ruled by an aunt
of yours. And you have a letter from your mother."

He took it and read it quickly. A smile flickered on his
face, which told Madeleine a lot about his relationship
with his mother. "She wants to meet you."

"She said as much in her letter to me."

He looked at her. "You may travel to Castle Gaillard if
you wish."

"Alone?"

"I'd provide an escort."

"She wants to see you as well," Madeleine pointed
out.

"I can't go just yet."

"Then neither will I." She was terrified that once she
left, he would make contact with the rebels again, and end
up in chains.

He tapped the parchment on his fingers. "Why the
nuns?"

"They are to help me with the management of the estate."

He nodded. "Well thought of. But with them here you
can be spared. I'd have thought you'd be happy to escape."

Madeleine's patience finally cracked. "Baddersley is not

a prison, my lord, but my home.'' She swung around and marched away.

''Madeleine.''

She froze but did not turn, waiting half hopefully for his retaliation.

''If you change your mind about visiting Normandy,'' he said, ''let me know.'' He didn't stop her as she walked away.

It was very tempting to run away to Normandy and be pampered as a new daughter, but Madeleine couldn't do that unless Aimery was safe at her side.

With the advent of Sister Gertrude and Sister Winifred, work at Baddersley speeded up. Sister Gertrude was an expert on agriculture and soon had the estate in the best shape possible, with plans underway for a much better performance the next year.

''There's no reason,'' she declared cheerfully, ''that this place should not show a profit next harvest.''

Her first project was to attack the kitchen garden near the hall, and the field down near the village which was supposed to be cultivated by the villagers for the lord.

The state of both had made Madeleine angry, for even with a shortage of sturdy laborers, more could have been done in the spring to provide crops for the summer. All they had now was a scant number of plants struggling to survive, and it was too late to put in most crops. Madeleine had tried some late cabbage. If it could only be preserved through the summer heat, and if the winter was not too hard too soon, there could be green stuff at Yuletide.

Sister Gertrude approved this effort and set in other crops, making some of the younger children responsible for carrying water from the stream to the plants. Sister Gertrude explained to them that on these plants their survival could well depend, but she also made it a game to fill the channels that ran down between the rows so the children laughed and giggled as they worked.

Sister Winifred's expertise was household management

and preserving. She complimented Madeleine's efforts and then improved on them, encouraging Madeleine to devote herself to her work of gathering wild foods. "Nearly everything can be dried and used, Lady Madeleine," she said with a radiant smile that was typical of her. "Truly, God is bountiful."

Sister Winifred ordered half the rich summer milk to be made into hard cheeses, which would be wrapped carefully and stored in a cool place. After careful thought she and Madeleine decided the best place was the chapel, their only stone building other than the armory. It was cool and secure.

Father Cedric was completely willing to lend its use as a storage place. "Christ provided the wine at Cana, Lady Madeleine. He will be happy to provide cheese in January."

Madeleine gave two men responsibility for turning the cheeses and guarding them from every hazard, for she knew people could live well on cheese even if there was no meat.

As for that, Winifred was drying meat as well as plants. She explained it would not be as palatable as smoked and salted meat but would keep longer. It could be pounded to a powder and added to boiled grains and herbs to make a nourishing porridge.

Madeleine felt as if a burden had been lifted. Starvation seemed impossible with the sisters here. They were always cheerful and energetic. Problems which had nearly overwhelmed Madeleine seemed to them an exciting challenge. They infected all the castle people with their enthusiasm, and everyone worked as never before. .

In addition, the two nuns were a relieving presence. They spent their due time at their office, often chanting their prayers as they worked, but at evening meals they were lighthearted and ready with merry stories—and their stories were not, like Hugh's, of war.

Was it Madeleine's imagination, or was even Aimery soothed by the sisters? She was sure of it when they talked him into offering a song one night. He had not played his lyre since their marriage, though Geoffrey and Hugh had asked now and then. Madeleine swallowed tears as she listened to his lovely voice. He wasn't yet singing a song for her, but he was singing, and that was something.

When he put the lyre aside he seemed relaxed. He and Madeleine were still at the high table, but the sisters had gone to sit by a window to catch the last of the light for their needlework. Hugh and Geoffrey were with the men in the hall, comparing techniques for sharpening blades.

At any moment, if the pattern of previous evenings held, Aimery too would find reason to leave her, but Madeleine sensed this could be a moment when she could find some kindness, some closeness in him.

"How is the work on the keep going?" she asked.

"It's nearly done. It won't withstand an army, but then, nothing here will."

"What else needs to be done to the defenses?" In truth, Madeleine didn't care, but she couldn't think of another topic of conversation.

"We can continue to strengthen the walls, but other than that there's only the moat. It depends on whether you want the stream diverted."

"I don't know."

He gave her a look which clearly said that in that case he was wasting his time talking to her.

"What I mean," she said quickly, "is I don't understand the implications for the village. Will it affect the drainage, or the irrigation of the fields?"

She had his attention, and a touch of respect. "It needs to be considered. I don't think most Normans do—they leave the people to adjust as best they can."

Her words had not been thought through, but now she saw they were important, and he admired her for it. Her heart lifted. "I think we should ask the villagers at one of their meetings. The moot, don't they call it?"

"Yes." He studied her as he drank from his goblet. "Aren't you afraid of becoming a little too English, asking the opinion of peasants?"

"I am English," she said firmly. "Norman-English, but English all the same. This is my home."

"So it is."

He drank again. Madeleine lifted her own goblet, searching desperately or a new topic of conversation. "How is your hand?" she asked.

After the first few days, once it was certain the wound would heal, he had taken over its tending himself. But today, for the first time, he was wearing the bracelet. The design was clearly revealed on the back of his hand. It was distorted by the scars, but she had done a fine piece of work. Once one recognized it, the design was clearly a hart with fine, broad antlers.

She caught her breath. Her fine work could lead to his death. No wonder he hadn't wanted it sewn.

"It's healing well," he said.

"It does not pain you to wear the bracelet?"

"No."

Madeleine took a deep breath. "If I had not sewn it, that design would have been ruined."

His eyes met hers. "So it would."

Madeleine licked her dry lips. "What is done," she said carefully, "could be undone."

He did not pretend to misunderstand. "I could slash myself with a knife, or lean carelessly against hot iron in the forge. I will not force my *wyrd.*"

"And what is that supposed to mean?" she asked in irritation. Such an accident would be a tiny hurt compared to his punishment if caught.

"The English adhere to the Norse idea of fate, Madeleine. Our *wyrd* cannot be changed. Our only choice is whether we face what comes with honor and courage, or disgrace ourselves by trying to flee."

"But you are Norman-English." She stated it as a challenge.

His eyes dropped to his goblet, and he turned it slowly. "Am I?"

An icy chill shot through her at such an admission of guilt. "You had better be."

His eyes came up sharply. "It would be unwise to threaten me, Madeleine."

"Would it? Does it not occur to you that *I* might have a sense of honor? And courage enough to act as I think right."

He was still. "And do you?"

"I pray God I do."

He took a deep breath. "And so do I."

"What?" Madeleine asked in confusion.

"Above all else," he said seriously, "what I ask for in a wife is honor and courage."

Madeleine caught her breath. He was talking to her, really talking to her, and coming close to the subject she wanted to address—their feelings for each other. "Even if it leads to your death?" she asked.

He smiled slightly. "Even then."

Madeleine felt her heart speed and a tingle in her hands. Suddenly it was not easy to think straight, and yet was so important that she do so. "Do you doubt my courage?" she asked.

He considered it. "No, I think you brave."

"Do you then doubt my honor?"

He did not answer, which was answer enough.

Madeleine searched for an explanation. He had been angry that day in the hut about the cruelty to the people. "It was Uncle Paul who caused the suffering here. I did what I could, but I was as powerless as the rest. Once, when I tried to challenge him, he threatened to whip me."

"I understand there was little you could do."

"What then?" She racked her brain further for the fault. "I was a virgin when I wed you. You know that."

His eyes crinkled, but it was a cruel humor. "But only just."

Madeleine leaped to her feet. "Is that what you're ob-

jecting to?'' she demanded. "That day by the stream?''
She realized she had attracted attention and lowered her
voice. "Now that's a case of the pot calling the kettle
black if ever I heard one.''

He gripped her arm. "There's a difference between men
and women, and well you know it.''

"Yes,'' she shouted, pulling against his grip. "Men
wouldn't know honor if it hit them in the face!''

Silence fell. Madeleine looked round to see outrage and
anger on the faces of the Norman men. Oh, Lord.

She found herself upside down over Aimery's shoulder,
bouncing her way to the solar. He dumped her on the bed.
She scrambled off—after a momentary hesitation in case
his intentions were amorous.

They weren't. He was unbuckling his belt.

"Angels and saints preserve me,'' she whispered, and
looked around for an escape. She could leap out of the
window, but he'd catch her in a moment. She backed away.
"Don't. I'm sorry. I shouldn't have said it.''

He walked forward, then swung the belt hard so that it
thwacked down on the bed. "Scream,'' he said.

Madeleine gaped, then bit her lip against a giggle. Then,
at the third stoke, she let out a faint scream.

"Is that the best you can do?'' he asked. *Thwack.*
"Haven't you ever been beaten?'' His lips were fighting
to smile.

Thwack.

"Ow!'' Madeleine shrieked and began to get into the
spirit of things. "Stop, please stop! Mercy!''

He was smiling. She loved the sight of it.

Thwack.

"Nooo!'' she wailed, and knocked a heavy wooden
bowl to the floor. "Mercy!''

Thwack.

"You've already said that,'' he pointed out, his eyes
brilliant with hilarity.

"So?'' she hissed.

Thwack. "So, be more creative.''

"When I'm in such pain," she muttered, "it's hard to be creative." She flung her arms wide and screamed, "Argh! You're killing me!"

Thwack.

"Spare me, lord of my heart!"

Thwack.

"I will worship you on my knees all my days!"

He stopped wielding his belt and leaned against the wall in tears of laughter, holding his sides. It was infectious. She began to whoop with it. She was sure in the hall it sounded like the wildest tears.

She recovered, belly aching, to find him still leaning against the wall, but calm now, arms folded. Amusement lingered on his face.

Giggles bubbled up again. "You'll have a terrible reputation."

"That's the idea." He turned serious. "I can't rule those men if they think my wife can insult me, and them."

She nodded. "I'll watch my tongue."

"You'd better. If you put me in a position where I have to beat you, Madeleine, I will."

She acknowledged it but couldn't hold back a teasing smile. "But not so hard, please, lord of my heart."

He choked on laughter and buckled his belt again. "You deserve far worse. You had best keep to your room tonight and look suitably subdued tomorrow." At the door he turned, still smiling. "I look forward to seeing you worshipping me on your knees."

Chapter 14

A imery had to work hard to look harsh as he entered the hall. Some of the men cheered but stopped abruptly when he stared at them. Hugh was frowning, and Geoffrey was as white as a sheet.

Aimery realized he had a problem. Clearly everyone expected Madeleine to be a bruised and beaten wretch. He didn't care about the men-at-arms; their misinterpretation might even increase the healthy fear he was building in them. He didn't, however, want Geoffrey to think that was the way to handle a wife.

He sat down between Hugh and Geoffrey. Geoffrey flinched slightly. "Some women scream a lot over very little," Aimery said.

"Yes, Lord." Geoffrey wouldn't meet his eyes.

"She'll be out here as good as new tomorrow."

Geoffrey looked at him, disbelieving but hopeful.

"My word on it." Aimery poured the young man some mead. "You'd be amazed at how few of those blows hit. Perhaps I should practice." He caught Hugh's eye, and the older man's lips twitched.

The next day Madeleine crept about the hall like a properly subdued wife, wincing slightly when she remembered. She was amused and even touched by some of the reactions. Geoffrey de Sceine hovered around her anxiously, Sisters Winifred and Gertrude spoke scathingly of men, and most of the hall women showed a pitying kind of sympathy which was as close to acceptance as Madeleine had experienced here.

Perhaps it was this sense of belonging that made it seem the sun shone more brightly, that the air was full of perfume and birdsong. Perhaps that was what made her want to dance and sing.

But it wasn't. It was the memory of that shared madness and laughter with Aimery.

She was in love. She had first called him lord of her heart in jest, but it was all too true.

It was bittersweet. He had not changed. He'd come to bed cold and breakfasted curtly. The barrier had cracked but been mended, and she still did not know what the problem was.

But she was in love with her husband, which wasn't all bad. And inside his iron-cold shell there was laughter and fire just waiting to burst free. She would crack that shell if it was the last thing she did.

In the meantime there was still work to do, and it seemed an excellent way to convince him of her honor. As she worked she waited for the evening meal when there might be an opportunity to chip away at his resistance.

That evening the nuns showed their disapproval of Aimery by sitting apart in silence, so the meal passed in the old way with talk of war, weapons, and hunting. Madeleine listened and waited. When the tables were broken down, Geoffrey and Hugh went to join a dice game. Aimery was cool, but he made no immediate move to leave the table. He poured them more wine. "It would be to your advantage to pay more attention to talk of warfare," he said.

"Why?"

"A convent obviously isn't the place to raise a chatelaine," he remarked. "If I am away, you will be in command of the castle, and though Hugh would organize any fighting, he should act at your command."

"Will you teach me?" she asked eagerly. In truth, it

was not so much the knowledge she sought as the time spent with him. Perhaps he recognized it, and that was why he hesitated. But then he rose. "Yes," he said. "Come outside."

They passed through the big hall doors into a bailey washed by the red of the setting sun. Most work was done, and those who lived in the castle were relaxing, chatting, or playing games. The villagers were drifting home. One man was whistling.

There was still a long way to go, thought Madeleine, but it was so much better than before. The people had hope.

She ventured a comment. "They seem much happier."

"They should be. We're spending a fortune feeding them." When he looked at her, there was almost a smile on his face.

He abruptly turned serious and strode toward the palisade. Madeleine had to scurry to catch up.

"The palisade and ditch are your main defense," he said briskly. "It's old-fashioned and won't keep out a force of any substance. In such a case you should sue for terms."

"What kind of terms?"

"As many lives as you can save. Yours above all." This was said without any trace of sentiment.

"That seems selfish."

"It's practical. The fate of the common people won't be changed by you staying or going. If you win free, you may be able to raise a force to recapture the place, and you won't be a hostage."

Aimery climbed up the steep stairs leading to the walkway at the top of the palisade and turned to offer her a hand. Madeleine did not need it, but took it for the touch, brief though it was.

He stood behind her in the narrow space, wide enough for only one man to squeeze past another, and with no rail to prevent a fall into the bailey. A brisk breeze blew her loose hair. He put up a hand to brush it from his face.

Feeling his body warm and hard behind her reminded her of the faery prince, his voice, his touch . . .

Madeleine was swamped by longing and closed her eyes, grateful that at least he could not see her weakness.

He cleared his throat. "You're unlikely to come under attack by a major force," he said rather gruffly, "and these defenses should deter marauders. The main thing is to keep the ditch free of debris and the land beyond clear of growth. That way no one can sneak up on you. The guards should be able to pick off any attackers with arrows, and they'll be off to seek an easier target."

"Such as the village," Madeleine said with disapproval.

"They'll raid that no matter what. With any kind of warning, the villagers will be off into the woods or up here for protection. That's why you have to be sure the watchcorn is alert. You carried a bow at the hunt. How good are you?"

Madeleine turned slightly to look at him. "Dreadful."

A flicker of humor lightened his face. "Then improve."

"Am I supposed to beat off invaders single-handedly?"

"It could come to that. But I was thinking we're going to need a lot of hares for the pot."

He turned to lead the way off the platform. Madeleine bubbled with optimism. The crack was not completely healed, and the fire within glowed in the evening light.

He guided her over to the small armory and unlocked the door. He took a bow and deftly strung it, then grabbed a handful of arrows and headed outside.

"I hope that's for you, not me," she said.

"Of course not. It's probably a little stronger than you're used to, but try it."

Madeleine accepted the weapon reluctantly. "The light's almost gone. How do you expect me to hit the target?"

"If you're as bad as you say, I don't."

She gave him a look. "If I kill someone, you pay the *wergild*."

"I pay everything around here anyway," he said, but lightly. He pointed at the side of the stables. "Hit that."

Madeleine gave a snort of disgust, drew, and loosed. The arrow thunked high into the log wall, just at the edge of the thatch.

"Well, you hit it," he remarked. "Just."

"Yes, I did," she retorted. *"Just* where I intended to."

"Did you? Then hit the same spot again."

Trust him to catch her out. Frowning with the effort, Madeleine tried to repeat her former movements. The arrow sailed up to bury itself in the thatch.

He shook his head. "When you release the string, you're not supposed to relax your left arm, too." He came and stood behind her, covering both her hands with his own. "For a short shot, hold your left hand on the target and don't let it move." He drew back the string and released it, not letting Madeleine jerk.

Madeleine tried to learn, but she was dizzy from being in his arms. The hard power of his thighs behind hers, the rippling muscles of his forearms before her eyes, were turning her own limbs to water.

He stepped away and handed her another arrow. She fumbled as she notched it, then got a hold on herself. With grim determination she kept her left hand on her first arrow and stiffened her arm until she feared it would break. She let the arrow fly, and it shuddered into the wood only a couple of feet from her target. "Stars and angels!" she exclaimed.

"An improvement. But if that had been a man, never mind a small animal, he'd be no worse for it, would he? I want you to practice every day."

It was such a brusque command, Madeleine itched to give a saucy answer, but she reminded herself she was proving her honor by perfect behavior. "Very well."

"And you should be able to defend yourself," he added. "After dinner tomorrow I'll teach you some tricks."

He unstrung the bow and went to put it away. Madeleine saw she had been dismissed, but she returned to the hall in an optimistic frame of mind. The embers were definitely glowing, and they were going to play these games again tomorrow.

Aimery took far longer than was necessary to put away the bow. In fact he skulked in the small stone hut like a coward.

It was all falling apart. Day by day he found it more difficult to remember why he must keep Madeleine at arm's length. He worked himself like a devil so he would sleep at nights and rushed from the bed in the morning before temptation overwhelmed him.

Putting his arms around her this evening had definitely not been a good idea, and yesterday . . .

He laughed at the memory of her shrieks. When he'd seen her rosy with laughter, he'd wanted her with more than lust. She was a witch . . .

But if she was, she was the cleverest witch in Christendom. He'd watched her like a hawk. She was skillful, industrious, patient, kind. She found food in the forest and gave it to the poor. Which was the truth? The cruel, deceitful witch, or the firm and kindly chatelaine? His heart said the latter, but his head demanded caution. She was undoubtedly very clever, and it would not be beyond her to pretend virtue in an attempt to enslave him.

The next morning Madeleine took her own bow out to the butts and, having made sure the area was well-cleared, practiced. She heard the suppressed chuckles from those nearby, but she did hit the target once, and it was good to hear laughter in Baddersley, whatever the cause.

She fumbled through her busy day thinking only of the lesson to come. She couldn't imagine what Aimery was going to teach her. Swordplay? She'd do her best, but she doubted she'd be able to swing a sword, never mind use it properly.

After dinner he took her not to the bailey, but into the solar. Madeleine looked around in puzzlement. It was the largest private room in the hall but still cramped for any kind of fighting.

He undid his belt. For a horrified moment she thought he was going to beat her, but he just slipped his sheathed knife off the belt and passed it to her. The hilt was beautifully bound with bronze and silver wire, and the pommel was a finely carved amber knob. She slid out the knife, and the blade gleamed wickedly sharp right down to the needle point.

"What do you expect me to do with this?" she asked.

"Kill if necessary."

Madeleine looked at him and shook her head. "I'm a healer, not a killer. It would be useful for digging things out of wounds, though."

"Use it that way if you wish, but be prepared to kill with it if necessary."

"I can't imagine wanting to kill."

"Can't you? What if your life was in danger, or that of a child?" He held her eyes. "What if some man was trying to rape you?"

Madeleine remembered Odo's attack and admitted there were times for violence. She shrugged. "Teach me what you can, but we'll not know if I can hurt someone unless the need arises."

"I have no doubt about it. You're a healer. You are already trained to hurt people when necessary."

"That's different."

"You'll find it's not. Find a comfortable grip. The hilt is doubtless too thick for you. I'll have something smaller made for you when I can. Your grip should be firm but not rigid . . ."

He worked with her for an hour, mainly pointing out the most effective places to strike.

"Pretend I'm attacking you," he said at last. "I'm unarmed, and you have a knife."

Madeleine looked at the vicious knife. "I'm afraid of hurting you."

He gave a sharp laugh at the notion and began to advance. Madeleine stuck the knife out to hold him off. A feint and he had it off her.

"Never extend your arm like that. You've no power left to strike." He returned the weapon and advanced again.

Madeleine kept her arm bent and closer to her body as he had told her earlier, watching for a chance to stab but still worried she might manage to wound him.

"I'm overconfident." He sauntered forward. "I don't think a woman dangerous. You can use that against me. I'm ogling your body instead of watching the weapon."

He appeared to be, too, which made it hard to concentrate on what she was supposed to be doing. Heavens, if he wanted her body, she was more than willing. Playing along, she thrust her breasts forward and swayed her hips invitingly. She heard him catch his breath and smiled to herself. Perhaps she had weapons she'd never been aware of.

She kept her mind on her lessons, however, and when he casually grabbed for the knife as an unsuspecting man might, she dropped to her knees and drove it toward his thigh.

She was on the ground cradling an aching wrist. The knife lay across the room.

He knelt beside her and took her wrist in an unsteady hand. "I'm sorry. I really did underestimate you. Is it broken?"

She flexed her wrist and shook her head, trying to re-create what had happened. It had been too fast. He must have knocked her hand away. "How did you do that?"

He helped her to her feet, keeping a hand under her arm until he was sure she could stand. "A lifetime of training. But you would have succeeded if I had been as cocksure as I pretended. If you'd hit the right spot, I would have bled to death."

Madeleine shuddered. "Then I don't have to do this anymore?"

"Of course you do. There are many more things I can

show you, and the stronger you are, the less of a liability you'll be to me.''

That put the whole thing in a bleak perspective. Had she imagined that moment of power over him?

He went to pour her some wine. Madeleine prepared to flaunt her body in front of him again, her mouth dry with nervousness and longing.

He put the goblet in her hand. "You should probably bind that wrist up," he said. "I'll send your woman."

Then, Devil take him, he was gone.

Once out of the room, Aimery took a deep, shuddering breath. It would be wiser to return to the earlier days, keep his distance, speak to her only briefly and of practical things. It was no longer possible.

He sought reasons to be alone with her. He was aware of her all day long. Despite tiredness, he had hardly slept last night as his body demanded hers and his mind insisted on control. He wasn't sure what would happen tonight.

If he once lost himself in love with Madeleine, he would be lost forever. Sweet Savior, the quickness and courage of her. The wit, the beauty, the strength . . .

Once he was gone, Madeleine discovered her wrist ached badly. She wrapped a damp cloth around it and cradled it. Then she saw the knife on the floor. It was a gift from Aimery and she treasured it, so she picked it up and slid it into its sheath. The hard leather sheath was gilded and lined with sheepskin to keep the blade lubricated and sharp. This was a valuable weapon.

She put it aside for the moment, but since he wished it, she would wear it on her girdle. So far, she thought ruefully, she had received bracelets and a knife from her husband. He seemed well on the way to turning her into a warrior, but if that was what he wanted she would do her best to please him.

Then Dorothy was there, fussing and muttering about brutes and tyrants. Dorothy did not think much of Aimery these days, but Madeleine had decided not to tell her the truth about the beating. If the story got out, it would raise his reputation in the eyes of the women, but it might lower it in the eyes of the men. Now Dorothy thought he'd brutalized her again.

The maid prepared a soothing compress under Madeleine's direction and tucked her into bed. The wrist still ached and screamed whenever she moved. After a while, Madeleine knew she would never sleep.

"I think I had best have a little of the poppy, Dorothy."

Madeleine drank it, and soon drifted into a deep sleep so that Aimery had little choice as to his actions that night. His mind told him it was just as well. His body ardently disagreed.

The next day Madeleine's wrist still ached, and she had to bind it. She was irritated by the way it hindered her and made short-tempered by the poppy and the nagging pain. At breakfast she snapped at Aimery. He snarled back and strode out of the hall.

Madeleine released her frustration on a clumsy maidservant and then regretted it. Her head throbbed, and she decided she deserved a day of rest. Since she couldn't even sew properly, she indulged in reading. Aimery came in at midday, clearly concerned. She reassured him that her wrist was not badly hurt.

To prove it to him, she went out to check on the work around the manor and found the open air did her good. Her head cleared, and her wrist didn't pain her unless she tried to do heavy work. She also noticed yet more sympathetic looks from the women and used this to gain their confidence.

By the time of the evening meal, Madeleine was in good spirits. She deliberately left her bandage off, so as not to remind Aimery of the problem. What, she wondered optimistically, would this evening bring?

She listened impatiently to a boring discussion about fighting formations. Then the meal was over, and she and

Aimery were alone. She smiled at him. "I think everyone is seeing my wrist injury as evidence of further cruelty. May I tell them the truth?"

"That I've been teaching you knife fighting? I think not. Most men would think me mad."

"In case I decided to try out the weapon on you?"

He was cool. "You have seen what the consequence would be."

Consequence or not, Madeleine would use a blade to try to cut through his forbidding manner if she could. It was as if the last few days had never been. "So," she said purposefully, "what do I learn tonight?"

"I think you should give your wrist time to heal," he said, and went off to join Hugh and Geoffrey.

Madeleine sighed and moved over to sit with the sisters until it was time for bed. She harbored faint hopes that something would change there, and even toyed with ways to use her body to entice him, but when she made her way to the solar he joined her. "One of the mares is about to foal. I'll spend tonight in the stables."

Madeleine found she didn't sleep at all well without him beside her in the bed.

The next day she took advantage of the new sympathy among the women and gathered a group of them to go into the woods with her in search of wild herbs and fruits. It was a hot day, and they all wore just their shifts and kirtles. As Madeleine always dressed simply for work, she appeared to be one of them except that she alone wore her hair uncovered. No one—such as Aimery—objected to this practice, and she found a veil or wimple got in the way, but now she wished she had worn a head-rail. She felt set apart.

The women were all married and kept their hair covered. She had a thick, uncovered braid like a maid.

They all had at least one child with them, either trotting alongside or carried in a sling on the back. Madeleine's womb was empty. She had had her courses since her wedding.

They all had men who mated with them often, some-times—to Madeleine's surprise—more often than they'd like. Listening to their frank, salty gossip, Madeleine was filled with an aching longing to be a true wife. She'd love to be pestered after a hard day.

As usual she smothered her pain in work. She taught the women about plants which were new to them, and she listened carefully as they explained their own traditions.

She was returning to the castle with her basket full of herbs when she saw Aimery talking to one of the peasants near the cornfields. Unable to resist, she sent the women on ahead and walked over to speak to her husband.

His companion looked up and saw her, said something to Aimery, and was dismissed, but not before Madeleine had recognized him. It was the other Saxon from that day when Odo had attacked her.

Her mouth dried, and a chill touched her as if clouds had blotted out the sun. She had convinced herself his treason was over, but perhaps it was not so.

She stopped, unsure what to do or say.

Aimery came over. Like her, he dressed simply for work. Today he wore a tawny linen tunic girdled with a plain leather belt. His only weapon was a long scramasax, and his only noble ornaments were his two rings and the bracelet on his right wrist.

"We need more hands here if anything is to be improved," he said in a businesslike tone. "Now that the defenses are adequate, I'll visit our other properties, and Rolleston. I'll find some more cottars and arrange for supplies."

"And leave me here?" she asked.

"You'll be safe with Hugh and the two sisters."

The place would be an empty shell if she didn't have the comfort of knowing he was about, and she'd live in fear that he was being entangled again in matters that could destroy him. "I think I should travel with you," she said. "I've never seen the other manors which make up the barony. And I would like to visit Rolleston."

There was a flash of irritation in his expression. "If it hasn't escaped your notice, woman, half the country is up in arms. William may have taken Warwick and put down unrest there, but Gospatric has raised Northumbria, Edwin and Morcar are still making trouble not far from here, and the Welsh and Scots are on the move. It's hardly the time for a pleasure trip."

"Then why are you going?" she demanded, half expecting a slap for her impudence.

"I've told you why," he said curtly and walked away.

Fear-sparked fury burned in her. "I won't be left here!" she shouted at his back.

He swung round and strode back. "You will do as you're told, as a good wife should."

"Wife!" she scoffed. "I'm hardly wife to you, Aimery de Gaillard."

He grabbed her by her thick plait. "Miss the bedding, do you? I suppose you do. You were quick enough to learn the business." With a leg behind her knees and a tug on her hair, she was flat on her back on the long grass with him on top of her.

Chapter 15

Madeleine was knocked out of breath, but she wasn't complaining. His shell was properly cracked now, and the fire was burning high. Her body anticipated what was to come, what she hoped was to come . . .

"You don't always have to throw me down, you know," she said, daring to tease.

A flash of amusement lit his eyes before it was shielded. Emboldened, Madeleine raised a tentative hand to brush his damp hair off his cheek. Her body was humming with delicious expectations.

He shook her hand off. "A man needs to vent his seed from time to time. That's what a wife's for." But his eyes betrayed him. At this moment he desired, and he desired her.

"I'm willing to be used that way," she said softly. "I would like a child. I've had my courses since the last time." She could see the battle waging in him and didn't know which way it would go; she feared cruelty and hungered for tenderness.

Aimery looked down on Madeleine beneath him, and impossibly wild desire surged in him. She was nut-brown from the summer sun, but her soft lips were deep rose and open to him, smiling. Her warm brown eyes spoke of desire. Her body beneath his was firm and round and willing. He imagined it rounder, rounded with his child. He eased to one side and ran his hand over her flat abdomen.

She trembled under his touch. His hand was none too steady. His desire of her was a weakness, and one he had resolved to fight, but he already knew he had lost the battle.

It was hard to remember what the battle was.

He had taken no other woman, for he would not do that in his wife's house, and his desire for her had been, at times, an agony. And here she was beneath him, weakening him with her dark eyes and soft lips, with the tentative movements of her hips.

She was willing? He'd take his pleasure then, but with no thought for hers.

He pulled up her skirt. Her legs fell open at a touch. He adjusted her body and entered, swift and smooth. The first sheathing was so exquisite he stopped with a groan to savor it. How slick she was, how ready. He looked at her and saw no resentment of his treatment of her, only the flushed cheeks of wanton rapture.

It fired his blood beyond all control.

She gasped, and her body shuddered and tightened around him, drawing him higher. As he pulled back, the tightness of her slid along him, stirring him into a half-crazed mist of agonized delight.

To which he totally surrendered.

When he slid into her, as hard as iron, Madeleine gasped with perfect relief to have him where he belonged at last. A shudder passed through her, and she felt her muscles tighten, heard him groan.

She stared up at him. Against the high, burning sun he was all golden—bright golden hair, duller gold on the skin, and tawny in his linen shirt. He shuddered as he drew out of her body slowly and then slid in again. His eyes were closed, and this time she kept hers open, watching this thing she could do to him.

She saw color flush his cheeks and sweat leap to his brow. She could almost see the gasping breaths pass over his lips. Gasping breaths which matched her own, heat and sweat that surely marked her, too, and the movement of him . . .

The sun beat down. The sky above was infinite, a perfect blue. Somewhere a skylark trilled and trilled as if rejoicing in their soaring passion.

An ember roared into flame.

He threw back his head and gave a choked cry as rippling tension passed from his body to hers. A cry of her own escaped as his seed burst into her. She wrapped her legs and arms around him as shudders shook them both.

His eyes opened, more black than green. His mouth came down on hers, hot and hungry, devouring her, and she sought to be devoured. They lost themselves in this new union.

His mouth slipped off hers to her ear. Her hand cherished his smooth neck, his sweat-slicked, scarred shoulder beneath thin, damp cloth. Her fingers found the valley of his spine and wandered down it to his hard buttocks.

She wished he were naked.

His lips trailed gently down her neck, gathering her sweat as she wanted to do to him, causing her to shiver, heat on heat, wet on wet. Then his mouth went further, to her breast to nuzzle softly at her sensitive nipples through the cloth. At the first touch there she shuddered, and when his teeth closed gently on her, she tensed.

He was still inside her, and hard.

"Sweet Jesu!" she gasped, and was not sure herself whether it was delight or trepidation. "Again?"

"Again," he said, looking up at her with hooded eyes. "Chastity does strange things to a man."

Madeleine lost her doubts. Delight, definitely delight. She wrapped her legs back around him possessively. "It does strange things to a woman, too."

"What sort of things?" he asked lazily as his clever hand wandered up and down her body and his hips made small, tantalizing movements against her.

"Oh, things," said Madeleine shyly, looking away.

"Tell me, Madeleine," he coaxed. "A man likes to know how a woman feels. Sometimes," he added dryly.

Her head was spinning, her body aching. "It feels wonderful. I like it." After a moment she admitted, "I thought we'd be doing it every night."

He choked on a laugh. "Perhaps we will. It seems a terrible shame not to. Who knows how long we have?"

A chill drove away some of the fever. His words echoed all too closely her own fears. Madeleine tightened her legs on him protectively. "What do you mean?"

He looked up. "Life's a chancy thing at best, that's all. I could be called upon to fight at any time." He lowered his head to drop kisses along the line of her jaw. Then his mouth lowered slowly to her breast again.

There was more to his words than that. Madeleine took a grip on his hair and pulled. He tightened his teeth and resisted. She felt herself stretch to the point of pain, gave a little cry, and let go. He looked up, laughing. "You wanted something?"

How strange that the small pain could bring back the fever so strongly. Madeleine certainly wanted something. She wriggled her hips against him, encouraging him to feed the hungry ache, but he went still. Hard inside her, but still.

"What did you want?" he insisted.

"Later. I can't think now!"

"Yes, you can," he said. His fingers began to torment her nipples again, causing her to whimper.

He grinned. "I'm not going to pleasure you until you tell me."

Then what did he think he was doing?

But she knew what he meant.

She struggled to organize her dizzy mind, even as her body shuddered and her breath wavered. "Who?" she gasped at last. "Who will call you to fight? The rebels?"

His fingers pressed painfully on her, then left her. He pulled out of her and out of the bondage of her legs.

"No!" she wailed, scrambling to her knees and reaching for him. How could she feel so icy-cold on a hot summer's day?

He knelt before her. "You think me a traitor? Then you surely don't want to give your body to such as I."

Madeleine ached and throbbed with a need she could never have imagined. It left no dignity. She begged. "Please!"

He was half-gone in passion, she could tell, but far more in control of himself than she. He gripped her wrist. "Am I a traitor?" he demanded fiercely.

Madeleine wanted to say no, but honesty is a hard habit to break. "I don't care," she whispered, tears falling down her hot cheeks. In the face of his implacable silence she added, "I don't know."

He gave a sigh and released her. "Nor do I," he said. "But I won't fight for the rebels. You have my word on that."

He pushed her gently back down and moved above her, holding himself high on strong arms. Madeleine's entrance felt like a hungry mouth, aching to devour him, yet he paused there against her. She could feel him at the opening and raised her hips, but he moved back a little.

"Please," she begged. "I need you."

"Remember me," he said softly and eased down into her, filling tight the aching void. Madeleine gave a great, shaking shudder of relief and closed her eyes. Nothing existed in the world for her except him in her. She worked with him fiercely, matching thrust for thrust until she succeeded in obliterating the feverish pain and replacing it with shattering, fear-devouring delight.

She lay limp and exhausted, felt him leave her, rearrange her skirt, felt the sun bake her. Through her closed lids she saw endless red.

A fly landed on her nose. She brushed it away. It returned. She opened her eyes to see him, sitting crosslegged beside her, tickling her with a scarlet poppy. "You'll burn," he said lazily, "and there's work to be done."

There was none of the cold indifference that had followed their last mating. She felt joined to him as never before. And he'd given her a promise. He wouldn't fight for the rebels. She took his hand and kissed it.

She smiled and received a smile back. It wasn't full and open, but it was far better than cold indifference.

She remembered that moment when it had all been threatened, but then smiled again. He'd given her a promise. He wouldn't fight for the rebels.

He rose smoothly to his feet, extended a hand, and pulled her up, then picked bits of grass from her hair and gown. He put a finger beneath her chin. "Feel more like a wife?"

She tilted her head. "I thought wives were for bed. What does a whore feel like?"

He grinned. "They're all different. Some hard, some soft . . ."

She playfully slapped his hand away, then turned to pick up her basket.

She gave a tut of annoyance when she found all her herbs scattered. He moved to help her. "Do you need more herbs? We should be able to buy some in Lincoln or London."

"Can we afford it?"

"No, but it's doubtless a necessity."

They began to amble toward the castle, savoring a sweet moment and each other.

Madeleine hated to disturb this time together, but she wanted to be rid of all the doubts that hovered between them. "What did he want?" she asked.

"Who?"

"Golden Hart's friend."

He gave her a considering look. "It was just a message. Nothing to bother you."

He drew her into his arms. "I gave up Golden Hart some time ago. There could be trouble if that all comes out, but it's unlikely now. After all," he said with a smile, "you were always the one most likely to expose me."

An answering smile tugged her lips and turned into a grin. "Mmm," she murmured, looking him over. "Speaking of exposure . . . I want to see you naked again."

"I've never seen you naked," he said. "Will you stand in the sunlight in just the glory of your hair and let me worship you?"

Madeleine blushed. "If you want," she said shyly.

He grinned. "If you'd understood English that day in the woods, you'd know what I want."

"What did you say then?"

He swung her around so that her back was against him and held her as he had then. There was no cloak to confine her, but Madeleine had to give a little thought to her poor herbs.

"I told you how beautiful your curves felt," he said in English, running his hands over her. "How sweetly heavy your breasts. How I wanted to lick their fullness all over and tease your nipples to aching, then suck them soft, suck them hard until you were wild for me."

Madeleine's body leaped within his confining arms. "You didn't do that then," he said. "That's how I knew you didn't understand."

"My body didn't understand then," she said.

"I confess, I thought you knew the language of love."

"What else did you say?" she asked breathlessly.

He laughed and slid his hand down to her thighs. "I told you how warm and moist you were, just waiting for me. I promised to be slow in loving you, to stroke you softly to your pleasure, then when you couldn't bear it anymore, I'd take you hard and strong."

Madeleine pressed back against him. "I can't bear it anymore . . ."

He laughed against her neck, kissed her nape. "Insatiable wanton. Have pity on the poor male."

She could feel the bulge of his desire and shifted her bottom against it, heard his breathing falter. He turned her slowly. Madeleine heard the herbs fall but didn't care.

Their heated kiss was interrupted by a shout. They broke apart and saw one of the castle guards trotting over to them.

Madeleine was flooded with embarrassment to be caught in such an embrace. Then she remembered she'd recently made long, desperate, passionate love at the edge of a path where anyone could have seen them.

Aimery glanced at her red face and laughed. "If anyone did see us, they doubtless only felt jealous. I'd better go and see what's amiss while you take time to recover your composure." His eyes were warm and loving, and he touched her cheek gently. "Later," he promised.

Madeleine watched him stride away. She welcomed the chance to accustom herself to the wonderful thing she had found, a union that went beyond bodies to hearts and souls. She was reluctant to return to the castle and disrupt this idyll with day-to-day concerns. She picked up her herbs, then wandered a bit more, gathering a few more plants but mostly gathering dreams of a golden future.

When, much later, she entered the bailey of Baddersley Castle she asked the guard where Aimery could be found.

"He rode out, Lady," said the man.

She stared at him. "Out? Where?"

"Don't know, Lady. He went on a journey with three men."

An icy foreboding assailed Madeleine. But no. She wouldn't think that of him.

"Just three men?" she demanded of the guard. "He didn't take Lord Geoffrey?"

"That's right, Lady."

"He must have left a message," she said.

"Doubtless with Lord Hugh, Lady."

Madeleine hurried to the training grounds, desperate for reassurance. "Hugh, what message did my husband leave for me?"

He raised his sweaty brows. "None with me, Lady Madeleine."

She deliberately summoned the memory of Aimery's tender parting like a ward against evil. "Do you know where he's gone?"

"No. He said he'd likely be gone a sennight, maybe longer. He may have left word with Geoffrey."

"A sennight?" Madeleine echoed with horror.

The squire was her next quarry. "Geoffrey," Madeleine demanded, "where has Aimery gone?"

The young man paled. "Er . . . he didn't say, Lady."

"Doesn't that strike you as strange?"

She saw him swallow. "He said earlier he thought of visiting the other manors . . ."

"Without you? With only three men?"

He bit his lip, then offered hopefully, "It was doubtless something to do with the messenger, Lady Madeleine."

Madeleine's fears abated. At last. An explanation. She poured herself a beaker of ale. "What messenger?"

"A messenger passed through from the queen en route for the king. He spoke to Lord Aimery."

The beaker never reached Madeleine's lips. "The messenger didn't bring a written message to Baddersley?"

"No, Lady Madeleine."

Madeleine put the beaker down untouched and went into the solar, remembering at last that when she'd admitted she didn't know whether he was a traitor or not, he had not affirmed his loyalty, but said, "Nor do I."

The whole golden scene fell into a new, bleak pattern. As soon as she'd moved to thwart his plan to join the rebels, he'd turned her up sweet and rutted her senses clean out of her. What a fool he must think her.

How convenient that a royal messenger had passed through at such a time, doubtless just stopping for refreshment. What would Aimery claim the message had been? A request for some vague minor service which would cover his journey to meet Hereward and Edwin? What a fool he must think her. No royal message came by word of mouth and he wouldn't go on legitimate business without Geoffrey.

Tears of betrayal burst in her eyes and she threw her much-abused basket at the wall just as Dorothy came in. The woman hurried to pick up the spilled herbs.

"I'll gut him!" Madeleine muttered. "I'll put teasels in his braies so he'll dance from here to London." She tore off her kirtle and shift. "He won't have to worry about the king gelding him, I'll do it myself!"

"Who? What?" The woman stared at her.

Madeleine realized she was standing stark naked and grabbed clean clothes from a chest and put them on. "Aimery de Gaillard, the low, scheming bastard." She scrubbed at the tears streaming down her face. "He played on me like a lyre—a right pretty tune, too—then sneaked away . . ."

"Lord Aimery rode out in armor with three men and two packhorses, Lady."

Madeleine swung on her. "And what has that to do with anything? He said he wouldn't go!"

Dorothy rolled her eyes and poured her mistress a goblet of wine. "Drink this, Lady. You've been too long in the sun."

Madeleine took a deep draft. She felt painfully used. Then she had a worse thought. All his recent thaw dated back to the time she'd threatened to betray him to the king. Was that all it had been, a way of besotting her out of her honor? Her misery was as sharp as a blade.

There was a rap on the door. Dorothy opened it, and Geoffrey entered hesitantly.

"Yes?" said Madeleine curtly.

"Lord Aimery did leave a message, Lady Madeleine."

Hope burst in her, full-blown. "What?" she demanded. "How could you have forgotten?"

"It is not to do with his journey," Geoffrey said. "Or not about where he's gone . . ."

Madeleine could have screamed. "What is it?"

Like a boy repeating a lesson, Geoffrey said, "He said he was sorry. And he'd pick up where he left off on his return.'' The squire looked at her and added warily, ''He departed in a mighty hurry, Lady.''

Geoffrey, too, left in a mighty hurry, a hair's breadth ahead of a flung goblet.

''Oh, he will, will he?'' muttered Madeleine. ''Over my dead body . . .''

''Lady Madeleine!'' moaned Dorothy, wringing her hands.

''He'll never do this to me again,'' said Madeleine fiercely. ''No matter how my body clamors, I will not be used like this again.'' She seized the carved crucifix from the wall. ''You are my witness, Dorothy. I promise—nay, I *vow*—never to lie with Aimery de Gaillard again until he proves he is true to the king and me both!''

Dorothy went pale and crossed herself. ''Oh, Lady, take it back. You can't deny your husband.''

Madeleine hung up the crucifix again. ''It is done. Well. Let's get back to work.''

As she checked the kitchens and the pens of poultry awaiting death, Madeleine's thoughts were all of Aimery.

He'd ride into Baddersley in a week or so, and she'd be able to tell him then just what she thought of him.

He'd ride into Baddersley with a perfect explanation of his absence, and she would happily beg his forgiveness for her wicked doubts.

He'd be sent back to Baddersley in pieces . . .

A wave of nausea passed over her at the thought of him blind, or without hands or genitals. She sent up fervent prayers for his safety. ''Only send him safe home to me,'' she whispered, ''and I'll make sure he does not stray again.''

How she was to achieve that she didn't know.

Someone cleared his throat. Madeleine looked around to see a soldier. ''Lord Hugh sends to say Odo de Pouissey approaches with four attendants. Are we to admit him?''

Odo? What more shocks could the day bring? He was

someone she'd rather not see, but she couldn't refuse hospitality. "Of course. I will come to greet him."

The man trotted off. Needing something to bolster her dignity, Madeleine took the time to enter the solar and drape a wimple over her head and shoulders. By the time she reached the hall doors, Odo was swinging off his horse in the bailey. He came over and gave her a familiar kiss on the cheek, then looked around. "I see you and de Gaillard have been working on the place, but it's not much even so. A proper stone castle and walls. That's what a man needs these days."

As she led him into the hall, he went on about the glorious campaign underway to crush the English rebels once and for all, and to build castles to keep them in order. "The king's ordered one built at Warwick and is giving it into the charge of Henry de Beaumont. I have no doubt I can soon win such an honor."

Madeleine ordered food and ale for him and his men, and provisions for his horses. Odo's was a clear case of sour grapes and wishful thinking, but she didn't ill-wish him. If he could achieve glory and win himself a castle, she had no objection, as long as it was in another area of the country.

One part of his monologue did interest her, however. "So the rebellion is over?" she asked. If so, Aimery would be in no danger.

Odo tore a large lump of pork off the bone with his teeth and washed it down with ale, half-chewed. He wiped his mouth and belched. "All but. William has only to appear before a city for it to open its gates and beg pardon. If I were him, I'd lop a few heads and stick them on pikes and have done with this once and for all."

Aimery's head on a pike . . . . "And what of that Hereward?" Madeleine asked, refilling his flagon. "I heard he was to join Earls Edwin and Gospatric."

He turned on her with surprising alertness. "Where heard you that?"

"Rumors, no more," said Madeleine cautiously, praying he would say something of what was on his mind.

She needn't have worried. Odo was incapable of keeping quiet about anything which might be to his own self-aggrandizement. He grinned. "I heard rumors, too, as I was riding south. More than rumors. I received sure word that Hereward is out of the Fens. He and a large force are lurking in Halver Wood not far north of here. Too many for my men to tackle, but I sent word to the king. He'll send a force and that will be the end of that weasel."

Madeleine fought to hide her sick dread. Hereward was out of the Fens and had sent for his nephew. "Do you intend to wait here until then and take part in the fighting?" She heard the thinness of her voice and cursed herself.

He smirked, unobservant as always. "Lonely, are you? Where is your fancy husband anyway?"

"East," Madeleine said quickly. "He's gone to visit his estate of Rolleston."

Odo shrugged. "It was always clear he didn't want you, so you've no cause for complaint if he's neglecting you." He looked over her plain dress. "And you haven't even cajoled out of him any of that gold that dazzled you. He probably has a buxom Saxon Danelaw wife tucked away at Rolleston, dripping with his spare jewelry."

Madeleine pinned a faint, unconcerned smile on her face, while splinters of bitter jealousy tormented her. Was it possible? A *manno Danico* marriage didn't block a Christian one. King Harold had been married in the Danish style for twenty years to Edith Swannehals and had taken Eadgyth of Mercia at the church door to solidify support for his claim to the throne.

But what did that matter anyway if her husband was riding to his death?

"Aimery and I are dealing together very well," she lied. "Do you intend a stay here, Odo?"

He shook his head. "Though the food's improved. I'm

under orders south to the queen,'' he said importantly, ''to be captain of the advance guard to bring her north.''

''Bring her north?'' Madeleine queried in surprise. ''Into the middle of a rebellion? She's eight months pregnant.''

Odo shrugged. ''The rebellion's as good as over, and the king wants her with him when the child is born.''

Madeleine thought darkly of men and their lack of consideration, but a large part of her mind was on Aimery.

Odo had sent word to the king about Hereward. William would surely send an army, maybe go with one himself, to finally capture that thorn in his flesh, and find he had Golden Hart in his grasp, too.

Aimery had surely guessed something of this. She remembered him saying, *Remember me,* even as he thrust into her. As if he were going to oblivion.

She swallowed tears. What was she to do?

Let him stew in his own juice, said a bitter part of her, but it was only a very small part.

She turned to Odo. ''Do you ride on immediately then?''

He nodded. ''Just thought I'd stop since we were passing close, and find better food than we carry. And a spare horse if you have one. One of ours has a sore leg.''

Madeleine arranged for a fresh mount and soon had the satisfaction of seeing him on his way. Then she went into the stables, ostensibly to check on the injured horse.

''Just a strain, Lady,'' the stable groom said. ''Soon remedied.''

''Good.'' Madeleine leaned against a post and said idly, ''Do you know where Halver Wood is, John?''

''Aye, Lady,'' he responded readily and without suspicion. ''It be north of here half a morning's ride. Off the old road a bit and toward Gormanby.''

Madeleine left armed with directions which were doubtless clear enough to the local people but mystifying to her. Half a morning's ride. Aimery would already be there then. But even if she couldn't stop him, someone had to warn him of the danger. How?

She went into the solar and pressed damp hands together

nervously. She had sworn to expose Aimery if she had proof of treason, but here she was trying to abet him. If the king could capture the magical symbol who was Hereward, and the other who was Golden Hart, he could break the back of English resistance to Norman rule. It was her duty to support that in every way possible.

But she couldn't let Aimery be taken. Could she send Geoffrey to warn him? Could she trust Geoffrey? He was a pleasant young man, but Norman to the core and surely not so besotted as to contemplate dishonor as she was doing.

Besotted. Part of her objected to that word, but she shrugged away such nonsense. She was madly in love with Aimery for all he was a traitor. So, she had to save him.

Would one of the local people help? They surely were mostly in favor of Golden Hart and Hereward, but a few were ready to betray their own kind for favor, and she could not be sure which was which. And would they believe her, a Norman, on such a matter?

The only possibility, she realized, was for her to go alone. The prospect scared her to death.

Chapter 16

~~~⌒⌒⌒⌒~~~

Since her well-escorted journey to Baddersley, Madeleine had never ventured beyond the paths of the nearby woods, and had never left the castle alone. Now she was planning to ride off through strange and hostile country in search of a poorly identified place which was infested by Norman-hating traitors.

She opened a box and removed Aimery's maps of the estate. Ah. By the old road, John must have meant the Roman road called Ermine Street which passed not far north of Baddersley. But there was no marking for Halver Wood or Gormanby. Well, it was surely possible to ride a couple of hours and then ask for further directions.

Alone? Asking English people for help finding Hereward? It seemed impossible, yet she must do something, and speedily.

She deliberately put aside future problems and considered the immediate—how to get out of Baddersley with a horse and without guards. After discarding any number of fanciful plans she simply ordered her horse saddled and fitted with panniers, and told John she was going to collect some special roots for her medicine chest.

As she rode across the bailey, Geoffrey hurried forward. "Do you require an escort, my lady?"

"No need," she said, grateful it was he and not Hugh who had been informed of her enterprise. "I am only go-

269

ing to the other side of the village, Geoffrey, and the horse will carry my load back for me.''

She could see he wasn't happy with the situation but lacked the confidence to insist. She rode out at a trot before he found it.

Beyond the village she took the north path which led, according to the map, to Ermine Street. Very shortly she was out of sight of Baddersley and all alone in the light woodland. She must be mad.

She remembered that not so long ago the people hereabouts had been malevolent toward her. That had faded since the king's visit and her marriage, but had they really changed? She shrugged. She had resolved to do this thing, and she would not falter. She eased Aimery's knife in its sheath and urged her horse through the trees, trembling at every rustle in the undergrowth.

Soon she came to the road and sighed with relief to be in a more public spot. The heavy old stones were still in place and could occasionally be seen through the cover of dirt and weeds. They formed a solid base in all weathers— a marvel to everyone, who all wished the way of making such a surface was still known.

The road was busy with ox-carts, riders, and foot traffic. A few travelers were soldiers, but most were clearly traders of one kind or another, which suggested that there was no warlike trouble in the area. Madeleine hoped to be taken for a trader herself with her panniers.

She set off north at a brisk pace, trying to gauge ''a half-morning's ride'' in John's terms. She was tempted to ask one of the drivers of the slow-moving carts whether he had seen Aimery and his men going past, but the less attention called to herself and him the better. She did, however, stop after a while and ask a man if he knew a place called Gormanby. He shook his head and regarded her speculatively.

Madeleine rode on. She cursed her southern looks, inherited from her mother. Her darker skin and brown eyes

marked her out among this fair-skinned race, and she was
sure her careful English had a foreign tone.

However, she had to take the chance and ask help again
or she'd end up riding Ermine Street all the way to Lincoln. When she came to a small monastery which served
as an inn for travelers, she waved away the offer of food
and asked after Gormanby. "Yes, my child," the monk
said readily. "But you have passed the track. Go back a
little way, and by some cherry trees and an oak you will
see a path go west. It is not far."

Madeleine mounted again and turned back with relief.
Both she and the horse were weary, but the end was in
sight.

She soon found the oak and cherry trees, and a path
next to them. She turned onto it eagerly, but she couldn't
help noticing that the woodland here was heavier than
around Baddersley. It was more difficult to see into and
more likely to hold danger both from man and beast. The
tall trees grew close to the narrow path, which was only
just wide enough for a cart to pass along. In fact, the ruts
from such carts were deeply ground into the earth. Above,
the leaves met to form a heavy green roof, cutting off the
sun and making the place dark and chill.

Uneasiness crept into Madeleine, and she would willingly have taken any excuse to turn back, but she pushed
on. She had another concern now. Even if there was no
personal danger, how was she to find anyone in this forest?
She might have to wait for Hereward to find her.

When a man ran out from the woods and neatly pulled
her off the horse, she was startled but not vastly surprised.
She hadn't, however, expected a sharp knife at her throat.

"Well, Lady Madeleine. Have business hereabouts, do
you?"

Madeleine gasped. It was the Saxon, the one who had
been with Aimery. He was grinning, but his eyes were
hard, and she knew he would slit her throat without hesitation if he decided it was meet.

"I need to contact Aimery," she whispered.

"Aimery? Lady," he said with a leer, "I would have thought he'd contacted you enough for one day."

This man had watched! Madeleine's face flamed, and she glared at him, knife or not. "I wish to *speak* with him. Or Hereward."

The grin was wiped away, and the knife pricked. Madeleine cried out and tried to jerk back, but his hold was like iron. She felt blood trickle down her skin.

"What do you know of Hereward, Norman bitch?"

"He is here," she choked out. "It is known. Word has been sent to the king."

"And you've come to warn him? A likely tale."

"I've come to warn Aimery."

"Now, that's more likely. You'd not want him to lose the bits you like best, would you?" He dragged her into the woods. She fought, but he swung the knife up to her face and she stopped. He only dragged her as far as his horse.

He pulled a rope from his pack, formed a noose, and slipped it over her head. Was he going to strangle her?

But he mounted up and told her to walk. When they returned to her horse, he told her to mount.

"I'm going to take you to Hereward," he said. "He'll know what to do with you. Try to escape and you'll throttle."

With the heavy, coarse rope lying on her shoulders and fretting at her skin, Madeleine needed no further warning. They rode along the track for a little way before turning off into the dark woods. If this was the treatment meted out by the man, what could she expect from the master?

She told herself Hereward was Aimery's uncle, and an English nobleman, but she wasn't reassured. He was an outlaw rebel and surely hated all Normans. He'd find it very convenient to slit her throat. Then Aimery would have possession of Baddersley without the burden of her presence or the threat of her telling someone about Golden Hart.

Despite everything, though, she couldn't believe Aimery would condone her death.

She began to say very earnest prayers that Aimery was with Hereward. Even though that would confirm his treason, and he'd be furious with her for following him and discovering his treachery, he'd protect her.

They turned off the well-worn path onto tracks which were scarcely visible. The dense wood seemed peaceful and empty of all but birds and insects, but then suddenly a man was before them. He said nothing, just took in her companion and nodded, then melted back into the undergrowth.

A little later, she saw her captor raise a hand. She looked around, then up to see another watcher in a tree.

It was a well-guarded camp. Hereward was no fool.

Then they were entering the camp of Hereward the Wake. It was not in a clearing but merely a gathering among the trunks of great old trees. Odo may have overestimated the size of the force, but it was still substantial. There were two tents, at least thirty rugged armed men, and a number of others who appeared to be servants. There were no women.

There was no Aimery.

Madeleine's mouth dried as she became the focus of hard eyes in ruddy, bearded faces. A lone Norman woman among men who hated Normans. What mad impulse had brought her here?

A few wore mail, but most wore only leather armor; they all, however, had weapons to hand—spear, bow, sword, ax. They all wore gold. Not as much or as splendid as Aimery's, but gold all the same—signs of a great ring-friend.

A man moved out of the group and came forward. He wore no armor at all, only a finely worked tunic over braies. A sword hung at his belt in a magnificent scabbard of gold and jewels, and his bracelets and arm bands were the finest she had ever seen.

Madeleine knew she faced Hereward of Mercia.

He bore a distinct resemblance to Aimery. He had a beard and moustache, and his long blond hair was silvered at the temples, his eyes a clear blue, but in the bones of his face and body she saw how Aimery would look twenty years hence. There was a power to this man. His movements were quick and light, and energy shone in him like a beacon.

"Gyrth," he said, looking at her captor, "have you found an unwilling bride?"

Gyrth swung off his horse and knelt. "Nay, Lord, except it be Aimery's bride." With a smirk he added, "And him the unwilling one, according to Baddersley gossip."

"And you bring her here haltered?" Hereward's fist connected with his man's jaw, laying him flat out. He ignored Gyrth and turned to help Madeleine off her horse, then gently eased the rope over her head.

"My deepest apologies, Lady Madeleine. Niece. You will be treated with nothing but honor here." He drew her over to a cloak on the ground at the base of an oak and urged her to sit, then turned to his men.

"This is Lady Madeleine, wife to Aimery, my well-loved nephew. Treat her as my niece or surrender your rings." The men quietly returned to their activities.

He sat down beside her. "Can I have anything brought for you? Mead? Pure water? Food?"

Madeleine shook her head, which felt full of lambs-wool. "I need nothing. I . . . I thought Aimery would be here."

The blue eyes fixed on her questioningly. He suddenly reminded her of William of Normandy, who had just such a piercing look. What a pair they would make if they ever came to a meeting. "And why would he be here, Madeleine? He has not come near me since William invaded England."

Madeleine forced her wits to clear and faced him. "I expected him to be here because you sent for him."

His eyes twinkled. "I send for him regularly, and despite the fact that he wears my ring, he does not come."

Madeleine worked at hiding an onslaught of uncertainty. This man was saying Aimery was loyal. Was it possible that Aimery had gone about his proper business despite the message from Gyrth; that she had ridden into this nest of outlaws for no reason? After all, he'd left hours ahead of her and was not here. It was a frightening prospect, yet she was filled with joy.

He was not a traitor!

"Even if you thought Aimery had come to me," Hereward said gently, "how did you know *where* to come?"

Held by those powerful eyes, Madeleine forced herself not to warn him of the danger of attack. If Aimery wasn't here, she *had* to let the king prevail, even at cost of her own life. But it was hard to deny Hereward of Mercia anything. No wonder the Normans feared him as no other.

"Have you ever met William?" she asked.

He didn't press for an answer to his question but smiled. "Indeed. Back in 1051 when he came to visit Edward." His face reflected genuinely pleasant memories. "We were bold young men and found pleasure in each other's company. Even though we knew this day would come."

"You couldn't have known."

"No? Edward would have no children, and it was clear he'd promised William the crown."

"Then he has the right," Madeleine asserted, raising her chin. "Why do you fight him?"

He shook his head. "He has no right, Madeleine. A king of England is chosen by the people through the Witan, and they chose first Harold, then Edgar Atheling, who is therefore the true king. But we knew in other ways what was to come. William knew what he wanted, and I see the future."

He said the words so calmly it took a moment for them to register. "No one but God can see the future. That's blasphemy!"

He smiled, unmoved. "Not to my god."

Madeleine crossed herself in horror. "You are a pagan. What are you going to do with me?"

He laughed, showing teeth still white and healthy. "Sacrifice you on an altar to our bestial deity? I would not so distress my nephew." He made a sign and Gyrth came over. To Madeleine's surprise he sat companionably on the cloak, showing no resentment of that earlier blow, though he flashed an angry look at her.

"How did she find her way here?" Hereward asked him.

"I don't know. I saw her heading north on the old road and followed. She asked directions to Gormanby twice and found the track. I took her in charge. She says the Bastard has word of our being here."

Madeleine cursed herself for giving that information.

Hereward raised a brow. "A bit slow in telling me, aren't you?"

"Took a while to get my senses back," said Gyrth wryly.

Hereward turned back to Madeleine. "So, William is coming," he said thoughtfully. "Why do you say that?"

Madeleine refused to answer.

"What do you think, Gyrth?" mused Hereward. "Pull her fingernails out? Apply a hot iron to her feet? Or is she tender enough to crumble under a hard spanking?"

Madeleine closed her eyes and prayed for the strength not to be a greater traitor than she already was.

"Ah," said Hereward. "And here's the man for the job."

Madeleine told herself she could surely endure a spanking, even a vicious one. But a hot iron? She'd seen brave men scream under a cauterizing iron. *Sweet Mary Mother, help me in my hour of need!*

"By all that's holy, what are you doing here?"

Madeleine's eyes flew open to see an astonished, angry husband. She leaped to her feet and flung herself into his arms.

She heard him say, "What have you done to her?" and was amazed anyone dared take that tone with Hereward.

"Teased her, that's all. But it's not a teasing matter.

She says William has word of our presence and is planning an attack, but she won't give any details.''

Madeleine found herself pushed away and down onto the cloak, where Aimery settled in front of her. ''The whole story,'' he said curtly.

Madeleine stiffened, remembering her grievances against him *and* the fact that his presence here now proved him to be a traitor. ''There's no need for torture,'' she snapped. ''I came to rescue you, though I don't know why when I think of the way—''

His hand closed tightly on her arm. ''Stop that and tell your story.''

She took a deep, steadying breath. He was right. Time enough for recriminations later. ''Odo passed through Baddersley,'' she said. ''He'd heard rumor of Hereward being here and sent word to the king.''

Aimery looked at Hereward. ''Odo de Pouissey. There'd be no reason for him to lie.''

Hereward nodded. ''There's a traitor in Gormanby needs ferreting out, then.'' He made a sign and two men slipped off to the task. Madeleine shivered. ''And we'd best be away. When I face William, it will be on my own terms.''

''You're not joining Edwin and Gospatric?'' Aimery asked.

''Their rising is already dead. I wait for the right time, when all England will come together.''

Aimery shook his head. ''That will never be. England lost its chance in the first days. Then you could have flung us back, but not now.''

''And would have done, had I been here,'' said Hereward with bitter certainty. ''It was a cursed *wyrd* that took me to Byzantium that year.''

''It was *wyrd* all the same,'' said Aimery. ''Fate cannot be changed. You drummed that into my head. I am trying to follow that path. Are you?''

Hereward looked coldly at his nephew. ''I know the future. I know what it will be. I saw Harold die but not when. I saw William king, but not for how long. I see a future where English, not Norman French, is the language of this land again, for high and low. That day will come, and I will bring it here.''

Aimery nodded. ''If you have seen it, it will be so. But it will come about in its own time, not because you force it.''

Hereward shook his proud head. ''We will prevail.''

''How?'' demanded Aimery. ''With the likes of Edwin and Gospatric? Edwin, who just wants pretty clothes and a royal bride, and Gospatric, who's obsessed with keeping Northumbria from Waltheof. I swear he's only in this uprising out of fury that Waltheof got Judith of Huntingdon. These men will bring back English rule?''

Hereward looked beyond his nephew, beyond the woods, almost, it seemed, beyond the edges of the world. At the expression in his eyes a shiver ran down Madeleine's spine. ''William's line will not last in England even as far as his sons' sons,'' he said. Then he looked back, focused on them once more. ''The king of Denmark will aid us.''

''Danish rule instead of Norman?'' said Aimery with exasperation, but he did not scoff at the prophesy. Madeleine herself was badly shaken by it. William had three healthy sons and a fourth, possibly, on the way. There would be grandsons in time, so perhaps the Norman hold on the English throne would fail.

''Cnut was Danish,'' said Hereward. ''He came and lived within English laws, unlike the Norman who brings his own ways. Tell your royal godfather that Hereward will bow the knee when William the Bastard accepts English laws and throws out these French brigands he had brought over to steal our land.''

''Those French brigands won England for him and must be paid.'' Aimery stood and brushed off his clothes. ''Did you bring me here with a lie or do you need me?''

Hereward rose to join him. They were of a height, and though Hereward was heavier, the resemblance was astonishing. It was clear they also had the same stubborn will.

"No lie," said Hereward. "Will you help?"

"Of course." Aimery looked at Madeleine and drew his uncle off a ways before continuing the conversation. Angrily, she leaped to her feet to follow, but her husband glared back at her. "If you value your skin, sit down and keep your eyes and ears to yourself."

She obeyed, happy to let her weakened legs collapse. Oh, Sweet Mary, it was true. For all that he didn't appear to wholeheartedly support his uncle's beliefs, Aimery was willing to help him. It must be the ring-bond. She could understand. Had she not come here to commit treason out of love and the loyalty of the marriage bond? But the consequences, the consequences if his part ever was discovered.

Gyrth sat next to her like a guard. He had taken out his vicious knife and was sharpening it lovingly on a whetstone. She looked around and saw many of the men eyeing her as if she was a juicy morsel for the pot. But as her gaze met theirs they looked away.

She was safe, she supposed, under Hereward's protection, and Aimery's. Of course, that left the question of how safe she was from Aimery, though all she'd done was save his miserable skin. She knew enough about men, however, to know they hated to be in the wrong.

The conference ended, and Aimery rejoined her. "Come on. Let's get you out of here."

She scrambled to her feet. "And what about you?"

"That is none of your business." He stalked off toward their horses, and she had to follow or be abandoned. She was stopped by Hereward.

"I am delighted to have been given a chance to meet you," he said in perfect Norman French. "I hope we can meet again in happier days."

"Under English rule?" she queried. "I doubt I would be welcome."

"Aimery's wife will always be welcome, though I'm afraid I will have to relieve you of Baddersley."

Madeleine answered instinctively. "Over my dead body!"

He grinned. "If necessary. But then, perhaps I would allow you and Aimery to continue to care for the place for me." He laughed deeply. "How your eyes flash! I rejoice in you, my dear. I think perhaps you are worthy of my nephew." He kissed her lightly on both cheeks. "May your *wyrd* be Balder's way."

With that he left her, and she hurried to where Aimery was waiting. He looked preoccupied and exasperated, although not particularly with her. He helped her into her saddle. "Don't let Hereward charm you," he said bluntly.

She sniffed. "How could I? He's just an older version of you."

He glared at her and swung into his own saddle. They rode out of a camp which was already breaking up, the men ready to disappear back into the Fens. They followed the paths she had traveled with Gyrth. Did he know that the man had haltered her? Did he care? Would *he* have struck Gyrth down for the insult?

"Where are your men?" she asked him.

"Left north of here. That's why it took so long for me to get here. I didn't have the luxury of riding straight here, announcing my destination all along the north road."

"Don't snap at me. I came to save your wretched life!"

"The king's men could thresh around in this forest for months without finding Hereward if he didn't want to be found. You came after me because you wanted to come and I wouldn't let you."

She hissed through her teeth. "And what a fancy way you found to stop me."

"Believe me. Next time I'll just lock you up."

"If your mission here was innocent, there was no reason not to bring me with you!"

He reined in his horse and faced her. "Bring you into a nest of outlaws? And you a staunch Norman . . ."

"Are you saying you're *not* a staunch Norman?"

His hand flashed out and snared the front of her tunic.

Madeleine squeaked as she found herself inches from him. "You have a mischievous tongue, my lady."

"Let go of me," she said. "You have no right to bully me this way."

"I have every right in the world, Lady, do you force me to it." He let her go and urged his horse forward again. "We can reach Baddersley before dark if you are willing to ride hard. What excuse did you make to get out of there?"

Madeleine was bone-achingly weary after her day's adventures, but she made no complaint. "I said I was going to gather roots."

"Then claim to have been lost."

"What of your men? Shouldn't we collect them?"

"They'll wait. The fewer people who know you or I have been in this locality, the better. That's why we're going to slip through the forest for a while."

They rode in silence along deer tracks and footpaths, heading south, but often in winding ways. Then they rejoined the road and galloped. There was little traffic now that the sun was sinking, and they made good speed. Madeleine's body was one big, weary ache, her mind a fog of exhaustion, but she clung on, too proud to beg for a rest, and hoped her horse could follow him home.

At last they swung off onto the narrower road to Baddersley. Madeleine survived on the thought that their journey was nearly over.

Aimery drew up just out of sight of the castle. "You should be safe from here."

"You're not coming with me?" she exclaimed. He was going back, she knew it.

"I have matters to attend to which your foolishness has delayed."

"My *foolishness!*" If she hadn't been so weary, Madeleine would have hit him. "I promise you, Aimery de Gaillard, this is the last time I try to help you."

"I'd welcome that if I had any faith in your promises." He turned his horse sharply.

Madeleine shouted, "Well, have faith in this. You won't cozen me with your false lovemaking again. I know all your tricks now!"

"Do you think so?" She saw his white teeth flash in the gloom, but didn't know if it was a grin or a snarl. "Our next meeting should be interesting then, wife."

He galloped off into the dusk.

Chapter 17

A imery did not return. Madeleine had to face the fact that he had joined Hereward and was now serving him.

Hereward had asked, "Will you help?" And Aimery had answered, "Of course," without a trace of hesitation.

Madeleine spent sleepless nights and fretful days waiting for news of his capture, dreading his return to take up her challenge, longing to see him again.

When, three days after her mad adventure, Madeleine received her expected summons to join the queen, she was relieved. As she packed her chests with her finery and her medicinal supplies, she told herself that Aimery de Gaillard would be justly served. When he made his laggardly way home to his wife—with or without his *secrets*—and found her gone.

She had, after all, made a vow. A vow that she would not lie with him until she was sure he was loyal. And then she had told him she wouldn't be tricked by his lovemaking skills. Both promises would be much easier to keep with half of England between them.

Matilda had sent an escort for her. Madeleine had only to consult with Geoffrey, Hugh, and the good sisters to be sure the work at the manor would continue properly, then organize enough packhorses for all her baggage before she and Dorothy could enjoy a tranquil and easy day's journey to Hertford. There they would find the queen, who was resting before the journey north to join the king.

Six days after her parting from Aimery, Madeleine entered Hertford. The queen's train was lodged throughout the town, with the queen living in the sheriff's substantial house. Matilda greeted her warmly. "A married lady now, and wife to Aimery de Gaillard, of whom I have always been fond. I'm sure he is treating you well. He always had a way with the ladies."

Madeleine gritted her teeth behind her smile and politely agreed. "And you, Your Majesty. How are you?"

"As well as can be expected for a woman in my condition," the queen said wryly. "I carry babes easily, but at this stage it is easy for no woman."

Madeleine chanced a protest about the projected journey. "I cannot think it wise for you to be traveling at this stage of your pregnancy, Your Majesty."

But Matilda waved that away. "If I had let childbearing restrict my movements, I would have accomplished little. I go north by easy stages and will rest when I think it necessary. William wants the child to be born in York. It will be so."

York, thought Madeleine, but she could see Matilda was as determined on this path as her husband. But York. Not only was it far to the north, but that part of the country was barely under control as yet. The queen, however, went briskly off to attend to other business and left Madeleine in the hands of her daughter and niece.

Madeleine was delighted to meet Judith and Agatha again, though the latter seemed sullen and subdued. There was nothing subdued about Judith, however, who was blooming.

"So," the beauty said, "you have married Aimery de Gaillard. Lucky woman. He fired my blood, I must confess. I would envy you if I had not done as well or better."

"Your betrothed pleases you?"

Judith's sigh was eloquent affirmation. "I only wish we were married." She drew Madeleine a little way from

Agatha. "It will be such a relief to have you here," she whispered. "Poor Agatha is so upset because the king won't settle her betrothal. And now that the Earl of Mercia has fled to raise rebellion, she's terrified he's going to be executed. I wouldn't have thought Edwin had it in him to pose that much danger to my uncle, but people can be surprising. Look at Agatha. She was even talking at one point of running off to join the earl and live with him out of wedlock!"

"That would stir the country." Madeleine glanced in surprise at the girl, who had always been so quiet and shy. "And could well cost Edwin dearly if the king did not let them wed as a result."

"Cost him his balls, you mean," said Judith bluntly, causing Madeleine's face to burn. "Jesu," added Judith. "Over a month wed, and she can still blush. I was hoping you could extend my education, but you still seem a little nun to me."

Madeleine thought of a lovemaking session by a cornfield and wished blushing were under human control. "I should think your education will be extended soon enough," Madeleine countered. "When is the wedding to be?"

Judith sighed. "Later. After my new cousin is born. I hope at least by Christmas." She lowered her voice. "I burn for him, Mad. Do you know what I mean?"

Madeleine nodded. She certainly did. And now, even if they should happen to meet, she had a sacred vow between her and Aimery which was likely to keep them apart forever. She couldn't exactly regret her vow, for it was right. She must be firm against treason, and he was so easily able to use her lust against her.

But she burned.

"Perhaps Agatha feels the same," she suggested to Judith. "You should sympathize."

Judith pulled a face. "I just find her and Edwin such unlikely tragic lovers, and it's not as if she actually carried out her plan. An attack of the gripe dampened her ardor.

She's only just emerged from her room after it . . ." She broke off and grimaced. "What a cat I am. She really was ill, for there was no sign of her for nearly a week, just Aunt Matilda constantly dashing into the sickroom quite haggard with concern, and these moaning noises. I did offer to assist, but they feared it was catching. But now that she's recovered, she has abandoned her plan. If they tried to separate me from Waltheof, I would go to him no matter how weak I was."

"Do you both go north, then?" Madeleine asked, intrigued by this Waltheof, for she had thought Judith too aware of her own charms to be so smitten by a mere male.

"No. That's Waltheof's hereditary land, though he doesn't have the title. I don't think the king trusts him there, for he's much loved. We're to go to Winchester under heavy chaperonage and guard. Agatha, too." She sighed. "Even though I sympathize with her, you can see she is hardly the person to want to chatter of love and kisses these days. I welcome the time we have together, you and I."

Madeleine thought she would disappoint in that regard, but she dutifully listened to Judith's ecstatic description of Waltheof—his amazing strength, his wit, his learning, his power to stir the blood.

She formed a picture of a gigantic saint and was bemused when she was finally introduced to the man. He was only a little heavier built than Aimery, and yet his strength was legendary. If he was learned, he did not demonstrate it before her. But his ability to stir the blood, that she could appreciate.

He was handsome and remarkably graceful in his movements, but there was something in his deep-set amber eyes which caused even her nerves to flutter. Judith, she saw, was close to swooning. It was to be hoped the effect diminished when this passion was allowed to run its course, or Judith was unlikely to be any use to anyone for the rest of her born days.

Waltheof sat beside his betrothed and took her hand as

if that were the most natural thing for a man to do. Aimery had never done such a thing. "I'm delighted to meet the Baddersley heiress at last," he said to Madeleine in excellent French.

Perhaps it was the way he sat so close to Judith, the way he held her hand, the way he smiled at her that turned Madeleine sour. "And I'm delighted to meet the man who's supposed to be descended from a bear," she taunted.

He took no offense but smiled enigmatically. "I grow fur at the full moon, Lady Madeleine." He raised his betrothed's hand and kissed the tip of one finger, holding Judith with his golden eyes. "I'm sure my wife will find it amusing. She can comb it." Madeleine could almost see Judith melt. "But remember," he added lightly, turning back to Madeleine, "my grandmother was not a bear, but a faery-bear. It makes a difference."

Madeleine cast a startled glance at Judith, who seemed to be swallowing this tale whole, in as much as she had a sane thought left in her lustful head. Madeleine had expected this sophisticated man to treat his mythical ancestry as fanciful nonsense, but that wasn't so. Did he believe in faeries?

"You should sympathize, Lady Madeleine," he said. "You, too, were a creature of legend not so long ago. Speculation about your fate was our principal entertainment."

"Did you win or lose?" asked Madeleine tartly.

He laughed. "I don't gamble. I judge Aimery de Gaillard to have won, however."

It was a pretty compliment, and Madeleine bit back a sour response. She was alarmed by how easy it was to be acerbic in the face of Waltheof and Judith's unity. She began to sympathize with Agatha, and wondered if the girl's plan to flee hadn't been inspired as much by a desire to get away from these two as a desire to join Edwin of Mercia. Madeleine certainly felt the need to escape. Even a week of the gripe appeared attractive. She made her excuses and left.

One thing she had noted was that Waltheof carried a skin mark on his right hand, as Aimery said they all did. She thought it was a bear. It reminded her of the ever-present danger of someone recognizing the design and linking it with Golden Hart. At least when Aimery was with Hereward that danger was lessened.

She realized she'd left the lovers together and wondered if she was supposed to play chaperone. She decided Judith and Waltheof were either controlling themselves or nothing on earth would restrain them. Or him, rather. Madeleine thought that if anyone was in control, it was Waltheof.

Was his apparent love genuine, she wondered as she went in search of the queen's chamberlain to discover her quarters. As long as she had been with Waltheof and Judith, she had been certain the feeling between them was real, and on Judith's side she was sure that was so. But on his?

She had reason to know men could play a pretty part when it suited them, and it must suit an Englishman like Waltheof to be so closely linked with the Norman royal family. Perhaps she should extend Judith's education and explain to her just how deceitful men could be, and how easy a skillful man found it to cozen a woman.

With this in mind she told herself she was fortunate to be free of Aimery. She would be with the queen's train for at least three months. Her lust for her husband should have burned out by the time they met again.

She found Gilbert, the chamberlain, and asked where her baggage should be put, expecting it to be in the queen's solar or perhaps in an ante-room with the other attendants. "You have a chamber, Lady Madeleine." He summoned an attendant to guide her.

Madeleine was surprised and gratified by the honor. A private room, no matter how small, in such a crowded place was a mark of distinction. She followed the servant

up steep wooden stairs to the second floor. They passed
through two rooms with curtained beds—one possibly occupied, as the curtains were drawn. As well as the beds,
the rooms were full of chests, pieces of armor and clothing, and straw mattresses. Hertford was definitely crowded.
She must have misunderstood Gilbert. She was doubtless
being taken to share a room with half a dozen other
women.

Then the man flung open the door to a corner room
which would offer much valued privacy, as it was at the
end of the house. The clutter was markedly less, and there
were only two chests and a few other items in the room.

Masculine items.

A gold armband left carelessly on top of a small jewel
chest caught the sun and her eye. She knew that snarling
dragon with its emerald eyes. She knew that chest.

Madeleine turned to the man. "Lord Aimery . . . ?"

"Is out, Lady. But he will return for the evening meal.
I will send your baggage and people here to you."

Madeleine looked around numbly.

But he was with Hereward, doing that "service" he
had promised. How could he be here? Straight from that
encounter with Waltheof, she began to think of faery crea-
tures who could be in two places at the same time. Then
more unpleasant thoughts pushed out the whimsical. Could
his service for Hereward be the basest form of treachery—
spying?

She walked about the room among his familiar possessions and smelled his familiar aroma, which she hadn't
been aware, till then, of missing. Her foolish body
hummed with delight when she touched his red tunic, as
her mind wondered how she would keep her vow and turn
him from treachery.

She couldn't stop fingering things. His bone comb with
blond hairs still in it. A wool cloak tossed carelessly on a
chair. The heavy gold armband lying on top of his jewel
chest. She tutted at such carelessness. The chest, as she

had supposed, was locked, and so she picked up the precious item.

What to do with it until her own chest was brought up? She tried putting it on her arm, but it was far too large. After a moment, with a mischievous smile, she stretched it a little more and clasped it just above her knee. She felt it there as if it were his hand. He'd never placed a loving hand on her thigh. When she came to think of it, Aimery de Gaillard had never touched her with gentleness except to serve his own devious plans.

No, that time when he'd thought he'd broken her arm, he'd been gentle for just a moment then.

She knew it would be wiser to take the thing off, but there was wanton delight in having it there. Dorothy bustled in, commanding servants carrying chests, and it was not the time to be raising her skirts.

It took some time to place the chests out of the way and remove the items which would be needed. Gowns had to be hung so the creases would fall out. Some of Aimery's possessions had to be moved. Madeleine looked for a mattress for Dorothy and found none.

"You will have to arrange for something to sleep on," she told the maid as she took off her traveling kirtle and tunic and her heavy linen wimple. She remembered the armband around her thigh, but she could imagine Dorothy's expression if she were to remove it in her sight. Hastily, she pulled on a blue silk kirtle fine enough for court and a darker blue silk tunic. It was richly embroidered in dark red and silver and set with blue-glass plaques to form the bodies of fish around the neck and sleeves. It was second only in richness to the tunic she had worn for her wedding, and unused since her days at the queen's court in Rouen.

If she had to face Aimery, she would do it proudly.

Dorothy began to comb out her hair. "There's a maids' room downstairs, Lady. I am to sleep there."

Aimery and she would be here alone? "I think I prefer

to have you closer in case I need anything." Such as protection.

"What would you need in the middle of the night, Lady? I haven't slept in your room since you married."

"You will be more comfortable here than crushed together with the maids," Madeleine protested.

"Think to your own comfort and that of your husband," Dorothy retorted as she began to form two fat plaits in Madeleine's hair. "The queen has apparently gone to some effort to put such newlyweds together. You can't spoil it for her."

Madeleine felt in a very spoiling mood. "Does Lord Aimery know I am summoned?" she asked.

"I don't know, Lady, but I doubt it. I was speaking to Maria, the queen's laundress, and she said it was to be a surprise for him."

"How wonderful," said Madeleine bleakly.

By the time the bell rang for the evening meal, there had been no sign of Aimery other than the eruption into the room of a lanky youth with freckles, who jerked to a halt, started to apologize and leave, and then looked around and realized he was in the right room after all.

He gave a hesitant bow. "My lady?"

Madeleine suppressed a grin. "You must be in Lord Aimery's train," she said tactfully, not sure if he was servant or squire. "I am Lady Madeleine, his wife."

The young man went pink and bowed again. "My apologies, Lady. We were not expecting you, I don't think."

"And you are?" Madeleine prompted.

"Thierry de Pontrouge, Lady." He bowed again. "Squire to Lord Aimery." From his bashful pride she judged it was clearly a very new appointment. It was not surprising though, for Geoffrey was of an age to become his own man.

"Greetings, Thierry. I hope you will be willing to do me a small service now and then when your duties to Lord Aimery permit."

He smiled widely. "Oh yes, Lady."

"Well then," said Madeleine, affecting a casual air, "do you know where my husband is?"

"He went out to find more horses for the baggage train, Lady. He will be back at any time."

He was not back, however, by the time the second bell told Madeleine she had to go down for the meal. They would meet in public then. Was that a good thing or not?

She was halfway down the stairs when she felt the rub of the gold band around her leg. Jesu! She stopped to run back and lock it in her chest, but then the last ring of the bell summoned, and she ran down instead before she was late. Matilda hated people to be late for meals.

Though she had been unaware of the gold enough to forget about it, now it seemed to burn her skin, and she imagined everyone in the hall was able to see it there, feel its weight, hear the slight rub of it against the linen of her shift.

What would Aimery think if he ever found out? There was no reason he should . . . But he might miss it . . . He might believe it stolen . . .

She was seriously thinking of making some excuse and rushing back upstairs when she was firmly directed to a place at the high table beside Agatha. She saw no sign of Aimery, though a space remained empty at her side which could be for him. She began to fret that his wickedness might already have caught up with him, imagined him already in chains.

As the food was served a trio of musicians played on pipe, horn, and drum. It was music to encourage order and tranquility. Matilda managed her court with a firm hand. Madeleine was surprised by a twinge of nostalgia for the meals during the king's stay at Baddersley—the flowing drink, the loud voices, and the hearty songs of war and lust.

She talked to Agatha in a desultory manner of fashion and a cure for croup. Agatha certainly wasn't lively company these days. As the time passed, her concern over Aimery grew pressing.

She saw him as soon as he entered. It was as if a bell rang and torches flared. He had not stopped to freshen himself and was windblown and dusty, but hale and hearty. Madeleine felt a spurt of pure irritation, followed by a surge of pure relief.

He bowed to Matilda but slipped into a place at the far end of the room among the men-at-arms. Madeleine wondered if he was avoiding her, but there was no indication he'd even seen her. He'd doubtless chosen his place just because he was dusty and late. She watched him.

He was more at ease than she'd ever seen him—healthily tired and hungry, relaxed among men. He seemed popular. His corner of the hall became a beacon of high spirits and laughter. Madeleine glanced anxiously at Matilda, but the queen looked indulgent. Again Madeleine wondered how Aimery could bear to work against two people who loved him so, who were willing to shower him with favors.

Madeleine waited for him to become aware of her as she had been instantly aware of him. It didn't happen. Then finally—perhaps as a result of her fixed gaze—he looked up. He found her. A piece of meat halted on its way to his mouth.

Did the room really hush, the music stop? Did her heartbeat echo in the silence?

His smile set, then relaxed. He inclined his head, popped the food into his mouth, and turned to speak to the man on his right.

Madeleine realized the activities of the room had not been disturbed, though she felt as if she had passed through a whirlwind.

Over the course of the meal she glanced frequently over at her husband and never caught his eyes on her.

When the meal was all but over, a page was sent to summon Aimery up to the queen. Madeleine hoped he would be scolded for being late and untidy, but Matilda smiled and laughed with him before gesturing Madeleine to his side.

"Madeleine," said the queen, "this cannot be quite the surprise I planned, since Aimery was obliged to be away when you arrived, but I hope you will not find your time attending me so arduous with your husband by your side."

"Attendance on you could never be arduous, Your Majesty," said Madeleine. Dear Lord, did this mean he was to be part of the queen's escort all the way to York?

"And you, Aimery? I know you have often found court duties tedious, but I was sure you would rather endure that than be deprived of your new wife for so many weeks."

"We thank you for your consideration, Your Majesty." He took Madeleine's hand and squeezed it, a similar action to Waltheof's but in this case threatening. It said, act pleased.

Madeleine forced a smile. "Indeed yes, Your Majesty." She turned the smile at Aimery. "We have had so little . . . *intimacy.*" She tugged to free her hand. His grip tightened until she was forced to stop.

His smile widened. "Our weeks of marriage have flown, have they not, love? Except the last week when we have been apart. Have the days dragged for you, the nights seemed bleak?"

"I have been sleepless," she admitted, hoping he caught the edge. "Lying awake wondering where you were . . ."

"Only a call to service could have taken me away."

Madeleine could not suppress a gasp at his audacity. She raised her chin. "No true woman would begrudge the monarch the *loyal* service of her man."

"And no true monarch," broke in the queen, amused, "would begrudge her vassal the *service* of his or her spouse. You have permission to retire and find a place more suitable for . . . private conversation."

There was no way to protest. Madeleine meekly went with Aimery out of the hall and up the stairs toward their room. As soon as they were out of the queen's sight, however, she hissed, "Would you care to stop breaking my fingers?"

Chapter 18

He released them, but it was clear she had only one acceptable destination. If she attempted any other it would be back to finger-breaking. Madeleine stalked ahead of him toward their chamber. The queen's intention had been perfectly clear. Would he try to take his ease on her body again?

Once in the room and with the door closed, he stood against it with his arms folded. "What's wrong?" he asked.

"Wrong?"

His suspicious eyes judged this innocent response and found it wanting. "I was surprised to see you here. You can't have been as surprised to see me. So why were you snarling at me down there?

She turned away. "I can't help but wonder when I find you have accepted a position at the queen's court with never a word to me. What exactly is your role here?"

"Marshal. My messenger must have crossed your party." He was close behind her. His hands were on her shoulders before she expected them, sending a shock of feeling she could not disguise. It was combined with another shock. Marshal? He was in *charge* of the queen's journey north? Surely she couldn't allow this. Not when she knew him to be plotting against the king. She resisted his hands, but he turned her around. He saw her expression and frowned, but then smiled. "Could it be you're jealous?"

Madeleine opened her eyes very wide. "Is there someone I should be jealous of?" He was feeling amorous, damn him. So was she, but she had a vow which held even more strongly now. What was she to do?

"That's for you to find out," he teased. "Having a wife along will doubtless restrict my activities. I don't know. I've never tried it before." His hands flexed gently over her collarbones. His knowing fingers played at her nape. Madeleine could feel her wanton body fight the restraints she was forcing on it.

Her breathing could not be controlled, nor her color. She saw his eyes darken, his cheeks flush with desire . . .

She twisted out of his hold and stalked across the room. "Don't let my presence bother you too much," she said tartly. "I have a job to do, and so do you. I doubt we'll see much of each other."

It was as if she'd pulled a weapon on him. His eyes turned cold, and he moved as a man moves with a sword.

"Do you?" he said, stalking her. "Yet you've traveled with a court and know how it will be. Especially with a heavily pregnant woman. Slow, stately, lots of time for . . . amusements."

He was barely an arm's length away, and she had placed herself against the wall with nowhere to retreat. He'd warned her about that. She tried to hold him off with words. "I'm not going to allow you to use my body."

He stopped. "Allow?"

Madeleine swallowed but did not reply. She was breathing in deep drafts as if fighting for her life.

The danger passed and he relaxed, looking merely curious. "Is this because of the last time, and what I said? I confess, I didn't want to admit how much I desired you that day. I thought I'd made it up to you. If not, I will." He moved a relaxed step forward.

Madeleine whipped out her knife. His knife. His gift. "I have vowed not to lie with you."

He froze. "Unless you intend to try to kill me," he said quietly, "put that away."

Madeleine didn't know how she had come to this pass. He was angry now as she'd never seen him. Coldly angry. With every sense alert for the disarming she knew she could not avoid, she said, "You taught me to defend myself against rape."

He was absolutely still. "A man can't rape his wife."

"Call it what you will. My body will feel the same."

She could see his chest rise and fall with every breath he took. "I give you my word, Madeleine, I will not force you. Put away the knife."

"You gave me your word you'd not fight for the rebels!" she cried with all the agonized betrayal in her soul.

But that moment of anger fractured her concentration. His foot brought her down as his hand wrenched the blade free and sent it spinning to quiver in the wooden wall.

Madeleine was flat on her back at his feet. She closed her eyes. What now? Rape? A whip? Both?

Eventually she couldn't bear the waiting and looked hesitantly up the long length of him till she found his set, somber face. "Never do that again," he said, then turned and left the room.

Madeleine rolled over and buried her head in her hands. She wished she could weep, but her grief was a cold stone in her chest, not liquid at all.

Eventually, she pushed wearily to her knees and then to her feet. She saw the knife in the wall, and went to take it. It would not pull free. She had to work with both hands for some time to get it out. The depth to which it had been driven into the oak told of his leashed fury.

He hadn't touched her. Perhaps he hadn't dared to.

And she would have the battle to fight again next time.

Madeleine didn't know where Aimery had gone, but she knew he would have to return. She dreaded that moment.

She picked up a book, then needlework, but could apply herself to neither. She ran over the quarrel again and again in her mind. She shouldn't have bared a blade, but she was honor-bound to uphold her vow to the death. If he tried to demand his rights, she would have to do the same again. She shivered at the thought.

He had promised not to force her. But he'd promised not to fight for the rebels, and she'd heard him say he would help Hereward . . .

He wasn't actually *fighting* for the rebels, but he'd never promised not to *work* for them, help them, spy for them.

All this meant she might be able to trust his word, but in other respects it terrified her. Exactly what service was Aimery de Gaillard doing for Hereward the Wake as marshal of the queen's party?

The light was going when Dorothy tapped and entered coyly. The woman stopped, astonished to find Madeleine alone. She had brought a jug of hot water and some food and wine.

"Lord Aimery just left for a few moments," Madeleine explained, then saw Dorothy take in her undisturbed clothes and the undisturbed bed. Madeleine was still in full court dress after over two hours here, supposedly with her husband. There was no explanation to offer, so Madeleine tried none, but allowed Dorothy to undress her.

When she was in her shift, Madeleine remembered the armband and hurriedly requested the woman to brush her hair. She had to get the band off. It would be infinitely better to reveal her foolishness to Dorothy than to Aimery, but she hoped to avoid both. How soon could she reasonably tell the woman to stop the brushing and leave?

She was about to speak the words when Aimery walked into the room. He checked himself slightly but then continued in. "Dorothy, I hope you are comfortably situated here."

Dorothy bobbed a curtsy. "Yes, Lord."

"Good. You may seek your bed then."

Madeleine thought of objecting, but it would merely postpone the confrontation.

When the door closed on the woman, he said nothing.

He ignored Madeleine, casually stripped off his still-dusty clothing, and dropped it in a corner. He'd never stripped in her presence before. She'd longed to see his naked body, but now it was an insult. He kept his belt in his hand and took a key out of his pouch. He went over to his jewel chest and opened it to put away his ornaments.

She saw him frown thoughtfully and look around.

There was no putting it off. She tried to ease her shift up slowly and slip the armband off but found she needed two hands to loosen it.

He watched, astonished.

She held it out, helplessly silent.

He took it and considered her bare leg thoughtfully.

Madeleine drew her skirt down and climbed under the bedcovers. He placed his bracelet in the chest and locked it, then came over and joined her in bed, not touching.

"You believe I will not rape you," he said flatly.

He was an ominous presence, and yet she did trust his word. "Yes."

"That is something." He turned away to sleep.

A bell woke the household the next morning.

Madeleine was surprised to find she had slept, but a day's traveling and all the subsequent strains had finally pushed her into oblivion. Aimery had appeared to sleep immediately, but if so he had slept long, for the bell dragged him unwillingly from sleep.

He stretched, touched her, flinched away.

Warily, their eyes met. He looked away, up at the canopy. "What is this vow you have made?"

Madeleine also looked up, at a spot some two feet from the spot which interested him. "Not to lie with you until I am sure you are loyal."

"You've lain with me all night," he pointed out.

"You know what I mean."

"I wondered how literal you were going to be." There was a trace of humor in his voice. She sensed he was going to try a softer approach and steeled herself against it.

"It is a vow, and I will keep it," she said firmly. "You must be true to the king."

"I promised not to rape you, and you laid down with me in a bed. If I give you my word that I am completely loyal to William, will you not believe it?"

Madeleine closed her eyes. "How can I?" she asked wearily. "I heard you with my own ears promise to help Hereward."

She felt the bed move and looked to see him standing there, naked and beautiful. And cold. "You needn't worry about your vow," he said. "I will not *lie* with a woman who will not take my word as true."

He turned away, pulled some clothes out of a chest, and dressed. As he buckled his belt he spoke in the calm, detached voice which had become so familiar to her during those terrible weeks at Baddersley. "The queen fancies us lovebirds, however. It would be cruel to disillusion her, especially so late in her pregnancy, when I understand all women, even queens, are inclined to be emotional. If I can play the part in public, can I expect you to cooperate?"

They would have to meet hour by hour, day by day, then come together each night in a bed. "Yes," she said.

Without another word, he left.

Madeleine threw herself into the work of the court, and stayed close to the queen and her ladies. She worked with them on altar cloths, read aloud to the queen as she rested, played games with Judith and Agatha, and helped Dame Adele, the midwife, organize all that would be necessary for the birth and the care of the babe.

This portly lady was scathing. "Traipsing about the country at such a time. No good will come of it, mark my words. And who'll be held to blame? We will."

Madeleine feared the woman was right, and she had the shocking thought that the easiest wickedness to accomplish on this journey would be to cause both queen and babe to die. Would Aimery sink so low?

He appeared to be working hard to secure Matilda's comfort, gathering supplies and inspecting carts, pack-horses, and men. In the first few days, he and Madeleine met only at meals, and he showed no sign of a guilty conscience. They spoke pleasantly to each other, but it was easy to avoid a show of intimacy. In fact, Matilda complimented Madeleine on her discreet behavior, contrasting it favorably with Judith's.

Madeleine saw more of Odo than she did of Aimery. Odo had command of the advance guard, but seemed to find nothing to do by way of preparation. Madeleine remarked on this fact one day.

"Good set of men," said Odo complacently. "Used to this kind of thing. We're all ready to go when your husband stops twitching around like a nervous nun."

Madeleine drew herself up. "I can tell you from experience, Odo, that nuns are not of a nervous disposition, having great faith in the Lord. It would be the act of a fool to set off to the northern wilderness unprepared."

"Playing the dutiful wife?" he sneered. "I don't forget how reluctant you were. Rumor said you had to be beaten to it."

She colored. "Rumor lies, as always."

He looked at her. She knew that even though he pretended not to want her or Baddersley, the loss still stung, and he resented being under Aimery's command. He'd do him harm if he could. Thank heavens he'd not find a way, unless he discovered Aimery's treason. She realized he would expect her to mention his plan to capture Hereward. "By the way," she said with studied indifference, "what happened in that matter of the rebels?"

"Which matter?" he said with a scowl.

"When you stopped at Baddersley, didn't you say you'd sent word to the king about rebels nearby, perhaps even Hereward? Were they caught? Were you rewarded?"

He turned red. "All England would be ringing with

news of Hereward's capture, and do I look as if I've been magnificently rewarded?''

She worked at appearing as if her mind was really on other matters. "It was a mistake? That's unfortunate, but surely you acted as you should.''

He studied her as if seeking to strip away layers. "Or perhaps they were warned. But how would they be warned?''

Madeleine knew she would have been wiser not to have raised the subject, but she met his eyes blandly. "A goodly part of England sympathizes with Hereward and his sort, Odo. I doubt William's army could advance with nobody noticing.''

"By the time William's army approached, they were long gone. Rumor says they left the day after I passed through the area, the very day I spoke to you about it.''

She shrugged. "Perhaps their business was done.''

"Or perhaps they were warned,'' he said again, "by a friend of Golden Hart.'' There was no doubt that he was suspicious. "The man who sold me the information was found spread-eagled.''

Madeleine swallowed. "What does that mean?''

He laughed sharply. "Ask your Saxon husband, whom you defend so well.''

Madeleine was left trembling. She wouldn't have thought Odo shrewd enough to put the pieces together, but she'd underestimated him. He had nothing except spite and envy to go on, but he was suspicious. If Aimery tried anything treasonous with Odo nearby, Madeleine might not be able to shield him from detection.

Especially as her main task *had* to be to protect the queen and her babe.

That evening after the meal, she found herself apart with Aimery for a little while. They stood close and smiled, Aimery holding her hand, playing their part for the queen.

"Odo suspects something about that business at Halver Wood,'' she said, peeping coyly up at him through her lashes.

"He'd be a fool if he didn't, and he's not that much of a fool." He dropped a warm kiss on her knuckles, and it still softened her, even though it was only done for effect.

"You are not to kill him," she said, looking straight into his eyes.

Those eyes flashed angrily, though he held the smile. "I have never killed to conceal my activities, and never will."

"Very noble when you have others do the killing for you," she retorted. "The informer in Gormanby was found spread-eagled. What does that mean?"

He paled and looked away toward the crowded room. "It's an old Viking custom. A man's breastbone is slit so that his ribs spring. He suffocates."

Madeleine couldn't maintain her smile. "That's horrible."

"No more so than blinding with hot iron, or chopping off feet and hands."

"But it was done for you."

He turned back. "It was done by Hereward for his cause. A clear message to all that such petty betrayals are not worth the silver. He'd have spread-eagled you or me if he thought it advantageous."

"I don't believe that!"

Aimery smiled again, but it was wry. "Caught you, did he? Be warned. Hereward is noble and kind and can snare hearts and minds with a word. He is also utterly ruthless in pursuit of a cause. He would despise himself to be less. His mind is more Norse than English, and he truly believes life is nothing—the experience of a bird who flies in one window of a hall and shortly flies out of another. The only significance in death is that a person meet it nobly and gain *iof*, the fame that lives forever."

Madeleine wondered just how much of this philosophy Aimery shared. "And yet you serve him," she said.

"I am his ring-friend, oath-bound to him."

"You have other oath-bonds."

"And I honor them. Smile, wife, or people will think us less than deliciously happy."

Madeleine smiled, though it hurt. "You can't serve two warring masters!"

He snared her and pulled her against him. Madeleine stiffened, but here in the hall she could not struggle. "I honor my vows—all of them—as best I can."

She would have argued, but his lips silenced her. Madeleine tried to be passive, but the taste of his mouth, the warmth of his body, stirred her like a love philtre. The pain of desire suddenly shot through her, arching her like a bow in his arms. He held her tight.

Then abruptly he pushed her away, turned, and left. Madeleine shakily returned to the safety of the queen's side, wondering what would happen when it was time to retire. She was so easily overcome.

They had established a pattern which was generally safe. Madeleine always removed to their room first, going up when the queen went to bed. Aimery came later, and she pretended to be asleep. He left the bed as soon as the bell rang. She stayed in it until he had left the room.

That night she lay there nervously, waiting for him to come. She was bracing herself to fight while her body begged for the release of love. She heard the door open, listened to the familiar sounds of him undressing. She felt the bed move as he joined her and knew by the careful distance and his stillness that this night would be just like all the others. Tears dampened her lashes.

Later she woke from a lovely dream to find it real. Her body was fitted against his, her back to his warm torso, his arm around her, brushing her nipples with each breath she took. His head rested against her shoulder, and each of his sleeping breaths stirred her hair.

She knew she should move, but instead her arm came up to cradle his against her. How had they come to this pass? How could she find a way out for both of them? Only by turning him away from treason.

When she awoke in the morning he was already gone,

and she had no idea if they had slept that way all night, or if he knew it.

The next day Matilda summoned Aimery to her solar to play for her. The queen's back was aching, and Madeleine was rubbing it. Aimery sat to tune his lyre.

"Come now," said the queen. "You may greet your wife with a kiss, Aimery. Don't stand on formality with me."

He came over and dropped a soft, warm kiss on Madeleine's lips. She accepted it as a proper wife should and smiled at him demurely. The queen nodded, then relaxed under the influence of the massage and the music.

Eventually she indicated Madeleine could stop, and called one of her ladies to make music. Aimery was not dismissed, however, but subjected to a thorough review of the plans for the journey.

"So all is in order," said Matilda at last.

"Yes, Your Majesty."

"Then we had best be on our way. I fear this child will be a hasty one, and it is to be born in York."

Madeleine and Aimery shared a glance. Did Matilda think she could keep the child in her womb by force of will? Doubtless she did.

"How many miles a day do you think we will make?" the queen asked.

"I hope for twenty, as long as we are on the old roads and the weather is good."

Matilda grimaced. "It would be a great deal simpler if I could ride." She flashed a humorous look around her ladies. "I warn you, you will have to take turns with me in the litter, reading to me and playing chess."

It was clear some of the ladies would be only too pleased by that duty, but Madeleine sympathized with the queen. She hated a dawdling journey in a curtained box.

"After Lincoln," said Aimery, "you could travel to York by water if you wished."

The queen considered this idea with great interest.

"Water travel would be much more comfortable. There is a good waterway?"

"Indeed, yes. There is a Roman canal from Lincoln to the Trent, which links with the Ouse at Airmyn. That river will take us to York. But we would not be able to take all the escort by water, just your ladies and a personal guard."

The queen considered it. "But the rest of the men surely could keep pace with us, and be not far away."

"Yes."

Matilda nodded. "Then make the arrangements, and let us be on our way. The sooner we are in York, the better."

The next day the queen's train finally worked its way out of Hertford.

In front was Odo's advance guard, who were to be sure the road was passable and safe.

The main party consisted of ten carts containing provisions, bedding, animals, and the more elderly servants. At the center was the queen's gilded litter. It was hung with fine silk curtains to allow her to see out while being shielded from the dust, and heavier blue damask curtains for privacy. Nearby rode those ladies and clerics who chose not to use the carts.

This central group was watched over by the queen's personal guard under the command of tough old Fulk d'Aix.

Behind were some mounted servants and a rear guard commanded by Allan de Ferrers, a young but taciturn nephew of the queen's.

Madeleine knew there were also men out on foot, some of whom had left days before to scout the countryside and woodland all along the queen's route and ensure there were no lurking rebels or outlaws. It would take a small army to face this entourage.

Madeleine was pleased to be on horseback instead of in a bone-shaking cart or a confined litter. As she looked at the party, with its banners snapping in the breeze and the gleaming spears and mail, she felt pride that this was Aimery's work. She had to admit he had done well.

She had been watching him carefully. After all, if he was up to no good, the simplest thing would be for him to mishandle his job so that the queen became easy prey for Hereward.

It would not be so simple, though. Odo was suspicious, and Fulk would certainly notice any shortcomings in the queen's protection and move instantly to correct them. Nor could Aimery give wrong orders at the time of an attack, for though he was in overall command, his role was much more administrative than military. It was for the guard captains to react to threats. Aimery's job was to anticipate and prevent danger and get this cumbersome entourage to York before the babe's birth.

Madeleine looked ahead to where Aimery was riding alongside a cart, speaking to the driver. It was a wonder he wasn't turning gray with the responsibility.

Nor could he be comfortable. He, like all the fighting men, was dressed in full armor—chain mail to the knees, leather boots reinforced with metal plaques, and a conical helmet with a nosepiece. All this was worn over leather and wool. In the August heat, he must be sweltering. Thierry rode proudly nearby with Aimery's shield hung at his saddle, and when he caught Madeleine's eye he gave a cheery wave.

She waved back.

They stopped the first night at Royston, no great distance from Baddersley. There was no question of privacy here. Madeleine slept with the queen's ladies and had no idea where Aimery slept.

She missed him, and tossed and turned all night.

The next day she was irritable and weary as they trundled their way to Huntingdon.

"Come, come," Matilda teased during the midday break. "So ill-humored, Madeleine, after one night away from your husband's arms? Pity we poor ladies who have not seen our men in a month or more."

Madeleine knew her face was fiery. "It's not that, Your Majesty," she muttered. "I just did not sleep well."

"Maybe," said Matilda. "But Huntingdon is spacious. We must ensure you have a chamber tonight."

Madeleine looked around at all the smirks and burned with embarrassment. There was no point in protesting for it would only upset the queen.

This romantic interference was not typical of Matilda, but the midwife, Adele, had told Madeleine it was often so. Women grew slower in the last weeks, and an active woman grew bored and was likely to take up a petty interest. Madeleine's marriage appeared to be Matilda's petty interest.

In Huntingdon, therefore, Madeleine and Aimery were allocated a private room.

Chapter 19

As Dorothy found the few things they would need for one night, Madeleine eyed the bed. It was considerably smaller than the one at Hertford. She doubted it would be possible for two people to lie in it and not touch. Her skin tingled. She would like to lie against him again, even if that was all they could have. She longed for more. She longed for ease, and laughter, and love, and the expression of it in mating. There would be none of that, however, until she could give him her trust.

She tried to debate with her conscience. Could she not say he had proved himself honorable? After all, he was protecting the queen as a true knight should . . .

But she dismissed such sophistry. She had already decided he had had no opportunity as yet for mischief. Perhaps if they finally arrived in York without incident, she could accept it.

But in that case, how was she to apologize to him for her misjudgment?

Aimery came in, out of armor and damp from a wash. He paused as he took in the size of the bed, but his face remained expressionless. He pulled out a green and gold tunic and put on some jewels.

Madeleine was standing close by, choosing her own decorations for the evening meal. He ignored her so completely when they were alone together that she had ceased being wary and ached for any scraps of closeness. As her fingers fumbled among her jewels, she drank in the aroma of his body, relished every fleeting moment of contact . . .

She sensed something and looked at him. He was staring at her. Suddenly he grabbed her and flung her against the wall. His mouth covered hers with forceful heat. He leaned heavily against her, his body hard and warm.

After the first shock, Madeleine surrendered. As soon as he sensed her response, his lips softened. The hand that had grabbed her plaits to restrain her became a caress which sent magic down her spine.

He rubbed his body against hers, causing a shudder of longing to ripple through both of them. The kiss went on and on, preventing any protest, driving the last scraps of resistance out of her mind.

Madeleine's legs began to buckle, and Aimery caught her to him, cupping her buttocks and pulling her close, moving her against him so that her fiery ache was pressed to his.

He dragged his lips from hers, and they both sucked hungrily for breath. Madeleine was almost swooning with passion and lack of air. He rolled them onto the bed, and his hand between her thighs plunged her deeper into a dizzy pit.

But an icicle of conscience stabbed.

"No," she whimpered.

He gentled his touch.

"No!" She pushed with all her might and squirmed away, then leaped off the bed.

He stared at her, wide-eyed.

"No," she repeated again like a chant against evil, staggering back against the far wall. "No. No. No. No . . ."

He rolled over to bury his face in his arms, his breathing deep and ragged.

Madeleine fled the room, tears streaming down her face. She stopped to scrub them away. Refuge. She needed refuge, but in the crowded castle there was no privacy. She passed along corridors and through rooms, smiling fiercely, praying for a quiet corner in which to huddle. She ended up in the stable sheds.

There were few men around, for the horses had already been tended to and settled. She slipped into her mare's stall and leaned against the animal's warm bulk. The tired horse just snuffled and dug into its hay.

"Oh, sweet Jesu," Madeleine prayed. "Give me strength."

Something had been opened by that wild assault, and the key had been Aimery's need. She couldn't bear that he needed her so. It woke a fire of need in herself. Even standing here, her knees were weak and an empty ache of longing tormented her. How could she bear it when she saw him again, when next she was alone with him?

The horn sounded for the meal. It called her to go and be with him before the whole court. How could she when a tremor of need vibrated through her like the wind through an aspen tree? Yet she must. Duty, cursed duty, called her.

As she left the stable shed, a voice softly called, "Lady Madeleine!"

She looked around.

A man sidled round the corner of the shed. A low-born man. English.

"What do you want?" She put a hand on the knife she wore in her belt and kept her distance.

"Your aid, Lady Madeleine. I be Hengar, the forester."

She relaxed a little. Aldreda's husband. "There's trouble at Baddersley?" she asked.

"If there be trouble at Baddersley," he muttered, "it comes of that Golden Hart." He was a slightly built, wiry man, and at the moment his eyes were shifty. Madeleine wondered what he was about.

"Golden Hart is a myth," she said.

"Nay, he be real. Reckon the queen'd pay silver for his name, Lady."

Madeleine's mouth dried. Hengar must be the Baddersley traitor! What in God's name was she to do now? "Who is he, then?" she asked as calmly as she could.

The man licked his lips. "My word be for the queen, and for silver."

"I cannot get you to the queen," said Madeleine, "but I can tell her."

"Nay," he said. "I'll only tell the queen."

She saw a flash of vicious amusement in his eyes. He thought her ignorant of Aimery's alter ego and was enjoying the notion of using her for her husband's ruin. The naked malice of it shocked her. "Why are you doing this?"

"I be loyal to the king," he said with smirking insincerity. "He be God's anointed, bain't he? It be our holy duty to be loyal."

"Then what about the silver?" she queried dryly.

"A man must live."

Madeleine regarded him coldly. "If you want me to help you, Hengar, you must tell me the real reason you are doing this."

He scowled and his eyes shifted. "That Golden Hart," he muttered at last. "Stealing my wife, he be."

Madeleine's heart constricted, but she kept her face blank. "Why do you say that?"

"Because it's true," he snarled into her face. "Ever since he came back she's been after him like a bitch in heat, wanting him in her again. Bad enough the first time, but I don't have to put up with it again."

"Again?" Madeleine asked shakily, stepping back.

He spat into the straw. "My girl, the only child Aldreda's quickened with in all these years. She's not mine. She's the lord's child."

"Frieda?" Madeleine remembered the fine-boned blond girl and felt chilled as if it were winter.

"Aye, Frieda. And now Aldreda says she'll take the child away to be his daughter. I hate the little runt, but he'll not have her! I'll tell who he be and where he's to be found. By the time Aldreda catches up to him, the king'll have made sure he's no use to a woman again.''

Madeleine retreated from his malice, back into the stable, but he followed her. She dimly heard the supper horn, heard the stable grooms head cheerfully off to the meal. She could call for help, but that would give Hengar the audience he wanted.

"You get me in to see the queen, Lady," said Hengar. "If you don't, I'll see to your destruction, too."

Madeleine stopped and put her hand on her knife. "Don't threaten me."

"Think you're safe?" he sneered. "You'll see."

Madeleine needed time. Time to think. Time to tell Aimery of the danger. "Hengar," she said firmly, "you must return to Baddersley and cease this foolishness. I'll have words with Aldreda."

He laughed. "You reckon she'll heed you? Nay, if you'll not help, I'll ask another. There'll be somebody here willing to help a loyal subject."

He turned away. She couldn't let him go.

"Hengar! Stop." He hesitated. "I'll give you silver to go back home and keep silent."

He turned. "So you know, do you? Traitor to your own kind, just like him."

"Don't claim to be so holy," Madeleine snapped. She took off her golden fillet. "Here. Take this and go."

He shook his head. "What use be that to me? No one'd believe I came by it honestly. I want silver for my news, and Aimery de Gaillard destroyed."

Madeleine finally thought of a weapon to use against him. "You daren't betray him, Hengar, because I would make sure everyone knew it was you. How long do you think you'd live to enjoy your wife and your silver? They spread-eagled an informer in Gormanby."

He went pasty white, then let out a howl and leaped for her. Madeleine whipped out her knife by instinct alone. She felt it bite bone as it burst into him, heard his choked

cry. Frantically, she pushed his jerking body away and
staggered back.

He crumpled, clutching the agony that was the knife in
his chest, blood blossoming about his fingers. His legs
scrabbled as if he would flee, then stilled as he died.

Madeleine looked numbly at her work, at the blood on
her hands. She had killed a man. She was damned.

She looked down at her clothes and was surprised to
find them free of blood. It had taken a few vital seconds
for the blood to gush past the knife. There was plenty of
blood now, spreading through his clothes, beginning to
pool in the dirt. What was she to do?

The knife. She had to get the knife which would betray
her identity.

She looked around, but the area was still deserted. She
rinsed her hands in the water bucket and hitched up her
skirts into her girdle. Then she stepped gingerly over to
the body, avoiding the pooling blood. She leaned down
and pulled. The knife didn't move. It was jammed in bone
as it had been jammed in wood that day Aimery had taken
it from her. Where had she found the strength to match
his? It had been the force of Hengar's own attack that had
driven in the knife.

But she had to get the knife out. It would mark her as
the killer as clearly as if she signed her name.

She gritted her teeth and used two hands. The body
lifted, but the blade would not come free. Then, over her
own curses, she heard voices.

With a whimper of panic she grasped one of Hengar's
feet and dragged him back into an empty stall, grateful he
was a small man. She pushed straw over him. She ran
back out and scattered fresh straw over the blood. It still
looked clear as sunlight to her guilty eyes.

Her heart was beating so hard and fast that she feared
at any moment it would burst. She pressed into a corner
as the voices grew louder. Two stable grooms walked past
and went into the next shed.

Madeleine almost fainted with relief. But what was she

to do? She would already have been missed at the meal with no excuse for her absence. When the body was found, it would be clear she had killed him. Perhaps the reason for her deed would come out, and Aimery would be dragged down to ruin.

She should hide the body more securely but couldn't think where. Her teeth were chattering and her brain felt like wool.

Aimery. Aimery would help. She flung more straw over the bloody patch, restored her skirts, and slipped furtively out of the stables. Once away from her crime, she stopped in a quiet corner in the bailey to calm herself.

She began to think. She should have tried again to get the knife out. Perhaps she should go back.

Her teeth started to chatter. She couldn't.

"Are you all right?"

She started, and turned to see Aimery nearby. Her throat seized up and she couldn't speak the words to tell him she was a murderess.

He came no closer. "You don't look well. Is it because of what happened earlier?"

Madeleine shook her head. His attack seemed eons ago.

"I think it is. I'm sorry for it, but this situation is driving me mad. If I ask the queen to release you from your duties, will you go?"

Where could she go now? She shook her head again, needing his comfort. When he made no move toward her, she flung herself into his arms. He caught his breath, then held her tight, but she wanted it tighter, tighter, to drive out thought. She clung to him, trembling.

"What is it? Madeleine, has someone hurt you?"

"No," she gasped. "Kiss me!"

When he hesitated, she grabbed his head and kissed him with bruising, desperate force. After a startled second he responded.

Madeleine pressed closer. He lifted her against him. She opened her legs and wrapped them around him as if she could take him into her despite their layers of clothes.

He broke the kiss and looked dazedly at her.

"Yes," she said. Her vow had been washed out in blood, for she was now his accomplice in treason, and she needed him.

"I won't be able to stop," he warned.

"I won't want you to." She tightened her legs and pushed at him. "Please . . ."

"Our room . . ." he said unsteadily.

"No!" she cried as frantically as she had earlier, but objecting now to any delay.

He shuddered, looked desperately around, then carried her, still wrapped around him, into a wall-chamber full of barrels. He sat her on one and forced her legs to release him.

Madeleine slumped back against the rough, cold wall behind her and closed her eyes, but she saw only blood, visions of blood. She opened them to see his face, flushed with desire but troubled. His hands trembled as he pushed back her skirts, as he ran them up her thighs.

"Are you sure?" he asked.

She was trembling as if she had a fever. She didn't know if it was lust or guilt, but she needed him to drive it away. "Yes, yes. Fill me now!"

His hands left to adjust his clothing, then he was in her. They groaned in unison. Madeleine clung to him, feeling the tremors shuddering through him, too. They must be rocking the very castle walls.

"Wrap your legs around me again, love. Hold me tight."

She obeyed, using her legs to demand a fiercer loving. It wasn't enough. She could still see the blood. "Take me," she gasped. "Harder!"

"Mad . . ."

"Harder!" she cried. "Harder!"

He smothered her desperate voice against his chest. "Hush, love. Hush." But he responded to her urging and pumped into her, hard and fast.

At last it came, the oblivion she sought. He drove her

beyond speech, beyond thought, plunged her into an abyss of violent passion.

When reality returned, he had her cradled in his lap, safe in his strong arms. He was stroking her hair and singing a gentle, lilting song. He had never been so tender before, and she had so longed for it. Now it shot pain through her heart like an arrow.

"What is that song?" she whispered.

"It's a shepherd's song to a lost lamb he's found."

Madeleine moaned. "I . . . I always wanted you to sing just for me . . ." She broke into bitter tears.

He held her and stroked her and murmured anxious soothings until the tears stopped. Madeleine had never felt so cherished in her life, but it could not last. She would have to tell him. Still burrowed against his chest, she whispered, "I'm damned."

His hand stilled. "By the Rood, Madeleine," he said with careful patience. "Is all this over that silly vow?"

"It wasn't silly," she protested hopelessly, "but it doesn't matter anymore."

His hand stroked her again. "Good. So what has damned you?" It was lightly said, indulgently.

She came out of hiding and faced him. "I . . . I've killed someone."

He merely looked puzzled. "What do you mean?"

Madeleine suddenly realized the time that must have passed, and pushed out of his arms. "Oh, Mary. We've got to do something. I left your knife in him!"

He was staring at her, but more seriously now. "Who? What have you done?"

"Hengar, the forester. He was going to tell the queen you were Golden Hart. I killed him."

"With my knife?" he said alertly. "Where?"

"In the stables." She grabbed his hand. "Come on. We have to get the knife out!"

He caught her and held her. "Are you sure?"

"I know when someone's dead," she snapped.

He shook her. "Then we had best be careful. We can't

go charging down there. For one thing,'' he said with a little smile, ''we have just missed the meal.''

Madeleine looked around and realized people were leaving the hall. ''Oh, Jesu.''

''I think that's the least of our problems. Our excuse is that you were not feeling well. I'll escort you to our chamber, then I'll go and see to the corpse.''

''I'm coming with you.''

''No.''

After a look at his face, she accepted it and let him steer her gently up to their room. Occasionally he gave a word of explanation to someone, that she was sick.

Madeline felt strangely apart from everything, as if she were made of mist. It wouldn't surprise her to be invisible. She looked at her hand and was astonished that it still looked solid and strong.

He sat her on the bed and poured wine for her, forced her to drink it. She came back to reality, and misery.

''They'll burn me,'' she said.

''Not unless you're married to him,'' he responded, almost as if he was finding the situation amusing. ''Tell me exactly where you left the body.''

She described it. ''What will you do?''

''Get the knife. Once that's gone, there's nothing to connect him to you.'' He kissed her gently, then shook his head. ''One day I'd like to make slow, beautiful love to you in a bed, Madeleine.''

''I'm a murderess,'' she protested.

He grinned. ''I'm coming to like the thought that you killed for me, love.'' He rose to his feet. ''I'll be back as soon as I can.'' He stopped and returned to grasp her chin. ''You are not, under any circumstances, to confess your sin while I'm gone. Do you understand?''

She thought of arguing. She needed to tell the world of her wickedness, to be punished and absolved. But she nodded.

Once he had gone, she lay back on the bed. Fight it as she would, the memory of Hengar's death throes haunted her. He had been a horrible man, but that gave her no right to kill him, not even to save her husband.

Then she thought of that ferocious lovemaking and pressed her hands to her face. It had been as if she were possessed by devils. And he was disgusted with her. He wanted ordinary, orderly lovemaking, and she forced him to that.

The queen came to see her. Matilda was not angry at their absence, but roguish. "I send your husband to find you and lose the pair of you. Do you intend to feed on love?"

Madeleine knew her burning face told all. "I beg pardon, Your Majesty."

Matilda chuckled. "What it is to be young and lusty. I will have some food sent to you. You obviously need your strength. Where is Aimery?"

Madeleine swallowed. "He had to go and check on one of the horses."

"I'm sure he'll be back right speedily, so I will leave you in peace."

The food came, but Madeleine could not face it, though she drank steadily of the wine. Dorothy and Thierry both came to see if they were needed and were sent away.

At last Aimery returned. "We have a problem."

Madeleine sat up. "Someone found the body?"

He nodded. "Yes. And the knife was already gone."

Chapter 20

Madeleine stared at him. "But it was fixed tight in the bone!"

"A stable groom found the corpse, and he swears there was no weapon. I can see no reason for him to lie."

"What will happen now?"

"The sheriff is looking into matters. I identified Hengar—it would be suspicious if I didn't—but said he had no business here. Did anyone see you in the stables?"

She shook her head. "No . . . at least, I don't think so . . . I wasn't trying to hide . . ." Her teeth were chattering.

He came to sit on the bed and took her twisting hands. "Except from me. Don't fret, Madeleine. If they bring it all back to you, you must simply say he attacked you."

She pulled her hands free, remembering that this was all his fault. His treason. His adultery with Hengar's wife. "A lie? You don't like lies."

"True enough, but is it a lie?"

Madeleine shuddered. "He attacked me, but only because I said I'd tell all Baddersley what he intended. And what he intended was a loyal act!"

"What he intended was petty spite," Aimery said levelly. "Hengar is no lover of Normans."

Madeleine glared up at him. *"Was.* And you know a lot about him, don't you? If he was spiteful, it was because you can't keep your hands off Aldreda! For that you've dragged me down into treason with you.''

He stood up sharply. ''I haven't dragged you anywhere, woman. Next you'll be claiming I raped you this evening, when if anything, it was the other way around.''

Madeleine hid her face. ''Don't. I can't bear the thought!''

Why, she thought, were they squabbling when they were finally bound together, even if it was only in evil? She heard the door close and looked up to see he was gone. Madeleine shivered as if an icy wind had cut through her.

What was to become of them? What of her vow? She supposed it still stood, but in their present situation it had no meaning. He didn't need to seduce her into loyalty, for he now knew she was loyal to him to death and beyond.

He had said he would not lie with her if she did not trust him, but lust had overcome him. She felt the same way. More than ever she needed to join with him, as the only solid point in a quicksand world, but what kind of loving would come, she wondered, from such poisoned ground? More of that mindlessly violent rutting? She had needed it then, but now she cringed at the memory of her behavior. He said it had been like a rape, and he was right. Pray God she had not conceived a child in such a way.

There was a bath house in the castle, and Madeleine sought it out. The woman there filled a curtained tub with hot water, and Madeleine scrubbed herself fiercely, scrubbing away the memory of blood, the smell of sex, scrubbing until she was red and sore as tears washed down her face.

''Lady Madeleine.'' It was the voice of the bath woman.

''Yes?''

''The queen has sent for you.''

Madeleine froze. Had it all come out already? She stilled the sudden tremble in her hands. So be it. She must try her best to keep Aimery out of it, for he was the one in real danger. She could easily say Hengar had attacked her, and all would be well as long as no one looked too closely at his motives. She realized the most compromising feature was that she had not reported the attack.

She climbed out of the tub and accepted the drying-cloth. It would be easier if she had to face William, for she could pretend to be a gentle maiden overwhelmed by violence. She suspected Matilda would dismiss such an explanation.

Madeleine hurried to the queen's chamber. She was admitted and found Matilda in bed, and Aimery already in attendance. He smiled at her, but Madeleine couldn't tell if it was a feigned smile, or genuine reassurance.

"Madeleine," said the queen. "You have heard of this foul deed?"

Madeleine had to think quickly as to whether she should have heard. Heavens, she was no good at this sort of thing. "Yes, Your Majesty. I have no idea what the man could have been doing here."

"Nor has anyone," said Matilda. Madeleine could tell the queen was tired and out of patience. "It would have been more fitting for you to concern yourself over your forester than to go off to enjoy a bath!"

Madeleine colored. "I'm sorry, Your Majesty. I didn't think there was anything I could do."

"I forbade her," said Aimery smoothly. "She was not feeling well. We think she may be with child."

Madeleine flashed him a startled look before hiding her surprise. It was a clever thing to say. It distracted Matilda and gained her sympathy.

"Good news," the queen declared, then winced. "Though whether you'll think so in seven months or so is another matter." She rubbed her side. "This child is kicking my ribs to bits." She frowned thoughtfully, then nodded. "We must leave the matter in the hands of the sheriff then, and hope this death is not connected with our train. Take her away, Aimery, and care for her. Perhaps she should not ride."

Madeleine spoke up quickly. "I feel less sick when I ride, Your Majesty."

Matilda snorted. "So you don't like litters either. Go along with you."

Madeleine and Aimery said nothing until they were safe in their room.

"That was very clever," said Madeleine.

He shrugged. "It could be true. If not, such mistakes are easily made."

Madeleine felt bone weary. She rubbed her arms, though the night was warm. "Will it be all right? What if someone saw me there?"

He came and gathered her into his arms. "It will be all right. If your part comes out, we'll say he attacked you. If anyone contends it, I'll make a court duel of it."

"No! You can't risk your life for me."

"That's my duty as your husband." He grinned cockily. "Anyway, I'd win."

"But your cause would be unjust. The hand of God would be against you."

He sobered at that but shrugged. "Then that would be my *wyrd*."

"Curse your foolish *wyrd*." Madeleine shoved him away. "If only I hadn't gone to the stables."

"If only I hadn't tried to force you. But if you want to look for God's hand in this, look there. If you hadn't gone to the stables, Hengar would doubtless have found a more sympathetic ear, and I could even now be in chains awaiting William's judgment."

Madeleine looked at him. "I know. I didn't intend to kill him, but I think I would have driven the blade in deliberately if that was the only way of stopping him."

"I know. That's why I'll pledge my life to save your honor."

"But I'm damned. In intent, at least, I committed a terrible sin, and I can't repent!"

He shook his head. "Don't, Madeleine. We all kill if we have to. He was your enemy as surely as if he had faced you armed on a battlefield, and you cut him down.

If that's a damning sin, then heaven is going to be thinly populated. Get into bed before you collapse.''

Wearily, Madeleine obeyed. "But what of the knife?''

"That's the interesting question, isn't it?'' he said as he joined her. "Perhaps it was just filched by a petty thief. It was a valuable enough piece.''

"Maybe,'' said Madeleine, "but it feels more like the sword of Damocles.''

He took her hand. "I won't let it fall on you. Trust me, Madeleine.''

Trust, ah trust. "I'll try,'' she said, and let sleep take her.

Madeleine woke late and weary, for her sleep had been fragmented by tortured dreams. Sometimes she had been plunging the knife into Hengar, sometimes into Aimery. Once, at least, it had been a weapon aimed at her own heart. Dorothy's voice shocked her awake, and Madeleine immediately looked at her hands, expecting to see them covered with blood.

"Are you all right, Lady?'' Dorothy hovered anxiously.

"Yes, yes,'' said Madeleine, sitting up. "I just had a restless night. What hour is it?''

"Eight, Lady. Lord Aimery said you should sleep, but now there's little time. I brought you some food.''

Madeleine looked at the cold fish and ale, and her stomach rebelled. "I'd rather have some plain bread and mead. Fetch me some, Dorothy. I can dress myself.''

Madeleine saw from the look the woman flashed at her that the rumor of her pregnancy was already flying around the hall and had now been confirmed. Well, as Aimery said, it could be true.

She was dressed by the time Dorothy returned. Madeleine forced down some of the bread and mead, then left her woman to complete the packing and supervise the men who would load their goods into the carts. She knew what she must do. She went to seek out the sheriff.

The portly man was English, and she sensed his rever-

ence for Normans was only superficial. A few minutes talk
with him, however, made it clear he had no suspicion of
complex causes behind Hengar's death.

"Perhaps some personal feud, Lady Madeleine. Perhaps even theft, for he had no purse on him. I intend to
ride over to Baddersley today with the body to break the
news to his widow and see what can be learned." He
winked. "I have found these cases often come back to
the marriage bed."

Madeleine knew she'd started. Would stories of Aimery
and Aldreda be circulating in Baddersley? She looked at
the man in alarm, wondering if she'd just given herself
away.

He was red-faced. "I beg pardon, Lady," he said hurriedly. "I shouldn't have mentioned such matters, you being young and convent-bred."

"No matter," Madeleine said. "Please do your best to
find the culprit, but tell Hengar's wife that she need not
vacate the forester's cottage, and if the matter is not settled
soon, I will pay the *wergild.*"

The man bowed. "You are gracious and generous,
Lady. I will tell her."

Madeleine left the interview shaken, but she knew it had
been essential. It would raise suspicion if she was not to
inquire about murder in her own manor. A short while
later she rode out of Huntingdon, struggling to put the
whole incident behind her.

During that day's ride, Aimery stopped by her side frequently to offer support. Madeleine found on the whole
that this merely interfered with her efforts to block Hengar's death from her mind. In the end she bluntly told him
to leave her be.

The trouble was that pushing Hengar from her mind
only made room for thoughts of Aimery and Aldreda. She
was tormented by memories of Aimery standing with the
woman, familiarly close. She longed to confront her husband with it, but she was riding with a group of women

with no possibility of privacy. Besides which, she suspected even raising the subject would be unwise.

She couldn't keep it out of her mind, however.

Then there was the question of Frieda. Hengar had sounded certain of his facts, yet the girl must be at least ten. Aimery would only have been about fourteen himself at the time. Had Hengar perhaps been mad?

But Madeleine had always sensed something between Aldreda and Aimery. She remembered Aimery's need for her the day before, his need that day by the cornfield. Was it likely that he'd suppressed his body's demands for so long with Aldreda willing? What would he do now that the woman was an available widow?

Madeleine was snapped out of her personal worries when she noticed increased alertness among the men. In the heat, most of them rode bare-headed, but now mailed hoods were being raised, conical helmets put on, shields taken up.

Aimery rode by. "What is it?" Madeleine asked.

He drew his horse up. "Nothing to alarm you." He gestured to the east. "Just the Fens."

Madeleine looked. The land on their right had grown flatter as they journeyed, but now she saw it had the green of wetlands. It was empty and vast, with only the haunting cries of marsh birds to show any sign of life.

"Hereward?" she asked nervously.

Aimery did not show guilt or anxiety. "Is out there somewhere and doubtless aware of our every move. He won't attack us. We're too strong."

She had to know. "What would you do if he did?"

He flashed her a cold look. "Defend the queen." Then he was gone.

She wanted desperately to trust him, but the memory of his pledge to Hereward, the memory of the power in the man she had felt herself, always left a lingering doubt.

They arrived at Peterborough without incident, however, and settled in and around the mighty abbey of Saints Peter, Paul, and Andrew.

Madeleine went to the queen as Matilda climbed wearily from the litter, rubbing her back. "When this journey's over," Matilda said testily, "I want that cursed contraption chopped up and burned. I'll dance around the fire."

Madeleine giggled. Matilda flashed her a fierce look, but her lips twitched. "I'll send you on a pilgrimage, girl, in seven months or so."

"I beg pardon, Your Majesty." Madeleine looked at the queen and any humor faded. Matilda's face was growing puffy, and the woman looked exhausted. "Will you not consider stopping here, Your Majesty? We are well into the north, and the abbey has people skilled in medicine."

Matilda drew herself up, forcing away signs of fatigue by will alone. "*I* have people skilled in medicine, and this prince will be born in York." A hand resting on her bulging womb, she swept forward to greet the abbot.

Madeleine shared a shrug with Adele, who shook her head. "There's no stopping her, Lady Madeleine. Don't fear. I've attended all her births, and there's been no problem yet."

"I don't like that puffiness, though," said Madeleine quietly. "I saw a woman die once when she swelled up late in her pregnancy."

"Aye, but I think this is more from the lying around all day. See if you can get her to walk in the cloisters this evening."

So Madeleine spent the evening walking with Matilda, trying to keep the impatient queen amused. The ladies played music and offered riddles, and as the light faded, Aimery came to sing. He offered a long saga of parted lovers who eventually found happiness. Madeleine drank in his music as if he sang just for her, and when she caught his eye, she thought perhaps he did.

But by the time the queen retired Madeleine was exhausted and quite relieved to find the men and women were segregated. She had no energy just now for marital matters.

The next day it rained. The royal train slogged its way from Peterborough to Bourne, and the carts were often mired in mud despite the solid base of the Roman road. Along with everyone else, Madeleine huddled in her cloak and endured.

At Bourne there was only a village and a modestly fortified manor. Madeleine discovered this, too, had once belonged to Hereward and was now in the hands of Ivo Taillebois, who did not live there. The ladies crammed into the bleak hall while the men camped outside in the mud, forming an armed circle of protection. When they assembled the next morning, it was still raining, and few even bothered to put on dry clothes. They would soon be sodden again.

It was not a chill rain, but Madeleine was damp through. In this weather the armed men fared better than the ladies, for their mail and leather gave better protection.

As she watched the final assembly of the party, Aimery drew up beside her and offered her a wineskin. "If we were in a secure place I'd consider stopping," he said, "but not in Hereward's manor on the edge of the Fens."

Madeleine tipped the skin and drank. She wished they had time to devote to each other, but there was none, and no privacy at all. "You do think there's danger then?"

"Let's just say I don't want to tempt my revered uncle with too tasty a morsel. The people here are his to the death. Anyway, I broached the question to the queen and she refuses to consider any delay." He looked at Madeleine. "Do you think the birth is imminent?"

"Adele has more experience than I, and she's birthed the queen's other babies. She's concerned."

His hand tapped restlessly on the pommel. "If the queen goes into labor on the road, how will it go?"

"It will be in God's hands, but she bears babes well. It should go easily. But, please God, not in the rain."

"Amen to that. I hope to rest tonight at Sleaford, which won't be much better than here, but after that is the end of the Fens, and Lincoln. We can halt there in safety."

Madeleine saw that the weight of his responsibilities pressed on him, and touched his hand. "It will go well."

He smiled his thanks. "And you? How are you?"

She wanted so much to seek the comfort of his arms, but she merely pulled her damp cloak closer. "Too tired and wet to worry about anything personal."

He laughed, but then sobered. "I don't want to add to your concerns, but there is something you should know."

"About Hengar?" she asked in alarm.

"No, about Golden Hart."

She stared at him. Was he about to confess his plan?

"I tangled with some men of Robert d'Oilly's in the spring, but one survived. The king took an interest in him and appointed him to the castle guard at Huntingdon. I've just seen him in Odo's troop."

A hundred thoughts clamored in Madeleine's mind, but she said, "He will recognize you?"

"He's seen me before without making the connection, but if Odo has hired him, there has to be a reason. If Odo points me out, the man might see the resemblance."

"What will you do?"

"Nothing."

"How can you do nothing when they plan to destroy you?" He made no response, and she surrendered to the other thought bursting in her head. "How many did you kill?"

He was surprised. "Three. Gyrth took one."

"You said you had never killed to conceal your actions."

"Nor have I. I killed to save a man from death and his fellows from the ruin that comes of killing Normans." He sighed and touched her cheek. "Don't look so distraught. I doubt anything will happen before we join the king in York, and hopefully not immediately then. I have plans for York," he said softly. "I want to make long, gentle love to you in a bed, my wife. Will I be welcome?"

With death hanging over him, how could she deny him? "Aye," she whispered.

A light flashed in his eyes. "Then we will assuredly make York. The rest is in the lap of the gods."

Sleaford, was, as he had predicted, just like Bourne, but as they approached the rain turned to drizzle, and by the time they left the next morning the summer sun was shining once again, and the road was firm.

In dry clothes and warm sun, everyone's spirits revived. Aimery raised a song and everyone joined in merrily. They were headed for Lincoln, where they could expect a solid castle and everything that an ancient and civilized town could provide.

Adele was riding with Matilda, and Madeleine rode nearby, for though the queen asserted she had no signs of delivery, she rubbed at the bottom of her belly now and then, and found it hard to find a comfortable position in which to lie. Adele had told Madeleine she was sure the birth would come within days.

When she wasn't watching Matilda, Madeleine nervously watched the countryside to the east of the road, wondering if Hereward was there, and what he intended. She occasionally saw small boats fishing for eels, and even foot travelers who used poles to leap the frequent dykes, but no signs of armed men. Some of the party were beginning to think Hereward a figment of the imagination, but Madeleine knew for certain he was not. As the day went by, however, the terrain changed. Madeleine felt a burden lift when the dangerous Fens were left behind.

Lincoln was truly a welcome sight, sitting high and proud on the hill over the River Witham, the new castle already dominating the ancient town. William of Percy, who had been given the castle to man and guard, rode out to welcome the queen. He was a hard-looking man with a fearsome scar down his face, but he inspired confidence. Madeleine thought even Aimery was grateful to let someone else take responsibility for a while.

The castle had been hurriedly ordered to be built as part of William's current campaign to subdue the north, and it was stark, but within its protection were numerous hand-some houses where the queen's train settled to rest.

Aimery came straight to the queen to urge that she stay in Lincoln for a few days.

"Nonsense," snapped Matilda. "The worst of the journey is over. Water travel will present no problems."

"If the weather holds," warned Aimery.

"It will," said Matilda.

As Aimery left, Matilda again rubbed her belly.

"Your Majesty," said Madeleine desperately, "it would not be wise to give birth on the river."

"I have no intention of doing so," said Matilda, as if it were a matter completely under her control. "I know these aches. They come for weeks before the birth."

Adele came forward. "But they are aches, Lady?"

"Of course they are aches," snapped Matilda. "I ache all over. Anyone would ache after being in that cursed box for a week. The baby is *not* on its way."

Madeleine and Adele shared a look and a sigh.

"I will sleep here with you tonight, Your Majesty," said Madeleine.

"No, you will not. I have enough people to hover over me, and Aimery has only one wife. Stop fussing over me, girl, and go and fuss over your husband. He will doubtless appreciate it a great deal more."

There was no debating with Matilda in this mood, and so Madeleine went to find her quarters. Again, they had a small but private room. When he'd promised to make love to her in York, had Aimery forgotten the opportunities that would be provided by the halt in Lincoln?

William of Percy provided a magnificent feast that night for the queen and her party. Madeleine thought this must be hard for Matilda, but there was no sign of it. She was gracious and alert, paying special attention to the burghers of the town, currying their favor for her husband's cause.

Madeleine and Aimery were seated by local dignitaries, too, and did their best to make a good impression. Their

ability to converse in English was appreciated. Looking
around, Madeleine could see communication was stilted
in many places. Did it not occur to many Normans to learn
the tongue of this land? Apparently not. They were waiting for the English to learn French.

She remembered Hereward's prediction that English
would be the language here in the future. It seemed unlikely.

She looked nervously at the far side, where Odo's men
were seated. She had no way of knowing which was the
man who could recognize Golden Hart, and she saw no
one gazing their way with suspicion. She had to copy
Aimery and put the matter out of her mind or she'd go
mad, but she didn't have his training in fatalism.

Her worries were broken by a disturbance at the doors.
A party swept in, led by a striking blond woman of middle
years. She was not particularly beautiful, but there was
humor and character in her face, and she possessed snapping bright eyes. Madeleine's attention, however, was
caught by a figure trailing behind the woman and her
guards.

What was Aldreda doing here? Joining Aimery?

Aimery stood suddenly. Madeleine stared at him in
astonishment as he moved quickly toward the group,
delight on his face. Her pain was sharp. He would betray
her thus before the whole company?

He swept the blond woman into his arms. "Mother!"

Madeleine stood slowly, prey to a mixture of relief and
guilt. She looked again at Aldreda, and the woman's sharp
gaze met hers, and hardened. Why was Aldreda looking
at her as if Madeleine were a chicken for the pot?

But there was no time for speculation now. Aimery was
calling her forward, the queen was summoning them all to
her, the Lady Lucia's party was being settled and fed.

Madeleine found herself wrapped in a warm, cushiony
embrace. "My dearest daughter! You are so pretty. How
did the worthless wretch win himself such a lovely bride?"
As they went to the queen, Lucia explained, "I saw how

it would be. I could sit in Normandy and turn to stone before my husband or son gave a thought to me, so I came.''

Lucia curtsied respectfully to the queen, but said as she rose, ''Matilda, you must be crazed.''

The queen laughed. ''People have said that to me all my life. Sweet Savior, but it's good to have you here, Lucia. Sit here and tell me all the news. You can huddle with your son later.'' She waved Aimery and Madeleine away, but they heard her say, ''He's doing very well, by the way. You can be proud of him.''

''I always am,'' said Lucia. ''Are you in labor yet, or are you just waiting to burst like a pea pod?''

Madeleine and Aimery shared a grin as they resumed their seats. ''She's lovely,'' said Madeleine.

''Yes, but don't be deceived. Even Father shakes in his shoes if she takes up an issue. We may at last have hope of the queen seeing sense.''

''I pray it is so.'' Madeleine toyed with a pastry. ''Did you see Aldreda?''

He looked up. ''Where?''

His reaction was a relief to her. Madeleine pointed the woman out. ''She came with your mother.''

''Mother must have stopped at Baddersley then,'' he remarked without great interest. ''But why would she bring Aldreda?''

''And why,'' asked Madeleine pointedly, ''would Aldreda want to come?''

Chapter 21

The queen retired early, attended by all her ladies and Lady Lucia de Gaillard. Once the queen was settled for the night, Madeleine took Aimery's mother to find the chamberlain and obtain quarters for her.

The man was harassed. "I have nothing suitable, Lady Madeleine. Every inch is taken in the ladies' rooms."

"You mustn't concern yourself," said Lucia. "I am not so soft that I can't sleep in the hall or the stables."

"Oh, dear," said the man. "It isn't right." He suddenly brightened. "Perhaps the lady could share your room, Lady Madeleine."

Madeleine thought of the private room and knew it was right. Not only was it right that Lucia have some comfort, but it was right that she and Aimery not be tempted yet. It wasn't a question of a vow anymore, but matters must be truly settled between them if they were to find happiness. "An excellent idea," she said. "Come along, my lady."

When they arrived at the chamber, Lucia looked around and said, "This is yours and Aimery's."

"Yes," said Madeleine, "but your sleeping here will not inconvenience us, I assure you."

"That," said Lucia, "sounds most unnatural."

Madeleine's face burned. "We're both very tired these days."

"I can't say a day's travel would have stopped Guy and me. Or would now, were he here."

Madeleine didn't know what to say to such plain, lusty talk, and took silver goblets out of a chest.

"I know your marriage was strangely arranged," said Lucia. "Have you learned to deal together?"

Madeleine busied herself in pouring wine. "Now and then," she said, and passed a goblet to the older woman.

Lucia laughed. "And I should mind my own business. Forgive me, my dear. It's hard to have but one chick. He looks well, if tired."

Madeleine sighed but smiled. "Believe me, getting Matilda to York is enough to turn us all gray."

Aimery came in to catch the end of that. "True enough. Have you changed her mind, Mother?"

"No, and I doubt I can. She's as aware as any of you of the problems, but she's shaped her fate by force of will all her life and believes she always can." Lucia shrugged. "Knowing Matilda, I would say the chances of the babe being born in York as she intends are extremely high."

Aimery drained the wine Madeleine gave him. "So be it. We should make Gainsborough tomorrow, then Airmyn, then York. Only three more days and all on water. Now," he said, throwing himself down on a bench next to his mother, "tell me your adventures, and all the news from home."

Madeleine pretended she had forgotten a duty to the queen and gave them some time together. When she returned, Lucia smiled her thanks. A little later Aimery left to do his nightly inspection of his force, leaving the two women alone.

"He's grown so," said Lucia, half proud, half sad.

"I have not known him any other way."

Lucia lovingly folded the cloak Aimery had dropped on a chest. "It seems an astonishingly short time since he was a babe at my breast, and a mere moment since he was all legs and arms and a voice slipping out of control . . ."

She took a deep breath. "You must pardon a foolish mother . . ."

Madeleine hugged her. "I pardon you anything, for you have given me Aimery."

Lucia pulled back to look at her. "Is it so?" She smiled. "Then I am content. You will keep him safe. I worry about him being in England, and I know Guy has been deeply concerned. Even I find the situation here painful, and I am not called upon to fight."

Madeleine wondered just how she was supposed to keep Aimery safe, then remembered Hengar and shuddered. "Hereward is your brother, isn't he?"

Lucia clucked. "Yes, and if I have the chance I'll give him a piece of my mind. Men! There's no turning back time. He should bow to the inevitable."

As they undressed, Madeleine ventured the subject of Aldreda. "I saw a woman from Baddersley in your party. Why is she here?"

"The weaver? When I stopped there looking for you, she asked to come. She has recently lost her husband and needs to travel to a brother in York. Is there a problem?"

Madeleine shook her head. "Except that her husband was found murdered at Huntingdon when we stopped there. The culprit has not been found. Likely enough she does have relatives in York." But Madeleine wondered. She had never heard of such relatives. And where exactly was Aimery now?

Madeleine had to fight an urge to go in search of him, to check if he was with Aldreda.

Madeleine and Lucia shared the bed. As they settled there Lucia said, "Poor woman. Especially as she is expecting a child."

Madeleine stiffened. "She is? She shows no sign."

"No, but she said she is pregnant."

Aimery came in with a straw mattress and settled himself in a corner. Madeleine looked up at the painted beams. Aldreda had quickened with only one child, said to be Aimery's. Now she was with child again.

* * *

Madeleine had no opportunity to raise the subject with Aimery the next day, but as they all gathered at the side of the Foss Dyke canal, Aldreda approached her.

"Lady Madeleine," she said demurely, "I hope you do not mind my coming here with your lord's mother."

Madeleine faced the woman warily. "Of course not," she lied. "I understand you seek relatives in York."

The woman's eyes shifted, revealing the lie. "It's hard for a woman to lose her man, Lady."

"I'm sure it is. I will be happy to arrange another marriage for you. Did the sheriff tell you I will pay the *wergild?* Twenty shillings, I believe."

"Aye," said Aldreda, adding boldly, "and I'm wondering why you would do that."

"I am your lord in Baddersley," said Madeleine calmly. "Your welfare is my concern, and I fear your husband's murderer will never be found."

"Do you, indeed?" said Aldreda with a distinct sneer. "Time will tell. But thank you for the *wergild,* Lady. It will come in useful. After all, I have a daughter to settle."

Madeleine couldn't hold it back. "And another babe on the way, I understand. When is it due?"

"Next Eastertide, or thereabouts, Lady." Aldreda's smile was cat-like. "Conceived so little time ago."

"A blessing," said Madeleine tightly, "to bear a child after so many barren years. Did you say special prayers?"

The woman smirked. "I certainly did something special, Lady."

Aldreda bowed herself away. When next Madeleine saw her, she was talking to Odo, of all people. That made Madeleine very uneasy. First d'Oilly's man, now Aldreda. Though Odo's ambitions had taken other directions, Madeleine knew he would do her and Aimery a mischief if he could, and her instinct told her Aldreda was mischief incarnate.

* * *

Madeleine found she had little time to worry about Odo's plans or Aldreda's link with Aimery, for she and Adele, and all the ladies, were kept busy by Matilda. The queen continued to deny labor, and was probably telling the truth, but she was restless and irritable.

They traveled the Foss Dyke in two relays of small barges, then embarked on larger vessels at the port of Torksey for the trip up the Trent. During the wait at Torksey the women kept the queen active, but once they were on the water again, she was condemned to sitting still. Though the litter had been a trial to her, on the road she had been able to demand frequent stops to walk around. The barges were wide boats, but with the large number of passengers and the oarsmen, there was little room to move. Matilda was uncomfortable and let everyone know it.

If it hadn't been for the queen's complaints, Madeleine would have enjoyed the peaceful glide through green countryside, but as it was she was immensely relieved to see Gainsborough. She offered prayers that the queen's labor would come on her there and put them all out of their misery.

Despite all the signs, and the silent prayers of her attendants, the queen did not go into labor in Gainsborough. Madeleine and Adele even discussed using herbs which would bring on labor, but the risks probably outweighed the advantages.

Only probably. Madeleine was nervous of the queen giving birth away from a town with only her personal guard to protect her and the babe.

The further north they traveled, the further away she felt from civilization. This part of England was clearly less under Norman control, and the people looked more Norse than Saxon. Though Gainsborough seemed prosperous and peaceful, the inhabitants regarded the invaders askance, and muttered curses beneath their breath. If trouble was to occur, there would be many willing accomplices.

As Madeleine waited to board her barge, Aimery came to stand beside her. "You look worried."

She snorted with exasperation. "And you aren't?"

He laughed. "At a certain point, worrying becomes pointless. Odo has no head for geography and is too arrogant to listen to those who have. He got lost on his way here and arrived after the rearguard. Allan de Ferrers is so nervous to be in the wicked north he's racing ahead expecting two-headed monsters to leap out from behind every bush. It seems impossible to expect them to keep pace with the barges. I'm wondering what the penalties are for tying a pregnant queen to a post and keeping her here."

Madeleine couldn't share his humor. "This is a mad enterprise, isn't it? Perhaps Hereward was right, and the line will not survive. Perhaps this is the beginning of the end."

She saw him sober. "Hereward was right," he said simply. "Hereward is always right."

"Is he?" Madeleine asked, fear sharpening her voice. "Then why are you here with us, instead of with him?"

"Because it's my duty to get the queen safely to York." His voice had matched hers in sharpness, but now he moderated it. "Madeleine, I do not serve Hereward. We should have sorted this out long ago."

"You forget. I heard you promise."

She could see his patience straining. "Yes, but not what. I am oath-bound to secrecy, but the service was not disloyal, and it is long over with. Believe me."

She wanted to so badly. "You mean no harm to the queen or the babe?"

He was shocked. "Is that what you think?"

She bit her lip. "It was all I could imagine. I'm sorry."

He turned away, and it was as if a wall grew up between them. "Am I a fool for wanting your trust? Am I going to have to prove my honesty afresh every day of my life?"

"I had reasons for doubting you," Madeleine protested. "You can't deny that."

"You had my word that I was loyal." He looked back at her, and she thought it was all right. But then he merely said, "Get aboard," and walked away.

* * *

Madeleine prayed to be in York, where perhaps they would be able to talk matters through. Where she would finally be sure he was loyal. Where he was going to make long, slow love to her in a bed.

If he wasn't in chains.

The queen was less restless, though still like a surly bear. Adele hovered, sure the birth was imminent, but there was little for Madeleine to do. When Matilda wanted companionship, it was Lucia she called for.

Aimery, too, had little to do now other than try to anticipate problems. Though it was not a time to talk of dangerous matters, for there was no privacy, Madeleine saw an opportunity to clear away some misunderstandings. She worked her way to his side. He took her hand as if it were the most natural thing in the world. Madeleine felt her heart tremble.

"I wanted to tell you about Stephen," she said.

"Stephen?"

"Why I didn't marry him."

His lips twitched. "It wasn't just that you showed good taste?"

She put on a frown. "You were furious at the time. With reason. You were angry that I'd broken my word."

His thumb rubbed against her hand. "True. So, why did you not marry de Faix?"

Madeleine still found it hard to speak of. "That night . . . When the king summoned me . . . I went to the stables, but the king wasn't there. Stephen was."

"I'd guessed as much, but I'm surprised it turned you so violently against him."

Madeleine looked out over the water. "He wasn't with a woman."

"He wasn't?" Aimery was clearly waiting for more.

Madeleine looked around them and leaned closer to hiss, "He was with a man!"

Aimery burst out laughing. "By St. Peter! The cunning rogue!"

"Stephen?"

Aimery shook his head. "William. I'm sure he knew Stephen's tastes when he made him one of the suitors. We never had a chance, did we?"

Madeleine looked at him anxiously. "Do you still regret it?"

He squeezed her hand gently. "Not at all. In fact, at the time I was tasting bile at the thought of you in Stephen's arms." He kissed her knuckles, then said a little reluctantly, "If we're to tackle our problems head on, I think we should speak of the time when the Baddersley people were whipped."

"Why then?" asked Madeleine in puzzlement.

He played with her fingers for a moment. "The story was you asked for the whippings."

"What!" But then Madeleine hesitated. "I suppose in a way I did. But, Aimery, it was only to save them all from maiming. My uncle was in a mindless rage."

"Ah." He sighed. "And the people heard you begging for the whipping, but could not understand enough French to understand why. I think I should beg your pardon for having believed that of you."

"I confess, I am hurt. Did it seem likely that I would act in such a way?"

"Not until I saw you watching."

Madeleine looked a question and he said, "I went up to the castle while the floggings were going on. I saw you watching the whipping of the children."

Madeleine shuddered at the memory. "I felt so helpless," she recalled. "It had never crossed my mind that he would flog the children too. I tried to stop him, but it was no use. I felt the least I could do was watch . . ."

He gently wiped away a tear that had escaped onto her cheek. "Dear heaven, what a tangle we've been in."

"And is it over?" But then she remembered Aldreda, Odo, and d'Oilly's man. And her lingering uneasiness about his promise to help Hereward. Should she ask him about that now?

"It is at least good that we are in harmony at last." He touched her lips with his finger and she knew that he too longed to seal their new accord with a kiss. This wasn't the place, however, and soon he was summoned to discuss some matter with the boatman.

Soon, however, they would be in York. Madeleine wrapped new hope around her and settled to watching the passing countryside.

This was a fertile river valley and villages were strung along the river trading route like beads. The land looked lush and prosperous, but she noted signs of war. One hamlet was a burned, abandoned shell. It could have been destroyed by king or rebels, but that hardly mattered. Homes were gone, crops destroyed, and doubtless people had died. She hated war.

Matilda insisted that they pull to the shore at midday for food and a chance to walk. Aimery wasn't happy about the plan, and put Fulk's guard on full alert. Everyone ate while strolling about, trying to get the kinks out of their legs. Madeleine saw Aldreda, and on impulse went to speak to her.

"How are you faring, Aldreda?"

The woman flashed her a distinctly unfriendly look. "Well enough."

"What of your daughter? Who is caring for her?"

"Hengar's mam. Frieda's grandam." She smirked and added, "After a fashion."

Madeleine decided to take a risk. "I heard that Frieda was not Hengar's child."

"Whose else would she be, Lady?"

Madeleine wouldn't name Aimery. Taking a shot in the dark, she said, "Hereward's?"

Aldreda paled. "No good that," she said, "him being an outlaw and all."

Madeleine scented blood. "But is it true?"

Aldreda stuck her chin up. "Frieda is the lord's child, and all know it."

Hengar had used those words. "What do you mean, the lord's child?"

"I know what I mean," said Aldreda slyly, "and so do all who have any business knowing. A lord's child must be gently raised and married well. As Frieda will be." She moved her shawl slightly. Madeleine gasped when she saw the distinctive amber knob of her own dagger, the murder weapon.

"What is that?" she asked, but she knew she had betrayed herself.

"You recognize it, Lady," said Aldreda. "You know what it is, and what it did. If Frieda doesn't get her due, I'll tell the world who killed my husband, and why."

The meat pie Madeleine had just eaten rebelled in her stomach. "You have no proof."

Aldreda bit into her own pasty with relish. "There's proof in the hand that wielded the knife, and I know from the sheriff that Aimery was strangely missing when my Hengar died."

Madeleine struggled with this new twist. Aldreda thought *Aimery* had killed Hengar, and she was threatening not so much to accuse him of murder as to expose him as Golden Hart, with his skin mark as final proof.

Madeleine looked at the woman and hated her. "How can you do this to someone who was once your lover?"

Aldreda shrugged. "I wouldn't rightly call him a lover, a young lad like that. It were over in a minute. But he has a duty to Frieda, and to me. He stole my man and I want another."

"I will arrange a marriage for you," Madeleine said quickly, "and one for Frieda in time."

"Nay, Lady. I know my worth. Frieda must be raised a lady as is her right, and married well. And I want Aimery."

Madeleine stared at her. "You want to force him to your bed?"

"I wouldn't mind, though there are others. No. I want

a Danelaw wedding with Frieda acknowledged as his child.''

Madeleine thought she was going mad. ''Those days are past, and Aimery's Norman. He doesn't hold with such things. Anyway, you admitted the child could be Hereward's.''

Aldreda regarded her with dismissive superiority. ''You don't understand. How could you? But Aimery does. I'll have my due, or he'll be brought low.''

''What keeps you safe?'' Madeleine asked coldly. ''After one death, what does another matter?''

Aldreda backed away, but she answered boldly. ''My husband was a fool. I suppose he went straight to Aimery and asked for silver for his silence. And got steel instead. I've told another. Killing me will do no good.''

Madeleine felt sick. ''Whom have you told?''

Aldreda smiled. ''I'm not likely to tell you that, am I? You just tell your husband to be more reasonable and set me and Frieda up in the manner we're entitled to, and to acknowledge the new babe, too. Both my children will be the equal of yours.''

Madeleine wondered how she kept from screaming. ''You have spoken to Aimery already?''

Aldreda nodded. ''Over-proud he is. Don't like the fact I have the upper hand, but he'll come to it, or he'll come to ruin. We women are more practical, aren't we?''

''And what of your accomplice?''

''I'll handle him, never fear.''

Madeleine rebelled against the woman's smug spite and wondered if Aimery had felt the same. If they gave in, they'd have her around their necks forever. She summoned all her dignity. ''You would be well advised, Aldreda, to take what we are willing to give and disappear. We would be generous.''

''Perhaps, Lady, but I'll have my full due.''

Madeleine walked away. What in Mary's name were they to do now? Was Aldreda's accomplice Odo? That would be a disaster for sure. She looked for Aimery, but he was busy organizing the reloading of supplies, and there was never, ever any privacy. She could have screamed, but she pushed back her fears. Nothing dramatic was likely to happen yet—except the queen giving birth. She returned to Matilda's side.

Lucia stretched her back and winced. "I confess, I'm weary of traveling. I'm staying in York even if Guy is not there. He can chase after me for a change. If, that is, Northumbria is secure. I honestly don't understand how William keeps his hold among so many enemies."

"Aimery says it's because they won't pull together."

Lucia sighed. "I can believe it. Mercia fights Wessex. Northumbria fights itself. William would not have gained a toe-hold if Tostig hadn't betrayed his brother Harold. Harold was a fine man," she said sadly. "A marriage was proposed between us, but then I met Guy."

Madeleine sought to distract her. "Have you ever visited York before?"

"What? A Lady of Mercia venture into the land of boglins and hairy men? Heaven forfend!"

Madeleine grinned. "I gather you've never met Waltheof Siwardson."

Lucia raised her brows. "No, but I knew his father and can well imagine. It's the faery blood."

She seemed perfectly serious. Madeleine asked, "Is there faery blood in Mercia?"

"Certainly not," said Lucia, then slid a mischievous glance sideways. "Disappointed?"

Madeleine laughed. "A little. But only a little."

But when she saw Aldreda watching her again, Madeleine thought Aimery might need faery blood to escape the gathering storm.

That afternoon the barges were steered into the great water of the Humber estuary and traveled up it to where the Aire River joined it at Airmyn. They all climbed stiffly out, gratefully aware that one more day would have them in York. Madeleine could hardly believe it, but it seemed as if Matilda was going to achieve her end.

Madeleine was no longer sure if she wanted to reach York or not. It promised time at last for her marriage, but threatened Aimery's exposure as Golden Hart. After all, if Odo brought forward his witnesses before the whole court, William would have to act. At the very least, Aimery would be disgraced and banished.

She was fretting over this when she bumped into Odo. She had the disquieting feeling he had deliberately stepped in her way. "Excuse me, Odo. The queen has need of me."

"Of course," he said without moving. "How is Her Majesty?"

"Well, considering. Step aside, please."

"And you? Rumor says you, too, are with child."

She made herself face him boldly. "We hope it is so. Odo, what do you want?"

"Just greeting my dear cousin," he said, and finally moved out of her way.

Madeleine hurried on, her heart thundering. He might as well have been a fox toying with a chicken. He knew everything.

She had to push her worries aside as she tended the weary, uncomfortable queen. They all again tried to persuade her to stay where she was and send for the king. He could be in Airmyn in a short day, but Matilda would have none of it. As soon as the queen was settled, all Madeleine's personal worries came back to her, and she sought a private moment with Aimery. She opened the subject bluntly. "I spoke to Aldreda."

He was sitting at a table studying a map of the area. He didn't look up. "Ignore her. She'll come to her senses."

"I think you're wrong. She's like a vixen with one cub. Or perhaps two," she added darkly.

He glanced up. "And what's that supposed to mean?"

"Is it yours?"

She saw his jaw set. "No, it isn't mine. I haven't touched Aldreda since I was fourteen years old."

"I believe you!" Madeleine said quickly. She did believe him. Why had she even mentioned it?

"Kind of you. It's doubtless Odo's child. She was playing the whore with him at Baddersley before the wedding."

Madeleine thought back to her three suitors and shivered at the mistake she could have made. She paced backward and forward. "So why is she claiming it's yours?"

He sighed and put aside the map. "Greed," he said. "Everything comes down to greed, the most vile of sins. I've promised to do what I can for Frieda, but she wants more."

"I know. Is it reasonable?"

"A Danelaw marriage? No, even if it had any meaning anymore."

"But if you don't, she'll betray you to the king."

He shrugged. "If that is my *wyrd.*"

Madeleine hit him. She made a fist and hammered his shoulder, which made as much impression as if she'd hit an oak tree, but at least he paid her some attention. "What do you want me to do?" he asked.

Madeleine shook her head, and her hand. "I don't know. But you could at least worry. Odo's licking his chops, too."

He shrugged. "I am worrying. There are men on the move nearby."

"Rebels?" asked Madeleine sharply, also consigning Aldreda and Odo to the irrelevant.

"Not Norman. They may have no connection to us."

"But we would tempt a force if it were large enough."

He tossed the note aside. "True. I'll just have to spend the night drumming the next day's route into Odo and Allan and hope they'll keep in position and close." He stood and smiled. "York tomorrow."

Despite everything, the mere word sent a curl of warmth

through her belly. "A lot of good that will do us if you're in chains."

He grinned. "Merely tax our ingenuity."

She gave a watery smile and went into his arms. "I'm terrified, Aimery."

He rubbed her back. "Don't be. I'll protect you. It will be all right."

"How can you know that?" she asked with exasperation.

"Perhaps I have the sight, too."

She looked up. "Have you?"

He kissed her. "Not as far as I know, but I do know this. Nothing short of death will keep me from our tryst."

Madeleine shivered and kissed him fiercely.

Chapter 22

Madeleine slept uneasily on the floor by the queen's bed that night, expecting at any time to be woken for the birth, but the morning came without labor. Adele had stayed awake for most of the night, and she shook her head. "I've had my hand on her belly since dawn, and the tightenings come and go without pattern. It's not to happen yet."

The queen spoke up testily. "Stop talking about me as if I were a child. I will tell you when I am in labor. Who better to know?"

Madeleine and Adele both knew the queen would lie if it suited her. She was desperate to make it to York, a mere twenty miles away.

Aimery came to speak to the queen, then drew Madeleine apart. "Can she travel? I will refuse to go on if you think it best. The weather's none too promising anyway."

Madeleine looked out to see dull, low clouds. "You'd have to tie her up."

He beat his fist softly against a post in his concern. "She's not in labor yet?"

"Adele's sure."

"When labor starts, how long should it take?"

"Many hours. But we can't tell, when a woman's had so many children. It can be fast. But fast is usually good."

"The people here say this weather shouldn't amount to much, but I'm not sure they're telling the truth. They owe no allegiance to William, or Gospatric for that matter. Their loyalty is all to Waltheof. I find myself wishing we had him with us, but then I'm not sure whose side he's on either . . .'' He shook his head. "York is looming in my mind as the promised land for more reason than one. Let's go.''

Matilda surprised everyone by walking lightly to her barge. Her eyes were bright, and she was smiling. "See," she said to Lucia. "I said I would make it to York. A good omen. A good omen.''

Lucia pulled a face as she followed the queen, but she winked at Madeleine and said, "Never underestimate the strength of female determination.''

The air was chill with misty droplets which grayed cloaks and armor. As the day progressed, the mist thickened until they could hardly see the riverbanks. The fog muffled sound. It became hard to believe that there were people elsewhere in the world, or colors other than gray.

Despite the fact that they were on the river and could not be lost, Madeleine found herself murmuring prayers that they would arrive somewhere, anywhere . . .

She wondered how far the mist spread and what was happening to Odo and Allan. Their mere existence was an act of faith, for it was difficult to imagine there was more to the party than the barge in front and the barge behind. Madeleine shivered when she remembered this was a land of myth and magic. This was the homeland of Waltheof, who didn't laugh at the notion that his grandmother was a faery-bear.

The queen's cry seemed, in retrospect, inevitable. Madeleine squirmed through the ladies to the queen's side and heard curses. She realized then that what she'd heard was not a cry of pain but of rage.

"What is it?'' she asked.

Adele looked up. "Her waters broke.''

Matilda lay back, muttering. "A few more hours. That's all. Just a few more hours.''

"You don't have a few more hours, and you know it," snapped Adele. "You've been lying to me all day."

Matilda smiled. "Has there been anywhere suitable to stop?" Then she caught her breath and clutched at Adele's hand.

Madeleine could see the ripple of the tightening womb. Labor was well-advanced. "We'll have to stop."

She worked her way forward to where Aimery stood by Fulk, both scanning the mist for hazards, and gave him the news. "Sweet Jesus," he said. He consulted with one of the boatmen.

Aimery turned back to Madeleine. "As best we can tell in this, we're close to a hamlet called Selby. We should be able to find shelter there. Can we make it?"

Madeleine shrugged. "If not, the babe will be born on the boat." She smiled at him wryly. "Believe me, in matters such as this women know well the meaning of *wyrd.*"

She went back and had the ladies search through the baggage for the pads and cloths prepared for the birth. The labor had speeded with the breaking of the waters, and no force on earth would stop the babe from being born within hours.

As always with birth, it was now a matter between Matilda and God.

The boats pulled to the western shore. The abrupt sight of buildings was a shocking relief, and a re-affirmation that civilization still existed. Then, as they tied up at a small wharf, the relief evaporated. The place was deserted, the buildings battered and burned.

They disembarked. The men stood guard with bared swords, but the menace had come and gone from this place.

"Who?" asked Madeleine of Aimery.

"It's recent, but it could be the rebels or the king. Whoever it was has not left much intact to serve as shelter."

Then a voice came out of the mist, followed by a dark shape.

Aimery strode forward. "Who are you?"

Madeleine could see now that it was a man—a strange man with flowing hair and a beard, and coarse clothing. Was this the style of the people of Northumbria?

He was unafraid. "I am Benedict of Auxerre, a humble hermit," he said in courtly French. "How can I help you?"

Aimery said, "Where are the people of Selby?"

"Fled like sheep before wolves."

"And you?"

"I am a holy hermit, and thus safe from wolves."

Aimery hesitated, then said, "We have a woman in childbirth and need shelter."

The hermit smiled. "What a pity it is not Christmastide. Come. My hut is a simple place, but secure from the weather, and I have a fire burning."

"How far?" asked Aimery.

"Just beyond the houses, at the edge of the village."

Fulk directed his men for the security of the hamlet, and Aimery came to carry Matilda to shelter. He waited a moment for a contraction to pass, then gathered her up.

"I'm a fine mess," said Matilda ruefully, then caught her breath and clutched at him.

Aimery looked at Madeleine in alarm. "If you wait till the tightenings are over," she said, "you'll wait till the babe's born. Go!"

He went, with Adele hurrying alongside. Madeleine ran off to collect the birth requirements, and directed the women to find clean clothes for the queen for after the birth. She looked around. It was difficult to tell in this gray mist, but the afternoon must be well-advanced. The mist had slowed them. She wondered how close they were to York. Even if the queen could travel after the birth, would they be able to reach the city before dark? Her skin crawled at the thought of spending the night in this skeletal village.

Once in the hermit's hut, however, she felt better. It was a small, simple stone building with a beaten earth floor, but there was a fire in the central hearth, and it was cozy. People were already scurrying in and out with supplies. The queen was sitting on the hermit's simple straw mattress, which was now covered with fine linen sheets. She was sipping wine from a silver goblet between the squeezings of her womb. A man was setting up a branch of candles to provide light. Neither Aimery nor the hermit was to be seen.

Soon the place was as suitable as possible, and everyone was sent off the fend for themselves—other than Adele, Madeleine, Lucia, and Matilda's favorite lady, Bertha. The room was crowded.

At Matilda's request, Bertha and Lucia took turns reading from a history of Charlemagne. Madeleine rubbed the queen's back, while Adele kept watch over the progress of the birth.

Matilda groaned and grunted, and occasionally cursed, but there was none of the wild screaming Madeleine had sometimes witnessed. She wondered how she herself would behave when her time came.

Matilda lurched onto her knees, resting her hands on the mattress. "Press harder, girl," she snapped. "Harder!"

Madeleine knelt behind her and pressed on the queen's back with all her might. "Better," grunted Matilda.

Madeleine looked up at Adele, and the woman nodded. "That's right. Always takes her in the back, it does." She stroked the queen's belly. "Not long now, lovey," she crooned.

Madeleine pressed and pressed, thinking that in this situation, as in most of importance, it mattered not if one was queen or peasant. It was all the same.

The queen suddenly gave a new and different cry, and collapsed down to lie on her side. "At last," she gasped.

"Aye, at last," said Adele, suddenly purposeful. She pushed back the queen's stained and soaked skirts. "Here, Lady Madeleine, come hold up her leg."

When she obeyed, Madeleine could already see the bulge of the baby's head.

"Wonderful, wonderful," said Adele. "Lovely sight. Everything's fine, everything's fine . . ."

Madeleine looked at the queen's sweaty face. Matilda's mouth was slack as she breathed fast and shallow, her eyes half-closed as if she dozed. Could she hear the reassuring murmur? Madeleine was sure she could. Then Matilda strained and grunted. The bulge between her legs grew.

There was a cry. It came not from the queen, but from outside. A battle cry. The ringing clash of arms.

Madeleine looked at Adele in alarm, but it was as if the woman didn't hear. Bertha had paled, but she read steadily on. Lucia met Madeleine's eyes calmly. "There is nothing to be done. Trust Aimery."

Trust Aimery. Madeleine looked at the first sign of the baby's hair and did just that.

Matilda gave a guttural cry. Adele rubbed the bulging skin, and slowly a scowling baby's head appeared. "Lovely, lovely," crooned Adele as she wiped the babe's face with a soft cloth. "There's a pretty angel. Just another push, lovey, then you'll have your babe. Push well . . ."

The queen grunted and pushed. The shoulders slid out, first one, then the other, and then, in a slithering rush, the babe was born. A boy. He cried immediately.

"The atheling," said Lucia somberly.

The sounds of battle were outside the hut now: battle cries like the howls of wolves at the door, shouts in English and French, the clang of weapon on weapon. With a whoosh an arrow flew in the high window to drop harmlessly on the floor. Madeleine heard Aimery shout a command. Her heart leaped, then twisted at the thought that he was fighting out there. Fighting whom? Hereward?

Her hands were unsteady as she helped the queen onto her back. Adele wrapped the babe and put him in his mother's arms, then settled to wait for the afterbirth. Matilda, suddenly alert as all new mothers are, gazed at the babe for a sober moment. Then she loosened her gown, competently put him to the breast, and looked up. "Who?"

"We don't know," Madeleine said. "English."

Matilda wriggled and pulled a knife from her belt, and laid it on the bed close to her hand. "Find out."

Lucia and Bertha were both standing guard by the door. Bertha was holding a stool, but was pallid. Lucia looked ready for battle, having taken up the hermit's sturdy pole.

Madeleine pulled out her eating-knife, wishing she had the better one, the one Aldreda still possessed. Then she opened the door a crack. It was blocked by the solid bulk of Fulk's back. Two other guards stood beside him.

They'd built a fire outside the hut, and it lit the misty battle a sultry red. Madeleine could only see shapes, but the sounds were clearer. Swords rang against ax and shield. The occasional arrow or spear hummed through the air. There were howls of war cries and of pain.

"Mary, mother . . ." Madeleine breathed, her eyes seeking Aimery. "Who?"

"Rebels," grunted Fulk. "How fares the queen?"

"Well, and she has borne a prince."

Fulk nodded. "Fear not. We will keep them safe."

Madeleine knew he would die before any intruder passed through the door, but it could come to that. How many men were involved in this attack? Where were Odo and Allan? Obliviously heading for York? Where was Aimery?

Lucia appeared at Madeleine's shoulder. "Is Hereward out there?" she demanded.

"We don't know whose force this is, Lady," said Fulk.

"Get word if you can that Lucia of Mercia is here, and I'll geld my wretched brother with his own knife if he's responsible for this."

Fulk laughed. "Thanks to God you're on our side, Lady, but there's no talking to these. They mean death."

On the word, a spear flew. Fulk's shield moved a second late. The spear took him in the throat, and he crumpled, choking, to the ground. Madeleine knelt quickly, but there was nothing to be done. Within seconds Fulk was dead.

She had to do something. She had to find Aimery. Before the two shocked guards moved to block the door, Madeleine darted out into the misty hell.

She slipped past the fire and crouched down behind a broken wall, looking for Aimery, looking to see who the attackers were. If it was Hereward, perhaps she could appeal to him. She had little faith in such a move, but she had to try.

Then she picked out Aimery fighting with the sword against a heavier man armed with an ax. She edged closer. His opponent was a noble, judging from the quality of his armor, and blatantly English with his flowing hair and beard. He was not Hereward.

"Keep faith with your English blood," she heard the rebel shout as he blocked a mighty blow with his shield. "Will you let the Bastard spawn here at will?"

Aimery pushed forward. "I'm Norman, Gospatric, and I'll kill you here unless you flee."

The larger man laughed. "Northumbrians never flee!" He swung his great ax. Madeleine shuddered as Aimery took the blow on his shield. "You're the one who'll die here, de Gaillard, along with the Bastard's bitch and whelp. You're outnumbered with no help coming." Gospatric stepped back and grinned. "We interfered with your messengers, *Norman*. Your advance guard is making full speed to York. Your rearguard is camped far back. Surrender or die."

"Then I salute death," said Aimery, and attacked.

Madeleine watched the fight in horror, tears running down her face. They were all going to die here, now, when she finally had absolute proof of Aimery's honor.

Then the sounds of battle changed. At first she couldn't interpret it. It sounded as if more men had joined the attack. But after a moment Gospatric's attention wavered, and the shape of the whole battle shifted.

Aimery landed a blow on his enemy's mailed shoulder which made him howl and retreat. "Who?" Gospatric shouted over the sounds of battle. "Who comes?"

The answer floated back on the mist. "Hereward of Mercia."

In a moment the man was there, in mail this time, his eyes bright with battle. "Go, Gospatric. This field is mine."

Madeleine crouched down, unsure whether this was rescue or a case of wolves fighting over a kill. Aimery, too, was watching.

"Are you not with us?" Gospatric asked.

Hereward, too, was armed with an ax. He swung it lazily. "I have your interests at heart, Northumbria. William has you in the dust, my friend, but he'll pardon you if you talk sweetly enough. But not if you kill his queen."

The fighting had stopped as the leaders talked. There were only the groans of the wounded to break the silence.

"And what if she's borne a son?"

"That is no longer your concern. My men outnumber yours. Allan de Ferrers makes his laggardly way here, and even now help should be setting out from York, summoned by the advance. Leave while you can. The day may come when we can fight together to drive out the Normans, but not today."

The matter hung in the balance of fate. Madeleine could sense it was as much Hereward's force of personality as reason that was swaying Gospatric.

Then he cursed, bellowed to his men, and was gone.

Madeleine relaxed, feeling as if she was taking her first real breath in hours. Then she noticed that Aimery was still on guard.

"No thanks, Nephew?" asked Hereward lightly.

"In due course," replied Aimery, sword at the ready.

Hereward chuckled. "I'd like to think it was my shaping, but it's your damned father. Reinforcements really are on the way."

"Good. Then you can doubtless leave us to take care of matters here."

Now that Gospatric and his Northumbrian rebels were gone, Madeleine could see the large number of Hereward's men surrounding the weary Normans. Dear Lord, was it all to start again? What did Hereward want?

"And how is the Duchess of Normandy?" Hereward asked.

"The queen is well."

"Has she delivered her babe?"

"I've been too busy to inquire."

"I would be interested to know."

Madeleine rose from her hiding place. "The queen is safely delivered of a son, and Lucia says she will geld you with your own knife if you make mischief."

Hereward laughed. "Is my sister here then? Woden help me." He sobered. "It's a shame it is a boy, for I will have to take him."

Madeleine stepped forward, knife in hand. "You can't take a newborn from his mother!"

"I have a wet nurse ready. He will not be harmed, but he will not be an atheling either."

Aimery spoke up. "You have little faith in your own prophecy, it would appear."

"Who knows how it is to be served?"

"It will be served by me, then," said Aimery calmly. He pulled off his ring and tossed it into the fire, then placed himself between Hereward and the hut.

They faced each other as the ring flared on the glowing embers.

"And by me." Lucia appeared at her son's side, Fulk's sword in her two hands. It was clear she could hardly lift it, but there was nothing ludicrous in her challenge.

Madeleine moved to stand at Aimery's other side. "And by me."

Hereward considered them. "Is it thus? Is this the future, that English, Norman, and Norman-English stand together?"

No one answered.

"So be it," Hereward made a gesture, and Gyrth came forward to take his ax. Madeleine let out a breath, hoping for the first time for life, for a future.

The breath was knocked out of her again when Hereward pulled a knife from his belt. A knife with a carved amber knob for its pommel. "I took this from a woman who sought to twist our traditions for her own gain, and foist a Norman bastard on my line. She will trouble you no more."

Aimery lowered his sword tip to the ground and rested his hands on the pommel. "You killed her?"

"As was my right. Care for my daughter."

"You claim Frieda?"

"She is a lord's child, therefore mine. When I come into my own again, I will acknowledge her, as is right."

"You're blind, Hereward," said Lucia in exasperation. "The land is won."

Hereward made a gesture which encompassed more than the squalid setting. "Look around with more than your eyes, Lucia. You at least have the blood for it. The land is never won. It merely waits for those who deserve it."

He leaned forward gracefully and hooked the glowing ring out of the fire on the tip of the dagger. He walked forward to face Aimery with the ring between them. "I gave you woman, mark, and ring on the one day. Do you renounce me?"

"I must."

"Then you should have none of them." With lightning speed, he dropped the ring on Aimery's hand and pressed it there with the knife. By the time Aimery had knocked it off and raised his sword, Hereward was away and taking up his ax again. "Give my respects to Matilda," he called, "but tell her, breed as she will, no son's son of hers will rule England!"

The mist swallowed him and his men as if by magic. Aimery hissed and Madeleine turned to look at his hand. An angry circle was branded over the skin-mark. Aimery clutched it, but the pain on his face was more from the passing of a part of his life than from the burn.

There was no goose grease to hand, so Madeleine dipped

a cloth in water and bound it on. "Can you fight left-handed?" she asked.

"After a fashion."

"I'd practice if I were you," she said tartly, "because if this goes on, one of these days you're going to have no useful right hand at all."

He laughed and hugged her close. "We're alive! For a while there I had grave doubts."

"I was terrified, but," she said, looking up, "I trusted you."

He held her closer. "I merely prayed. And if you're wondering, to the God on the Cross."

Then they heard hoofbeats. Madeleine peered at the mist in dread. "Please, Mary, not more."

"I think, I hope, this is the relief party from York."

It proved to be so, with William in the lead. His quick eyes took in the scene. "The queen?" he asked.

"Is safe," Madeleine said, "and delivered of a son."

William grinned. "Good news! An atheling. Now all is secure. But who attacked you here?"

"Gospatric," said Aimery. "By mistake. He left when Hereward explained it to him."

Madeleine only just stopped herself from gasping at this version, but she knew Aimery must have his reasons.

"Hereward was here? How long since?" William was already looking around to organize the hunt.

"Not long, sire. He was the agent of the queen's safety."

William frowned at his godson. "You're over-fond of the man. What happened to your hand?"

"A burn."

"You aren't wearing his ring."

"No, sire."

William nodded. "Let Hereward go, then. The day of our meeting will come, and I will prevail. For now, I would rather see Matilda and my son." He swept into the hut.

"Why?" asked Madeleine.

Aimery sighed and stretched. "If Gospatric's aims were made clear, William would hound him to the death, and Northumbria would end up a bloody waste. If I judge aright, the Earl of Northumbria will be on his knees within the month, asking nicely to be forgiven, and that should be the end of things."

"Edwin, too?"

"Of course, particularly if William gives him Agatha. That will leave Hereward isolated, and he, too, will have to sue for pardon. Then, perhaps, England can have peace."

Madeleine shook her head. "You're as mad as your uncle."

"Indeed he is!" It was Count Guy, his mailed arm wrapped firmly about Lucia. "As mad as Hereward, but as fine a man as well." He gripped his son's arm. "You have done well this day, Aimery. I have to tell you, though, that the Lady Madeleine's cousin, Odo, is spreading a strange tale. He says you are the English outlaw, Golden Hart."

Aimery glanced at Madeleine. "Why would he do that?"

"For reward, of course, though he misjudges if he thinks any man will gain from forcing William to ruin you." Guy held his son's eyes. "Is it true?"

Aimery seemed perfectly calm. "That I am Golden Hart? What does William think?

"Does anyone ever know what William thinks? Odo de Pouissey claims he rode ahead to York when he had news that you were planning to deliver the queen to Hereward. He feared he would not have the authority to thwart your plans . . ."

Now that it had come, Madeleine found she was not so much afraid as purposeful. She felt like a sharp blade. That triggered a thought, and she looked at the amber-headed knife on the ground.

With a warning pressure on Aimery's arm, Madeleine slipped away from the group. She stooped to pick up the knife as she passed, then went to the wharf and onto the barge. By good fortune, her chest was on top of a pile. It took only a moment to find the gilded scabbard, slip in the blade, and fix it on her girdle.

She returned to Aimery's side just as a man came forward to summon them all to attend William.

It was crowded in the hut. William sat by Matilda, holding his son. Guy, Lucia, Madeleine, and Aimery stood where they could. Then Odo came in. He looked around at the group uneasily. Perhaps even he sensed there was no one in the room who felt kindly toward him.

"Ah, Odo," said William benignly. "You may congratulate me on my fine son."

Odo bowed. "I do most heartily, sire."

"And it would appear that your information was at fault, for Lord Aimery defended the queen most staunchly."

Odo flushed and looked around. "And yet he let that cur, Hereward, escape."

William looked a question at Aimery.

"We were outnumbered, sire. As Hereward appeared to intend us no harm, I thought it better to let him go."

"A wise decision, wouldn't you say, de Pouissey?"

"A cautious one," sneered Odo. "I find it odd that Aimery de Gaillard fought valiantly against Gospatric, but struck no blow against Hereward. There are those who claim they were on good terms, even clasping hands at the end."

William looked intrigued. "Are you saying it was all staged, with Hereward and Aimery saving the day in order to gain my favor?"

The thought had obviously never crossed Odo's mind, but he grasped it eagerly. "Yes, sire."

"What an exceedingly subtle mind you have. But Aimery already has my favor in full measure, and Hereward has merely to bend the knee to me to receive it."

Odo swallowed. "But what of the murder at Huntingdon?" he said desperately. "Where is the woman, Aldreda, who has the knife found in the body? It is de Gaillard's own knife, awarded to him by you.''

''What woman is this?'' asked William.

''Aldreda is a weaver from Baddersley,'' said Aimery. ''Her husband was found dead in Huntingdon. If Hereward is to be believed, she, too, is dead.''

''Dead!'' cried Odo. ''Foully murdered then. By you!''

''By Hereward,'' said Aimery, ''for reasons personal to them. I have had no opportunity for private death for many hours.''

Odo was red with rage and looking more like his father by the second. He was as foolish, too, for the king was clearly keen to overlook all if he was allowed. ''She should have the knife on her,'' Odo blustered. ''That is proof.''

Madeleine spoke up. ''I'm not sure how it would be proof of anything, but I thought *I* had the knife the king awarded to Aimery.'' She indicated the knife on her girdle.

Odo stared. ''Where did you get that?''

''From Aimery, weeks ago.''

''Let me see it.'' The king studied the knife and nodded. ''It is the same.'' He looked at Odo with a warning frown. ''I believe your intentions, de Pouissey, are loyal, but you have been misinformed. What motive could Aimery have to murder a peasant?''

Odo glared at Aimery. ''That peasant would have named him as Golden Hart, as would the weaver. He has killed them, but there is another, sire. Send for Bertrand, who was a man of Robert d'Oilly's. He is in my party, and once encountered Golden Hart, as you know. He will tell all.''

The king's face was coldly inscrutable as he had the man summoned. Guy and Lucia were pale. Aimery looked calm.

The man entered and fell to his knee, his eyes flickering about nervously. They were sharp eyes, though.

''Now, Bertrand,'' said the king, ''Lord Odo seems to

think you can identify someone here as the giant who attacked you at Banbury.''

The man looked around, and his eyes lingered for a moment on Aimery. ''Nay, sire. None here are large enough.''

''You lie!'' shouted Odo. ''You said to me two days past that Lord Aimery could be the man.''

''I said *could* be, my lord. So could any number of people. But Lord Aimery is a true Norman knight, as he's shown this day. The man I fought was lowborn.''

''But handled a sword well,'' said Odo.

The man was now quite cocky. ''*I* handle a sword well, and I'm lowborn.''

Odo would have said more, but the king interrupted. ''There is clearly nothing in this.'' He passed Bertrand some coins. ''You may go, my man, with our thanks.''

The king regarded Odo with cold humor. ''If this continues, de Pouissey, I might begin to think you carry a grudge against Aimery for winning the fair Lady Madeleine.''

Odo glared around, too furious to hear the warning in the king's voice. ''I only carry a grudge against traitors, sire. He has killed two witnesses and suborned another, but there is one witness that cannot be silenced. Aimery de Gaillard carries a mark on his hand that tells his guilt as clear as the gospels.'' He swung to face Aimery. ''I see you hide it under a rag. Show us that heathenish mark if you dare!''

Aimery calmly unwound the cloth and removed the bracelet from his wrist. The scar of the boar-wound ran from the middle of his hand a few inches up his forearm. Now it was surmounted by an angry red circle. The skin marks were a mere tangle of lines.

''So,'' said the king. ''Who can tell what that is supposed to be?''

It was unclear whether it was a question or not, but Lucia answered it. ''It was a horse, sire. Now it's just a mess with four legs. I don't see how Aimery could possibly be Golden Hart, even if he were so foolish, for as I traveled, I heard the outlaw was harrying shipping to France.''

''And I,'' said the king, ''have had certain word that he raided Lancaster two days since with a body of Scots.'' He looked at Odo. ''I fear this north country has turned your wits, de Pouissey. I bid you go serve with Lord William Fitz Osbern against the Welsh. That area may suit you better and enable you to gain the rewards you so clearly seek.''

With a sound perilously close to a snarl, Odo bowed himself out. There was a collective expiration.

William passed his child back to Matilda and looked at Aimery. ''And now, Golden Hart . . .''

Chapter 23

With a slight smile, Aimery knelt. "I am only a small part of the whole, sire, and never served you ill."

The king's eyes were cold. "You spawned a monster which troubles me."

Aimery met his anger calmly. "It would have spawned itself, sire."

The king smiled wolfishly. "If I truly wished to punish you, I would exile you to Normandy. Would you go?"

Aimery paled. After a heavy moment he said, "No, sire."

Lucia gasped.

"Would you join Hereward?"

"No, sire. I suppose I would truly be Edwald the outlaw."

The king exploded. "Doing what, by the Blood?"

"Helping the people."

William shook his head. "You try my patience sorely, Aimery." He sat staring at the young man. Madeleine felt as if everyone in the room was holding their breath; she knew she was. Except the oblivious baby, which suddenly gave a little squawk. The tension broke.

The king relaxed. "But you have served me well this day." He thrust his hand forward. "Help the people, then. Help *my* people, but do it as Aimery de Gaillard."

Aimery kissed the king's hand and rose.

"Now go away," said the king. "The queen and I will rest here for the night. You must fend for yourselves."

As they left the hut Guy groaned. "Lucia. Is your hair gray, too?"

"I'm scared to look."

Guy turned to Aimery. "I could flay you alive. Is it over now?"

Aimery shrugged. "I won't play Golden Hart anymore. The rest, I suppose, is *wyrd.*"

Guy muttered something and led Lucia away.

Madeleine went into Aimery's arms. "Are we safe?"

He kissed her. "As safe as we're ever likely to be. Which is to say, not very. But I have hope we'll at least make it to York."

She blushed. "Do you think of nothing else?"

His hands flexed on her shoulders. "Between protecting the queen, fighting for my life, and confessing my sins to William? No, I don't suppose I do. I'm beginning to let myself think of going home to look after Baddersley and Rolleston. Of watching you give birth to our first child. Of finding a way for England to prosper . . . Do you trust me?"

"Completely. I'm sorry."

"I never did tell you the service I did for Hereward."

"I don't care."

"I had permission to tell you days ago, and didn't. I wanted your blind faith, which was a weakness in me."

Madeleine had to be honest. "I couldn't be entirely sure until I saw you fight Gospatric and deny Hereward."

He kissed her again. "I know. I don't mind. I don't think blind faith is an admirable quality all in all. Give me a woman who uses her wits any day. I delivered a package."

"A package?"

"To be precise, Lady Agatha."

Madeleine looked at him. "What on earth are you talking about?"

He put his arm around her, and they began to stroll

about looking for some sheltered corner in which to sleep. "Silly little Agatha took it into her head to join Edwin, like the heroine from a ballad. With a couple of stupid guards—they'd have to be stupid to go along with it—she rode up the North Road asking for him. The men who captured her were going to try for ransom, but Hereward heard and took charge of her. He had no safe way of returning her to court and summoned me."

"That was Gyrth. Why didn't you tell me?"

"That was Gyrth, but I wasn't intending to go. I'd been refusing summonses from Hereward since Senlac, and I thought it a trick. Then the queen's messenger passed through on his way to York, with a secret urgent request that I use my contacts to find Agatha."

"So you went. But you could have told me something."

He laughed. "I left you a vague but reassuring message. I think it must have lost some meaning by the time it reached you."

"It did indeed. Poor Agatha. Dragged home in disgrace. No wonder she was so sullen when I saw her."

"Yes." They settled for a damp corner of a hut which at least still had part of a roof and a layer of straw. He lay with her in his arms. "And poor Aldreda. And Frieda. These are hard times."

"Yes," said Madeleine. "But there's always York."

York was none too simple, however. For his own good reasons the king made a grand entrance into the ancient city the next day. From river to castle, Matilda traveled in an open litter, and William rode beside her carrying the babe.

The route was crowded, but Madeleine could not judge the mood of the people. There were smiles, and even enthusiasm when coins were thrown, but she didn't trust the good humor to last. An occasional voice would cry, "The atheling!" and there would be a cheer, but not everyone cheered, and she suspected the ones who cried that important name were paid by William's men.

She glanced at Aimery, and he smiled back. The look in his eyes made her toes curl. She found she didn't really care about the settling of Northumbria as long as it didn't interfere with the coming night.

The king was lodging at the bishop's palace, and Madeleine was kept busy there helping to settle the queen and the baby. Eventually, however, Matilda noticed her. "Sweet heavens, child, have you nothing better to do? Go and see to your own lodging. You deserve a reward."

With a blushing smile, Madeleine went.

It took time and a number of inquiries to find the tiny room she and Aimery had been given. With the bed and their chests there was scarcely room to move, but it was private, it had a bed, and no one would suggest they include a third person in such a cramped space. It was perfect.

Madeleine wished she could stay here until Aimery came, then remain here forever, but there was the evening meal to get through. Dorothy dressed her in a fine kirtle and tunic and plaited her hair, covering it with an embroidered scarf crossed at the front and hanging to the waist behind. Madeleine chose her jewels—a gold collar and the bracelets Aimery had given her as her morning gift—then sent the woman off, telling her not to return.

She waited as long as she dared for Aimery to come and change, for she'd not had a private moment with him since the morning, but the second blast of the horn made her leave the room. Ah well, there would be later.

But as she walked along the narrow passageway she was snared and wrapped in a cloak, a cloak she remembered. Her heart leaped, and she tingled with expectation. "The meal?"

"We're excused," he said in English against her ear.

She leaned back against him. "I don't suppose by any chance you're naked, are you?"

He choked on laughter. "That would be rash, wouldn't it, here in the passageway?"

"But a lovely thought . . ."

His lips nuzzled the skin of her nape through the silk of her scarf. "I have hundreds of lovely thoughts, my dusky lady. Thoughts of your breasts heavy in my hands, your skin smooth beneath my fingers. I'm going to touch your breasts until they sing for me like music, and lick them till they reach for me."

He wasn't doing anything, but her breath was fractured, and she was hot within the cloak. "You promised me a bed," she said.

"In good time." His hand moved at last, moved to simply cover an aching breast, bringing more torment than relief. "I fear I've taught you to be impatient, love. Time to learn a different lesson."

"What lesson is that?" The third bellow of the horn meant everyone would be in the hall. They were truly alone.

"The delights of postponing delight. Do you remember what I said to you by the river?"

She moved against his hand. "I remember what you said you said."

"I said I was going to tease your nipples to aching, then suck them soft, suck them hard until you were wild for me." Again her body moved of its own will, begging for what it was promised.

Madeleine could not move her hands, but she pressed back against him and wiggled. She heard him catch his breath.

"I told you how hot and moist you were for me," he said hoarsely. "How much more so you would be when I touched you there. How I'd make you ache, and take your ache and turn it into fire. I'm going to love you slowly, my wife, very, very slowly, then when you can't stand it anymore, I'll take you hard and fast."

Her body burned for him. She ached already. "I can't stand it anymore," she whispered.

He chuckled. "You have a lot to learn."

He carried her to their room, unwound the cloak, then sat her firmly on the bed. Madeleine watched dazedly as he undressed himself. Finally he stood naked before her in full desire, all gold. Gold skin, gold hair, gold bands on strong arms. Her beautiful river god. Her faery prince.

He wore armbands, and a bracelet on his left wrist, but none on his right. Because of the wound, or because it was no longer necessary?

She touched gently near the blistered circle on the back of his right hand. "Hereward saved you with this."

"And doubtless knew it."

Madeleine thought of the magic that wove through this land. Was it part of the magic that was weaving through her now? She rose and ran a hand up a muscled arm, across his chest, and down the other. It was as if his flesh sang beneath her fingers. Was this how she felt to him?

She moved to undress, but he swung her against him again, her back to him. "Now I'm naked," he said softly. She knew it. His erection was hard against her back. Her heart was thundering. Her legs shook. How much more of this could she endure?

He put his hands over her breasts and rubbed them with the most tender touch, so she could scarcely feel it through three layers of cloth. It was as if fire surged through her veins. "Sweet heavens," she gasped.

"Sweet heavens indeed," he whispered as one hand slid down to press at the juncture of her thighs. She whimpered. He worked up her skirt until his hand could slide between her thighs. Her head fell back, then forward. A shudder took her, and only his strong arm held her up.

Gently he turned her, put her hands on his shoulders, and undid her girdle. Madeleine regained some of her wits and was able to cooperate as he stripped off her clothes in one layer, until she, too, was dressed only in her jewels— the heavy gold collar and the two bracelets.

His eyes traveled over every inch of her and adored her without words. Responding to that message, Madeleine spread her arms and turned before him, flashing him a triumphant smile. He laughed and captured her, lowered his head to lick first one nipple then the other until a shuddering wave passed through her. But that was all.

He began to unravel her plaits.

Playfully desperate, she reached for his erect shaft. He laughed, dodged, and in a moment she found her wrists bound with her silk scarf. "Aimery!"

"Just to keep you out of mischief for a moment," he said, and continued his work until her hair was a rich curtain around her. He rubbed one long strand over her right nipple and smiled. "I'll untie you, but if you touch me, I'll spill my seed. Then you'll have to wait even longer."

"Keep me tied then," she said, pressing forward. "But do it. I'm wild for you. Truly I am!"

"Do you think so? But I promised you long, slow love in a bed. We haven't even made it to the bed yet." Madeleine groaned as he led her there. He pulled back the covers and settled her on cool linen sheets. His hands began to wander over her, exciting and abandoning a host of delicious places.

"Come to me!" she gasped. "Is this love or torture?"

He grinned. "Which does it feel like?"

"I don't know!"

He flicked the silk off her wrists and rolled onto his back. "Then you take charge."

Madeleine stared at him. His manhood was hard and full and beautiful. She looked at the silk in her hands and wafted it gently over him, saw him tremble. With a mischievous grin, she bound his hands with the scarf, being careful of his burn. The bond wasn't even knotted, and she knew he could break it if it was, but she knew, too, that it would hold him as her prisoner.

Pulled by some force, she leaned forward till her heavy hair fell on him. She swayed her head so that the tresses brushed over his chest and thighs. She heard him catch his breath and looked up. "Is this love or torture?" she asked softly.

"I don't know."

She lowered her lips and touched the glistening tip of his shaft. It jerked. He groaned. She saw his hands clench.

She throbbed to have him in her, but she wanted this, too. This power. She touched him with her tongue, watching him. He looked to be in agony, and she repented. She loosed the scarf and tickled him with it again.

"Amazing what they teach you in a convent," he muttered, and confiscated the teasing silk.

Madeleine giggled. "It must be an instinct. But," she added, "tell me true. Do men suck fluid from a woman's breasts to stiffen themselves?"

He burst out laughing. "Believe me, I was stiff as a poker before I touched your breasts. But let's make sure."

His mouth was hot on her nipples, and he tongued and teased her until she moaned. Then, as he had promised, he sucked hard, so hard that she cried out and arched like a bow.

Then, again as he'd promised, he entered her hard and strong, watching her with dark, heated eyes. Madeleine tried to watch him, to see his ecstasy, but reality vanished for her as the fever roared. She knew only the heat and power of him as she flew apart into heavenly fragments.

She drifted together again and licked the salt sweat from his shoulder. "Could I live on this, do you think?"

He laughed. "No."

"Are we going to do it again right now?"

"No."

"Do you love me?"

"No."

Madeleine's eyes flew open. He smiled lazily. "You asked for that. Love is too mild a word. You are to me as my heart is to me."

"I don't think love is a mild word, Aimery. It's like the oceans and the storms, and the heat of the sun. It's the power of a leaf as it breaks free of the earth, and the flow of the river that grinds the corn. It's the joining in the bed, and the birthing of babes. With love we can do anything."

He disentangled them from her hair, and peeled their

damp bodies apart so that he could gather her into his arms. "Then let's use our love to grow things, sweet heart of mine. Both corn and babes. And a peaceful England for their future. God and *wyrd* willing."

Madeleine settled against him. "God and *wyrd* willing, dear lord of my heart."